Praise for *This Earl of Mine*

"Delicious, witty, and ripping good fun! Kate Bateman's
writing sparkles." —*USA Today* bestselling author
Laura Lee Guhrke

"Dashing, daring, and deliciously romantic!"
—*USA Today* bestselling author
Caroline Linden

"A riveting new voice for Regency readers! Kate Bateman
is now on my auto-buy list." —Janna MacGregor,
author of *The Good,
the Bad, and the Duke*

This Earl of Mine

Kate Bateman

St. Martin's Paperbacks

This is a work of fiction. All of the characters, organizations, and events
portrayed in this novel are either products of the author's imagination or
are used fictitiously.

First published in the United States by St. Martin's Paperbacks, an imprint
of St. Martin's Publishing Group.

THIS EARL OF MINE

Copyright © 2019 by Kate Bateman.

For information, address St. Martin's Publishing Group, 120 Broadway,
New York, NY 10271.

www.stmartins.com

ISBN: 978-1-250-30595-4

Our books may be purchased in bulk for promotional, educational, or
business use. Please contact your local bookseller or the Macmillan
Corporate and Premium Sales Department at 1-800-221-7945, ext. 5442,
or by e-mail at MacmillanSpecialMarkets@macmillan.com.

Printed in the United States of America

St. Martin's Paperbacks edition / November 2019

10 9 8 7 6 5 4 3 2 1

To my crazy, wonderful family,
especially my three lovely monsters,
and M, with much love.

Acknowledgments

Thanks to Jennie Conway and everyone at St. Martin's Press, and to my fab agent, Patricia Nelson, for doing all the stuff I hate to do, so I can get on with writing. And thanks to the wonderful ladies of the C.I.A. (you know who you are!) whose friendship, advice, support, and general kick-assery have been invaluable.

Chapter 1.

London, March 1816.

There were worse places to find a husband than Newgate Prison.

Of course there were.

It was just that, at present, Georgie couldn't think of any.

"Georgiana Caversteed, this is a terrible idea."

Georgie frowned at her burly companion, Pieter Smit, as the nondescript carriage he'd summoned to convey them to London's most notorious jail rocked to a halt on the cobbled street. The salt-weathered Dutchman always used her full name whenever he disapproved of something she was doing. Which was often.

"Your father would turn in his watery grave if he knew what you were about."

That was undoubtedly true. Until three days ago, enlisting a husband from amongst the ranks of London's most dangerous criminals had not featured prominently on her list of life goals. But desperate times called for desperate measures. Or, in this case, for a desperate felon about to be hanged. A felon she would marry before the night was through.

Georgie peered out into the rain-drizzled street, then up, up the near-windowless walls. They rose into the mist, five stories high, a vast expanse of brickwork, bleak and unpromising. A church bell tolled somewhere in the darkness, a forlorn clang like a death knell. Her stomach knotted with a grim sense of foreboding.

Was she really going to go through with this? It had seemed a good plan, in the safety of Grosvenor Square. The perfect way to thwart Cousin Josiah once and for all. She stepped from the carriage, ducked her head against the rain, and followed Pieter under a vast arched gate. Her heart hammered at the audacity of what she planned.

They'd taken the same route as condemned prisoners on the way to Tyburn tree, only in reverse. West to east, from the rarefied social strata of Mayfair through gradually rougher and bleaker neighborhoods, Holborn and St. Giles, to this miserable place where the dregs of humanity had been incarcerated. Georgie felt as if she were nearing her own execution.

She shook off the pervasive aura of doom and straightened her spine. This was her choice. However unpalatable the next few minutes might be, the alternative was far worse. Better a temporary marriage to a murderous, unwashed criminal than a lifetime of misery with Josiah.

They crossed the deserted outer courtyard, and Georgie cleared her throat, trying not to inhale the foul-smelling air that seeped from the very pores of the building. "You have it all arranged? They are expecting us?"

Pieter nodded. "Aye. I've greased the wheels with yer blunt, my girl. The proctor and the ordinary are both bent as copper shillings. Used to having their palms greased, those two, the greedy bastards."

Her father's right-hand man had never minced words

in front of her, and Georgie appreciated his bluntness. So few people in the *ton* ever said what they really meant. Pieter's honesty was refreshing. He'd been her father's man for twenty years before she'd even been born. A case of mumps had prevented him from accompanying William Caversteed on his last, fateful voyage, and Georgie had often thought that if Pieter had been with her father, maybe he'd still be alive. Little things like squalls, shipwrecks, and attacks from Barbary pirates would be mere inconveniences to a man like Pieter Smit.

In the five years since Papa's death, Pieter's steadfast loyalty had been dedicated to William's daughters, and Georgie loved the gruff, hulking manservant like a second father. He would see her through this madcap scheme— even if he disapproved.

She tugged the hood of her cloak down to stave off the drizzle. This place was filled with murderers, highwaymen, forgers, and thieves. Poor wretches slated to die, or those "lucky" few whose sentences had been commuted to transportation. Yet in her own way, she was equally desperate.

"You are sure that this man is to be hanged tomorrow?"

Pieter nodded grimly as he rapped on a wooden door. "I am. A low sort he is, by all accounts."

She shouldn't ask, didn't want to know too much about the man whose name she was purchasing. A man whose death would spell her own freedom. She would be wed and widowed within twenty-four hours.

Taking advantage of a condemned man left a sour taste in her mouth, a sense of guilt that her happiness should come from the misfortune of another. But this man would die whether she married him or not. "What are his crimes?"

"Numerous, I'm told. He's a coiner." At her frown, Pieter elaborated. "Someone who forges coins. It's treason, that."

"Oh." That seemed a little harsh. She couldn't imagine what that was like, having no money, forced to make your own. Still, having a fortune was almost as much of a curse as having nothing. She'd endured six years of insincere, lecherous fortune hunters, thanks to her bountiful coffers.

"A smuggler too," Pieter added for good measure. "Stabbed a customs man down in Kent."

She was simply making the best out of a bad situation. This man would surely realize that while there was no hope for himself, at least he could leave this world having provided for whatever family he left behind. Everyone had parents, or siblings, or lovers. Everyone had a price. She, of all people, knew that—she was buying herself a husband. At least this way there was no pretense. Besides, what was the point in having a fortune if you couldn't use it to make yourself happy?

Pieter hammered impatiently on the door again.

"I know you disapprove," Georgie muttered. "But Father would never have wanted me to marry a man who covets my purse more than my person. If you hadn't rescued me the other evening, that's precisely what would have happened. I would have had to wed Josiah to prevent a scandal. I refuse to give control of my life and my fortune to some idiot to mismanage. As a widow, I will be free."

Pieter gave an eloquent sniff.

"You think me heartless," Georgie said. "But can you think of another way?" At his frowning silence, she nodded. "No, me neither."

Heavy footsteps and the jangle of keys finally heralded proof of human life inside. The door scraped open, and the low glare of a lantern illuminated a grotesquely large man in the doorway.

"Mr. Knollys?"

The man gave a brown-toothed grin as he recognized Pieter. "Welcome back, sir. Welcome back." He craned his neck and raised the lantern, trying to catch a glimpse of Georgie. "You brought the lady, then?" His piggy eyes narrowed with curiosity within the folds of his flabby face.

"And the license." Pieter tapped the pocket of his coat.

Knollys nodded and stepped back, allowing them entry. "The ordinary's agreed to perform the service." He turned and began shuffling down the narrow corridor, lantern raised. "Only one small problem." He cocked his head back toward Pieter. "That cove the lady was to marry? Cheated the 'angman, 'e 'as."

Pieter stopped abruptly, and Georgie bumped into his broad back.

"He's dead?" Pieter exclaimed. "Then why are we here? You can damn well return that purse I paid you!"

The man's belly undulated grotesquely as he laughed. It was not a kindly sound. "Now, now. Don't you worry yerself none, me fine lad. That special license don't have no names on it yet, do it? No. We've plenty more like 'im in this place. This way."

The foul stench of the prison increased tenfold as they followed the unpleasant Knollys up some stairs and down a second corridor. Rows of thick wooden doors, each with a square metal hatch and a sliding shutter at eye level, lined the walls on either side. Noises emanated from some—inhuman moans, shouts, and foul curses. Others were ominously silent. Georgie pressed her handkerchief to her nose, glad she'd doused it in lavender water.

Knollys waddled to a stop in front of the final door in the row. His eyes glistened with a disquieting amount of glee.

"Found the lady a substitute, I 'ave." He thumped the metal grate with his meaty fist and eyed Georgie's cloaked form with a knowing, suggestive leer that made her feel as though she'd been drenched in cooking fat. She resisted the urge to shudder.

"Wake up, lads!" he bellowed. "There's a lady 'ere needs yer services."

Chapter 2.

Benedict William Henry Wylde, scapegrace second son of the late Earl of Morcott, reluctant war hero, and former scourge of the *ton*, strained to hear the last words of his cellmate. He bent forward, trying to ignore the stench of the man's blackened teeth and the sickly sweet scent of impending death that wreathed his feverish form.

Silas had been sick for days, courtesy of a festering stab wound in his thigh. The bastard jailers hadn't heeded his pleas for water, bandages, or laudanum. Ben had been trying to decipher the smuggler's ranting for hours. Delirium had loosened the man's tongue, and he'd leaned close, waiting for something useful to slip between those cracked lips, but the words had been frustratingly fragmented. Silas raved about plots and treasons. An Irishman. The emperor. Benedict had been on the verge of shaking the poor bastard when his crewmate let out one last, gasping breath—and died.

"Oh, bloody hell!"

Ben drew back from the hard, straw-filled pallet that

stank of piss and death. He'd been so close to getting the information he needed.

Not for the first time, he cursed his friend Alex's uncle, Sir Nathaniel Conant, Chief Magistrate of Bow Street and the man tasked with transforming the way London was policed. Bow Street was the senior magistrate court in the capital, and the "Runners," as they were rather contemptuously known, investigated crimes, followed up leads, served warrants and summons, searched properties for stolen goods, and watched premises where infringements of bylaws or other offences were suspected.

Conant had approached Ben, Alex, and their friend Seb about a year ago, a few months after their return from fighting Napoleon on the continent. The three of them had just opened the Tricorn Club—the gambling hell they'd pledged to run together while crouched around a smoky campfire in Belgium. Conant had pointed out that their new venture placed them in an ideal position for gathering intelligence on behalf of His Majesty's government, since its members—and their acquaintances—came from all levels of society. He'd also requested their assistance on occasional cases, especially those which bridged the social divide. The three of them not only had entrée into polite society, but thanks to their time in the Rifles, they dealt equally well with those from the lower end of the social spectrum, the "scum of the earth," as Wellington had famously called his own troops.

Conant paid the three of them a modest sum for every mission they undertook, plus extra commission for each bit of new information they brought in. Neither Alex nor Seb needed the money; they were more interested in the challenge to their wits, but Benedict had jumped at the chance of some additional income, even though the work was sometimes—such as now—less than glamorous.

He was in Newgate on Conant's orders, chasing a rumor that someone had been trying to assemble a crew of smugglers to rescue the deposed Emperor Napoleon from the island of St. Helena. Benedict had been ingratiating himself with this band for weeks, posing as a bitter ex-navy gunner, searching for the man behind such a plan. He'd even allowed himself to be seized by customs officials near Gravesend along with half the gang—recently deceased Silas amongst them—in the hopes of discovering more. If he solved this case, he'd receive a reward of five hundred pounds, which could go some way toward helping his brother pay off the mass of debt left by their profligate father.

He'd been in here almost ten days now. The gang's ringleader, a vicious bastard named Hammond, had been hanged yesterday morning. Ben, Silas, and two of the younger gang members had been sentenced to transportation. That was British leniency for you: a nice slow death on a prison ship instead of a quick drop from Tyburn tree.

The prison hulk would be leaving at dawn, but Ben wouldn't be on it. There was no need to hang around now that Silas and Hammond were both dead. He'd get nothing more from them. And the two youngsters, Peters and Fry, were barely in their teens. They knew nothing useful. Conant had arranged for him to "disappear" from the prison hulk before it sailed; its guards were as open to bribery as Knollys.

Several other gang members had escaped the Gravesend raid. Benedict had glimpsed a few familiar faces in the crowd when the magistrate had passed down his sentence. He'd have to chase them down as soon as he was free and see if any of them had been approached for the traitorous mission.

Benedict sighed and slid down the wall until he sat on the filthy floor, his knees bent in front of him. He'd forgotten what it felt like to be clean. He rasped one hand over his stubbled jaw and grimaced—he'd let his beard grow out as a partial disguise. He'd commit murder for a wash and a razor. Even during the worst scrapes in the Peninsular War, and then in France and Belgium, he'd always found time to shave. Alex and Seb, his brothers-in-arms, had mocked him for it mercilessly.

He glanced at the square of rain visible through the tiny barred grate on the outer wall of his cell. Seb and Alex were out there, lucky buggers, playing merry hell with the debutantes, wives, and widows of London with amazing impartiality.

The things he did for king and bloody country.

And cash, of course. Five hundred pounds was nothing to sneeze at.

Tracking down a traitor was admirable. Having to stay celibate and sober because there was neither a woman nor grog to be had in prison was hell. What he wouldn't give for some decent French brandy and a warm, willing wench. Hell, right now he'd settle for some of that watered-down ratafia they served at society balls and a tumble with a barmaid.

A pretty barmaid, of course. His face had always allowed him to be choosy. At least, it did when he was clean-shaven. His own mother probably wouldn't recognize him right now.

Voices and footsteps intruded on his errant fancies as the obsequious voice of Knollys echoed through the stones. A fist slammed into the grate, loud enough to wake the dead, and Benedict glanced over at Silas with morbid humor. Well, almost loud enough.

"Wake up, lads!" Knollys bellowed. "There's a lady 'ere needs yer services."

Benedict's brows rose in the darkness. What the devil?

"Ye promised ten pounds if I'd find 'er a man an' never

say nuffink to nobody," he heard Knollys say through the door.

"Are they waiting to hang too?" An older man's voice, that, with a foreign inflexion. Dutch, perhaps.

"Nay. Ain't got no more for the gallows. Not since Hammond yesterday." Knollys sounded almost apologetic. "But either one of these'll fit the bill. Off to Van Diemen's Land they are, at first light."

"No, that won't do at all."

Benedict's ears pricked up at the sound of the cultured female voice. She sounded extremely peeved.

"I specifically wanted a condemned man, Mr. Knollys."

"Better come back in a week or so then, milady."

There was a short pause as the two visitors apparently conferred, too low for him to hear.

"I cannot wait another few weeks." The woman sounded resigned. "Very well. Let's see what you have."

Keys grated in the lock and Knollys's quivering belly filled the doorway. Benedict shielded his eyes from the lantern's glare, blinding after the semidarkness of the cell. The glow illuminated Silas's still figure on the bed and Knollys grunted.

"Dead, is 'e?" He sounded neither dismayed nor surprised. "Figured he wouldn't last the week. You'll 'ave to do then, Wylde. Get up."

Benedict pushed himself to his feet with a wince.

"Ain't married, are you, Wylde?" Knollys muttered, low enough not to be heard by those in the corridor.

"Never met the right woman," Benedict drawled, being careful to retain the rough accent of an east coast smuggler he'd adopted. "Still, one lives in 'ope."

Knollys frowned, trying to decide whether Ben was being sarcastic. As usual, he got it wrong. "This lady's 'ere to wed," he grunted finally, gesturing vaguely behind him.

Benedict squinted. Two shapes hovered just outside, partly shielded by the jailer's immense bulk. One of them, the smaller hooded figure, might possibly be female. "What woman comes here to marry?"

Knollys chuckled. "A desperate one, Mr. Wylde."

The avaricious glint in Knollys's eye hinted that he saw the opportunity to take advantage, and Benedict experienced a rush of both anger and protectiveness for the foolish woman, whoever she might be. Probably one of the muslin set, seeking a name for her unborn child. Or some common trollop, hoping her debts would be wiped off with the death of her husband. Except he'd never met a tart who spoke with such a clipped, aristocratic accent.

"You want me to marry some woman I've never met?" Benedict almost laughed in disbelief. "I appreciate the offer, Mr. Knollys, but I'll have to decline. I ain't stepping into the parson's mousetrap for no one."

Knollys took a menacing step forward. "Oh, you'll do it, Wylde, or I'll have Ennis bash your skull in." He glanced over at Silas's corpse. "I can just as easy 'ave 'im dig two graves instead of one."

Ennis was a short, troll-like thug who possessed fewer brains than a sack of potatoes, but he took a malicious and creative pleasure in administering beatings with his heavy wooden cudgel. Benedict's temper rose. He didn't like being threatened. If it weren't for the manacles binding his hands, he'd explain that pertinent fact to Mr. Knollys in no uncertain terms.

Unfortunately, Knollys wasn't a man to take chances. He prodded Benedict with his stick. "Out with ye. And no funny business." His meaty fist cuffed Ben around the head to underscore the point.

Benedict stepped out into the dim passageway and took an appreciative breath. The air was slightly less rancid out here. Of course, it was all a matter of degree.

A broad, grizzled man of around sixty moved to stand protectively in front of the woman, arms crossed and bushy brows lowered. Benedict leaned sideways and tried to make out her features, but the hood of a domino shielded her face. She made a delicious, feminine rustle of silk as she stepped back, though. No rough worsted and cotton for this lady. Interesting.

Knollys prodded him along the passage, and Benedict shook his head to dispel a sense of unreality. Here he was, unshaven, unwashed, less than six hours from freedom, and apparently about to be wed to a perfect stranger. It seemed like yet another cruel joke by fate.

He'd never imagined himself marrying. Not after the disastrous example of his own parents' union. His mother had endured his father's company only long enough to produce the requisite heir and a spare, then removed herself to the gaiety of London. For the next twenty years, she'd entertained a series of lovers in the town house, while his father had remained immured in Herefordshire with a succession of steadily younger live-in mistresses, one of whom had taken it upon herself to introduce a seventeen-year-old Benedict to the mysteries of the female form. It was a pattern of domesticity Benedict had absolutely no desire to repeat.

In truth, he hadn't thought he'd survive the war and live to the ripe old age of twenty-eight. If he *had* ever been forced to picture his own wedding—under torture, perhaps—he was fairly certain he wouldn't have imagined it taking place in prison. At the very least, he would have had his family and a couple of friends in attendance; his fellow sworn bachelors, Alex and Seb. Some flowers, maybe. A country church.

He'd never envisaged the lady. If three years of warfare had taught him anything, it was that life was too short to tie himself to one woman for the rest of his life.

Marriage would be an imprisonment worse than his cell here in Newgate.

They clattered down the stairs and into the tiny chapel where the ordinary, Horace Cotton, was waiting, red-faced and unctuous. Cotton relished his role of resident chaplain; he enjoyed haranguing soon-to-be-dead prisoners with lengthy sermons full of fire and brimstone. No doubt he was being paid handsomely for this evening's work.

Benedict halted in front of the altar—little more than a table covered in a white cloth and two candles—and raised his manacled wrists to Knollys. The jailer sniffed but clearly realized he'd have to unchain him if they were to proceed. He gave Ben a sour, warning look as the irons slipped off, just daring him to try something. Ben shot him a cocky, challenging sneer in return.

How to put a stop to this farce? He had no cash to bribe his way out. A chronic lack of funds was precisely why he'd been working for Bow Street since his return from France, chasing thief-taker's rewards.

Could he write the wrong name on the register, to invalidate the marriage? Probably not. Both Knollys and Cotton knew him as Ben Wylde. Ex-Rifle brigade, penniless, cynical veteran of Waterloo. It wasn't his full name, of course, but it would probably be enough to satisfy the law.

Announcing that his brother happened to be the Earl of Morcott would certainly make matters interesting, but thanks to their father's profligacy, the estate was mortgaged to the hilt. John had even less money than Benedict.

The unpleasant sensation that he'd been neatly backed into a corner made Benedict's neck prickle, as if a French sniper had him in his sights. Still, he'd survived worse. He was a master at getting out of scrapes. Even if he *was* forced to marry this mystery harridan, there were always alternatives. An annulment, for one.

"Might I at least have the name of the lady to whom I'm about to be joined in holy matrimony?" he drawled.

The manservant scowled at the ironic edge to his tone, but the woman laid a silencing hand on his arm and stepped around him.

"You can indeed, sir." In one smooth movement, she pulled the hood from her head and faced him squarely. "My name is Georgiana Caversteed."

Benedict cursed in every language he knew.

Chapter 3.

Georgiana Caversteed? What devil's trick was this?

He knew the name, but he'd never seen the face—until now. God's teeth, every man in London knew the name. The chit was so rich, she might as well have her own bank. She could have her pick of any man in England. What in God's name was she doing in Newgate looking for a husband?

Benedict barely remembered not to bow—an automatic response to being introduced to a lady of quality—and racked his brains to recall what he knew of her family. A cit's daughter. Her father had been in shipping, a merchant, rich as Croesus. He'd died and left the family a fortune.

The younger sister was said to be the beauty of the family, but she must indeed be a goddess, because Georgiana Caversteed was strikingly lovely. Her arresting, heart-shaped face held a small, straight nose and eyes which, in the candlelight, appeared to be dark grey, the color of wet slate. Her brows were full, her lashes long, and her mouth was soft and a fraction too wide.

A swift heat spread throughout his body, and his heart began to pound.

She regarded him steadily as he made his assessment, neither dipping her head nor coyly fluttering her lashes. Benedict's interest kicked up a notch at her directness, and a twitch in his breeches reminded him with unpleasantly bad timing of his enforced abstinence. This was neither the time nor the place to do anything about *that*.

They'd never met in the ton. She must have come to town after he'd left for the peninsula three years ago, which would make her around twenty-four. Most women would be considered on the shelf at that age, unmarried after so many social seasons, but with the near-irresistible lure of her fortune and with those dazzling looks, Georgiana Caversteed could be *eighty-four* and someone would still want her.

And yet here she was.

Benedict kept his expression bland, even as he tried to breathe normally. What on earth had made her take such drastic action? Was the chit daft in the head? He couldn't imagine any situation desperate enough to warrant getting leg-shackled to a man like him.

She moistened her lips with the tip of her tongue—which sent another shot of heat straight to his gut—and fixed him with an imperious glare. "What is your name, sir?" She took a step closer, almost in challenge, in defiance of his unchained hands and undoubtedly menacing demeanor.

He quelled a spurt of admiration for her courage, even if it was ill-advised. His inhaled breath caught a subtle whiff of her perfume. It made his knees weak. He'd forgotten the intoxicating scent of woman and skin. For one

foolish moment, he imagined pulling her close and
pressing his nose into her hair, just filling his lungs with
the divine scent of her. He wanted to drink in her smell.
He wanted to see if those lips really were as soft as they
looked.

He took an involuntary step toward her but stopped at
the low growl of warning from her manservant. Sanity
prevailed, and he just remembered to stay in the role of
rough smuggler they all expected of him.

"My name? Ben Wylde. At your service."

His voice was a deep rasp, rough from lack of use, and
Georgie's stomach did an odd little flip. She needed to
take command here, like Father on board one of his ships,
but the man facing her was huge, hairy, and thoroughly
intimidating.

When she'd glanced around Knollys's rotund form and
into the gloomy cell, her first impression of the prisoner
had been astonishment at his sheer size. He'd seemed to
fill the entire space, all broad shoulders, wide chest, and
long legs. She'd been expecting some poor, ragged, cowering scrap of humanity. Not this strapping, unapologeti-
cally male creature.

She'd studied his shaggy, overlong hair and splendid
proportions from the back as they'd traipsed down the
corridor. He stood a good head taller than Knollys, and
unlike the jailer's waddling shuffle, this man walked with
a long, confident stride, straight-backed and chin high, as
if he owned the prison and were simply taking a tour for
his pleasure.

Now, in the chapel, she finally saw his face—the parts
that weren't covered with a dark bristle of beard—and
her skin prickled as she allowed her eyes to rove over
him. She pretended she was inspecting a horse or a piece
of furniture. Something large and impersonal.

His dark hair was matted and hung around his face almost to his chin. It was hard to tell what color it would be when it was clean. A small wisp of straw stuck out from one side, just above his ear, and she resisted a bizarre feminine urge to reach up and remove it. Dark beard hid the shape of his jaw, but the candlelight caught his slanted cheekbones and cast shadows in the hollows beneath. The skin that she could see—a straight slash of nose, cheeks, and forehead—was unfashionably tanned and emphasized his deep brown eyes.

She'd stepped as close to him as she dared; no doubt he'd smell like a cesspool if she got any nearer, but even so, she was aware of an uncomfortable curl of . . . what? Reluctant attraction? Repelled fascination?

The top of her head only came up to his chin, and his size was, paradoxically, both threatening and reassuring. He was large enough to lean on; she was certain if she raised her hand to his chest, he would be solid and warm. Unmovable. Her heart hammered in alarm. He was huge and unwashed, and yet her body reacted to him in the most disconcerting manner.

His stare was uncomfortably intense. She dropped her eyes, breaking the odd frisson between them, and took a small step backward.

His lawn shirt, open at the neck, was so thin it was almost transparent. His muscled chest and arms were clearly visible through the grimy fabric. His breeches were a nondescript brown, snug at the seams, and delineated the hard ridges of muscles of his lean thighs with unnerving clarity.

Georgie frowned. This was a man in the prime of life. It seemed wrong that he'd been caged like an animal. He exuded such a piratical air of command that she could easily imagine him on the prow of a ship or pacing in front of a group of soldiers, snapping orders.

She found her voice. "Were you in the military, Mr. Wylde?"

That would certainly explain his splendid physique and air of cocky confidence.

His dark brows twitched in what might have been surprise but could equally have been irritation. "I was."

She waited for more, but he did not elaborate. Clearly Mr. Wylde was a man of few words. His story was probably like that of thousands of other soldiers who had returned from the wars and found themselves unable to find honest work. She'd seen them in the streets, ragged and begging. It was England's disgrace that men who'd fought so heroically for their country had been reduced to pursuing a life of crime to survive.

Was the fact that he was not a condemned man truly a problem? Her original plan had been to tell Josiah she'd married a sailor who had put to sea. She would have been a widow, of course, but Josiah would never have known that. Her "absent" husband could have sailed the world indefinitely.

If she married this Wylde fellow, she would not immediately become a widow, but the intended result would be the same. Josiah would not be able to force her into marriage and risk committing bigamy.

Georgie narrowed her eyes at the prisoner. They would be bound together until one or the other of them died, and he looked disconcertingly healthy. Providing he didn't take up heavy drinking or catch a nasty tropical disease, he'd probably outlive her. That could cause problems.

Of course, if he continued his ill-advised occupation, then he'd probably succumb to a knife or a bullet sooner rather than later. Men like him always came to a sticky end; he'd only narrowly escaped the gallows this time. She'd probably be a widow in truth soon enough. But how would she hear of his passing if he were halfway across the world? How would she know when she was free?

She tore her eyes away from the rogue's surprisingly tempting lips and fixed Knollys with a hard stare. "Is there really no one else? I mean, he's so . . . so . . ."

Words failed her. Intimidating? Manly?

Unmanageable.

"No, ma'am. But he won't bother you after tonight."

What alternative did she have? She couldn't wait another few weeks. Her near-miss with Josiah had been the last straw. She'd been lucky to escape with an awful, sloppy kiss and not complete ruination. She sighed. "He'll have to do. Pieter, will you explain the terms of the agreement?"

Pieter nodded. "You'll marry Miss Caversteed tonight, Mr. Wylde. In exchange, you'll receive five hundred pounds to do with as you will."

Georgie waited for the prisoner to look suitably impressed. He did not. One dark eyebrow rose slightly, and the corner of his mobile lips curled in a most irritating way.

"Fat lot of good it'll do me in here," he drawled. "Ain't got time to pop to a bank between now and when they chain me to that floating death trap in the morning."

He had a fair point. "Is there someone else to whom we could send the money?"

His lips twitched again as if at some private joke. "Aye. Send it to Mr. Wolff at number ten St. James's. The Tricorn Club. Compliments of Ben Wylde. He'll appreciate it."

Georgie had no idea who this Mr. Wolff was—probably someone to whom this wretch owed a gambling debt—but she nodded and beckoned Pieter over. He took his cue and unfolded the legal document she'd had drawn up. He flattened it on the table next to the ordinary's pen and ink.

"You must sign this, Mr. Wylde. Ye can read?" he added as an afterthought.

Another twitch of those lips. "As if I'd been educated at Cambridge, sir. But give me the highlights."

"It says you renounce all claim to the lady's fortune, except for the five hundred pounds already agreed. You will make no further financial demands upon her in the future."

"Sounds reasonable."

The prisoner made a show of studying the entire document, or at least pretending to read it, then dipped the pen into the ink. Georgie held her breath.

Papa's will had divided his property equally between his wife and two daughters. To Georgie's mother, he'd left the estate in Lincolnshire. To her sister, Juliet, he'd left the London town house. And to Georgie, his eldest, the one who'd learned the business at his knee, he'd left the fleet of ships with which he'd made his fortune, the warehouses full of spices and silk, and the company ledgers.

His trusted man of business, Edmund Shaw, had done an exemplary job as Georgie's financial guardian for the past few years, but in three weeks' time, she would turn twenty-five and come into full possession of her fortune. And according to English law, as soon as she married, all that would instantly become the property of her husband, to do with as he wished.

That husband would *not* be Josiah.

Despite her mother's protests that it was vulgar and unladylike to concern herself with commerce, in the past five years Georgie had purchased two new ships and almost doubled her profits. She loved the challenge of running her own business, the independence. She was damned if she'd give it over to some blithering idiot like Josiah to drink and gamble away.

Which was precisely why she'd had Edmund draw up

this detailed document. It stated that all property and capital that was hers before the marriage *remained* hers. Her husband would receive only a discretionary allowance. To date, she'd received seven offers of marriage, and each time she'd sent her suitor to see Mr. Shaw. Every one of them had balked at signing—proof, if she'd needed it, that they'd only been after her fortune.

She let out a relieved sigh as the prisoner's pen moved confidently over the paper. Ben Wylde's signature was surprisingly neat. Perhaps he'd been a secretary, or written dispatches in the army? She shook her head. It wasn't her job to wonder about him. He was a means to an end, that was all.

He straightened, and his brown eyes were filled with a twinkle of devilry. "There, now. Just one further question, before we get to the vows, Miss Caversteed. Just what do you intend for a wedding night?"

Chapter 4.

Heat flashed across Georgie's skin, both at the impertinent question and the way the rogue's cheeky gaze moved over her. Laugh lines crinkled the corners of his brown eyes. She was used to such speculative ogling from her years in the *ton*, but not once had her body reacted as it did to this blackguard's leisurely perusal. Her breath quickened.

Pieter growled again and took a step forward, but the man grinned and held up both hands in an expression of innocence.

"Can't blame a chap for trying." He chuckled. "Jus' tryin' to scratch an itch."

"There will be no wedding night," Georgie said firmly. "I want your name, Mr. Wylde, not your—"

"Cock?" he suggested cheerfully.

"—company," she finished, proud of her cool tone.

His teeth flashed white as he smiled. "Why not? You'll never see me again. No one will know. Exceptin' these fine gentlemen, of course, and I'm sure they'd give us a few moments of privacy—"

"I am not having . . . marital relations . . . in a dirty prison with a stranger I just met!" she ground out.

His eyes twinkled. "Aww. Have pity. Give a poor wretch one last, 'appy memory of England. I might not even make it to Australia. I could be wrecked, or taken by sickness—"

Georgie narrowed her eyes. "I know precisely how perilous the oceans are, Mr. Wylde. My father died at sea."

The teasing laughter disappeared from his eyes. "Forgive me. I am sorry for your loss."

She waved away his sympathy. "In any case, my answer is still no."

"Will the marriage be legal if it ain't consummated?"

Georgie bit back a curse. She had no idea if consummation was actually required, but this man wasn't going to be around to cast doubts on the validity of their union. And she certainly wasn't going to mention it to anyone. "I'll take the chance, Mr. Wylde," she said briskly. "Now shall we begin?"

He bent at the waist in a parody of a gentleman's bow, which somehow managed to look entirely natural. "Why not, Miss Caversteed?" There was an ironic edge to his voice. "I have nothing else planned for this evening, save counting the lice in my cell."

On shaking legs, Georgie approached the makeshift altar and felt a gust of warm air as the prisoner came to stand beside her. The hairs on her arm rose, as if she'd brushed against a cobweb. She glanced down at her feet; there was an indentation in the flagstones, a concave dip where the stone had been worn smooth. Thousands of others had stood here over the years, pledging their own vows of fidelity.

Cotton opened the Bible to begin the ceremony, and Knollys and Pieter stood to one side to act as the witnesses. Georgie quelled a moment of panic. This was not something to be taken lightly. What was she doing, marrying a stranger? Making a mockery of this solemn institution? Swearing to love, honor, and obey this one man until death? She would probably be struck by lightning for uttering such falsehoods in a sacred place.

The darkness, the flicker of candles, the oppressive cave-like walls, made her feel as though they were participating in a far more ancient ritual. Something primal and profound that included fire and blood and the bonding of hands. Of souls.

She shook her head to banish the thought.

The preacher began.

She did not class herself as a romantic—she left that to her younger sister, Juliet—but this was not how a wedding should be. No flowers, no choir or hymns or beaming, benevolent vicar. No family and friends. Instead, there was this cold, echoing, slightly musty-smelling chapel. Cheap tallow candles instead of the more expensive beeswax they used at home.

Warmth permeated her side as the prisoner shifted closer to her, almost as if he were offering silent support. His hip and shoulder pressed against hers and lent her strength.

Her voice didn't shake when she spoke her vows. This was a matter of self-preservation, of protecting Mama and Juliet. She would not falter. The man at her side was not Josiah.

The prisoner repeated his vows, his voice low and confident, his accent less pronounced. Perhaps he was making an effort to speak properly for the occasion.

Pieter had purchased two plain gold rings, which he

laid flat on the open Bible in the ordinary's hands. Cotton launched into a blustering speech about the sanctity of this and submitting to that; Georgie barely listened. But her heart jolted as the prisoner took her left hand and slid a ring on her fourth finger. The metal was cool, but quickly warmed to her skin.

His own hands were large and capable; she felt the heat of his palm, the strength in his long fingers, as they reversed positions and she threaded the ring onto his left hand. It stuck on his knuckle, but she wriggled and twisted, and it finally slid on. Instead of letting her hand drop, his fingers threaded through hers, steady and oddly comforting.

And then it was over. Cotton added their names to the marriage license Pieter had obtained from a bribable clerk at Doctors' Commons. The prisoner released her hand to sign the register, the gold ring on his finger glinting in the candlelight. Georgie bent her thumb inwards and touched her own band. It felt strange, foreign. She would remove it as soon as she was in the carriage.

The prisoner straightened and caught her eye. "In the absence of anything more rousing, may I be permitted to kiss the bride?"

Her pulse leapt, but she saw no reason to be churlish. She had what she'd come for, after all. She adopted an expression of bored resignation. "Oh, very well."

He leaned forward. Georgie sipped in a breath and held it, determined not to inhale his undoubtedly repulsive odor. She pursed her lips and closed her eyes. Martyr-like, she waited.

And waited.

She heard him chuckle. His fingers settled on either side of her face and tilted her chin up. His thumb brushed the indent at the corner of her lips.

Her stomach flipped. She opened her eyes, caught a brief glimpse of his dark irises as his face descended to hers, and waited for something like Josiah's greedy lechery: a wet, sloppy assault.

He did not kiss like Josiah.

His mouth brushed hers, his lips a shockingly soft counterpoint to the prickles on his jaw. Something hot and achy bloomed inside her, from her breastbone to the pit of her belly. It was a tease of a kiss; a light, questioning touch that somehow managed to both madden and promise at the same time. His lips moved on hers as if testing his welcome, and Georgie found herself leaning up into him, enthralled. Wanting more. She softened her mouth just as his tongue traced the seam of her lips. Seeking entry. *Tasting* her. She jolted back in shock, suddenly recalling where she was. Who he was.

Heat flooded her face. Thoroughly mortified, she stared up into his laughing eyes.

"Hello, Mrs. Wylde," he whispered, just for her.

She ignored her hammering pulse and the weak sensation in her knees and tried to appear entirely unaffected by the kiss. Good God, that was her name now. *Mrs. Wylde.* She took a decisive step back. "*Goodbye*, Mr. Wylde," she said firmly. Her lips still tingled. "And thank you," she added. "You have done me a great service this night."

The corners of his lips twitched, and he swept her another magnificent bow, as perfect as if they stood in the receiving line at Carlton House. "My pleasure, Mrs. Wylde."

She did not fail to detect the sarcasm in his tone. They both knew he'd taken no "pleasure" from her.

"Any time you need another 'service,' do ask. I would be honored to assist." Those wicked eyes flicked to her lips and back up again.

Georgie turned away, flustered, and gestured to Pieter. "Let's go." Suddenly, all she wanted was to be home. She needed to think, and her wits seemed to have gone begging in the presence of this exasperating man.

Pieter collected the marriage license from Cotton and tossed a jingling purse to Knollys, who grinned and touched his forelock.

"Nice doin' business, milady," he sneered. He crossed to the prisoner and began to refasten the manacles around his wrists. Wylde submitted to the imprisonment without comment, and Georgie bit her lip to quell an instinctive protest. There was nothing more she could do for him now.

She took one last glance at the prisoner. What did one say to a handsome stranger you'd just married and would never see again? It was not a situation often covered in etiquette books. She couldn't very well wish him a good life.

"I wish you a safe journey," she said at last. And then, on a whim, added the words she'd always said when taking leave of her father, "Fair winds and a calm sea."

Those dark eyes met hers and held her captive for a long moment. "Thank you, my lady. If fortune is kind, perhaps we'll meet again—under more auspicious circumstances."

It was all she could do to nod.

Once the outer door of the prison clanged behind her, Georgie took a deep, cleansing breath. Her hands shook as she raised the hood of her domino, but a mad sense of relief washed over her. She'd done it! For six long years, she'd endured awkward matchmaking and unconvincing proposals, the never-ending sting of gossip and speculation. Josiah's thinly veiled threats and disapproval. She'd bowed to convention, done what others expected of her, from the moment she'd entered the *ton*. Now, for the first time in her adult life, she was free to start doing exactly as she pleased.

Ben Wylde, criminal rogue, had given her freedom.

Chapter 5.

A disturbance in the hallway and the angry scuffle of feet was the first indication of Cousin Josiah's arrival. His voice, low but threatening, carried through the half-open salon door.

"No, curse you, I'll announce myself!"

Georgie sat a little straighter in her chair and braced herself for what was bound to be an unpleasant interview. Anything concerning Josiah was unpleasant.

He flung himself through the door, brandishing the brief note she'd sent him like an Old Testament prophet. "What is the meaning of this, Georgiana? It says here that you've married. What do you mean by writing such twaddle?"

Georgie set down her book—*Robinson Crusoe* by Daniel Defoe—and glanced over at Pieter, who'd followed Josiah into the room and positioned himself in the corner, a silent but effective bodyguard. She looked up at her cousin's irate face impassively, but inside, her heart was racing.

"It's quite true, Josiah. I am married. Three days ago, as a matter of fact. I wanted you to be one of the first to know."

The irony in her tone was lost on Josiah. He'd removed his hat but hadn't handed it over in the hallway before he'd barged his way up to the salon, and his knuckles gleamed white as he crushed the curled brim in his hand. He slapped it against his thigh in an impatient gesture and exhaled with a chiding half laugh. "You are a tease, Georgiana."

Georgie lifted her chin, grateful that her mother and sister were out shopping. "Far from it. I would never joke about something as important as marriage. I wed by special license. Pieter can vouch to the truth of it."

Josiah's face grew red and mottled as his lips compressed in a furious line. "Who is he?" he demanded. "This husband of yours? Not one of 'em fortune hunters who've been sniffing 'round your skirts? You couldn't stand the sight of any of 'em!"

Georgie refrained from adding, *Fortune hunters like yourself?* Instead she said, "He's a midshipman on one of my frigates. We met at Blackwall three years ago. And we've been meeting in secret each time he's been back in port."

She silently congratulated herself on that little embellishment; she'd been inspired by her sister's favorite book, *Romeo and Juliet.*

Josiah looked as though he'd swallowed something repugnant. "A midshipman! You've pledged herself to a common sailor?" His eyes ran over her in disgust, as if he were viewing her in a whole new—and distinctly more unflattering—light. "Which ship?" Disbelief fairly dripped from his tone.

"I don't believe I'm under any obligation to tell you. I doubt the two of you will ever meet."

Georgie smiled as an overwhelming sense of triumph poured through her, a feeling of weightlessness, of relief. She'd endured months, years, of Josiah's unsubtle, over-bearing attentions. The way he used his greater height and bulk to stand too close to her at every opportunity, invading her space, subtly aggressive. The way he some-times caught her wrist to restrain her or placed his sweaty palm at the small of her back to steer her in to dinner. Proprietorial, when he had no cause to be. Now, all his fawning obsequiousness had come to nothing.

"But what of your fortune? The honor due to your family?" Josiah spluttered.

Of course, her money *would* be his primary concern. It was the only reason he'd ever paid her any attention. He took a menacing step toward her, and Georgie shrank back; he looked as though he wanted to throttle her. She glanced over at Pieter in a silent, pointed reminder that she was amply protected, and breathed a sigh of relief when Josiah spun on his heel and paced away.

"Your mother agreed to this farce?" Josiah demanded. "You cannot convince me of it. She's always wanted an aristocratic title for you. And for Juliet. I doubt she'd have given her blessing to the Prince Regent himself!"

Georgie raised her brows and dodged the question. "I needed no one's permission. I am of legal age to make my own decisions, especially those which concern my future happiness. In three weeks, I shall turn twenty-five."

"You've lost your wits, girl! You should be sent straight to Bedlam. A sailor?" Josiah repeated incredulously. "Good God, what will the world think?"

"I haven't the slightest intention of finding out. There's no reason for anyone in the *ton* to know about my mar-riage. My affairs are my own, as are my wits. Besides, I doubt my husband will ever set foot in a ballroom, once he returns to these shores. We plan to retire to Lincoln-shire." She sent Josiah a sweet smile and twisted the verbal knife. "I know I can rely on your discretion, Josiah. Such an undesirable connection might reflect badly on you."

Her cousin was as obsessed with the family's social standing as her mother. He'd spent his entire life trying to ingratiate himself with the *ton*, glossing over what he saw as the family's "shameful" background in trade. In his opinion, a fortune that had been earned was of far less merit than one that had been inherited. He would never lower himself to actually *work* for a living—which was good because as far as Georgie had seen, he had no discernable skills, save perhaps a talent for overindulgence. He spent his time trying to emulate his betters, lounging in gentleman's clubs, playing cards and dice, attending prizefights, and patronizing eye-wateringly expensive tailors and boot makers he could ill afford.

"You have as much to lose as I do if word of this comes out," she reminded him quietly.

Josiah shook his head and his lip stuck out stubbornly. "I simply don't believe you, Georgiana. This all some ridiculous joke at my expense. But mark my words, I *will* discover the truth."

Georgie shrugged. "Believe what you will, but my marriage is fact." She gestured to the door. "That is all, Josiah. I'm sure you have plenty of other places to be. Pieter will show you out."

As the door slammed behind him, Georgie breathed a sigh of relief. Pieter returned and gave her a meaningful glance from under his bushy brows.

"He won't be taking your word for it, Georgie. Not when he's been after you for so long. No man wants to think he's been pipped to the winning post."

"Especially when he thought he was the lead horse in

the race," Georgie finished dryly. She tossed her head. "He won't find out anything. And besides, even if he does, my marriage was perfectly legal. There's nothing he can do about it. He's just furious because the Caversteed fortune has slipped through his greedy, grasping fingers."

Chapter 6.

Lady Langton's ballroom was the usual wash of vapid chatter, politics, rivalries, witticisms, and gossip. Georgie stood next to her mother and feigned polite interest in the assorted comings and goings.

She was happy. Really. Everything was wonderful. Today—her twenty-fifth birthday—she'd finally become sole, legal owner of Caversteed Trading and Shipping. The family's future was secure. Josiah's plans had been stymied.

So why did she feel as if she were in an odd sort of limbo?

She'd blame it on the usual melancholy of being another year older and still unwed, but she *was* wed, wasn't she? Maybe that was the problem. She was a married woman without a husband. A wife, yet still a virgin. What a mess.

She gazed across the dance floor and tried to ignore the sense of dissatisfaction that had plagued her ever since she'd left Newgate. According to her original plan, she should have been a widow by now. Instead, she had a husband, somewhere out there in the world.

Her stomach gave an anxious flutter every time she thought of the rogue she'd married. Their encounter had left her with a restless awareness of her own body, a strange yearning. Looking back, she was amazed at her own boldness. Her memories of that night had taken on elements of a dream, or a bout of madness.

She had to stop thinking about him.

It had been three weeks since she'd summoned her mother and sister into the library and calmly explained that she'd married a convict to avoid Cousin Josiah. Mother had taken the news surprisingly well. She'd long ago abandoned any hope of Georgie landing a decent husband, and she'd never particularly liked Cousin Josiah, so she sympathized with Georgie's aversion to marrying him, if not her choice of alternative.

In addition, Mother was blessed with a talent for simply ignoring things she didn't want to acknowledge, like outrageous dressmakers' bills, the ruinous cost of claret, and wayward eldest daughters who secretly married criminals. Her main concern had been that the *ton* might find out about Georgie's "foolish act," as she called it. No scandal could be allowed to jeopardize Juliet's chances of a brilliant match. She'd pronounced the whole affair an "unfortunate incident best forgotten," and had sworn both Georgie and Juliet to secrecy.

"Do try one of these flans, Georgiana."

Georgie turned. Only her mother ever called her Georgiana. And Pieter, of course, whenever she did something outrageous.

"I wonder if it would be possible to abduct Lady Langton's pastry chef?" Mother muttered around a delicate mouthful of éclair. "He's French, you know. These are divine."

Georgie smiled, well used to such flights of fancy. "I don't think it's legal. And even if it were, it sounds expensive. I bet you'd have to lay out a tidy sum for a kidnapping. Even for a lowly pastry chef."

Her mother chewed thoughtfully. "Hmm. You're probably right. Besides, Cook wouldn't like it if we let a revolutionary invade her kitchen." She poked Georgie in the ribs with her folded fan. "I hope you're not going to discuss trade routes with Lord Galveston again. This is supposed to be a party. No one wants to talk about latitude and longitude. Eccentricity is all very well in a ninety-year-old spinster, but it is hardly becoming in a woman who is only twenty-four."

Georgie managed not to roll her eyes. "Twenty-five, as of today," she murmured.

Mother had decided that Georgie would soon be a widow—thanks to the short life expectancy of criminals in the Antipodes. She'd been suggesting potential *second* husbands with depressing regularity.

"Oh, look, there's Clara Cockburn. Admiral Cockburn's wife." Her mother waved at a plump, dark-haired woman across the room then raised her fan to hide her mouth. "Odious gossip. I don't care what you say, Georgie, that woman has a mustache. I swear, in certain lights—"

"Shh!" Georgie smothered a laugh. "Someone will hear you! You wouldn't want to ruin Juliet's chances, would you?"

As if by unspoken agreement, they both turned to watch her younger sister, who was dancing in the center of the room. A tiny frown wrinkled the perfection of Juliet's otherwise smooth forehead. Mother sucked in a breath. "Oh dear. It doesn't look as if she's finding the Duke of Upton amusing."

Not for the first time, Georgie wondered how she could be related to such a beautiful creature. Juliet literally turned heads wherever she went. Just this morning, walking to Hatchard's, a distracted carriage driver had taken one look at Juliet and pulled so hard on his reins that his horse had crashed into a street vendor's stall. A torrent of apples had rolled down from the poor merchant's carefully constructed pyramid. A besotted young buck had rushed forward to shield Juliet from the fruity threat—ignoring Georgie in his haste—and when Juliet had thrown him an absent-minded smile of thanks, he'd backed away, bowing, until he'd bumped into a window cleaner's ladder. Both of them had toppled to the ground.

Juliet, as usual, had been oblivious to the trail of destruction that followed in her wake. It was, however, impossible to dislike her because she was completely free from vanity or conceit. No one was immune to her sunny charm, from the eighty-year-old vicar to the two-year-old in leading strings; one sweet smile from Juliet's rosebud lips and the hardest of hearts melted.

Georgie completely understood Juliet's appeal. Her own sense of humor was sometimes dry and at the expense of male pride, and she was often uncomfortably direct. Who wanted that when they could have Juliet's delicious folly?

Juliet's incredible clumsiness, however, had always been a source of slightly guilty pleasure. This, surely, was evidence of Mother Nature giving the less pretty girls a sporting chance. No one should be allowed that much beauty *and* coordination. It just wouldn't be fair. Even as she watched, Juliet turned the wrong way in the dance and stepped on her partner's foot. The duke didn't seem to notice. His rapt gaze never left her face, and he seemed genuinely crestfallen at the need to restore her to her family when the cotillion ended. Juliet gave him a sweet smile, nodded at his pleasantries—and expertly sent him on his way.

She turned to Georgie with a little huff as their mother excused herself to go to the powder room.

"Something wrong, Ju?" Georgie ventured.

Juliet gave an elegant shrug of her milky-white shoulders. "Do you know how tiresome it is to be constantly likened to classical deities? I swear, if one more person compares me to Diana or Aphrodite, I'll . . . well, I don't know what I'll do. But it will be bad."

She pursed her lips, and Georgie bit back a smile. If the men thought of Juliet as a Greek goddess, they probably considered *her* a Harpy or a Gorgon.

"Why must men be so silly?" Juliet sighed. "Lord Dunravin said he'd slay dragons for me. There aren't any dragons anymore, are there? At least, not in England."

"There are no dragons left in England," Georgie agreed, with a straight face. "Unless you count Lady Cockburn over there. How dare he offer to rid the world of imaginary beasts?"

"Well, what would you want a man to do for you?" Juliet asked, suddenly serious. "If not slay dragons?"

Georgie considered the question. She'd given up hope of a man wanting to do things for her about five insincere proposals ago. "I'd want him to make me smile," she said after a moment. "And make my stomach all giddy."

The way her prisoner had done.

"And be aware that there are no dragons in England," she added for good measure. "Intelligence in a man is always a welcome surprise." She nodded toward the duke. "You're not seriously considering Upton, are you?"

"Ugh, no. I know mother would love me to become 'Her Grace,' but I can't imagine marrying anyone except my darling Simeon."

Georgie suppressed a groan. Juliet had been besotted with Simeon Pettigrew, the vicar's son from Little Gidding, the Lincolnshire village closest to their family home, for years. Mother had hoped that Juliet's first London season would make her forget all about him, but nothing—not even the undivided attention of the unmarried male half of the *ton*—had done the trick. Worse, Georgie had promised Juliet that if she still wanted silly Simeon after a whole season, then she would lend her support to the union.

Juliet sniffed. "Don't look like that, Georgie. It's not my fault. I never meant to fall in love with a mere mister." She crossed her gloved hands over her perfectly proportioned bosom and sighed dramatically. "The heart has no discernment. Besides, Upton's awful. A lord with whom to be bored, as Simeon would say." She snorted at her own joke.

Georgie winced. Simeon's poetry was unaccountably bad. Byron, Shelly, and Keats could rest easy in their beds. Simeon had a habit of trying to make everything rhyme, with no regard for sense or meter, but that hadn't deterred Juliet, who thought him wonderfully romantic.

"I do wish Mother would relent. I miss him, Georgie." Her lower lip pushed out in a hint of a pout. "It's all right for you. You're safe from her matchmaking. Even when you married a *criminal* and she barely batted an eyelid."

"That's because she'd given up hope of me ever choosing a husband. And I wouldn't exactly say she 'didn't bat an eyelid,'" Georgie muttered. "She called me a headstrong, impetuous hellion far too much like Father."

"She meant it affectionately. You know how much she loved Papa. And she's secretly proud of the fact that you've inherited his talent for business, even if she dislikes you to show it in public."

So unladylike, Georgiana. No man wants a wife who dabbles in trade.

Georgie sighed. Maybe she should take a lover? She was twenty-five, for heaven's sake. Most girls had been married off at sixteen or seventeen. She'd missed out on seven years of knowing what physical pleasure could be had between a man and a woman. Such an arrangement might lack the steady friendship and loving support that her parents had found in their marriage, but at least it would be *something*.

She cast her gaze over the assorted crowd and tried to muster some enthusiasm for one of the titled fops who milled around. If she were to avoid a scandal, she needed a rake. A discreet rake. There were a few potential candidates in attendance. But Turnbull was too loud. Coster was too sweaty. Elton was too short. Woodford was too old. Wingate was attractive, but irredeemably stupid.

Not one of them made her heart thump in her chest or made her stomach swirl in that delicious way her prisoner's wicked gaze had done.

She'd dreamed of him. Alone at night, tucked in her lonely bed, it was his eyes she imagined, his big hands touching her skin. Their brief kiss haunted her, teasing her with a hint of how much more there was to experience in life. It was just her luck to discover she was attracted to rogues, instead of gentlemen. To lean, dark ruffians with soft brown hair and taunting eyes.

What he was doing, her pirate, her highwayman? She'd never actually discovered his crimes. Wherever he was, she hoped he was alive and well. It did her heart good to think of him laughing somewhere in the sunlight, thumbing his nose at convention, having adventures in the great wide world.

Part of her wished she could have gone with him. She wanted that freedom, the challenge of the great unknown, the excitement of knowing whole uncharted continents lay ahead, just waiting to be explored. She wanted to be Robinson Crusoe, or Gulliver, or Byron's Corsair, sailing "o'er the glad waters of the dark blue sea" to find some "Pirate's Isle." She owned ships that sailed across the world, to exotic locations like Alexandria and Ceylon, Calcutta and Peking, but she'd never been adventuring on any of them. She'd never even been over to France, given Britain's near-constant state of warfare with that country for most of her adult life.

Ladies don't do that, Georgiana.

But, oh, how she wanted to.

The closest she'd ever been to a life on the ocean wave was sailing her single-mast sailboat, *L'Aventure*, on the artificial lake Father had created back in Lincolnshire.

Lucky pirate.

It was a shame she'd never see him again.

Chapter 7.

He was back.

Benedict had spent three weeks chasing down leads, trying to glean something from the idle chatter in London's darkest and least salubrious taverns. But apart from some vague whispers about the plot to rescue Bonaparte from St. Helena, he'd learned little of value.

He'd rarely bothered with *ton* parties since his return from Belgium; he preferred to spend his free time in the card rooms at the Tricorn, listening to the gossip, but Alex had begged him to accompany him tonight, and he hadn't had the heart to refuse.

Ben glanced sideways at Alexander Harland, second son of the Duke of Southwick, the man who, along with Sebastien Wolff, had been his best friend since their first days at Eton. All three of them were younger sons, the "spares" as opposed to the "heirs," shipped off to receive a decent education without the stifling expectation of one day inheriting a title or having to take their seat in the House of Lords.

They shared a wicked sense of humor and an un-quenchable thirst for adventure, and their friendship had sustained them through school and their subsequent stud-ies at Cambridge. When they'd left university five years ago, they'd thrown themselves enthusiastically into town life, not rising until midday, drinking and flirting away the nights. They'd gleefully cultivated reputations as game-sters, reprobates, and all-around rogues.

But even London's endless whirl of dissipation had begun to pall, and when Nelson trounced Napoleon at Trafalgar, the three of them had signed up to the Rifles, looking for adventure, naively convinced the war would all be over in a matter of months.

But their "short stint" in the Rifles had turned into three long, grueling years—years which had included any number of close shaves, hellish conditions, moments of elation and despair, hardship and loss.

Benedict shook his head. War had made men of them, had shown their previous existence to be shallow and friv-olous. They'd made a pact, one evening, seated around a smoky campfire on a sodden field in Belgium, the dawn before Waterloo. A vow that when they returned—if they survived the battle ahead—they'd make their fortunes together.

Alex and Seb already had money, of course. Alex was wealthy in his own right, thanks to a generous maiden aunt who'd left him a tidy sum, and Seb was the younger son of a duke and had his own funds.

In stark contrast, Benedict's father had left his off-spring in dire straits. Benedict's older brother, John, had inherited the title Earl of Morcott, but little else save a monstrous pile of debt, which Benedict felt honor bound to help him reduce. John had sold off everything that wasn't entailed and had managed to retain the principle seat, Morcott Hall, and a few hundred acres, and was busy returning the estate to profitability. He was currently in town on the lookout for a wealthy wife, but Ben hadn't caught up with him for weeks.

He'd offered John the money he'd received when he sold off his commission and left the Rifles, but John had staunchly refused. Not out of pride—he appreciated the gesture, but he insisted that Benedict invest in something to secure his own financial future.

And so Benedict had put his money in with Alex and Seb, and they'd opened the Tricorn Club, named after the three-cornered hat favored by rogues and highwaymen. They'd deemed the name both appropriate—since there were three of them in the joint enterprise—and suitably disreputable. The club, after all, would be open not just to an elite few, like White's or Brooks', but to any who could pay the subscription fee, honor their gambling debts, and abide by the house rules. The Tricorn was the most progressive of clubs: It welcomed lords and ladies, actresses and tradesmen, bankers and lawyers.

Conant had been correct in his initial assessment; the Tricorn was a bridge between all levels of society, the perfect place for ferreting out secrets and overhearing gossip. Drink, pretty women, and an intimate atmosphere, all encouraged men to talk. Fortunes changed hands at the turn of a card, the roll of dice, and those who owed money could often be induced to divulge valuable snippets of information in exchange for forgiveness of their debts to the house. The owners of the Tricorn held a great deal of power. The power to tear up incriminating IOUs, or, conversely, the power to call in the debts and ruin a man completely.

Ben, Alex, and Seb had slipped back into their previous roles, appearing to the world as reckless, aimless pleasure-seekers, but this time they had a purpose. As ex-soldiers, they didn't flinch at encountering the darker elements of society, but they were also on friendly terms with all but the highest sticklers in the *ton*.

Benedict gave a wry smile as he glanced around the room. The disapproving matrons kept inviting him to their soirées, clutching their pearls in scandalized dismay. Most of them secretly hoped he'd show an honorable interest in their daughters. Or a dishonorable interest in *them*. He'd lost count of the number of married women who'd offered themselves to him over the years.

He ran his hand over his freshly shaven jaw, relishing the smoothness. His handsome face and family name had always allowed him access to the highest society. Scandalous and debt-ridden he might be, but he was still a member of one of the oldest aristocratic families in England. Still a catch.

At least, he would be, if he weren't already married.

Benedict's heart gave an impatient lurch. *She* was the real reason he'd braved Lady Langton's ballroom. His wife. Georgiana Caversteed. Or rather, Georgiana Wylde.

He'd relived the brief moments they'd spent together in the flickering torchlight over and over, trying to make sense of it. She must have been in considerable trouble to have resorted to such a plan, but that was no excuse. He didn't have time to become embroiled in some spoiled princess's machinations.

He'd been deliberately crass in Newgate to test her reaction. Everything about her—from her soft skin to her crisp voice—had proclaimed her a lady of quality. He'd wanted to shock her into reconsidering her plans. And yet she'd countered his raw cheekiness with a cool confidence he'd found amazingly attractive. Georgiana Caversteed was an extraordinary woman, no doubt about it.

Her stubborn intelligence intrigued him almost as much as the taste of her had aroused him. But that still didn't mean he wanted to be *married* to her.

The only consolation was the fact that she'd be as keen to dissolve their union as he was, once she discovered his true identity. He couldn't wait to watch those generous lips part in shock.

"What are you smiling about?" Alex shot him a side-long glance.

Benedict shrugged. "Women. Or rather, one woman in particular."

Alex's brows lifted. "I thought we were here to pick up rumors, not find you a new mistress."

Benedict sent him an enigmatic smile.

"She's not married, is she?" Alex asked warily. "Married mistresses are more trouble than they're worth, believe me. Widows are infinitely more amenable. No irate husbands to deal with, for a start." He eyed Benedict's evening attire with a severe eye. "You should have come in uniform. No woman can resist the allure of a military man. It's a basic law of physics. The amount of scarlet, gilt braiding, and medals on your chest is directly proportional to how attractive a girl finds you."

Benedict shook his head in mock disapproval. "So cynical."

His companion shrugged. "We escaped relatively unscathed from Boney, when you consider it. Not a missing limb between us. No dashing facial scars." He nodded across the room at a seasoned old soldier surrounded by a gaggle of admiring ladies. "Look at Uxbridge over there. Lost half his leg at Waterloo, and he's a bloody hero."

"I got a ball in the shoulder at Salamanca," Benedict reminded him mildly.

"And I have a sabre cut on my thigh and a blind spot

in my left eye," Alex finished. "My point is, you can't play the 'gallant wounded hero' sympathy card with injuries like ours. No one knows about my loss of vision unless I tell them about it. And by the time a lady sees my scar, we're already a long way past the sympathy stage." He grinned wickedly and tilted his head. "I wonder if I should contrive a limp?"

Benedict snorted. "As if you need any help getting women." Alex took after his mother, who had been a famous beauty, and his sulky good looks had females sighing and salivating over him wherever he went. "If you must know, I'm looking for one of the Caversteed girls." He enjoyed the look of surprise that passed over his friend's face; he should have waited until Alex had a mouthful of champagne.

Alex turned to the dance floor and unerringly picked out a girl who was dancing with the Duke of Upton. "What, the fair Juliet? She's a beauty, I'll give you that, but you don't stand a chance. She's turned down a whole raft of suitors. You're overestimating your charms if you think she'll have a fling with a scapegrace second son who's part owner of a gaming hell. The mother's after a title. A marquis, at least."

Benedict eyed his wife's younger sister as she swirled about the floor. The girl was undeniably beautiful, but her features seemed watered-down versions of the ones he'd found so arresting in her sibling. Her nose was too small, her eyes too doll-like, her rosebud mouth lacking the sensual generosity of Georgiana's.

Not that he'd been thinking about the damned woman's mouth.

Not more than once or twice a day, at any rate.

He wanted to divorce her, not sleep with her.

Actually, that wasn't true. He wanted to do both of those things. Divorce her. *And* sleep with her. But only one of them was going to happen. Bedding the prickly Miss Caversteed was not in the cards, even if she was, technically, at this very moment, his wife. That way, as Shakespeare so rightly put it, lay madness.

He was going to sort out this mess, then find someone far less complicated with whom to sate his seething lust, because every one of his finely honed battle instincts told him that tangling with Georgiana Caversteed would only lead to trouble.

He scanned the edges of the room impatiently. "Not her. I was looking for the other one."

Alex's dark brows rose in question.

"I'll tell you about it later."

Benedict hadn't yet told his two closest friends about his impromptu marriage. Miss Caversteed had honored her promise to send five hundred pounds to Seb, but Benedict had waved it off as the proceeds of a lucky run at the card tables and promptly sent it off to his brother to help with the more pressing bills on the Morcott estate. His profits from the Tricorn always went to helping John claw back what their profligate father had lost.

He'd returned to his rooms above the Tricorn determined to tell his friends everything when Alex had invited him to come out, and since there was a good chance that his unwanted wife would be present at tonight's event, Ben had agreed. If all went well, they'd be laughing about the whole thing over a game of cards and some good French brandy before the week was out.

The only reason to stay married to a woman like Georgiana Caversteed would be to take advantage of her immense fortune, which, God knew, he needed. Her money could pay off the mountain of debt his father had left behind, save Morcott Hall, and secure the livelihood of every worker who relied on the estate to survive.

She could have been the answer to his prayers. And

yet in one of the great ironies of the universe, which Benedict had come to accept as his due, he'd simultaneously married the richest woman he'd ever met and signed away his ability to get a single penny from her, all within the space of ten minutes.

He had better things to do than chase some headstrong heiress around town to demand a divorce. He wanted this marriage over and done with as quickly as possible.

And then he saw her, standing with an older woman who was probably her mother on the opposite side of the dance floor, and his pulse jolted with a rush of nervous energy, like a fencer *en garde*.

Her gown, a dark blue sheath embroidered at the edges with gold thread, molded to her slim curves with a subtlety that indicated the work of an extremely expensive modiste. Beneath the chandelier's glow her hair held an unexpected hint of copper he hadn't noticed in Newgate, and the thick mass had been swept up in some complicated knot on the top of her head.

His fingers itched to unpin it.

Her slate-grey eyes scanned the ballroom, and the expression on her face was a mixture of polite boredom and resignation. Benedict watched as she took a final sip of lemonade and grimaced at the taste. He'd wager she hated being here almost as much as he did, although for different reasons. He smiled in anticipation. Her evening was about to get a whole lot worse.

Juliet leaned closer to Georgie and raised her fan to hide her mouth, just as their mother did. "Oh, goodness. I don't believe it! They're here!"

Georgie tried to dredge up some interest in whoever had captured her sister's eye. "Who are?"

"The most scandalous men in London!"

"Oh. Is Lord Byron back from the continent?"

"No, silly. The Unholy Trinity. Well, two of them at any rate. Benedict, the earl of Morcott's brother, and Alex, the Duke of Southwick's son. They're the ones who've started that infamous gaming hell. Honestly, don't you read any of the scandal sheets?"

"I try not to," Georgie murmured truthfully, turning toward the refreshment table to dispose of her empty glass. Her attention usually drifted away when her sister read aloud. Juliet's love of gossipy fashion magazines and badly written gothic horrors had produced a hilarious ability to overdramatize any event. A simple walk to church could be reinvented as an attempted kidnapping—the innocuous-looking man loitering on the corner was undoubtedly a French spy. If one listened to Juliet, child-swapping at birth, abductions, and incarceration of mad, elderly relatives were regular occurrences.

"You must have heard of them," Juliet whispered. "*The Lady's Quarterly Gazette* reported that Wylde has only just been released from the Fleet!"

"Oh," Georgie said vaguely.

"He has a shocking reputation. Gambling. Horse races. Shooting contests."

Georgie she found herself rather envious of the man, whoever he was. He sounded like he was having fun. Clearly he paid no heed to the disapproval of the *ton*. How liberating that must be.

"They're both extremely handsome," Juliet breathed soulfully. "Nothing compared to Simeon, of course, but still, I can quite see why everyone keeps forgiving them."

Georgie finally glanced in the direction her sister indicated and caught her breath.

No. It couldn't be.

The man across the room was tall, dark, handsome—and horribly familiar. Her heart skidded to a stop then began galloping as if she'd run a steeplechase. Without a horse. She narrowed her eyes and studied the man's profile. No beard obscured his face now, but it was unmistakably the same tanned skin, the same straight nose and sharp cheekbones as her prisoner. His clean-shaven cheeks showed a hint of—not quite dimples, precisely, more like grooves—and a smooth line of jaw above a pristine cravat. Her mouth went dry.

It was merely an uncanny resemblance. The man she'd married was half the world away.

But an impeccable navy jacket accentuated the same broad shoulders she'd admired in Newgate. Tan breeches hugged the same long thighs and lean hips. His hair—still unfashionably long—was lighter now that it was clean: a mid-brown with a natural wave that curled around his ears and gave him a careless, windblown look.

There must be some mistake.

And then, as if aware of her perusal, his eyes snapped to hers, and her heart lodged in her throat. Those deep brown eyes held hers in a direct, challenging stare.

This could not be happening.

Georgie tore her gaze away and let out a shaky breath. "Who is that man?"

Juliet gave a little huff of frustration. "Haven't you been listening to a word I've been saying? That's Benedict Wylde, Morcott's penniless younger brother. The equally handsome man next to him is his best friend, Alex Harland. I was introduced to him last week at Caroline Brudenell's card party."

The leaden hand of doom crushed Georgie's chest. The room spun.

Benedict Wylde. *Ben* Wylde.

Her prisoner.

Her *husband*.

Dual images of the man juxtaposed one another in her mind: scruffy prisoner and immaculate aristocrat.

She risked another glance, almost against her will. Benedict Wylde. The most unsuitable man in London. He was still watching her. His brows rose in silent question, and his lips curved upward in a slow, wicked smile.

Her skin went hot, then cold, as if she'd been stung by a nettle, then jumped into a freezing pond. A surge of furious indignation assailed her. *The Lady's Quarterly Gazette* needed to check its facts. He hadn't been languishing in the Fleet, he'd been rotting in bloody Newgate!

Her stomach plummeted. Had she somehow been duped by a fortune hunter? Impossible. Wylde couldn't possibly have planned their meeting. And besides, he'd signed her contract, hadn't he? It was watertight. Her fortune was secure.

Georgie exhaled slowly and tried to think, but her pulse refused to calm. What was he doing here? And dear God, what had she done?

Chapter 8.

"Good heavens! They're coming this way."

Georgie barely heard Juliet's scandalized gasp. What should she do? Run? Scream? Faint? She'd never swooned before—that was Juliet's forte—but now seemed like an excellent time to start. She shot a desperate glance to her left, but the crowded refreshments table barred her way. Unable to move right without pushing Juliet into an urn full of foliage, she watched in mute horror as the two men approached. Wylde led the way, pausing as he was hailed by acquaintances, but still closing the distance inexorably, like a panther stalking its prey.

Perhaps, by some amazing coincidence, he had a twin.

Georgie bit the inside of her lip. Now she sounded like Juliet, making up fanciful tales.

Then he was there, bowing with the same athletic grace she'd witnessed in prison, and it was too late to run. Heat washed over her in waves. This was going to be disaster. He stopped right in front of her, impossible to ignore, but it was his friend who spoke first.

"Miss Georgiana Caversteed, Miss Juliet Caversteed."

They both bobbed a curtsey. At least, Juliet did. Georgie's knees simply buckled.

Juliet dimpled prettily. "Mr. Harland. How good to see you again."

The darker-haired man half turned to his companion. "And you. May I present my good friend, Benedict Wylde?"

The rogue nodded to Juliet then glanced at Georgie, a hint of devilry sparkling in his eyes, as if they shared a private joke. "Miss Caversteed, it is a pleasure to meet you."

Georgie waited for him to add "again," but mercifully he did not. Instead, he narrowed his eyes as if struggling to recall something and tilted his head as his gaze roved over her face.

"I must say, you look extremely familiar. Have we met?"

Oh, the beast. So, he'd decided to torture her, had he? Georgie swallowed and willed her voice to come out steady. "I can't imagine where we might have crossed paths, Mr. Wylde."

"You're right, of course," he murmured. "I'm sure I would have remembered such an encounter."

His voice might have lost its rough slang and harsh guttural edges, but it was still the same deep rumble that had played havoc with her pulse. Georgie glanced at Juliet and found her sister watching their byplay in open-mouthed astonishment. It was usually *she* who captured the attention of the gentlemen, but Wylde had barely spared her a glance.

He bent his arm at the elbow and offered it forward in unmistakable invitation. "Would you care to take a turn about the room, Miss Caversteed?"

The coiled tension inside her eased a fraction; he was going to pretend they've never met. Thank heaven.

"Or perhaps you'd care to dance?"

"Dance?" she repeated stupidly.

"It is a customary activity, at a ball." His eyes shone with silent laughter.

She'd rather dance with a Bengal tiger. While naked. But people were already watching them curiously; she couldn't turn him down without eliciting all manner of comment. "Yes, all right, then."

He bowed again, mocking her ungracious acceptance with his courtly manners. "My lady."

Was it her imagination, or had he placed a slight possessive emphasis on the first word? With great reluctance, she placed her hand on his arm and allowed him to lead her onto the dance floor. He took her right hand in his and slid his left hand around her waist to rest at the small of her back. The heat of his palm burned through the layers of her dress, and the warmth of his chest bathed her front, even though they were still several inches apart.

Georgie took a deep breath and inadvertently inhaled the scent of him, a subtly masculine cologne, clean and earthy, a million miles away from the stench of that hell-hole in which they'd first met. Her blood started a slow simmer.

Naturally, the musicians struck up a waltz. Fate would never be so kind as to provide a lively reel. She focused on the plain gold stick pin that fastened his intricate cravat.

"You, sir, are supposed to be on your way to Australia! What are you doing here?" She raised her head and met his amused gaze with a glare. "I don't know what happened in Newgate after I left, but somehow you bribed the jailers to let you escape. You probably used my money! Are you a wanted criminal? On the run?"

He shook his head. "Ben Wylde the smuggler is on his way to Australia, alone and unlamented." A dimple creased his left cheek. "*Benedict* Wylde, on the other hand, brother of the Earl of Morcott, is very much present and correct. And delighted to renew his acquaintance with you." He passed an idle glance around the room and lowered his head to her ear. "I do believe we're setting tongues wagging, Miss Caversteed."

Georgie shot him a cynical look. "I doubt anyone here will think it odd that a man known to be permanently in need of funds should be dancing with the richest single woman in the room."

Her acerbic response seemed to amuse him. "Ah. My reputation precedes me." He guided her into a turn, and she clutched his shoulder as the room spun. "As does yours. The *ton* still thinks you're quite the catch on the marriage mart. The rich Miss Caversteed, princess in her ivory tower, untouchable by mere mortals like myself."

His grip tightened on her waist, as if to give lie to the words: *He* was touching her. She missed a step, but plastered a smile on her face, intensely aware of the surrounding couples all shamelessly trying to eavesdrop on their conversation.

"You haven't told anyone you're married," he whispered.

She stiffened. Was that a threat? Did he mean to blackmail her? To demand money for his silence? "We need to talk, Mr. Wylde. Somewhere private."

His teeth flashed white. "Somewhere private? At a ball? Unlikely. What if we're caught alone together? Just *think* of the scandal." His tone was deeply ironic. "Why, we'd probably be forced to marry. Again."

Georgie dragged air into her constricted lungs. "No, thank you, Mr. Wylde. Marrying you once was quite enough."

They completed another turn, and she tried to ignore

how effortlessly they seemed to fit together, despite his greater size. He somehow managed to position his thigh intimately between hers with alarming regularity. Her entire body was warm, humming. The waltz truly was an indecent dance.

"I don't even know your full name," she hissed irritably. "Are we even legally married?"

He'd signed the name Ben Wylde in Newgate, but it seemed his given name was Benedict. That suited him— something lordly and autocratic. And rather fitting that it should include the word "edict." No doubt he was accustomed to bossing people around. Well, he wouldn't succeed with *her*.

"The name I gave in Newgate wasn't my full name, but yes, it was enough to bind us together. I checked. Our marriage is legal."

Georgie was finding it hard to draw a breath. She forced herself to look away from his sinfully inviting lips—even more noticeable now he'd removed that scruffy beard— and exhale slowly. "You know I had no expectation of you remaining in the country."

"I had no plans to be transported."

"Then why on earth didn't you say something?"

His fingers tightened on hers. "I don't recall having much say in the matter, madam, when I was dragged from my cell in manacles and forced to the altar."

A guilty heat warmed her neck. He had a point. She might as well have held a gun to his head, for all the choice she'd given him.

"We can't talk here," he murmured. "Come and see me tomorrow."

Georgie glanced around. Mother had rejoined Juliet at the side of the dance floor. Both of them wore identical expressions of avid curiosity. Georgie bit back the torrent of accusations that were on the tip of her tongue and shot them a bright, reassuring smile before turning back to Wylde. "What do you mean 'come and see me'?"

"I can't very well call on *you*, can I? Not if you want to avoid a scandal—which I assume is the case, since you've kept the news of our marriage from the *ton*." His gaze met hers. "I'm sure a woman who can arrange a clandestine visit to Newgate can get herself to the back entrance of the Tricorn Club in St. James' at ten o'clock tomorrow morning without being seen."

Georgie recognized the challenge for what it was. And she had absolutely no choice but to pick up the gauntlet. "All right. I'll be there."

The waltz ended, and they swirled to a breathless stop. Wylde's grip tightened for a moment before he released her. She tried to calm her racing heartbeat as he caught her hand and lifted it to his lips. Even through her gloves, the back of her fingers tingled. She snatched her hand away and held it behind her back.

His laughing eyes mocked her evasion. "Until tomorrow, Mrs. Wylde."

Chapter 9.

Alex, naturally, cornered Benedict as soon as they were alone and demanded an explanation for his sudden interest in the Caversteed girls. Ben refused to explain until they were back at the Tricorn—mainly so he wouldn't be forced to repeat the tale for Seb's benefit. He waited for the third member of their team to join them in the burgundy damask-lined private salon, poured all three of them a drink, and lowered himself into one of the three large leather armchairs in front of the fire.

"I'm married," Ben said curtly. "To Georgiana Caversteed."

Alex almost spat out his brandy. "The shipping heiress?" he spluttered. "The picky one? *That* Georgiana Caversteed?"

"The very same."

"Good God. When did that happen?"

"A few weeks ago, in Newgate."

"Bloody hell, Ben! Only you could land an heiress—and a gorgeous one at that—while locked up in *prison*."

"It's not a permanent arrangement," Benedict growled.

Alex shook his head, his expression one of wonder and admiration. "You should go and play cards immediately. You have the devil's own luck."

Seb raised his glass in an ironic toast. "Well, congratulations. It all sounds wonderfully irregular. Usually it's the penniless beauty who's maneuvered into marrying the rich-but-nefarious hero." His brows arched in good humor. "But here's our poor, pretty Benedict, forced to sacrifice himself on the altar of matrimony to an attractive hoyden worth more than all three of us put together." He sent Benedict a mocking look. "You poor child. Fate can be so cruel."

"Oh, go to the devil," Benedict said crossly. "It's only temporary. As soon as she gets here tomorrow, I'll find out what she's up to and put an end to this farce."

Alex raised his brows. A wicked glint appeared in his eyes. "She's coming here?"

"Your presence will not be required," Benedict said firmly. The last thing he needed was Alex and Seb's interference. He knocked back the remainder of his brandy and savored the warm burn down his throat.

"What are you going to do with her?" Alex swirled the amber liquid in his glass.

"Damned if I know. We can't *stay* married, that's for certain. Thankfully, I doubt she'll want to, now she knows who I really am. The woman wanted someone who was about to be transported or hanged. She should be more than willing to rectify the mistake."

"It's not that easy, getting rid of a wife, you know," Seb said. "They're like those prickly burs that stick to your clothes. Once they get their hooks into you, they're the very devil to shake off. Ask anyone."

Ben scowled at him. "You have plenty of experience with clinging wives, do you?"

"Hardly. I avoid them like the plague. Why bother with another man's wife when there are so many enthusiastic widows and single women out there?"

"I'm sure there are ways to get rid of a wife," Alex said. "Annulment. Divorce."

"Paying a highwayman to dispatch her," Seb joked. "Tying weights to her feet and dumping her into the Thames. Shipping her off—"

Alex ignored him. "I doubt she'll want her name dragged through the mud by a divorce, though. The Caversteeds might not be old money, but their standing in society is good."

"You could always leave the country," Seb said cheerfully, clearly relishing his role as devil's advocate. "Go on a nice extended tour of Europe. A few nights with those delightfully inventive ladies in Paris and you'll forget you even have a wife."

"I'm not going anywhere." Ben scowled. "We only just got back from Europe, remember? I've seen more than enough of France and Spain to last me a lifetime." He turned to Alex, determined to steer the conversation away from the vexing Miss Caversteed. "How's your investigation going?"

Alex had been asked by Conant to look into the suspicious death of an Italian diplomat.

"Slowly," Alex sighed. "It looks like he was killed by his own servant, who then fled the country, but the motive is still unclear." He glanced over at Seb. "Maybe the servant finally snapped after the count ruined his eighth cravat trying to create the perfect waterfall?"

Ben snorted. Seb's pride in his sartorial style was a running joke between them. "You know what those volatile Italians are like. Always so passionate, so hot headed."

Alex shot Seb a taunting smile, and Benedict tried unsuccessfully to suppress a grin at the way Seb simply raised his eyebrows and refused to rise to the bait. Seb was half-Italian and Alex delighted in teasing him about the "foreign" half of his nature—mainly because Seb was the complete opposite of a quick-tempered Italian. Despite his Mediterranean good looks, he had the coolest head of anyone Ben had ever met. There was nobody better to have at your side in a crisis. Even if he did spend twenty minutes perfecting his cufflinks.

He sent Alex a sympathetic glance. "You'll make a breakthrough soon, I'm sure."

Alex discarded his empty glass and rose. "Think I'll go and take a last look at the pit."

He was referring to the main room of the club, where the vast majority of gambling took place. A small balcony, shielded by a wooden fretwork screen, rather like a minstrel's gallery, was positioned high above one end of the gaming room. Accessed by a small staircase, it allowed the three owners to look out over the floor and watch the games in progress below—and keep an eye on the club's patrons. As former snipers, all three of them enjoyed the elevated position.

Ben got to his feet too. "I'm going to get some sleep."

Seb chuckled and drained the last of his brandy. "Sounds like you're going to need all your wits about you tomorrow, dealing with that wife of yours. Think she's ever seen the inside of a gaming club before? Maybe you should bring her downstairs and teach her how to play roulette. I'd be more than happy to—"

"She's not going anywhere near the public side," Ben said firmly. "And you're not going to be teaching her anything."

Seb gave a chuckle. "Spoil sport. In that case, I'll wish you good night. And good luck."

Chapter 10.

The Tricorn Club in St. James's was a newly established gentlemen's club, but in the few months it had been open, it had, according to Pieter, gained a reputation for deep card play and extravagance in both food and "gentlemanly entertainment," which Georgie took to be a euphemism for "attractive, available women."

At ten o'clock in the morning, however, this enclave of elegant depravity was remarkably quiet. Pieter turned the carriage into the stable mews behind the imposing stone-clad building.

"Georgiana Caversteed, this is a—"

"—terrible idea," Georgie finished with a grimace. "Yes. I know. I know."

She'd told Pieter of Wylde's reappearance, of course. The Dutchman had simply raised his bushy brows and said he'd warned her against her foolish scheme at the outset. He opened his mouth to say more now, but Georgie was in no mood for a lecture. She raised the hem of her cloak, stepped down onto the cobbles, and tried to ignore the butterflies churning in her stomach.

She'd barely slept a wink last night, turning over all the possible outcomes of this meeting in her mind. What did Wylde want? A monthly allowance? A lump sum? How much would this debacle cost her?

"Please wait for me here. I shouldn't be long."

The back door of the club swung open to reveal a mountain of a man dressed in black-and-gold livery. His size was such that Georgie wouldn't have been surprised to learn he was a former boxer or wrestler. Certainly, his crooked nose and cauliflower ear spoke of an interesting life.

Pieter stepped forward protectively, but Wylde appeared behind the behemoth and shot her a welcoming smile.

"Stand down, Mickey, the lady's here to see me."

The mountain nodded respectfully and stepped aside to let her pass.

"Good morning, Miss Caversteed," Wylde said, and for one moment Georgie imagined herself poised at the door of some sinister castle—like the one in Mrs. Radcliffe's *Mysteries of Udolpho*—a foolish, unsuspecting traveler about to discover something very unpleasant inside. She gave herself a mental shake. She had to stop sneak-reading Juliet's gothic tales. She was getting overly fanciful.

"I'll be right here," Pieter said gruffly. "If you're not out in half an hour, I'm coming in to get you."

Georgie nodded. She mounted the stairs, stepped over the threshold, and entered the lion's den. She followed Wylde's broad shoulders along a marble-tiled hallway, up a set of curving stairs, and into a surprisingly light and airy sitting room. Despite having always wondered what the inside of a gentleman's lodgings might look like, she wasted no time examining the furnishings. She sank into the seat he indicated and arranged her hands primly in her lap. "I'll come straight to the point, Mr. Wylde. What game are you playing?"

The corners of his lips twitched. "Not one to mince words, are you?" He crossed to an elegant French fauteuil and sat, one ankle resting on the opposite knee, the epitome of relaxed masculinity. "No game, Miss Caversteed. *You* found *me* at Newgate. Our meeting was purely accidental."

She raised her brows, inviting him to explain what he'd been doing there.

He tilted his head and fixed her with an accusatory look. "I, for one, had no plans to *marry* when I entered the building."

Guilty heat warmed her cheeks.

"I applaud your ingenuity," he said dryly. "There was no chance your suitor would escape, that's for sure."

She shifted uncomfortably in the chair. He deserved an explanation. "It was an unusual course of action, I know—"

He raised his brows, silently mocking the understatement, and she looked at her hands. "Until a few weeks ago I had no desire to marry anyone. Ever. I do not, after all, need the money. And I have no desperate hankering for a title."

"You might be the first woman of my acquaintance to say that and actually mean it," he replied amiably. "Few would deny the desire to be one day addressed as 'my lady,' or 'Your Grace.'"

"Not me."

His gaze flicked to her stomach. "So, why the sudden need for a husband? Are you anticipating a happy event in around nine months' time? Seeking a name for another man's brat?"

Georgie couldn't contain her gasp of shock. "What?

No! Of course not! I've never . . . I mean . . ." She trailed off, utterly mortified at the suggestion, and took a deep, steadying breath. She should have anticipated such an assumption. "No. That's not it at all. The problem was my cousin, Josiah."

"Ah."

His tone was neutral, and she tried to decide how best to phrase Josiah's steady campaign of harassment. "Josiah has been trying to persuade me to marry him for years, but as I neared my majority, he became increasingly in-sistent—so much so that I feared he would engineer some compromising situation so we'd be forced to wed."

She sneaked a glance at Wylde. A muscle ticked in his jaw.

"I could not face placing my future, or my business, in Josiah's hands, but there was no one else in the *ton* I trusted enough to marry. I was desperate. And then I realized that if I married a condemned man, I could con-trol my own fate. I could tell Josiah I was married and fail to mention I was also a widow."

She made a wry face at her own naivety. "Unfortu-nately, there were no condemned men in Newgate. When you were offered as an alternative, I reasoned that a liv-ing, but absent, husband would do. Josiah thinks I fell in love with a midshipman on one of my own brigs, who's currently away at sea."

"Very romantic. Swept off your feet by a burly sailor. How did your cousin take the news? Not well, I'd imagine."

"Pieter showed him the marriage license, but he still suspects a trick. He's probably trying to find a way to disprove it even as we speak."

Wylde tapped one long forefinger on the arm of the chair. "So, apart from your hulking manservant, the two witnesses at Newgate, and dear Josiah, who else knows we've wed?"

"Only my mother and my sister—and they only think I've married a convict. They do not know the convict is you."

"And you're in no hurry to tell them," he said wryly. "Because I'm even worse than a convict. Who'd want to be tied to someone like me?" His eyes crinkled at the corners in self-mockery.

She shot him an accusing glare. "Can you blame me? You do have the blackest reputation."

He inclined his head as if accepting a compliment, the perverse man. "Why thank you. One tries one's best. And yet I'm still welcome in the most select drawing rooms. It's most unfair. A man can behave atrociously and escape with an indulgent slap on the wrist, but the same behavior from a woman causes the *ton* to immediately close ranks and expel her."

Georgie nodded. "Which is precisely why I need to sever our association. If the circumstances of our marriage ever got out, the scandal would ruin my sister's chances of making a good match. She and my mother would be spurned and disgraced."

"And yourself," he added gently.

"Oh, well, yes. Of course."

If Wylde was going to blackmail her, she'd just given him the perfect opening. She waited with a grim sense of inevitability for him to demand a princely sum to keep quiet about the whole affair.

"Hmm," he mused. "I see your dilemma. So, what now?"

Georgie hid a frown of surprise. Was he truly not going to ask her for money? She was no stranger to tough negotiating, but he was almost impossible to read. Time to lay all her cards on the table. Honesty in business dealings, however painful, was vital.

She cleared her throat and assumed a brisk tone. "I was hoping we could deal with this like sensible adults. You cannot wish to be married to me. And I do not want to be married to you. An immediate annulment is therefore in both our interests."

"On what grounds? We're both of sound mind."

Georgie resisted the urge to snort. She'd doubted her own sanity almost daily during the past few weeks. "Josiah threatened to have me declared mentally incapacitated when I told him I'd married a sailor," she admitted wryly. "But that won't work. I have plenty of professional acquaintances who can attest to the fact that I'm competent."

She stole a glance at Wylde's chiseled profile. He really did have an extraordinarily nice jawline, now that it wasn't covered in bristles. Looking at his lips made her own tingle. A wave of disbelief washed over her. She, Georgiana Caversteed, was *married* to this Adonis! It was such an improbable pairing, like some Greek god come down from Mount Olympus to dally with an unsuspecting mortal. She took another wistful glance at his outrageously tempting mouth. Things rarely went well for the mortals in those stories, though. They all ended up being turned into rocks, or trees, or got ripped apart by hunting dogs.

Still, maybe it was worth it. He really was mind numbingly handsome.

Georgie shook her head and forced herself to concentrate on the disaster at hand. "I had hoped our marriage could be terminated on the grounds of nonconsummation, but according to my research, that in itself is not sufficient for an annulment." Heat rushed to her cheeks.

"In fact, to gain an annulment the husband—ah, that is, you—would have to be declared impotent."

A long, excruciating silence ensued. She didn't dare look at Wylde's face; she focused on the pale green swirls of the Aubusson rug instead. Was it possible for someone to burn up with mortification? She ignored the hellish flush creeping up her neck and stumbled on.

"In order for *that* to happen, the groom would have to share his wife's bed for three years, prove she's still a virgin at the end of it, and prove that he couldn't get aroused by two other women, such as, ah, professional courtesans, before an annulment would be granted."

She ran out of breath. When Wylde failed to answer, she glanced up to gauge his reaction. His heated gaze turned the tingle in her lips into a full-body flush. She curled her toes inside her shoes.

"Then it seems we have a problem, Miss Caversteed."

His eyes held hers, and Georgie found she was breathing rather too fast.

"Even if we shared a bed for three years, and managed not to touch one another in all that time"—his intent expression seemed to indicate the unlikeliness of that eventuality—"I would still be found more than capable of consummating our marriage." His brows rose in unmistakable challenge. "If you have any doubts, I am more than willing to prove my ability. Just say the word."

Chapter 11.

Georgie experienced a mad, irrational urge to blurt out, *Go on then*, but bit her tongue instead.

Wylde let the silence play out for another long, uncomfortable moment, then said, "So, no. An annulment due to my impotence is out of the question."

She dragged in a calming breath; she felt as if she'd survived a close encounter with a wild animal. "Well, the only other reason for an annulment would be on account of fraud. But you've already said that the name you signed on the register was enough to bind us legally, so I can't see how we could argue that. And we're both over the legal age of consent."

The ticking of the porcelain clock on the mantel seemed unnaturally loud and condemning. Georgie worried her lower lip as waves of guilt and shame rolled over her. She'd ruined this man's life—albeit unintentionally—by barging into Newgate and forcing him to marry her. An awful thought suddenly occurred to her. "Oh no! There wasn't anyone else you wanted to marry, was there?"

His mouth curved faintly. "No. Although I'm sure the ladies of the *ton* will go into mourning when they hear I'm off the market." His tone carried a cynical edge.

"Have you *never* considered marriage?"

"Honestly? No. I thought I'd die in France or Spain before I ever had to make a decision."

Her heart twisted at the blunt truth of his words. What horrors had he faced? She'd pored over Juliet's scandal sheets last night, gleaning every scrap of gossip about him. He'd fought in the Peninsular War and at Waterloo. Three years in the Rifles under General Graham. It was disconcerting to realize the depths of his worldly experience so vastly outweighed her own. He would be a formidable opponent. Or ally.

"Why were you in Newgate?"

"I never was, officially. As far as the *ton* is concerned, I was languishing in the Fleet for a gambling debt."

"So why—?"

"Since leaving the army, I've been working for Sir Nathaniel Conant, Chief Magistrate of Bow Street."

Her surprise must have shown on her face because he smiled. "Bow Street usually deals with lower and middle-class criminals, so when a case comes up that involves the *ton*, none of the regular runners can get very far. That's where I come in. I have access to all levels of society. I assist with any cases that require contact with the aristocracy."

Georgie's mind reeled. Why would a man like him choose to fight crime when he could be sunning himself like a gilded peacock on some country estate or living on credit and his aristocratic name and sponging off friends and relations, like half the *ton*?

"I'm trying to discover the connection between some wealthy nob, a bunch of Kent smugglers, and a plot to rescue Bonaparte from exile."

She sat back in her chair. Of all the tales she'd expected him to spin, this one topped the lot. What he was describing was dangerous work. "Why?"

He slanted her an ironic look. "Not from any burning sense of patriotism, I can assure you. Patriotism got me shot in Spain and nearly blown to pieces in Belgium. I need the money."

Disappointment made her stomach sink. Ah. He'd merely been biding his time before asking for cash. "Did you know who I was, when we wed?"

"I knew *of* you. Georgiana Caversteed, the shipping heiress."

She tightened her grip on her reticule. "Did you think you would become rich by marrying me?"

His lips quirked again. "Not after I read and signed your waiver. That was well done, by the way. Wonderfully emasculating. Although the five hundred pounds was most appreciated." He shrugged, as if the loss of the rest of her fortune was of no consequence to him.

Georgie didn't know what to make of that. No one had ever dismissed her money quite so casually. Her wealth usually hovered in the background of every conversation, a silent, unacknowledged barrier to true friendship and trust. She shook her head. Everyone wanted something, and Wylde was no different. She just had to find out what it was.

"So, we can't get an annulment. What about a divorce?" he asked.

"You would have to petition that I had been adulterous."

His quizzical gaze raked her, from the top of her head, down over her breasts, to her toes and back, as if he could somehow see whether another man's hands had touched her. "And that hasn't been the case?"

Heat rose and she squirmed in her seat. "No," she

managed breathlessly. "I have not broken my vows." She resisted the urge to ask the same of him. It was none of her business. "Besides, a divorce is out of the question. It would require an Act of Parliament, which would create precisely the kind of scandal I am trying to avoid."

In all honesty, Juliet would probably welcome a scandal; if Mother was forced to relinquish her dreams of a title, her sister could marry simpering Simeon instead. But Mother would be hurt. She truly cared about the opinion of the *ton* and loved the gaiety of London. She wouldn't want to be banished to the wilds of Lincolnshire. She'd experienced enough heartache when Georgie's father had died. Georgie refused to add to it.

Wylde tapped his fingers on the arm of his chair. "So, we can't avoid being married."

Georgie grimaced. "No. I'm sorry. It was never my intention to—"

He waved away her apology with an impatient flick of those long fingers. "What's done is done. We'll just have to make the best of it."

He said it in the same way a battlefield doctor might say, *We'll have to remove the leg, then*. With a sort of fatalistic resignation.

Georgie battled a paradoxical sense of pique. Surely being married to her wasn't *that* bad?

"You'll barely have to see me," she said brightly. "I'll return to Lincolnshire once the season's over and you can continue your, ah, gentlemanly pursuits here in town. We can lead completely separate lives."

There, that sounded suitably worldly and sophisticated. Precisely the kind of arrangement that would appeal to someone like Wylde.

There was something profoundly depressing about such an arrangement, though. Where was the companionship, the shared laughter and affection that had characterized her own parents' marriage? Where was the happy union she'd once dreamed of for herself? Georgie stifled a sigh. Six unsuccessful seasons had proved how little gentlemen desired a sharp-tongued bluestocking with an unladylike interest in commerce. She had to face reality.

Yet that niggling sense of dissatisfaction wouldn't go away. This was all so insipid. So logical. So unexciting. She wanted to start having adventures, to start living her life, instead of watching it go by as if it were all happening to someone else. A secret marriage of convenience would fend off Josiah, true, but she'd still be plagued by other bothersome fortune hunters. She'd still have to spend the next twenty years turning them down, being seen as an eternal spinster too picky to choose a husband. Eventually she'd be relegated to the side of the room with the wallflowers and the dowagers, an object of pity and scorn.

No, it was not to be borne. It was time to take control of her life.

"Wait," she said. "What if we *don't* keep our marriage quiet?"

Chapter 12.

Wylde's dark brows lifted. "What do you mean?"

Georgie thought quickly. "Well, we can't announce that we're already married, obviously. That would be far too scandalous. But what if we led up to it slowly? What if you courted me, quite properly, and 'proposed' at the end of the season? Then we could marry again—in public—and our relationship would be out in the open."

He didn't say anything, so she rushed on, amazed at her own audacity. "We can both still go our separate ways once we're out of the public eye. But this way, I'll have the status of a wife instead of a spinster. Single young ladies of the *ton* are guarded more heavily than any treasure in the British Museum. As a married woman, I'd have far more freedom."

She waved her hand in what she hoped was a nonchalant gesture. "I doubt any serious action would be needed on your part. A conversation or two at a party. A few smoldering looks across the dance floor. Drives in the park. Afternoon tea. The usual thing."

The thought of someone as gorgeous as Benedict Wylde lavishing attention on her—even if it was only for show—made her stomach flutter. He was a creature entirely outside her scope of experience. But she'd already had more excitement in the moments they'd shared than in the rest of her life put together. Why not seize this chance to enjoy the attentions of such a fascinating man? Even if it was only until the end of the season.

Wylde's expression was bland, but a faint hint of devilry twinkled in his eyes as he contemplated the idea. His lips curved in that provoking, teasing way. "Am I to pretend to fall catastrophically in love with you?"

She levelled him a look that indicated just how unlikely that was. "Of course not. Not a soul would believe it. You can, however, fall irrevocably in love with my bank balance."

He opened his mouth to protest, but she didn't let him speak. "The *ton* will assume you're a fortune hunter, yes, and I'll be pitied as a foolish, romantic dupe, blinded by your handsome face. But who cares? We'll both know the truth."

He chuckled at her cheerful cynicism. "Handsome, eh?"

She sent him a withering look. "Oh, don't pretend you don't know. You can't be oblivious to the hordes of women throwing themselves at your feet at every social engagement."

"It's hardly flattering for either of us, is it? And I think you're underrating your own charms." His eyes roved over her again, spreading heat wherever they touched. "I happen to find competence and self-possession extremely attractive in a woman."

Georgie did her best to ignore the incendiary effects of that look. "Nobody will be surprised if we separate soon after the wedding. They'll say it's the predictable outcome of a penniless aristocrat marrying a rich heiress. Utter incompatibility."

Wylde's chair creaked as he repositioned his long legs. "And what about your cousin? Won't he think it odd if you're flirting with me so soon after your 'wedding'? How can you become betrothed to me if you're already married to Jolly Jack Tar?"

Drat. She'd forgotten about that.

"My poor husband can die at sea."

Wylde ran his hand over his jaw, and Georgie held her breath, praying he would agree to her proposal.

"Chasing after you *would* provide me with a good reason to be back in the *ton*," he mused.

"There you go!"

He gazed out of the window for a long moment. "And I suppose if we married publicly, you'd also receive the dubious benefit of my name." He made a wry expression. "It's never done *me* any good—a family crest doesn't stop a bullet on the battlefield. I have a hole in my shoulder to prove it. But you might like the protection it affords."

Georgie tried to ignore the warm feeling his words produced. For a self-confessed scoundrel, he had his own—albeit slightly warped—sense of honor. He'd been enough of a gentleman not to demand money from her, but she couldn't expect a man like him to help her out of the goodness of his heart. He'd already admitted that lack of funds was the reason he undertook such dangerous work for Bow Street. Perhaps it was time to sweeten the deal.

Doubtless, the women he usually spent time with were beautiful and sophisticated; he wouldn't select them for their ability to broker a trade deal. Georgie might not be as attractive as her sister, but she would use what weapons she had—namely, her fortune.

"I'll make it worth your while, Mr. Wylde."

His gaze snapped back to hers. "In what way?"

"I would pay you for your trouble."

He stilled, and she prayed she hadn't miscalculated. Men, she'd discovered, were oddly unpredictable where masculine pride and money were involved. "You said you hoped to get a reward for foiling this plot for Bow Street? How much is it?"

His eyes narrowed. "Five hundred pounds."

"Well, then. I'll pay you double. A thousand pounds."

Another excruciating silence. Georgie eyed the door with longing. What was she doing?

"Let me get this straight in my mind," Wylde said slowly. "You want to *pay* me to flirt with you? Is that right?"

His voice held a certain dangerous edge. Was he insulted? Angry? Intrigued?

"To court me," she amended, then winced at how ridiculous that sounded. Still, she'd come this far. What was a little more embarrassment? "And only when we're in public."

They stared at one another for several long heartbeats, and Georgie quelled a rising sense of alarm. She'd been sure he'd jump at the chance to reduce his debts. She'd never faced a situation where the right amount of money hadn't solved the problem.

"I'm merely suggesting a mutually beneficial arrangement," she hurried on. "It would be useful to have you around to act as a buffer between myself and my cousin. And to deter other fortune hunters."

"I see."

She narrowed her eyes and fixed him with the look she usually reserved for tradesmen who tried to overcharge her simply because she was female. Those idiots assumed she was mentally impaired because she had squashy lumps on the front of her chest instead of something dangling between her legs.

"I do hope you're not one of these men who have difficulty dealing with a woman. This is no different from me engaging a shipwright to build me a brig, or a cobbler to make me shoes. You are known for your superior skills of social interaction, Mr. Wylde. I am merely offering to engage your services until the end of the season."

Benedict struggled to keep his face impassive as irritation warred with amusement. Pay him to woo her? What sort of woman suggested such a thing? He didn't know whether to pity her, laugh at her, or be very, very afraid.

His pride rebelled against her offer of money, but the brutal truth was, he didn't have the luxury of being able to refuse. Morcott's survival was more important than any personal humiliation he might endure.

He returned his attention to the woman who was turning his life upside down. This was the first time he'd seen her in full daylight. The morning sun that streamed through the window picked out the copper in her hair and highlighted the fine grain of her skin. She wasn't one of those women who needed the flattering glow of candlelight to appear to her best advantage. She looked small and fierce, and utterly delectable.

Benedict rearranged himself discreetly in his chair. He'd barely been able to concentrate on what she was saying; he kept getting distracted by those perfect pink lips, the thick sweep of her lashes, and those startling eyes. Every time she looked at him directly, he felt his pulse leap and his blood thicken. Her confidence and clever mind attracted him in ways he couldn't explain.

He'd never met a more self-sufficient woman in his life. Rather daunting, her intellect. Had she been a man in the army, she would have been a strategist to equal Wellington. A formidable opponent, Miss Caversteed.

Or rather, Mrs. Wylde. Thank God she had no idea how appealing he found her—she seemed quite prepared to use every weapon at her disposal to get what she wanted.

Still, she fidgeted under his prolonged gaze. Good. Despite her innocence, she was definitely aware of him as a man. She'd turned the most luscious shade of pink last night when he'd painted a picture of them together in some scandalous situation. He could use that to his advantage.

Benedict hid a smile of anticipation. Flirting with her would be a pleasure, not a chore. He was a scoundrel to take her money for doing something he needed absolutely no encouragement to do, but there was no harm in allowing the *ton* to think him focused on seducing her rather than ferreting out their secrets. Her thousand pounds would be a welcome addition to Bow Street's five hundred.

The suggestion that she needed to pay him to court her was laughable. He needed no incentive. His desire for her would pass, just as it did with every other woman he encountered, but there was no reason why they couldn't both enjoy this situation while it lasted.

She obviously liked to think she was all business, but anyone with half a brain could see she was a passionate woman. She'd lost her faith in mankind—specifically the feckless, fortune-hunting half—each time some idiot had refused to eschew her fortune. Now, she clearly thought of herself as the less desirable of the two Caversteed sisters. Benedict couldn't wait to show her just how passionate she could be. She'd unwittingly given him the perfect opportunity for a slow campaign of seduction; he'd lay siege to her defenses until she crumbled. It would be both a challenge and a joy.

There was no danger of her falling in love with him. She was far too sensible to fall for a penniless wastrel, and when their physical relationship petered out, they could go their separate ways, perfectly amicably, just as she'd suggested.

Of course, they'd both be stuck in an empty, loveless marriage like the one his parents had endured—something he'd tried his utmost to avoid. But his army years had taught him to accept those things that couldn't be changed and to make the best of what he'd been given.

Fate, it seemed, had given him Georgiana Caversteed Wylde.

It wasn't that he didn't believe in love. On the contrary, he was sure that it existed for some people, somewhere. But personal experience had shown him how rare and unusual a thing it was. How unpredictable and, oftentimes, unpleasant. No, he'd stick with good old-fashioned lust, which had served him perfectly well for the past decade or so.

He cleared his throat and felt the jolt as her eyes met his. He shot her the prisoner's cheeky, unrepentant grin. "I don't pretend to be perfect husband material, Mrs. Wylde, but I'll be a damn sight better than some poxy murderer from Newgate."

She let out a relieved breath, which brought his attention to the perfect curves of her breasts beneath her morning dress. Oh, this was going to be fun.

"How will you pay me?"

She shifted in her seat. "Um. An allowance, I suppose. Say three hundred pounds a month for the next three months? And the balance on the day we wed. Does that sound fair?"

He suppressed a triumphant smile. "More than fair. All right. You have a deal."

Georgie blinked as Wylde stood. She rose too, hating the disadvantage of her smaller size as he crossed the room in two large strides. Goodness, she'd forgotten how tall he was. How broad.

He smiled down at her. "Shall we shake on it?" That wicked twinkle was back in his eye. "Or should we seal our bargain as we did our wedding? With a kiss?"

She couldn't stop her eyes from dropping to his far-too-tempting mouth. What would it feel like to kiss him without all those prickles? Were his lips as soft as she remembered? "I . . . ah—"

He leaned down, blocking out the light, and she held her breath as indecision warred with desire. She ought to pull away. She did not move.

The front of his chest brushed hers. His warm exhalation fanned her lips.

And a commotion in the hallway ruined the moment.

Georgie silently cursed Pieter's timing as Wylde stepped back in a rush of cool air. A second later a knock sounded on the door and the mountain entered, followed by her loyal Dutchman.

"Are you done, miss?"

Georgie cleared her throat, certain her cheeks were burning. Good heavens, where were her wits? "Yes, thank you, Pieter. I was just taking my leave."

She risked a glance at Wylde, who looked as innocent as a schoolboy and not at all like a man who'd been about to kiss her. If he was disappointed, it didn't show. Perhaps he'd only been playing with her. Doubtless he affected every woman in this same, unnerving way.

"I shall see you soon, Mr. Wylde?"

He offered her a stiff formal bow and that pirate's smile. "You can be sure of it, Miss Caversteed."

Chapter 13.

"Georgie, will you walk with me in the park?"

Georgie looked up from her book and cast a frowning glance at the leaden sky beyond the bay window. "I think it's going to rain."

Juliet twirled her bonnet around by the ribbons and gave her brightest smile. "Nonsense. Not until this afternoon. Oh, please come. I can't ask Mother. She's gone to call on Mrs. Cox."

Her sister's flushed cheeks were highly suspicious. Juliet never volunteered for physical exercise. "What's going on, Ju?"

Juliet sank gracefully onto the chaise, almost fizzing with excitement. "It's Simeon! He's here, in London. I just received a note saying he wants to meet." She cast a beseeching puppy-dog look at Georgie.

"Can't he just call here, like all your other suitors?"

"You know he can't. Mother's likely to turn him away, and I don't want to go behind her back. You know how disapproving she is. Oh, *please* say you'll come. I promise it won't take long. I've missed him so much."

"Oh, all right. But wear a shawl."

As Juliet rushed off to dress, Georgie suppressed a twinge of envy. At least her sister had heard from *her* beau. She hadn't heard anything from Wylde for the past three days. Perhaps he'd reconsidered their outlandish deal. Perhaps that was for the best.

She'd been proud of the cool, logical way she'd presented her case, because when it came to Benedict Wylde, her feelings were thoroughly illogical—a confusing mix of wariness, mistrust, and heart-pounding attraction. She shook her head and went to find a bonnet and an umbrella in case her prediction of rain proved true.

It was only a short walk from Grosvenor Square, down Upper Brook Street to Hyde Park, and although grey clouds threatened, the day was surprisingly warm for March. They hadn't been in the park more than a few minutes, strolling down the long avenues and trailed by Juliet's long-suffering maid Charlotte, when disaster struck.

Juliet had just bent to sniff some early-blooming daffodils when she gasped.

"Oh! I see Simeon! Over there, on the other side of the pond!"

She waved her reticule at the thin figure, which had the undesired effect of disturbing a bumble bee that had been buzzing among the flowers, minding its own business.

"Aargh! A bee! Get off!"

Georgie tried to catch Juliet's flailing arms. "Just stand still. It's not interested in you. Once it realizes you're not a flower, it will leave you alone."

But Juliet was deaf to all reason. She flapped like a demented chicken. The blameless bee managed to get caught up in her shawl.

Juliet clapped a hand to the side of the neck. "It bit me!" she gasped.

"Stung you," Georgie corrected automatically. "Bees don't have teeth."

"I don't care!" Juliet wailed. "Oh Lord, I can't breathe!"

Georgie rolled her eyes. This wasn't the first time her sister had been, in her own words, "maliciously singled out for assassination" by a bee. The orchard back in Little Gidding was full of them.

Charlotte bustled up, her plump, kindly face the picture of concern. "Now, miss, you'll be all right. Come on, let's get you home."

Juliet turned and squinted expectantly across the pond at where Simeon had been standing. "Oh, this is perfect! Where is Simeon? He can come and rescue me. When Mother sees how kind and gallant he is, she's bound to soften toward him. Can you see him, Georgie?"

Georgie squinted across the lake. Simeon's thin figure was heading toward them. "He's coming."

Juliet swayed slightly. "I wish he'd hurry. I really *do* feel faint."

Her face had turned quite pale. Alarmed, Georgie put a hand out to steady her.

"Can I be of assistance, ladies?"

Georgie turned at the masculine voice, expecting to see Simeon, but it was Wylde's handsome face that had appeared next to them. "Mr. Wylde!"

"Miss Caversteed." He shot her an amused, sympathetic glance then turned to the flustered Juliet and offered his arm. "Miss Juliet, may I escort you home?"

Juliet clutched at his arm like the sole survivor of a shipwreck, her fear of fainting in a public place clearly greater than her desire to wait for Simeon's aid. "Oh, Mr. Wylde. Thank goodness. Yes, please. Your assistance would be most welcome."

Georgie glanced across the pond. Simeon had witnessed the entire incident but had been too far away to come to his beloved's rescue. He hovered at the edge of a small copse of trees, apparently in an agony of indecision now that his chance to play knight-errant had been usurped by another. She shooed him away with a subtle gesture of her hand and turned back to Juliet.

"Were you on your way somewhere, Mr. Wylde?" she asked, as they began to escort Juliet toward the park gate.

"As a matter of fact, I was, Miss Caversteed," he replied with exaggerated politeness. "I was on my way to call on you."

Juliet gave a little gasp, which Georgie ignored. "How very fortunate. We are honored, of course."

They were halfway home when Juliet's steps faltered, and she touched one hand to her forehead. "Oh! Oh dear. I really *do* think I'm going to faint."

Georgie groaned inwardly as her sister sagged elegantly against Wylde's side.

With a resigned sigh, he caught her before she could crumple to the ground. He bent, hooked one arm behind Juliet's knees, set the other around her shoulders, and swept her off her feet.

Charlotte gave a scandalized gasp.

He strode along Upper Brook Street like some well-dressed pirate, as if he barely noticed the weight of Juliet's slim body in his arms—which, considering his wonderful physique, was probably true. Georgie bit back a sting of completely irrational jealousy and tried not to imagine what it would feel like to be held in those strong, capable arms or cradled against that wonderfully broad chest. Darting in front of them, she ran up the front steps, opened the door, and ushered them into the hall.

Wylde, still carrying Juliet, turned this way and that,

then shot her a questioning look. "Where do you want her?"

Georgie glanced upwards. "The salon's upstairs, but you don't need to—"

He didn't wait for her to finish. He simply mounted the stairs two at a time and deposited Juliet gently on the chaise longue in the salon at the front of the house.

He wasn't even out of breath.

Juliet managed to settle, long-limbed and tragic, with one hand dramatically covering her forehead. Georgie was just about to pat her sister's cheeks when Mother burst into the room and started fluttering like an overexcited pigeon. She was so intent on Juliet that she didn't even notice Wylde, who had sensibly retreated to the corner of the room.

"Juliet! My love! What happened?" She caught Juliet's wrist to check for a pulse.

"She was stung by a bee in the park," Georgie said.

"Quick! My smelling salts. No! A feather. We must find a feather!"

"Why do you need a feather?"

"Why, to burn, child. She must be roused!"

Georgie grimaced. "Please don't. Burnt feathers smell awful. She's coming round on her own, look."

Juliet opened one eye and sent Georgie an incredulous look. "I really fainted? Oh, how mortifying! Where's Sime—"

Mother ignored them both. "Where can we get a feather? A pillow? Don't just stand there, Georgiana. Wait! I have it. My hat! There's a feather in my hat." She tugged the bonnet from her head.

Juliet, ever conscious of fashion, roused herself enough to protest. "No! Don't ruin it! It's such a pretty hat."

Mother was momentarily diverted. "Do you think so? I had second thoughts about it this morning when I looked in the mirror. I thought, 'Whatever could have possessed Madame Cerise to suggest mauve?'" She tilted her head and studied the offending garment with a critical eye. "You can have it if you like. It will suit you better than me."

Juliet wrinkled her nose. "No, thank you. Lavender makes me look ill. Maybe Georgie would like it?"

Georgie rolled her eyes. If Juliet was back to discussing fashion, she was well on the road to recovery. "Perhaps we should all have a nice cup of tea?" Georgie darted a quick, embarrassed glance over at Wylde to see what he was making of this introduction to her ridiculous family. From his expression, he appeared to find it highly amusing.

Mother frowned. "Tea? She needs laudanum for her excitable nerves!"

Wylde stepped forward. "Might I suggest a cold compress, to reduce any swelling, and some calamine lotion?"

Mother jumped as though she'd been shot, one hand pressed over her heart. "Oh, good gracious!"

"Mother, this is Mr. Benedict Wylde. He was kind enough to help Juliet back from the park."

Benedict bowed. "Your servant, ma'am."

Mother melted like a glacier under the midday sun. "Mr. Wylde! Of course. How can we thank you enough for coming to dear Juliet's aid?"

"I'm just glad I was able to help."

Mother preened under that irresistible smile. "It was an extremely romantic gesture." She glanced meaningfully from him to Juliet, and Georgie groaned inwardly. "How fortunate you were in the vicinity."

"Indeed," Georgie said dryly. "Extremely fortunate."

In all fairness, she couldn't accuse Wylde of engineering the disaster, but he'd doubtless been only too happy to play the gallant hero to someone as pretty as Juliet. The gossip mongers would have a marvelous time dissecting this. It was too much to hope that nobody had seen him carting her sister into the house like some medieval groom carrying his bride over the threshold.

"I'll have Mrs. Potter bring some tea up," Mother said cheerfully. "And the calamine and compress." She shot an arch glance at Wylde. "I'm sure you won't mind keeping Juliet company for a few moments, will you, Mr. Wylde?"

She bustled out of the room without waiting for an answer.

Chapter 14.

As soon as their mother left, Juliet raised herself weakly from the pillows. "Whatever happened to Simeon? Did he see what happened?"

"He saw," Georgie said. "He seemed rather surprised that you'd swooned into the arms of another man."

Juliet's face fell. "Oh dear. I truly didn't mean to. You don't think he'll be jealous, do you? He has no reason to be." She glanced over at Wylde. "No offense, Mr. Wylde, and I do appreciate your help, but my heart is already taken."

He smiled. "No offence taken, Miss Juliet."

"Did he follow us home? Look outside!"

Georgie crossed to the window. Sure enough, standing forlornly behind the iron railings that delineated the small garden in the center of Grosvenor Square, stood Simeon Pettigrew.

"Yes, he's there."

Simeon was only a year older than Juliet, nineteen to her eighteen, and was personally responsible for convincing Georgie that love really was blind. And quite possibly deaf and stupid as well. There was no other way to explain Juliet's inexplicable attraction.

Simeon had a long, thin face with eyes that drooped down at the outer corners and gave him the look of a perpetually disappointed puppy. Round spectacles perched on his long nose. Not because he needed them—the lenses were clear glass—but because he was under the erroneous impression that they made him look more scholarly. Unable to grow a full beard, he maintained the few straggly hairs that sprouted from his chin and a sad attempt at a mustache, which appeared as a shadowy, peach-like fuzz on his upper lip. He kept his wavy black hair deliberately long, chin length, so it was always getting in his mouth; he sucked the end of it absentmindedly when he was concentrating.

Without meaning to, Georgie glanced over at Wylde: a decade older in years, and a lifetime older in experience. A man, compared to a boy. Unlike Simeon's waxy pallor, his face was bronzed from his time spent abroad. The few lines that fanned from the corners of his wicked brown eyes only added to his unholy allure. Even at this hour of the morning, the dark hint of stubble on his jaw made Georgie's fingers itch to touch it, to feel the rough texture.

She pressed her hand to her chest and felt the lump of her wedding ring beneath her dress. She'd taken to wearing it suspended on a chain around her throat, a physical reminder that she'd taken control of her own destiny. It nestled against her skin, against her heart, like a secret. What would Wylde think if he knew? Would he think her sentimental? Longing for him? The thought brought a weakening sensation to her knees and a confusion in her stomach.

The sudden spatter of raindrops on the windowpanes snapped her out of her reverie.

"I should take my leave."

Georgie glanced at Wylde and frowned. "It's raining. Did you leave your carriage at the park?"

"I don't keep a carriage." He shot her a self-deprecating smile. "Too expensive. But it isn't far to St. James's. Walking takes twenty minutes. A carriage takes fifteen. It's almost the same."

"You can't have expected the rain, though," she persisted. He was wearing an extremely well-fitted morning coat of dark blue, a neatly tied cravat, white shirt, and breeches. None of which would benefit from a soaking.

He shrugged, an impressive feat considering the fit of his jacket. "I've been rained on before. In several different countries, thanks to Bonaparte. I shan't dissolve."

"Well, you're probably made of sterner stuff than Simeon out there."

Wylde moved to stand behind her. He glanced over her shoulder, and she became intensely aware of the warmth of his body, so close, the faint tang of his skin. A slow heat curled in her belly.

Simeon was still staring up at what he probably believed was Juliet's window. He was wrong; Juliet's room faced the back of the house.

"Lovesick idiot. He's bound to catch a cold," Wylde murmured. His tone clearly suggested, *You'll never catch* me *doing something so stupid for a woman.*

Simeon looked thoroughly miserable now, hunched against the drizzle. As they watched, he glanced upward, and his thin shoulders rose and fell in a sigh, as if such treatment was no less than he expected from the pitiless heavens. As if in response, the shower quickly became a deluge of biblical proportions. The rattle of carriages was drowned out by the hiss of the rain on the pavement as it collected in runnels and washed into the drains.

Juliet sat up, all lounging forgotten. "Oh, my poor Simeon! Is he getting terribly wet?"

"I'm afraid so."

Wylde caught Georgie's eye, and they shared an amused look.

"He's persistent, I'll give him that," he muttered. "Oh, I almost forgot. Do you have any plans for tomorrow evening? I'm meeting someone at Vauxhall. If we're seen there together, I can show you some conspicuous attention and get rumors flying."

Before Georgie could reply, Mother returned, accompanied by Mrs. Potter, the housekeeper, carrying a large tray.

"Will you stay for some tea, Mr. Wylde?"

"I'm afraid I cannot, Mrs. Caversteed. But I was hoping I might see you ladies at Vauxhall Gardens tomorrow night. I hear Madame Sacqui is performing her rope-walking tricks, and there will be fireworks at ten."

Mother shot a congratulatory look at Juliet. "That sounds lovely! Juliet's been wanting to see the fireworks for an age, haven't you, dear? If the weather is fine, we'll be there."

He bowed slightly. "Shall we say nine o'clock, by the rotunda?"

"Perfect."

"I'll see Mr. Wylde out," Georgie said, herding him toward the door.

The front hall was uncharacteristically deserted; Pieter was doubtless below stairs making a cold compress for Juliet. Georgie opened the front door—and came face-to-face with a sodden Simeon, who was standing at the bottom of the steps, apparently summoning the courage to knock. His black hair was plastered to his skull, and in one hand, he held a limp posy of flowers, presumably purloined from Hyde Park's borders.

She gave an exasperated sigh. "Oh, come in, Mr. Pettigrew, for heaven's sake."

She stepped back to avoid his sopping figure as he splashed up the steps and into the hall.

"You are an angel, Miss Caversteed," he breathed fervently. "An angel." He tried to possess himself of her hand, then changed his mind and sneezed instead. "I do beg your pardon, but I couldn't stay away. I saw what happened in the park." He glanced over at Benedict and frowned, then turned back to Georgie. "Is Juliet well? Bee stings are no trifling matter. And Juliet is such a delicate creature. Why—"

Georgie cut off what promised to be a long list of Juliet's attributes. "She will be perfectly well, I am sure, Mr. Pettigrew. But please, you must go, before Mother hears you. You know she disapproves of your association."

Simeon scowled. "My love for Juliet could survive anything! Even the direst of opposition—"

"Yes, yes," Georgie said impatiently, "that's all very well. But you're dripping on the rug."

Simeon looked down. "Oh, sorry." He stepped sideways onto the checkerboard tiles. A steady stream of water dripped from his hat and made a shiny puddle by his feet. He shot Wylde a beseeching look, as if to appeal to him man-to-man. "My love and I have been cruelly separated, sir. Like Romeo and Juliet. My heart is torn asunder, cleft in twain!"

"That's Hamlet, not Romeo and Juliet," Benedict said quellingly.

Georgie sent him a surprised glance—who'd have thought Wylde would know his Shakespeare?—then turned back to Simeon. "You must be perfectly miserable, Mr. Pettigrew. Why don't you go back to . . . wherever it is you're staying . . . and dry off?"

Simeon shot her a kicked-puppy look. "What is corporeal discomfort, Miss Caversteed, when the pain in my heart, nay, my soul is infinitely worse?"

"You won't say that when you have pneumonia," she said tartly. "Who will Juliet marry if you die?"

He brightened marginally. "You mean to say that you support our union?" He caught her hands in his own thin, wet fingers. She tried to tug them back, but his grip was surprisingly strong, despite the sodden bouquet.

She nodded. "I do. You seem to genuinely care for my sister. As this present situation proves. But you cannot go standing around in rainstorms. There is nothing romantic about the ague, I assure you."

He opened his mouth to argue. "But I—"

She shot a pleading glance at Wylde. "Would you escort him home?"

"It will be my pleasure." Benedict eyed Simeon darkly. "Let go of her hands, you."

Simeon glanced down and seemed surprised to find himself still clutching Georgie's fingers. He dropped them immediately. "Oh, sorry."

Benedict nodded and opened the door, ushering him out into the rain.

"Would you like to borrow an umbrella?" Georgie asked.

Wylde shook his head. "I'll be fine. Until tomorrow, then?"

"Yes. And thank you for your help today."

He accepted that with a tilt of his chin and a charming flash of a smile. "I can honestly say that I've rarely spent a more entertaining morning, Miss Caversteed. Good day."

Chapter 15.

Juliet caught Georgie's arm as they paid their shillings for entry and started toward Vauxhall's rotunda. The hum of the crowds and the bright sound of music masked her urgent whisper, but she still glanced at Mother, ahead of them on the wide tree-lined avenue.

"Georgie, I need your help."

Georgie raised her brows in silent question.

"I need you to occupy Mother while I see Simeon. I've arranged to meet him by the water cascade in fifteen minutes."

Georgie groaned. "Juliet!"

"I need to show him I'm fully recovered. He worries about me. It's so sweet. And I want to make sure he hasn't caught a chill after his drenching yesterday."

"All right. But just for a few minutes."

Mother turned with a bright smile. "Goodness, it's crowded this evening. I hope your new admirer can find us, Juliet."

Juliet sighed audibly. "He's not my admirer, Mother.

In fact, he seemed to be spend more time looking at Georgie than at me."

A frown creased Mother's brow. "Well, there's no point in him paying *Georgiana* any attention, is there? Seeing as how she took leave of her senses and married some highwayman without telling anyone." She shot Georgie a familiar, disapproving look.

"Midshipman," Georgie corrected absently. "He wasn't a highwayman."

Mother waved that away. "Same thing. My point is, you're already taken."

"I thought you wanted a title for Juliet?" Georgie couldn't resist saying. "Mr. Wylde is a younger son. His *brother* is the earl."

Mother sniffed. "The Morcotts are an old and extremely well-connected family. Mr. Wylde may not have the robust finances one might like, certainly, but he can trace his lineage back to the Norman conquest."

Juliet sent Georgie a horrified glance. Mother had clearly been studying her *Debrett's*.

"And there's nothing wrong with him showing an interest in Juliet," Mother continued. "His attentions will only make her other suitors, like Upton, more ardent."

Juliet winced, and Georgie have her arm a sympathetic squeeze. "Oh look," she said brightly. "Is that your friend Lady Cowper?"

Mother twirled. "It is indeed! I haven't seen dear Caroline in an age. Would you just *look* at that ostrich feather? Why, it's monstrous!" She waved merrily. "Why don't you two head toward the rotunda and see if you can find Mr. Wylde? I'll catch up with you in a moment."

Juliet sent Georgie a triumphant look. "Yes, Mama."

Benedict was standing under the trees in a shadowy corner of Vauxhall waiting for his informant when he felt an almost imperceptible nudge in the region of his coat pocket. He turned, caught the perpetrator's slim wrist in a punishing grip, and spun the potential thief into the light—then grinned when he saw the boy's familiar, grimy face.

"You'll have to be quicker than that, Jem." He chuckled. "Best stick to smuggling and selling information. Picking pockets isn't your forte."

Jem Barnes's lips split into a gap-toothed grin as he rubbed his abused wrist to restore the circulation.

"Easy, guv. I'm out o' practice, is all." He slunk back into the shadows out of habit and gave a low, impressed whistle as he took in Benedict's evening clothes and silver-topped cane. "Ho, look at you, dressed up all fancy," he cooed. "What you do? Rob a bank? Take up the High Toby?"

"Won a shooting contest," Ben said lazily.

The boy's gaze sharpened. "Sounds like you can afford to pay me a little sum'fin for what I know, then, don't it?"

Benedict hid a smile. Jem was a sharp one. He'd been one of the few members of Hammond's gang to escape the Gravesend raid. They boy was as slippery as an eel. "I'll pay you," he said evenly. "If you have anything worthwhile to tell me."

Jem wiped his nose on his ragged sleeve. "Shame about Peters and Fry. I 'eard they's 'eaded for Van Diemen's Land."

"They were lucky they didn't swing like Hammond, or die in the cells like Silas."

Jem spat on the ground, an eloquent dismissal of the vicious ringleader. "Ain't nobody gonna miss 'Ammond, that's for sure. But how come *you* ain't on a prison ship?"

"I bribed the Newgate turnkey."

The youngster shrugged, unsurprised by the fickleness of man. Ben withdrew a guinea from his waistcoat pocket and idly flipped it over in his fingers. Jem watched it like a starving dog at the butcher's shop window.

"So, what do you know?" Ben asked gently.

The boy smiled. "Being the enterprisin' cove what I am, I've found it pays to listen at doors." He puffed out his chest. "I always know what's goin' on, me. Listened in to 'Ammond, I did."

Ben nodded approvingly. "And?"

"Just before the Gravesend job 'e met with a cove called Johnstone."

"Go on."

"Well, this Johnstone was trying to get a crew together. Said 'e 'ad a job that'd make us all richer than the pope. Told 'Ammond to find 'im men who could sail anyfink and not ask too many questions, like."

"Plenty of those around. Half the navy's looking for work these days. Did he say what the job was?"

"Aye. That was the funny part. This Johnstone never sounded like a Frenchie—'e were as English as roast beef—but 'e said it were to get old Boney off some island." Jem wrinkled his nose. "Ain't we just spent ten years gettin' *rid* of 'im? Why'd anyone want to bring 'im back?"

Benedict shrugged. "He still has his supporters, both here and elsewhere. Did this Johnstone say *how* he planned to rescue Bonaparte? With just the one ship? Meeting up with others? Attacking the island?"

Jem shook his head. "Nah. Sorry."

Benedict flipped the guinea, and Jem snatched it from the air like a conjurer. It disappeared into the folds of his shapeless jacket.

"Did Johnstone say who was paying for this rescue attempt? Or mention any other names?"

Jem screwed up his face. "There was somefin' about a doctor. An Irish name, it was. Like O'Malley. Or O'Brien."

"When did Johnstone want to sail?"

Jem scratched his head with a dirty finger, no doubt dislodging several resident lice. "Soon. That's all I know."

Benedict cursed.

Jem shrugged. "You'll know for sure if I go an' find Johnstone, won't ye?" He gave a toothy grin. "Which I will 'appily do—for another guinea."

"Highway robbery!"

Jem's shrug was unapologetic. "A boy's got to eat."

Ben flipped him another coin. "All right. See if you can find this Johnstone. And then come straight to me."

Jem tipped a nonexistent hat in a jaunty salute. "Aye-aye, Cap'n." He disappeared soundlessly into the shadows.

Benedict checked his pocket watch and cursed. He was late to meet Georgie.

Georgie hurried down a shadowed walk and cursed her younger sister. Juliet hadn't been at the water feature, and Georgie strongly suspected she'd retreated somewhere more private with her beau.

So now here *she* was, sneaking through the distinctly less-populated part of Vauxhall Gardens. She'd already interrupted three different amorous couples—the darkness had concealed the worst of it, thankfully—and despite muttering copious apologies and hastening away, her cheeks still burned with mortification.

"Georgiana?"

Her stomach dropped as she recognized the masculine voice, and the dark shadow that accompanied it, as her cousin's stocky frame stepped out from behind a topiary bush.

"Josiah! What are you doing here?"

She couldn't say it was a pleasure to see him. It wasn't.

She glanced left and right, and stifled a series of unlady-like profanities. Had he been following her?

Her unease grew as Josiah strolled closer, and she saw his lips curved in a distinctly unpleasant smile.

"I could ask the same thing about you, Cousin. Are you meeting someone?"

She gave an exasperated exhale. "Of course not. I'm looking for Juliet."

"Come now, don't lie to me. You're here to meet your lover, aren't you?"

A trickle of fear mingled with her distaste as she caught the stale waft of alcohol on his breath. "Don't be ridiculous."

"Why is it ridiculous? Your new husband could barely have given you a taste of things before he set to sea. Maybe you're here to scratch an itch."

Georgie gasped. Josiah had always been unpleasant, but she'd never seen him drunk, nor heard him speak so crudely. She stepped back but was stopped short by the edge of a flower bed. Her heel sunk into the soft earth as he pressed closer, a belligerent expression on his face.

"All these years, I kept my distance. Tried to be re-spectful. You had us all fooled, didn't you?" He shook his head. "I should tell everyone your sordid little secret. The *ton* would love to know why you've been so picky all these years. It's not because you're too high in the in-step, is it, Georgie? It's because you like a bit of rough." He caught her upper arm in a painful grip. "You should have told me what you wanted, sweetheart. You didn't have to marry a filthy sailor to get it."

"How dare you!" Georgie tried to twist away, but he tightened his grip and yanked her forward. She stumbled and gasped in fury as he casually pawed her breast. The ripping sound of her lace fichu rent the night air.

"Your man isn't here to see to you now, is he?" Josiah

panted, pressing his wet lips to the side of her neck. "But I can give you what you need."

Fury and revulsion coursed through her veins. She shoved her palms hard against his chest. "Get off me, Josiah!"

He ignored her struggles.

"Step back, or I'll be forced to hurt you."

His disbelieving chuckle was her only answer. Georgie cursed. So be it. Josiah's wasn't the first unwelcome kiss to which she'd been subjected, and Pieter had taught her exactly how to deal with such irritations. She stopped struggling, let herself sag against her cousin's chest, and gave a moan that could be construed as encouragement. Josiah groaned against her shoulder as she swept her hand down over his hip and stroked back up, feigning a caress, even as her stomach churned.

"That's right, you little hussy," he breathed. "Let me show you—oof!"

Georgie lowered her knee from between his legs and stepped back as Josiah curled into a ball and collapsed sideways, clutching his groin in agony.

"I warned you," she sighed unhappily.

Chapter 16.

Unfortunately, Josiah did not stay down for long. Georgie barely had time to grab the slim knife she kept in her boot when he lurched to his feet with a snarl.

"You little bitch!"

She lifted the blade so it caught the light. "If you're wondering if I know how to use this," she said levelly, "let me tell you that Father *insisted* on it before he allowed me to accompany him to the docks. In case I got into any trouble."

Josiah stilled, clearly realizing she wasn't joking. They stared at one another for a long, breathless moment, and Georgie prayed he wouldn't try anything stupid. Stabbing one's own cousin—however deserving he might be—was most definitely *not the thing*.

The metallic hiss of a blade being unsheathed made them both turn in unison, and Georgie let out a surprised exhale as Wylde stepped out from the shadows, the lethal blade of a swordstick in one hand and the ebony cane that had concealed it in the other.

He faced Josiah. "I do hope you were about to bid the lady adieu," he said with sweet menace. "Because I don't believe she requires your presence."

Josiah glared at him but raised both hands to his shoulders in a gesture of surrender. "Indeed I was, sir."

Georgie didn't take her eyes away from her cousin, but her words were for the man who strolled forward until he stopped a few feet from her side. "Good evening, Mr. Wylde. Thank you for your assistance, but I have this under control."

"I can see that," he said amiably. "I'm just providing a little backup in case this gentleman decides to chance his arm." He gave Josiah a slight, mocking bow that was a perfect insult. "I don't believe we've met. Benedict Wylde. Late of the Rifles. I'm a sight better with pistols than I am with a sword, but I'm quite willing to use this on you if you don't back away. Right. Now."

Josiah curled his lip but did as he was ordered. "We'll talk again, Cousin," he promised Georgie darkly, then turned and stalked away.

Georgie noted his limping stride with no small degree of satisfaction. When she was certain he'd gone, she released the tension in her shoulders and let the hand holding the knife fall to her skirts. She turned to Wylde with a slow exhale of relief.

"Well, that was—"

"A stupid bloody thing to do?" he supplied. "What in hell's name was that?"

He glanced around the shadowed clearing with a frown, as if scanning for further danger. "Good God, woman! Where did you learn a trick like that? And what are you doing, carrying a knife in your boot?"

"Pieter showed me how to handle myself," she said, secretly amazed that her voice didn't wobble. Now that the danger was past, her hands were shaking and she felt decidedly nauseous. Relief that Wylde had come to her aid was slowly giving way to embarrassment that he'd seen her in such an awful position, and consternation at how close she'd come to disaster.

Her own blood relative had *assaulted* her. What had Josiah been thinking? And how foolish was she, to have underestimated the depths of his resentment? She smoothed the front of her skirts and tried to calm the frantic pounding of her heart.

"I think it shows a great deal of common sense. I regularly visit my ships and warehouses at Blackwall. I don't know if you're acquainted with the dockside wharves, Mr. Wylde, but they aren't the most salubrious of neighborhoods. One cannot be too careful."

Wylde sheathed his sword inside the walking cane with a practiced swish and glared at her. "What are you doing out here? We were supposed to meet at the rotunda."

"What are *you* doing?" she countered. "Lurking about in the bushes?"

"I was meeting an informant. Where's your man Pieter?"

"It's his day off. He goes to spend it with his sister in Bloomsbury."

"You shouldn't be out here alone."

Georgie tilted her blade. "I'm not exactly defenseless."

His eyes narrowed dangerously in the dim light, and he suddenly looked far less like a gentleman of leisure and far more like the ruthless killer she'd thought him in Newgate.

"Yes, you are."

Benedict took a deep, steadying breath and tried to banish the jolt of primitive possessiveness that had seized

him when he'd stepped through the trees and discovered
Georgie in the arms of another man.

A split second later, when he'd realized she was being assaulted, fury had overwhelmed his jealousy. He'd
actually reached over his shoulder for his rifle, a move
so instinctive he did it without conscious thought. He'd
cursed when he realized he wasn't carrying his Baker.
He'd spent years with it never far from his hand; he felt
naked without its familiar weight.

But since going around armed to the teeth was frowned
upon in polite society, he'd had to settle for carrying a
foppish swordstick. It could skewer Georgie's lecherous cousin quite effectively, but Ben had been tempted
to simply rip the bastard limb from limb instead. He
would have been outraged at finding any woman being
mistreated, but somehow the fact that it was Georgie, his
woman, increased his fury tenfold. How dare that bastard
touch her?

Her disheveled appearance only made him more furious. Her cousin's assault had dislodged the combs
from her hair—it spilled in haphazard disarray over her
shoulders—and her fichu was ripped where it had been
pulled from her bodice. Benedict cast a scathing, dismissive glance at the knife she still held in one small fist.

"That little thing might have been enough to scare
your cousin, but it won't deter anyone with more experience with a blade."

His stomach clenched as he imagined her coming up
against one of the murderous scum he regularly encountered in his line of work. Men like Hammond and Silas.
Smugglers, cutthroats, murderers, thieves. They'd have
gutted her like a fish and never even paused for breath.
God. The thought of her coming up against one of those
back-alley bastards was enough to make him want to
retch.

She needed to be protected from all that ugliness. From that harsh, dirty portion of the world. She might have caught a glimpse of it in her business dealings, but she hadn't seen humanity at its worst, as he had. She hadn't seen the ferocity, the barbarism, the depths men desperate to survive were capable of. The terrifying ease with which a human life could be snuffed out. He wanted to lock her away in her ivory tower, somewhere safe and as lavishly appointed as her money could afford.

Her dismissive shrug only increased his irritation. Did she truly not know the danger she'd been in? Long years of warfare had shown him just how vicious and bestial a man could become. Murder and rape were daily occurrences in the backstreets of this city.

She wiped the back of her hand over her mouth. "Ugh. I can't believe Josiah tried to kiss me."

Blood pounded in his temples. "How can you be so naive?"

She frowned, and he bit back what he'd been about to say: *Of course your cousin wants to screw you. Any man with eyes would want to.*

I want to.

He took a step toward her and caught her wrist. In a quick, practiced move, he twisted her arm back and up, and squeezed. She dropped the knife with a soft cry of dismay, and he let her go, ignoring the glare she sent him. "See? Lucky for you, I have more honor than your cousin."

Bloody foolish woman, to put herself in such a dangerous position.

If she was humiliated by how easily he'd disarmed her, she didn't show it. She huffed out an indignant breath. "Josiah doesn't want me. He only wants my money because he's gambled his own away." She bit her lip. "Perhaps I should just give him a lump sum, so he'll leave me alone."

Benedict ground his teeth. "You are not to give that

cockroach a penny, do you hear me? He's a grown man. He can make his own way in the world, just like every-one else. Christ, I saw men lose limbs in the war. They're back here now, making lives for themselves." He shook his head in silent fury. "Your cousin has no idea how lucky he is. He could work, as you do, instead of drink-ing and gambling his days away."

He glared down at her. "And why do you always think you have to buy your way out of any problem, hmm?"

She lowered her chin and stared at his chest. "Because it's the only way I know."

Her defeated tone made something in his chest twinge uncomfortably.

"Father always wanted me to marry a man like him-self." She sighed. "A man with drive, with his own money. So whenever someone offered for me, he made it clear that any husband of mine would only receive an annual income of a thousand pounds. The rest would remain under my control." She gave a small, wry smile. "How-ever much those men professed to love me, when it came right down to it, none of them would agree to that. My money is the most compelling thing about me."

She was wrong. There was so much more to her than her fortune. Benedict was about to tell her so, but then she looked up into his face. Her eyes were huge in the dim light, her face pale. He'd seen that same look on the faces of raw recruits after their first taste of battle—delayed shock.

He was an idiot. Scolding her, frightening her with his strength when he should be offering comfort and reas-surance. He opened his arms. "Oh, come here. It's all right."

She closed the distance between them with a frus-trated little sniff, as if annoyed by her own weakness. He pulled her into an easy hug, and she leaned against him for a brief moment, her palms pressed against his shirtfront. He tried to ignore the warming effect it had on his body.

"Thank you for coming to my rescue," she mumbled. She pulled back a fraction and met his eyes, and in the space of a heartbeat, the air between them changed. Her eyes darted down to his mouth then back up in unmistakable entreaty, and his gut tightened. Before he could think better of it, he lifted his hand and ran his thumb across her lips, tugging them apart the way he'd dreamed of doing since the first moment he'd seen her in Newgate.

Her eyes widened but didn't pull away.

Soft, so soft. So close.

She pressed herself more firmly against him, and he nearly groaned aloud. He wanted to kiss her so badly. His body hardened to the point of pain, a splendid, urgent ache. He felt drunk on the feel of her of her, her scent.

To hell with it.

He cradled her nape, tilted her head to the perfect angle, and leaned down to kiss her.

"Georgie? Are you there?"

The feminine hiss brought Benedict back from the brink, even as he cursed the interruption with every fiber of his being. He pulled back and met Georgie's startled eyes. Shaken at what he'd almost done, he released her and stepped back just as her sister's shadowy form emerged from the other side of the bushes.

Good God.

His heart was pounding as if he'd just survived a French cavalry charge, but he shot her a cocky grin to prove how unaffected he was.

Georgie blinked as if waking from a stupor. She bent to the ground, retrieved her blade from where she'd dropped it, lifted the hem of her skirts, and replaced it at her ankle. "Over here," she croaked, stalking past him without a second glance. "Where on earth did you get to, Juliet? I've been looking for you everywhere."

"Did you find Mr. Wylde?" Juliet asked innocently.

Benedict bit back a snort.

Oh yes, she most certainly did.

Chapter 17.

Benedict watched Georgie until she'd reached the safety of her mother, then headed toward the rotunda, where two semicircular "piazzas" opened up, illuminated by hanging lanterns. Seb and Alex had secured one of the curved, open-fronted supper boxes and were partaking of a fine dinner.

Seb raised his wine glass when he caught sight of Benedict. "Ah, there you are. Come and have a drink. Did you meet up with your little contact?"

"Jem? Yes. He's still as slippery as ever. The little bugger even tried to pick my pocket." Ben took a long drink of the wine Seb poured him and noticed with some amusement that his hand was still shaking. That dratted woman.

Seb indicated the lavish spread laid out on the table. "Alex is paying for dinner. He's just been given three hundred pounds for recovering some antiquarian coins for General Sir Charles James Fox."

Benedict gave him a jaunty salute with his glass. "Good work."

Alex accepted the compliment with a lazy nod. He leaned back in his chair, indolently watching the crowds parade past the open front of the booth. The more subtle ladies contented themselves with peeping coyly at them from behind their fans. The bolder ones shot them saucy, suggestive glances that even a blind man couldn't have misinterpreted.

A group of expensively dressed women swept past, as colorful as a flock of exotic parrots with their parasols, fans, and shawls. Their accents pronounced them to be Americans, and at least three of the younger ones peered into the box with undisguised interest.

Alex sent them a cheeky smile and a silent toast that had them blushing and hushing one another in a frenzy of flustered giggles. "Thank God we've stopped being at war with everyone," he said fervently. "We've been deprived the company of French and American ladies for years."

"I wouldn't say you've exactly been deprived," Seb drawled. "What about that pretty Spanish widow near Salamanca? Or that little French actress you've been meeting at the Theatre Royal?"

Alex raised a brow. "Who? Claudette? She's as French as you are, which is to say, not at all. Her real name's Sally Tuffin, and she's never been farther than Covent Garden."

Seb, who always made it his business to know everything about everyone—his personal motto was "knowledge is power"—inclined his head at the departing flock of ladies. "Those are the Caton sisters from Maryland. They're filthy rich; father's a tobacco baron. They're on the hunt for titled husbands. Wellington dotes on them."

Alex's gaze followed them appreciatively. "Very transatlantic. Maybe we should take a leaf out of Benedict's book, Seb, and get ourselves rich wives?"

"Neither of you have titles," Benedict pointed out.

"Maybe one of 'em will fall for your brother?" Seb mused. "That would solve all his problems. I'm all in favor of introducing fresh stock into the *ton*. Anyone familiar with animal husbandry will tell you that too much inbreeding produces an unhealthy population. Look at the Hapsburgs. Or our own dear King George. Mad as a bunch of hatters, the lot of them. That's what happens when you keep marrying your cousin."

Ben shook his head at his irreverence. "John doesn't stand a chance. I expect the Misses Caton are aiming rather higher than an impoverished earl."

Seb smiled. "We should thank God there's no need for either of us to get leg-shackled to some whey-faced harridan just to clear a debt, Alex."

Benedict chuckled at his friend's vehemence, but Seb wasn't finished.

"I'm serious. Choosing a bride in the *ton* is worse than selecting a horse at Tattersall's. At least at Tat's, you get to look at their teeth." Seb subtly inclined his head toward the next female to stroll past. "Shall I try to get Miss Asquith to smile so you can get a glimpse of her pearly-white gnashers?"

Alex gave a theatrical shudder. "Please don't."

Benedict scanned the crowd, searching for Georgie, and finally located her coming down one of the tree-lined walks. It was time to set tongues wagging about the two of them. He downed his drink, vaulted easily over the low wall at the front of the booth, and stalked toward her.

She saw him approach, and then pretended she didn't, and he smiled at her evasion. She hadn't been so coy when she'd kneed old Josiah in the crown jewels earlier. He stepped into her path and bowed low to her mother, who preened a little at the attention, then at Georgie and her sister.

"Ladies, what a pleasure to see you all again. I hope you're having a pleasant evening?"

"Oh, yes," Mrs. Caversteed enthused. "It is a little chilly, perhaps, with this breeze, but the fireworks were wonderful. And did you see Madame Saqui descending her rope? Extraordinary."

Benedict caught Georgie's eye. "It has been a most enlightening evening."

Color rose in her cheeks as she caught his double meaning, and she shot him a chiding "don't-you-dare-say-anything" look from behind her mother's back. He sent her a bland, angelic smile in return.

"May I walk with you a little way, Miss Caversteed?" He offered her his crooked arm, and after a small hesitation she took it, leaving Juliet and her mother to follow on behind.

He steered them away from Seb and Alex's avid interest and along a row of vendors' stalls, pointing out various foodstuffs and trinkets along the way, and making sure to smile brightly at every gossipy old biddy he encountered while simultaneously keeping his head bent toward Georgie as if enchanted. It wasn't as difficult as he'd imagined; watching her expressive face as she enthused over such simple things as toasted chestnuts or a gaudy fan was entertaining in itself. She seemed to find delight in everything.

They stopped to watch a Punch and Judy show, laughing as the shrill-voiced puppet of Judy battered her poor husband over the head with a rolling pin and tried to prevent an incongruous crocodile from stealing a string of fabric sausages.

"Poor Mr. Punch," Benedict murmured under his breath.

"I do hope you won't treat your own husband quite so poorly, Miss Caversteed."

Georgie chuckled. "Only if he deserves it, Mr. Wylde."

He smiled down at her. "I do believe we've just given Clara Cockburn something to discuss at her next dinner party. I've spent a conspicuous amount of time escorting you through one of London's most popular attractions, in the very proper company of your sister and mother. Not once have I attempted to lure you off the path of virtuousness and into the shrubbery. People will be wondering what's wrong with me."

As one they turned, and sure enough, Lady Cockburn's fan had whisked up to cover her mouth as she leaned in to speak to her companion. Her eyes flashed over at Georgie and Ben with speculative interest.

Benedict raised Georgie's hand and kissed the back of it in farewell, just to fan the flames. Her cheeks pinked charmingly.

"I can guarantee that within a quarter of an hour Whites' betting book will be filled with speculation as to whether you're to be my next mistress . . or something more permanent," he said.

"Well then, I suppose we can call the evening a success," Georgie murmured back. "Since that is precisely what we set out to achieve. Your work here is done, Mr. Wylde. At least for tonight. You are released from your duties."

"Your servant, ma'am," Benedict said, with only a trace of irony. He bowed and left.

Chapter 18.

Georgie was still trying to decide what to do about Josiah's assault and Wylde's almost-kiss two days later.

Mother had finally yielded to Juliet's moping and allowed Simeon to call at the house, but since she was upstairs with a headache, Georgie had been designated as her sister's chaperone. She was now trapped in the upstairs parlor pretending to read a book and being forced to listen to Simeon compose his latest masterwork: "The Ballad of the Bee Sting."

Georgie was seriously considering singeing her own skirts as an excuse to leave the room when Mrs. Potter announced a new caller. She glanced up, pathetically grateful for any interruption, and her heart stuttered as Wylde stepped into the room. His hair was windblown, and he looked as devastating as ever in a pair of buff breeches, a snowy-white shirt, and a forest-green jacket.

"Good afternoon, ladies."

"Oh, hello, Mr. Wylde," Juliet said listlessly, and immediately turned back to her beau.

Simeon looked up from the bureau and sent him a cool nod of acknowledgment. "Wylde."

Benedict returned the nod solemnly. "Pettigrew." He crossed the room and took a seat next to Georgie on the sofa. "Afternoon, Miss Caversteed. I trust you've recovered from your adventures at Vauxhall?"

Georgie cleared her throat and tried to ignore the heat that spread through her limbs every time she recalled their almost-kiss. "Yes, thank you, Mr. Wylde." She glanced at the small bunch of flowers in his left hand, a posy of tiny dark purple violets and drooping snowdrops, the kind sold on street corners by ragged flower girls. They looked comical and fragile in his large masculine hands. She recalled those hands on her and her blood heated.

He offered them forward with a self-deprecating look. "What does one get for the girl who has everything?"

The men trying to court her usually sent great overblown bouquets, huge hothouse flowers that always made her a little sad. Everyone assumed she'd scorn something cheap, but she greatly preferred these hand-picked weeds. They had personality.

"Thank you. They're lovely," she said, and genuinely meant it.

Wylde glanced over at Simeon and Juliet. "So these are the star-crossed lovers, eh?"

"Mr. Pettigrew has impressed Mother with his 'stalwart persistence.' She's decided to give him a second chance, although he'll find it hard to convince her he's a more acceptable match than someone with a title and a fortune."

"It doesn't look like his drenching did any lasting harm."

"No."

Juliet was perched delicately on the chaise longue nearest Simeon, one elbow resting on the scrolled arm as she gazed worshipfully at him. The morning sun haloed her dark hair and showed off the smooth perfection of her skin. She looked luminous and delicate, like one of the porcelain Meissen shepherdesses on the mantelpiece. Doubtless Wylde, a connoisseur of the female form, was enjoying the view.

"I think Simeon sees you as something as a threat for Juliet's affections," Georgie whispered.

He raised his brows. "There's no danger of that."

She shot him a disbelieving look. "Are you seriously telling me that you don't find my sister attractive?"

He shrugged. "Oh, she's beautiful, I grant you. A diamond of the first water. But not my type, at all. She's too young, for starters. And too docile. I like my women with a little more spark." His smile could have melted rock. "Someone who knows her own mind and isn't afraid to stand up for herself."

Georgie's body warmed at his insinuation, then reminded herself that he was being paid to be attentive. His flippant charm meant nothing. It was as natural to him as breathing.

"Simeon is writing me a sonnet, Mr. Wylde." Juliet sighed soulfully. "Isn't that romantic?"

"I'm sure you think so, Miss Caversteed," he said politely.

Georgie fought a snort. Her idea of romance wasn't a man composing her sonnets. Romance was a strong man standing aside, letting her fight her own battles, and only stepping in if she needed help. What would Simeon have done if he'd been faced with Josiah at Vauxhall? Hit him over the head with a poetry book? She suppressed a smile at the ridiculous image. They said the pen was mightier than the sword, but she'd take Wylde's sword-stick over Simeon's pencil any day.

"I have immortalized the events in verse," Simeon announced grandly. "I shall read it to you if you like, Mr. Wylde."

"Oh, God, no," Benedict groaned, *sotto voce*.

"That would be lovely, Mr. Pettigrew," Georgie said with a wicked glance at Wylde. She lowered her voice. "Juliet thinks Mr. Pettigrew is extremely talented."

He sent her a droll glance. "Yes, but I bet Juliet also thinks rainbows are made from magical fairy dust and that dragons live in Scotland," he muttered.

"Who's to say she's not right about the dragons?"

"Basic common sense? Complete lack of empirical evidence? Zero credible sightings for hundreds of years?"

"There are plenty of wild, unexplored places in the world—"

He shot her a wicked, glinting look from under his lashes and raised his eyebrows. "I have Wylde places you can explore any time you like, Miss Caversteed."

She fought an answering smile. Really, it was scandalously improper, to be flirting with him like this. Even worse to be enjoying it quite so much.

Simeon cleared his throat.

"O, thou naughty stripy felon,
Round thou art, just like a melon."

Wylde gave her a horrified, disbelieving look, and Georgie stifled a laugh. She'd been the unlucky recipient of Simeon's performances before.

"You are a wicked little fellow,
With your stripes of black and yellow.
Your tiny body is covered in fuzz
And the sound you make is 'buzz, buzz, buzz.'"

Simeon styled himself very much on his hero George Gordon, Lord Byron. Georgie assumed his hairstyle—if, indeed, it could be called a style—was meant to be romantically wind-tossed, but he succeeded only in looking unkempt. Wylde, on the other hand, managed to make the same style look completely effortless. And eminently touchable. She fastened her fingers together in her lap to avoid temptation.

Simeon was in full flow now, waving his paper all over the place.

"I love the way you tilt your cheek up,
I love the way you hold your teacup.
I love—"

Wylde turned to her, a pained expression on his face. "Can't someone stop him?" he whispered. "Isn't there enough terrible poetry in the world without some adolescent fool adding to it?"

"He adores the role of lovesick swain. Back in Lincolnshire, he was very taken with the Arthurian legends. Troilus and Cressida, Lancelot and Guinevere. He spent an entire week last summer splashing around in the lake looking for some mystical sword."

"Well, I wish he'd go and search for the holy grail of poesy somewhere else. All that sighing and languishing. It's exhausting just watching him."

"I believe he's cultivating a fashionable ennui."

"Bloody hell. Since when was it fashionable to drape yourself over the furniture and spout godawful verse? What is the country coming to?" He shook his head. "Is this the sort of watery whelp I fought hand-to-hand at Waterloo to protect? What happened to British manhood while I was away?"

Georgie bit her lip. "He's what they call 'a sensitive soul.'"

Wylde cast Simeon a disapproving glare. "Ten minutes in the Rifle corps would toughen him up. He'd probably faint if he ever had to hold a loaded gun."

Simeon was still going strong.

"If I were a bee, and you were the clover,

I'd drink of your sweetness and—" He paused, searching for a suitable rhyme.

Benedict leaned in close. "That has to end with 'and bend you right over,'" he whispered.

Georgie's cheeks flamed. The man was outrageous. Every time he looked at her like that, she experienced a strange, melting, squirming sensation just below her ribs, not entirely pleasant, but not particularly comfortable either.

Simeon scribbled something, then crossed it out and frowned. Twin lines furrowed his bushy brows.

"Having trouble, Mr. Pettigrew?" she enquired desperately.

"Indeed. I'm trying to find a satisfactory rhyme for 'lady luck.' But my muse has deserted me."

"Thank the Lord," Benedict murmured.

"How about Puck?" Georgie suggested. "Shakespeare's character from *A Midsummer Night's Dream*?"

Wylde glared at her for encouraging him. Her gaze dropped to his mouth, and the word "suck" popped into her brain. She imagined catching his lower lip between her teeth and—

Stop it.

Wylde was watching her. His lips twitched, as though he guessed the wicked direction of her thoughts. He glanced over at Simeon with a bland look. "Maybe if you go through the alphabet? Buck. Chuck. Duck. Nothing starting with *E*, of course."

Georgie wasn't fooled by his innocent expression. The next letter was *F*. And she knew *precisely* which word he was thinking of, even though a gently bred woman shouldn't. She'd spent too much time around foul-mouthed sailors. They'd bellowed that profanity enough times when they'd thought she was safely out of hearing. A very emphatic, Germanic word.

Wylde bit his lower lip with his top teeth, beginning to form it in slow motion. His eyes twinkled in delight, and he looked like he was about to break out laughing. "F—"

"Gluck!" she blurted out, too loudly. "You know, the German composer?"

Wylde looked comically crestfallen that she hadn't fallen into his verbal bear pit and made a face that clearly said "spoilsport."

"That's not how you say it," he murmured. "It rhymes with book, not luck."

Pettigrew, of course, was oblivious to the scalding undercurrents in the room. He chewed the end of his pen. "No. I don't think I can put a composer in here. Perhaps I can insert a chicken? And use 'cluck.'"

Benedict clapped his hands. "Excellent idea, Mr. Pettigrew. I've yet to encounter a poem that wasn't immeasurably improved by the inclusion of a chicken. Carry on." He waved his hand like a royal pardon, then caught Georgie's elbow and steered her toward the window seat on the other side of the room. "A moment of your time, Miss Caversteed."

As soon as they were safely out of earshot, Georgie turned innocent eyes on him. "Don't tell me you're not a fan of poetry, Mr. Wylde?"

"That is *not* poetry," he growled. "That is a mangling of our great and noble language. I've heard better verses in St. Giles."

She raised her brows.

"There's one by Prinny's favorite, Captain Charles Morris, that starts, 'The Dey of Algiers—'"

"I'm sure I don't want to hear it," she said swiftly. "I doubt it's suitable for a lady's ears."

"Why not? It's amusing. And at least it rhymes. It celebrates the Dey's magnificent—"

"Naval victory?"

"—manly appendage," Wylde finished, completely unrepentant. "But perhaps your 'gentle ears' aren't ready for such profanity."

Georgie suppressed a snort. He *knew* she'd been thinking of that dreadful word earlier. And unlike every other man of her acquaintance, he found it amusing, instead of censuring her for it. How liberating, to be able to share a joke with someone of equal wit and flexible morals.

"All right, what about this one by Robert Burns?" he pressed.

Tom and Tim on mischief bent,
Went to the plains of Timbuctoo;
They saw three Maidens in a tent,
Tom bucked one, and—"

"Let me guess," Georgie said dryly, determined not to let him discompose her, "'—and Tim bucked two'? How original. At least Mr. Pettigrew's verses are about more than . . ." She strove for an appropriate word and settled on ". . . tupping."

"No, they aren't. They might be couched in obfuscation and circumlocution, but at the heart of every one of them is tupping. Or screwing. Or whatever else you want to call it. The hero of any courtly romance, whether he admits it or not, is pining for a good, hard—"

"Kiss," she finished emphatically.

"No. Not a *kiss*, Miss Caversteed. I can tell you quite candidly, that there's not a man alive who would turn around after killing a bloody great dragon or vanquishing some horrible witch and be happy with a kiss on the cheek."

"So die my dreams of courtly love," she sighed, emulating Juliet's breathy tone to perfection.

"Courtly love isn't what populates the world," he finished darkly. "If you ever want a demonstration of what *does*, I'll be happy to show you."

His gaze caught hers, and Georgie thought her body would go up in flames. Good God, what did one say to that? "That's very magnanimous of you," she managed weakly.

The corner of his mouth curled upward. "Isn't it? Now, tell me honestly, when you came up with your lunatic plan to marry a criminal, surely you didn't intend to eschew male company for the rest of your life?"

"As a matter of fact, I'd planned on taking a lover once I returned to Lincolnshire. A widow can do as she pleases, as long as she's circumspect."

Georgie marveled at her own boldness. What was it about him that made her say whatever was on her mind, however indiscreet?

He nodded, entirely unperturbed. Did nothing shock him?

"And now I've ruined your plans by refusing to be hanged or shipped off to Australia. I do apologize." His roguish grin was in no way apologetic. He leaned forward again. "As your legally wedded husband, one could almost argue that it's my duty to teach you such things."

Her happiness evaporated. Of course. That's all she was to him—a duty. An entertaining one, quite possibly, but a duty nonetheless. Theirs was a marriage in name only. Any emotional entanglements—which would naturally ensue if she agreed to such an outrageous offer—would only complicate things when it came time to part ways.

If only it wasn't so tempting to say yes.

"That aspect of our union is not something I require your help with," she said.

He accepted her withdrawal with a good-natured

shrug. "All right, but if you ever change your mind, do let me know."

Georgie decided it was time to steer the subject into safer territory. "Did you learn anything of import at Vauxhall?" The only thing *she'd* discovered was how nice it felt to be in his arms, how quickly he could turn her blood to fire and her brain to mush.

She had to stop thinking about it.

"I did. My contact gave me a lead to a man who could be involved." He glanced over at Simeon and Juliet, but neither of them was paying any attention. A bomb could have gone off, and they wouldn't have noticed.

"And—?" Georgie prompted. "Who is it?"

He frowned at her. "I'm not sure I should tell you. Issues of national security, and all that."

She shot him a pointed look. "You don't think I can keep a secret, Mr. Wylde?"

"Good point, Mrs. Wylde," he whispered.

"So who's the lead?"

He sighed in defeat, as if sensing her determination. "A man named Barry O'Meara."

"Never heard of him."

"There's no reason why you should have. He's the Royal Navy surgeon Napoleon selected to remain on St. Helena with him as his personal physician. O'Meara recently returned to these shores, full of sympathy for the emperor's cause, and has been lobbying intensely in favor of Bonaparte being freed." Twin creases formed between his brows. "O'Meara will be familiar with the security arrangements on the island. If he thinks his petitioning is falling on deaf ears, he'd be in a perfect position to advise on a rescue mission instead."

"He does sound a likely candidate. What do you plan to do?"

"Find evidence to support the theory that he's plotting something."

"How?"

"By searching his house."

"Will you wait until he goes out?"

Wylde grinned at her persistence. "No, I plan to do it while he's at home, with thirty or forty other people in attendance." Georgie raised her brows incredulously and he chuckled. "O'Meara's having a card party next Tuesday evening. There'll be deep card play, plenty of drink, and lots of available women. I've managed to get myself invited."

"The Westons' ridotto is on Tuesday night too," Georgie said. The Westons' annual masked ball was usually her favorite event of the season; since every guest wore masks and dominos to conceal their identity, she could pretend she was somebody ordinary for a night. People actually flirted with her and spoke to her because they wanted to, not because she was a rich heiress to be envied or entrapped. She loved the thrill of anonymity. Even so, Wylde's evening sounded far more exciting.

A sudden determination not to be left out seized her. "I have a suggestion."

It was his turn to raise his brows. "I'm all ears."

"I should come with you to O'Meara's house," she said firmly. "I can attend the Westons' party, but slip away to O'Meara's to help you, and be back before my mother even notices I'm missing."

"And why would I let you to do that?"

She gave what she hoped was a winning smile. "It will be far easier for you to sneak around a house party with a woman in tow. Think about it. A lone man loitering around might be seen as suspicious, but nobody will bat an eyelid if a couple are seen disappearing off into the shadows."

His eyes glinted wickedly. "And what do you know about disappearing into the shadows with gentlemen?"

She fought to contain her blush. "Nothing at all. But I'm sure if O'Meara's guests are as disreputable as you suggest, they'll think nothing of it. Especially considering your reputation as a rake."

His smile made her blood heat. "You mean nobody will be shocked if we're caught kissing on the billiard table?"

Georgie's breath caught, but before she could remind him that there would be no kissing, or anything else for that matter, he said, "Actually, you make a good argument. O'Meara only lives a few streets away from the Westons. And you'll be masked, so there's no chance of you being recognized. It shouldn't be too risky. All right, you can come."

She quelled a little crow of elation. She hadn't really imagined she'd be able to persuade him, but here, suddenly, was her chance for an adventure!

Her heart thudded against her ribs as she saw the challenge in his eyes, and she had a sudden vision of what he must have been like in the war. Flashing that devil-may-care grin, sneaking off to do something dangerous that might just get him killed. She had no doubt his men would have followed him anywhere, even into hell itself. His charisma was magnetic, irresistible.

He smiled. "I'll take my leave. I've had quite enough bad poetry for one day."

"Shall we arrange to meet somewhere specific at the Westons'?"

His gaze roved over her face as if committing it to memory. "No. I'll find you."

Georgie wasn't sure if that was a promise or a threat, but her heart took a long time to regain its normal rhythm after he left.

Chapter 19.

Her eyes glittered with excitement through the holes
of her black half mask. Georgie took one last satisfied
glance in the cheval mirror then swept her floor-length
domino over her shoulders and descended the stairs to
find Mama and Juliet already in the hall, and Pieter, in
his coachman's livery, waiting by the door.

Juliet appeared equally pleased to be going to the
Westons'. She'd arranged to meet Pettigrew—who would
sneak in without an invitation—and take advantage of
the opportunity to dance more than the permitted two
dances together. Or to steal a kiss somewhere private.

It took fifteen minutes of queuing just to reach the
front steps of the Westons' mansion, and Georgie smiled
in relief. It was a perfect crush; it would be easy to slip
away in such a crowd. Hopefully Mother would be too
busy trying to keep track of Juliet to notice her eldest
daughter had gone missing.

Her heart pounded. She felt deliciously naughty, sneaking off to experience an entirely different side of life. This

might be just another work assignment for Wylde—he probably spent half his life unearthing incriminating evidence in exciting places—but for her, it promised a night of unparalleled adventure.

She slipped away from Juliet and Mother in the crowded entrance hall and entered the main ballroom. The heat and press of warm bodies was stifling and the hum of excited chatter almost overwhelmed the orchestra, but her spirits lifted. The whole place buzzed with energy, with people determined to enjoy the night to the fullest.

She'd just started to edge around the side of the room, squeezing herself through the throng, when a highwayman stepped into her path. He was dressed almost entirely in black, from his shining Hessian boots and billowing cloak, to the black fabric mask tied over his eyes and the tricorn hat perched jauntily on his head.

She gasped as he caught her arm and tugged her against his broad chest.

"Evening, wife," he rumbled.

She'd half expected him to say, "Stand and deliver."

"How did you know it was me?" She still wore her domino with the hood pulled up over her hair, which concealed her from head to toe.

His lips curved in an enigmatic smile as he lifted her chin with his finger, as if readying her for a kiss. "I'd know you anywhere, Georgie girl. This way."

Her stomach somersaulted. That was the first time he'd ever called her Georgie. It sounded strangely intimate in his deep masculine voice.

He took her elbow and weaved his way through the crowd, which parted as if by magic in front of him. She couldn't help but notice how the women's gazes followed him, drawn by the magnetism of his body, even when they couldn't see his face. He exuded power and mystery, the promise of danger, an irresistible combination.

Georgie was seized by the ridiculous urge to shout: *He's mine. He's married to me.* She shook her head. He probably had a mistress. Or a whole string of them.

When they had navigated the sea of guests and slipped back outside, Wylde hailed the foremost cab in the semicircular drive and gave the driver an address. His large fingers closed around hers as he helped her up into the carriage. The contact burned, even through her evening gloves.

"Let me do the talking tonight, understand?" he said as he settled on the seat opposite her. She nodded, her stomach churning in trepidation.

It was a short drive to O'Meara's house. Lights blazed from the windows and the sounds of a raucous party emanated from the open front door. Georgie followed Wylde up the steps, where he handed his cloak, hat, and mask to a waiting footman.

She'd been anticipating this moment all evening. She waited until he glanced back at her, undid the tie at the neck of her domino, and let it slide over her shoulders. She suppressed a smile of pure feminine satisfaction when his mouth dropped open in shock.

"What the devil are you wearing?" he growled.

"Don't you like it?" She feigned innocence. "Since you said I was to be your 'lady companion,' one of possibly dubious morals, I thought I should dress the part."

It was the most scandalous dress she'd ever owned. She'd never worn it in public—the color and style hardly befitted an unmarried woman—but when she'd seen the rolls of teal silk being unloaded from one of her ships, she'd been unable to resist. She was sick of wearing demure, unflattering pastels. She'd ordered Madame Cerise to make her something extraordinary, and Madame Cerise, a true Frenchwoman, had risen admirably to the challenge. This was the dress of a bold, confident woman, a daring gown to go with a daring adventure.

Wylde looked like he wanted to shove her straight back into the carriage.

Or strangle her.

Or devour her.

Excellent.

His eyes seemed to be fixed on her chest. Or perhaps on the diamond and emerald necklace she'd chosen to match the outfit. The jewels had belonged to a minor European royal until the turbulent years of the revolution had forced them to sell. Georgie always felt like a princess when she wore them, despite the covetous looks she received from the other girls in the *ton*.

"Holy hell, woman!" he growled. "Do you *want* to be robbed?"

Fine words from a man dressed as a highwayman. He looked quite capable of stealing her jewels *and* her virtue. She wouldn't miss either.

She waved him away. "Nobody will think they're real, not on a courtesan. They'll assume they're paste. Stop worrying."

A muscle ticked in his jaw, and she congratulated herself on having discomposed him. There was something decidedly satisfying about shaking his usual air of cool confidence.

"Well for God's sake, keep your mask on," he grumbled, ushering her up the stairs.

The rooms were crowded with both men and women, all instantly recognizable as belonging to a lower social stratum than Georgie usually encountered. Their laughter was louder, the ladies' dresses too gaudy. Many of them wore rouge and lip paint.

And yet everyone seemed to be having far more fun than at a society party. The laughter was genuine. The buzz of conversation ebbed and flowed naturally; there was no whispering of malicious gossip or cruel tittering behind fans. The rhythmic slap of cards emanated from one room, along with the general hum of jovial conversation and the chink of glasses.

Wylde caught her wrist and steered her in that direction, weaving in and out of the throng. He stopped at a baize-topped gaming table just as another man rose to vacate his seat.

"Mind if I join you for a hand, gents?"

None of them objected, probably glad to have fresh money in the game. He sat and Georgie positioned herself behind him, hovering unobtrusively at his elbow. As the game got underway, she studied the other players at the table and with a horrified start recognized the player on Wylde's left as one of her former suitors.

Thank goodness she was wearing a mask.

Sir Stanley Kenilworth had offered for her the year she'd come out. He had seemed genuinely surprised when she'd declined the privilege of settling his numerous debts in exchange for him "overlooking her city roots."

He'd grown even fatter since then. His bloodshot eyes indicated a dedication to drinking, and his slack mouth and red jowls made her thankful she hadn't accepted his suit. This would have been *her* money that he was drinking and gambling away.

She stifled a squeal of indignation when he leaned back and casually pinched her bottom.

"Who's this little beauty, Wylde?" he slurred. "Lucky dog. You always do find the prettiest wenches."

The old coot didn't know who she was. His lecherous eyes ran over her, and Georgie dodged his hand and edged closer to Wylde. The dress was having the desired effect, but on the wrong man. She didn't know whether to be insulted, alarmed, or perversely flattered.

Wylde smiled easily and dealt the cards with practiced skill. "Keep your hands off, Kenilworth. I don't share."

His tone was pleasant enough, but there was an underlying thread of steel the other man didn't miss. Sir Stanley raised his palms in a gesture of surrender. "No offense, old man. Just saying, she's a pretty bit o' muslin."

Wylde's lips twitched. "She is. But trust me, you can't afford her."

Another man at the table laughed. "Well, I certainly can't. You've cost me a pretty penny this month, Wylde. I lost a pony when you bested Millington in that horse race to Brighton. I bet you'd never make it in under three hours."

Wylde shrugged. "What can I say? I ride as well as I shoot."

Georgie raised her brows. So that was how he augmented his meagre earnings from Bow Street; he took part in games of skill. The man was a scandalous disgrace, permanently without funds, but he didn't seem particularly concerned. She envied his assurance, that mantle of confidence honed by generations of aristocratic forebears.

Genteel poverty like his was quite commonplace amongst the *ton*. The entire monetary system ran on promises and debts, unpaid bills and gambling IOUs. She'd bet everyone in this room owed something to someone. Except for her.

She accepted a glass of wine and took the opportunity to study the rest of the room as Wylde played. She identified their host, O'Meara, moving smoothly between his guests. He seemed genial enough, with dark curly hair styled à la Brutus and rather hooded eyes. When he reached their table, he greeted the men and paid her scant attention; his gaze slid over her and dismissed her as mere ornamentation. Good.

To emphasize her role as Wylde's consort, she casually rested her hand on his shoulder. His muscles tensed under her fingertips, but after the slightest pause, he turned back to the small pile of winnings in front of him and threw down a card. Seized by a wicked impulse, Georgie trailed her fingers up toward his neck and toyed with the lock of hair that curled behind his ear.

He half turned his head as if to say something to her, then apparently decided against it.

She glanced at his cards over his shoulder and bit back a frustrated groan. Why had he discarded that queen? Really, he was making the oddest decisions. With her head for numbers, she'd always found calculating the odds of cards relatively easy, but she doubted Wylde would appreciate her interference in this instance.

Her fingers stroked the thick hair at his nape, just above his cravat, and her heart pounded at the illicit thrill of it. Wylde cleared his throat, repositioned himself in his chair, and threw down a ten, ruining any chance he might have had of winning the hand.

Georgie stifled a giggle. Was she distracting him? The idea was delightful.

The hand finished, and he stood and gathered his paltry winnings. "Excuse me, gents, but I've ignored my lady long enough. I do believe she'd appreciate a tour of the house."

This was met with knowing ribald laughter. "Oh, aye. I hear the doctor's billiard table's very sturdy," Kenilworth snickered. "Well worth a detour."

Georgie flushed beneath her mask. They all thought Wylde was taking her off somewhere for . . . nefarious purposes.

If only.

She hadn't been able to stop thinking about his ridiculous offer to introduce her to physical pleasure. The idea had taken root, a wicked, intriguing possibility. Had he been serious? What would he have done if she'd actually taken him up on it?

His cheek brushed hers as he leaned over to whisper in her ear. "They'll be imagining us *in flagrante delicto* in less than five minutes. Come on." He looked at her and away, leaving an instant's burn in his wake. As he ushered her out of the room, Georgie tried to banish the hot, sinful images he'd conjured.

They dodged another couple sneaking upstairs and a servant carrying a swaying tray of glasses. Wylde sent her a casual, intimate smile over his shoulder that perfectly communicated his delight in the unholy thrill of risk-taking. His eyes were glowing with excitement. Georgie's matching sense of elation left her almost breathless.

This was what made this man so dangerously attractive. When he called on someone to join him on an adventure, he was well-nigh irresistible.

Chapter 20.

Benedict tried to still his racing heart as he ushered Georgie down the corridor, into O'Meara's library, and closed the door behind them with a click.

The woman was driving him insane. He hadn't taken a decent breath since he'd seen her in that fever-dream of a dress. Its color emphasized the smooth skin of her bare shoulders and made him want to kiss the indent at the front of her throat, where her collarbones met. The dangerously low-cut bodice invited him to cup the lush mounds of her breasts, to press his face to them.

And if the dress hadn't been enough, while *he'd* been trying to concentrate on piquet, the little wretch had started fondling him. Her light, teasing touches had produced a flash of heat on his neck and an instant stiffening between his legs.

He had no idea what hand he'd played; his complete attention had been on her fingers in his hair. He imagined her closing her fists, gripping his hair as he thrust into her, and his hands trembled. The scent of her, an intriguing mix of perfume and skin that was uniquely hers, teased his senses, so delicious he wanted to lick her. Everywhere. He felt befuddled.

He needed to concentrate, to look for evidence. Not throw her up onto O'Meara's leather-topped writing desk. With a decided effort, he strode over to the desk in question and produced his pocket knife from his waistcoat. The lock to the top drawer yielded to its pressure with only the slightest splintering of wood, and he exhaled in satisfaction. "Let's see what the good doctor is hiding."

He rifled through the drawers, discarding most items until he came to a roll of large papers tied with a slim blue ribbon. The size alone indicated they were maps or plans of some sort. He pulled down one corner, took a brief glance, and decided they merited a closer look. He glanced over at Georgie, who'd made her way over to one of the walls of books, and beckoned her forward. As soon as she got close, he dropped to his knees and took hold of the hem of her skirts.

She sucked in a scandalized breath. "What are you doing?"

"I can't very well walk out of here with these stuffed in my jacket, can I? We'll have to hide them in your skirts."

She made a little squeaking sound, but he'd already exposed her stockinged shin. He inhaled a waft of warm, perfumed skin that made his head swim and caught a tantalizing glimpse of gartered knee before she pushed her skirts down with her hands.

"Stop being such a prude," he scolded.

She gave huff of irritation, or perhaps embarrassment. "Get off! I'll do it."

He sat back on his heels and reluctantly handed her the roll of papers. She turned her back to him and hiked up her skirts, using the strings from her inner hanging pocket to secure the scroll. She let the fabric fall with a swish, then turned and took a few experimental steps. The roll rustled almost imperceptibly as it banged against her thigh, but the folds of her skirt hid its presence very well.

"There. I—"

Voices in the hall made them both freeze. The door-knob rattled. He hadn't locked it. Before she could protest, he grabbed her upper arms, pushed her back against the nearest bookshelf, and smothered her "oomph" of surprise with his mouth.

In some dim recess of her mind Georgie realized Wylde was only kissing her to distract from their true purpose in the library, but as his lips molded to hers, she could barely think. Panic at the thought of discovery height-ened her sense of urgency, and with a little moan she returned his embrace with desperate fervor.

Somewhere near the door, she heard an embarrassed laugh—"Oh! sorry, old man, didn't mean to interrupt"—but Wylde's tongue delved into her mouth, hot as sin, and thinking became too much.

With the mask on, all she could feel was his lips on hers, the slight, thrilling rasp of his stubble chafing against her jaw. Two mouths pressing together in the darkness. His body was hard, his weight pinning her ef-fortlessly against the shelves, and she writhed against him shamelessly, wanting more. His hands came up to cup her face, then slid down her throat and over her breasts, and Georgie bit back a gasp of shock. Her nipples peaked, and her breasts seemed to swell into his hands.

He moved lower, his lips leaving a trail of fire down the side of her neck and across her collarbone, and Geor-gie tilted her head, wordlessly begging him to continue. She couldn't stop her hands from straying over his body, over wool and linen, down the front of his chest, then around his waist and under his jacket. Her seeking fingers slipped beneath his waistcoat and shirt and then she was touching the hot, bare flesh of his back. His muscles leapt and flexed beneath her palm.

He gave a heartfelt groan. "This dress, woman, God, I—" He seemed incapable of finishing the thought. His hot breath fanned the swell of her breast just above the neckline of her dress, and Georgie's knees almost buckled as his tongue flicked out and tasted her skin. Like in a whirlpool at sea, she let herself be dragged down, beyond hope of rescue, helpless against the undertow.

The abrupt crash of shattering glass brought the world back into focus with a sharp, unpleasant jolt. Someone had dropped something down the hall.

Cool air rushed into the space between them as Wylde stepped back abruptly. Georgie sucked in a breath, glad of the bookcase to support her rubbery legs. Her lips throbbed, her breasts felt achy and full, and her heart was thudding painfully against her ribs.

He retreated another step, tugging at the bottom of his waistcoat to straighten it. His hair was rumpled from where she'd run her fingers through it.

He cleared his throat. "Right then. Good job." His gaze dropped to her chest, which was still rising and falling in agitation, and he shook his head as if to clear it. "Excellent distraction, Mrs. Wylde. Top notch. Now, let's get out of here."

Georgie pushed off from the bookcase and tried to match his insouciant manner as she followed him back out into the hall.

The fortuitous broken decanter in the card room had diverted everyone's attention. It was an easy enough matter for them to gather their things and take their leave. Wylde hailed a cab, one with a closed roof, and handed her inside.

She could barely see him in the dim interior. He was a shadowed form on the opposite seat, but his masculine presence filled the space, impossible to ignore. She could hear his breathing, slow and steady, totally in control, as if the passion that had flared between them only minutes before had never existed.

The memory of her enthusiastic response made her cheeks burn. His kiss had just been part of the game. It meant nothing to him. Maybe he'd thought to give the innocent little virgin a bit of excitement to round off the evening.

And yet, he'd kissed her for far longer than necessary.

Glad of the concealing darkness, Georgie edged forward on the seat, tugged up her skirts, and unfastened the rolled papers. The wash of cool air on her upper legs made her acutely aware that she was exposing herself. She thrust papers in his general direction. "Here."

His hand closed over hers unerringly. God, how much could he see in the dark? She hurriedly fluffed her skirts back down—and was sure she heard him chuckle. The coach slowed as it joined the back of the queue at the Westons'.

"Are you coming in?" she asked.

"No. I want to take a look at our ill-gotten gains."

She quashed a wave of frustration. She deserved a look at those papers too. But she could hardly demand that he take her back to his lodgings. She'd been absent long enough. "I want to know what's in them."

"I'll call on you soon."

The door swung open, and the coachman let down the step. Wylde, half-lit by the sudden shaft of illumination, took her hand and kissed her knuckles. Her heart gave a funny little thump.

"Thank you for your help tonight," he said huskily.

"My pleasure," she breathed.

It *had* been her pleasure, she realized wryly. Illicit. Exciting. Fun. Exactly the type of adventure she'd always dreamed of. Being married to Benedict Wylde was turning out to be far more interesting than she'd ever envisaged.

She found her mother by the Westons' refreshments table.

"Ah, there you are, Georgiana. I've been looking for you everywhere."

Georgie mumbled something about needing to see to her dress. Her mother raised her brows as she got a good look at the gown, and Georgie braced herself for a scold, but to her amazement her mother tilted her head and smiled.

"Is that a new dress? I must say, that color suits you very well. Madame Cerise has excelled herself. But you do look a little flushed. I hope you haven't been overexerting yourself?"

It was all Georgie could do to stifle a snort. Kissing Wylde had been exertion of the sweetest, most dangerous kind. And it was one exercise she wouldn't mind repeating on a regular basis.

Chapter 21.

Georgie spent the following morning in a frenzy of anticipation. She declined to accompany her mother and sister to Bond Street, certain that if she went out shopping, she would miss Wylde.

They were partners in crime now. Last night's events had shifted their relationship. But had she merely imagined the flash of newfound respect in his eyes? Were they becoming friends?

She almost jumped out of her seat when the front knocker banged, and footsteps sounded on the stairs. But it wasn't Wylde who entered the drawing room. It was Josiah.

"Cousin."

Georgie sent him a thin smile of welcome in front of the maid, but as soon as Tilly left, she allowed even the pretense of civility to drop. She glared at him. "What are you doing here, Josiah? I can't imagine why you think you'd be welcome after what you did to me at Vauxhall."

His answering smile was as fake as her own. His obvious lack of remorse was infuriating. "Tilly informs me that your mother and sister are out shopping. That's good. It's you I wanted to see." His oily voice matched his greasy hair.

Georgie eyed him dispassionately. He wasn't an unattractive man, at least not physically, but the dark rings under his eyes and the yellow tinge to his skin made him look far from his best. She wondered if he'd been drinking or frequenting the numerous opium dens that abounded in the city. He certainly looked as if he hadn't slept for days. Her lip curled in distaste. "What do you want?"

He eased back into a chair with a smile that chilled her to the bone. "Simply put, money."

She gave an incredulous laugh. "And you think *I'm* going to give it to you? Have you taken leave of your senses? I wouldn't throw a bucket of water on you if you were on fire."

His smug expression didn't waver. "Oh, I think you will, Georgie. To protect the family's reputation. Because let me tell you, I'm up to my ears in debt. Quite drowning in the River Tick, as they say." He gave a hapless shrug, as if none of that were his fault. "I have moneylenders hounding me day and night—quite unpleasant fellows some of 'em—and debts I can't repay. If I don't settle them soon, I don't doubt I'll be challenged to a duel or thrown into debtor's prison." His expression grew crafty. "And we can't have the family name dragged through the mud, can we? Not while Juliet's still trying to land herself a title."

Georgie gritted her teeth and cursed his uncanny ability to hone in on the very things she cared about most. His roving gaze felt like an assault and raised goose bumps on her arms. It was nothing like the pleasant, warming sensation she felt when Wylde looked at her.

He uncrossed his legs and stood. "You're going to write me a bank draft, Georgie. For five hundred pounds.

Because if you don't, I'm going to tell everyone in the *ton* you're married to a sailor."

Georgie mirrored his stance, but inside she was shaking with fury. Wylde had told her not to give her cousin a penny, but she had no doubt that Josiah was telling the truth about his debts. He might be bluffing—his own precious reputation would be blackened by association if he told the *ton* about her marriage—but she couldn't take the chance and risk hurting Juliet or Mama. Josiah certainly seemed desperate enough to do as he threatened. He'd be ruined anyway, if he didn't pay his debts, so what did he have to lose?

"Very well."

He raised his brows at her ready answer and watched closely as she crossed to the drop-front escritoire in the corner. Her writing was shaky with suppressed fury, but she managed to sign five hundred pounds over to him. He snatched the paper from her hand and studied it suspiciously, as if she might be cheating him somehow.

"It's good," she said bitterly. "But this is the last time I will ever give you any money, Josiah."

He folded the bank draft into his inside jacket pocket, patted it, and sketched her a sarcastic bow. "Nice doing business with you, Cousin. I'll see myself out."

Georgie let out a sigh when he'd gone and sank into the nearest chair. Her limbs still quivered with outrage and dismay, both at her cousin's daring and her own pathetic inability to refuse him. He'd bullied her neatly into a corner, and she hated the feeling of having been taken advantage of. With a sudden cry, she jumped up and rang for her maid. "Tilly, will you get my hat and gloves please? I'm going out."

The servant bobbed a curtsey. "Yes, ma'am. Pieter's not back from the stables yet, if you're wanting the carriage brought around."

"No, thank you. I'll just take a walk in the park. I need a little fresh air."

Georgie didn't wait for a maid to chaperone her. She reached Hyde Park, hailed a cab, and instructed the driver to convey her to the Tricorn Club, St. James's.

If Wylde wouldn't come to her, she would go to him.

Benedict glanced up from his desk at the knock on his apartment door. "Yes, Mickey, what is it?"

The ex-boxer's huge head appeared around the door-frame. "There's a woman 'ere for you."

Ben frowned, even as his heart gave a little skip. It was bound to be Georgie. He should have known she wouldn't have the patience to wait for him to call on her. "What kind of woman?"

"The same one as was 'ere last time."

Ben sat back in his chair. "That's what I was afraid of. Bring her up."

She swept into his parlor like a tiny whirlwind, all bustling skirts and windswept coiffure. Beneath a lunatic confection of a bonnet, strewn with all manner of fashionable bows and ruffles, her cheeks were flushed a becoming pink, and her eyes sparkled with a strange, almost combative light.

His brain immediately wondered what *he* could do to make her cheeks that pink—and he was glad he'd stayed seated, so his crotch was hidden behind the desk.

"Mrs. Wylde," he said. "To what do I owe the pleasure?"

"You know perfectly well." She tugged at the ribbon bow by her ear, removed her bonnet, and tossed it onto a chair. She must have left her cloak with Mickey. Her morning dress was a delicate sprigged muslin that molded to her body with fashionable and unnerving faithfulness. Benedict prayed for strength.

"You promised to share the contents of the scroll we stole last night. I have been waiting in all morning."

She sent him a chiding look; he was clearly not dressed for an imminent visit to her house. He wore only a white shirt and breeches, covered by his favorite long, deep-red banyan robe.

He drew himself up in his chair. "As a matter of fact, I've only just returned from a meeting with Admiral Cockburn."

She pounced on that. "The Admiralty? Why? What did we steal?" She stalked impatiently to the desk and tried to get a look at the opened scroll he'd been studying.

"Plans."

"For what?"

He tried to ignore the heady scent of her perfume as she came closer. "Plans for a submarine," he said, his throat suddenly dry.

Her eyes widened. "Really? Let me see."

She placed her hands flat on the desk and leaned over to get a better look, unwittingly providing him with a magnificent view of her cleavage.

A gentleman would have politely averted his gaze, but Benedict rarely behaved like a gentleman these days. He bit back a moan and tried to forget those wonderful moments of madness in O'Meara's library, when he'd put his mouth to those pert little mounds. He'd been *so* close to—

She turned the paper to study it the right way up, and her nose wrinkled in concentration. Ben leaned back in his chair and watched her.

Since the war, he'd developed a new appreciation of such simple pleasures. On the boat back from Belgium, after Waterloo, he'd made a promise to himself that he would seize as many moments of happiness as he could. He'd never take them for granted again. In a strange way, it was his memorial to all those who'd lost their lives. He owed it to them to do all the things that they could not. To enjoy life to the utmost, to taste it. To *live* it.

The feel of the sun on his face was all the sweeter now for having been hard-won; he'd come so close to never seeing another sunrise. He appreciated the grey drizzle, the astonishing greenness of the fields, the relentless bustling optimism of the metropolis, everyone so intent on their lives, the thrust of commerce, the urgent yells of the street vendors. He savored the first sip of his morning coffee, the yeasty taste of fresh bread.

And he savored the woman in front of him.

He'd endured months of abstinence during the war, eons without the soft touch of a female. He'd rarely accepted the dubious attentions of the camp followers; he'd feared infection more than he'd craved the momentary release, so he'd made do with his own hand and his imagination. Since his return to England, he'd spent a few evenings with women, but while they'd satisfied his physical demands, they'd left his heart and mind untouched.

But here was a beautiful, infuriating woman, in his rooms. In his life. It was springtime, a time of hope and renewal, and the world was coming alive again. *He* was coming alive again, as if the emotions that had been deadened during the war were being coaxed forth by her presence.

A profound sense of gratitude swept through him. He wanted to get on his knees and glory in the miracle of having survived. He wanted to carry her through into his bedroom, throw her down on his bed, and show her just how wonderful it was to be lusty, healthy, and alive. His body throbbed in definite agreement, and he found himself calculating the number of steps to the bedroom. Mentally unbuttoning and unhooking.

Georgiana Caversteed Wylde, however, was completely oblivious to the heated direction of his thoughts. She was far too engrossed in the hand-drawn cross section in front of her. Benedict bit back a wry smile. No doubt she'd grasp the technicalities of it far better than he could. She presumably knew her way around all manner of seafaring vessels, what with owning her own shipping line.

He suppressed a sigh and willed the ache in his groin to subside. Work before pleasure. His mantra.

"The Admiralty have intercepted several plans to rescue Bonaparte since he was placed on St. Helena," he said. "Some of 'em more harebrained than others. One included the crew of a notorious privateer named the *True Blooded Yankee* invading the island from Brazil. Cockburn believes Bonaparte plans to travel to the United States, where his brother Joseph now lives, should a rescue attempt be successful."

Georgie's captivating grey eyes met his, and he fought to keep track of the conversation in the face of the distracting length of her eyelashes. This close, he noticed she had two little freckles on the bridge of her nose.

"How extraordinary," she said.

Concentrate, Wylde, he reminded himself. He tapped the plans in front of her. "This suggests our friend O'Meara is involved in something similar."

Chapter 22.

Georgie studied the technical drawings in front of her and shook her head in amazement. "These are incredible."

The plans they had stolen from O'Meara showed the design for a boat—or rather, a submersible vessel—of about twenty feet in length. The hull was divided into three chambers, with a central section for the operator and controls, and two end sections that could be filled with water or air as ballast to sink or rise. Despite her extensive knowledge of ships, she'd never seen anything quite like it. The revolutionary concept made her heart beat faster.

"Who designed this? And what did Admiral Cockburn say when you showed him?"

Wylde smiled at her evident enthusiasm. "He wasn't best pleased, as it happens because he's seen these plans before. They were stolen from the Admiralty about a year ago."

Georgie blinked. "The Admiralty is developing a submarine?"

"They *were*, when we were at war with France."

He indicated the seat behind her, and Georgie sat, then leaned forward, eager to hear the story.

"Around fifteen years ago, France paid an American inventor named Robert Fulton to develop a submarine to use against us," he said. "He did so, but the Treaty of Amiens in 1802 put an end to the war. When hostilities resumed a year later, the French had lost interest in the project, but our own Admiralty had taken note. The government was terrified Napoleon would invade, and they thought Fulton's innovations could help derail that, so they brought him over to our side."

Georgie raised her brows. "Very sneaky."

"All's fair in love and war. Fulton moved to London and signed a contract with Prime Minister Pitt and Lord Melville, First Lord of the Admiralty, to attack fleets using his 'submarine bombs.' By October 1805, he'd actually succeeded in blowing up a brig with this 'torpedo' system."

Wylde's mouth twisted wryly. "Unfortunately for Fulton, Nelson destroyed the French fleet at Trafalgar that very same month. The Admiralty told him to stop work, believing the threat eliminated. He demanded to be paid in full, despite his invention never having been used. Some bitter negotiating ensued, which resulted in the vessel being broken up and Fulton returning to his homeland, very unhappy, in 1806."

"What a shame!"

"That's not the end of the tale, though. When war broke out with France *again*, four years ago, the Admiralty decided to revisit the idea. Since Fulton was working for the Americans by then, they contacted an acquaintance of his who'd helped make the original vessel, a character called Tom Johnstone."

Georgie bounced in her chair. "This is fabulous! Just like one of Mr. Defoe's adventure novels! Who is this Johnstone fellow?"

"A smuggler and an adventurer, by trade. But the Admiralty turned a blind eye to that and commissioned him to work on a new vessel using Fulton's original designs." He indicated the papers spread out on the desk. "These designs. They gave him enough money to start building and the use of a shipyard at Blackwall Reach on the Thames."

"I have warehouses at Blackwall!" Georgie exclaimed. "This has all been going on right under my very nose! Did Johnstone build the vessel?"

"Not quite. Once again, the war ended before work was completed. Johnstone, like Fulton, was ordered to stop work, and went back to smuggling on the Kent coast. Until a few months ago, when Bow Street sent me to investigate rumors of a smuggler who was trying to engage a crew of competent sailors for a mysterious voyage."

"You think it's Johnstone?"

He rested his elbows on the arms of the chair and nodded. "I do. He and O'Meara are in league together. When the Admiralty's plans went missing, suspicion fell on a man named John Finlaison who was keeper of their records at the time, but nothing was ever proved. It turns out that Finlaison is a good friend of O'Meara's. They corresponded regularly the entire time the doctor was stationed on St. Helena."

"Aha! So O'Meara got hold of the plans and contacted Johnstone to build him a new submarine?"

"Precisely."

Georgie tilted her head toward the papers and frowned. "But this design is extremely challenging, even for an experienced shipwright. It would take months to construct. You have plenty of time to find your man."

Wylde shook his head. "Ah, but here's the rub, as Shakespeare would say. Johnstone doesn't have to build a whole new vessel. He only has to finish the one he started a few years ago."

Georgie blinked. "What?"

"The Admiralty didn't destroy Johnstone's second model. It was put in dry dock in one of the navy's warehouses—and then lost."

"Lost? How does one lose a *submarine*?"

He chuckled. "I believe the actual phrase Admiral Cockburn used was 'temporarily unaccounted for,' but it's the same thing. When the plans were stolen, they sent someone to check on it, but it wasn't where it was supposed to be."

Georgie let out a slow breath. "You think Johnstone and O'Meara have stolen it, don't you?"

"That would be my guess."

She sat back in a whoosh of skirts. "But this is unbelievable!"

His devilish grin brought out the roguish dimple on his cheek. "Isn't it just?"

They sat in a companionable silence for a few moments, contemplating the unusual situation, then Georgie said, "It's rather ironic, don't you think, that someone is planning to rescue the French emperor with a British-made submarine designed by an American?"

He gave a world-weary shrug. "War's like that. Nothing makes sense. Things always come back to bite you in the arse."

She smiled at his cynical assessment. "So, what's to

be done? I assume Bow Street wants you to prevent any rescue attempt?"

He nodded. "Indeed. Unfortunately, being a smuggler, Johnstone is an expert at avoiding the authorities. I've been chasing him for months with no luck—that's how I ended up in Newgate."

She sent him a teasing smile. "We have him to thank for our introduction, then?"

His eyes crinkled at the corners. "I suppose so. I'll thank him, if we ever meet. Bow Street has men following O'Meara now, but he'll be wary of leading us to Johnstone." He exhaled slowly, and Georgie stifled the urge to lean over and kiss the scowl off his handsome face. He looked adorably frustrated.

"We need to find the submarine and stop it from sailing," he said. "But neither Bow Street nor the Admiralty have enough manpower to start searching thousands of warehouses—assuming it's even being stored here in London." His hair flopped forward as he raked his hand through it. "Where would you even start?"

The question was rhetorical, but Georgie answered it anyway. "You have to narrow down your search. Have you considered that these plans might provide a way to trace him?"

"How?"

"Well, in the first instance, it's unlikely the submarine has been moved very far from its original location. Blackwall is a busy place—ships unload at all hours of the day and night. Such an unusual vessel would be extremely conspicuous, which suggests they would have limited the time it was visible to the public. Plus, it has to be built close to the river, because they'll need to test it, so that narrows your search even further."

He rested his elbows on the desk, mirroring her position.

"All that makes perfect sense, Captain Caversteed"—his lips quirked at the teasing nickname—"but even if it *is* somewhere near Blackwall, there are still hundreds of wharves and warehouses to look at."

Georgie pulled the paper toward her and pointed at the craft. "Johnstone cannot be building this alone. Look at how complicated it is. It takes a whole team of men to make something even as simple as a rowboat. You need carpenters and block makers, caulkers to pitch the seams, rope makers, riggers to fit the spars and sails, anchor smiths and blacksmiths to provide the chains and all the brass fittings. That's before you even get to these more unusual, bespoke parts." She drew her finger over the section that detailed various complicated-looking portholes, piping, and mechanical instruments. "This requires all sorts of gauges and valves."

She glanced up, and the blood rushed to her face as she realized Wylde was watching her with an amused, intent expression. It was the same kind of look she imagined visitors to a zoo bestowed on some perplexing new creature they'd never encountered before.

Oh, wonderful. Young ladies were supposed to go into raptures over the latest fashion plates in the *Journal de Desmoiselles,* not display an unseemly interest in technical drawings.

Well, she wasn't going to hide her curiosity. Wylde would just have to take her as she was.

She cleared her throat. "I know many of the tradesmen who supply the shipbuilding yards, and I can tell you there are very few with the skills to make such complicated bits of machinery."

His slow smile made her stomach flutter. "I think you might be onto something, Mrs. Wylde. Go on."

She tried to ignore the feeling his appreciative gaze produced; it was as if she were basking in the warm glow of his approval. But it was a rare thing, to encounter a man who was neither astonished nor disgusted by her knowledge.

"The man who makes the instruments for my ships would be one of those experts," she said. "His name is Mr. Harrison. Perhaps he can give you some insight. He may have supplied parts for this submarine or be able to suggest the name of someone else who might have."

"That is a capital idea." Wylde slapped his palms on his knees and stood, apparently having decided it was time for her to leave. Georgie did the same, swallowing a twinge of pique. She'd been enjoying their discussion.

He stepped around the desk, picked up her bonnet, and handed it to her. "Since you know this chap, and where he works, that makes you the ideal person to accompany me and make the introductions. Shall we say tomorrow, ten o'clock?"

She paused in the act of retying the ribbon of her bonnet and tried not to let her inner leap of excitement show. "You want me to pursue this case with you?"

He placed his hands on his hips in a vaguely combative stance. "What of it? Fate, or luck, or whatever else you want to call it—maybe some higher power with an exceptionally warped sense of humor—seems to have thrust you, someone with an exceptional knowledge of seafaring matters, into an investigation that requires precisely those same skills. Who am I to ignore that kind of assistance, hmm?"

She had no answer to that.

"Don't think you'll be getting half the reward money if we catch Johnstone, though," he cautioned. "This is still my case. You're just assisting."

"I wasn't even thinking of it," Georgie protested truthfully.

"Well, good. You have quite enough money of your own."

She choked back a surprised laugh. Nobody had ever dismissed her fortune with such casual levity before.

He tilted his head and surveyed her from head to toe. "I never thought you'd end up being *useful*, Mrs. Wylde. Decorative, yes. Irritating? Undoubtedly. But useful? Never."

Georgie opened her mouth to berate him, but he laid his index finger over her lips, and she sucked in a little gasp of surprise. Her stomach swooped as if she'd just driven over a jolt in the road or cleared a fence on her horse. The contact of his warm skin made her lips tingle.

"Perhaps if we're successful, I'll quit Bow Street and we can set up a rival agency: Wylde and Wylde, independent investigators. No job too small. No reward too big."

He was joking, of course. The idea of them having such a close association once the season was over was impossible. But his crooked smile did funny things to her insides. He lifted his finger and tapped her playfully on the nose, and Georgie laughed to cover her confusion. She'd hoped he was about to kiss her.

"Do you think you'll be able to get away from your mother tomorrow?"

"Yes. I visit our own warehouse every month, so she won't be surprised if I go to the docks. I'll have to bring Pieter with me, of course, but we'll pick you up on the way."

Wylde ushered her to the door, and Georgie suppressed a sigh. Here she was, an unchaperoned young lady in the private rooms of a rogue—a rogue, moreover, to whom she was legally married and had kissed quite comprehensively several times—but who apparently had no inclination to further their acquaintance.

Had he only been teasing when he made his offer to introduce her to passion? Or had he changed his mind, having kissed her and found her wanting? Perhaps he looked at every woman with that same hungry look he sometimes sent her. The thought was rather demoralizing.

Still, she was looking forward to tomorrow.

Chapter 23.

Georgie donned her most practical dress for their visit to the wharves. Pieter, seated up front of the nondescript carriage she'd purchased precisely for her monthly visits to Blackwall, made his opinion of her fraternizing with a "disreputable cove" like Wylde evident with an eloquent, disapproving sniff.

Wylde was ready when they pulled up in front of the Tricorn Club. He bounded down the front steps, leapt up into the carriage before Pieter could get down from the box, and settled himself on the opposite, rather thread-bare seat across from Georgie.

"Morning, Georgie girl."

She curbed the urge to call him "Benny boy" in retaliation and adopted a businesslike tone. "Good morning, Mr. Wylde."

He gave her modest attire a lingering look that somehow made her feel as if she were wearing something far more alluring than a plain blue worsted dress. Or wearing nothing at all.

Her skin tingled. She'd never met anyone who had such an effect on her. It was animal attraction, obviously, the kind described in dramatic prose in Juliet's gothic romances. The kind that made otherwise sensible people do foolish things in Simeon's epic poems.

Wylde himself was clothed equally plainly, in buff breeches, boots, and a navy jacket—none of which lessened his unholy appeal. He should have looked like a tradesman or a schoolteacher, someone dull and anonymous, but if anything, he appeared to greater advantage without the distraction of exquisite tailoring. His natural confidence shone through, as it had in Newgate.

He had the athletic body of a manual worker, lean, yet muscled. He certainly didn't need the padding, sawdust, or male corsets used by many gentlemen to improve his figure. Instead of a cravat, he'd knotted a neckerchief casually around his strong throat, and Georgie tried not to notice the way the thin linen of his shirt clung to his chest.

She fidgeted in her seat as they rattled along the Strand and past Somerset House, the venue for the Royal Academy of Arts annual exhibition, then indicated the cardboard tube he'd placed on the seat. "The plans, I take it?"

"Yes. This Harrison of yours will need to take a look."

They bowled down Fleet Street, then past Doctors' Commons and along Thames Street, with the river on their right. As soon as they passed London Bridge, Georgie leaned forward to see one of her favorite sights on the whole trip: the vast open-air fish market of Billingsgate.

Even with the window closed, the overpowering odor of the place—a vile combination of roach and plaice, flounders and eels—permeated the carriage, and she wrinkled her nose.

The lively scene always fascinated her. She caught a glimpse of an auctioneer standing on a barrel next to the stalls that had been set out around the dock, reducing the sum he requested until one of the rowdy fishwives thrust up a hand to bid for a parcel of fish. A grey-haired old crone sat on a basket smoking a clay pipe, while another took a swig from a dark green bottle. A couple of cats wound hopefully around their legs.

The reassuringly solid walls of the Tower of London appeared next. The route was familiar to Georgie; she and Pieter took it at least once every month, but the sheer variety of sights it offered never failed to entertain.

The houses became more crushed together as they headed east. Many had upper stories that were wider than the ones below. They leaned so close, they almost touched, blocking out the light to the narrow alleys they created below. Churches squeezed in cheek by jowl with shops and taverns, and the streets teemed with sailors and merchants' wives, coaches and horses, clergymen and whores. Georgie smiled as they passed a ragtag child driving a cart pulled by a rangy dog. The pair narrowly missed a liveried footman on an errand and a laundress with a basket of clothes balanced precariously on her head.

As they skirted the rough edges of Limehouse and Cheapside, she breathed a thankful prayer that she'd been born to a life of comfort instead of misery in such a squalid place.

Considering how aware she was of Wylde's presence, she'd thought the journey would be awkward, but they'd settled into a companionable silence. Mama and Juliet always seemed to feel the need to fill every minute of a journey with chatter, but he seemed content to gaze out of the window and savor the view. Every so often, he would point something out to her—like a woman in a ridiculously oversized bonnet battling against the wind—and they would share a smile. The tension that always seemed to fizz between them was still present, but it was layered with an odd sense of easy contentment. She felt as if they were becoming friends, and yet she knew so very little about him.

"Tell me about your family," she said suddenly.

His muscles tensed, and she cursed herself for ruining the convivial atmosphere, but then he shrugged.

"There's not much to tell. My parents had a classic marriage of convenience. I have an older brother, John, eighteen months my senior. Not long after I was born, my mother declared that she hated the country. She promptly decamped to the London town house, where she lived quite separate from my father until she died a few years ago. John and I grew up on the estate, and since Father paid us very little attention until we were old enough to play a decent hand of cards, we were left to a succession of nannies, nursemaids, and tutors."

He glanced up and must have seen the pitying look on her face because he sent her a reassuring grin. "It was an idyllic childhood, truly. Those nannies and tutors were easy to escape. John and I spent much of our time romping in the fields and woods on the estate, riding, fishing, and swimming."

Georgie frowned down at her hands. "That's so different to my own experience. It sounds as though your parents had nothing in common, as if they barely tolerated one another, whereas my parents' marriage was a love match. Mother was devastated when Father died so suddenly."

Georgie quelled a sad little smile. It seemed both their parents' marriages were cautionary tales; her own parents' against the risk of loving and potentially losing, his about marrying with no love on either side.

Benedict nodded. "My parents didn't dislike one another, per se, it's just that they had different interests, different lives. They stayed on friendly terms—at least until

the extent of father's gambling losses became apparent."
A shadow crossed his face. "I was away in Portugal when
everything came to a head, but Mother died just before
he lost the London house in a game of whist. Things got
worse after that. Father refused to stop gambling. When
he died, only a year later, there was nothing left except
that which was entailed."

"Is that why you need money?" Georgie asked quietly. "To help your brother repay your father's debts?"

He nodded. "John shouldn't have to shoulder it alone.
We both grew up at Morcott Hall. Its servants and tenants practically raised us, they're as much family as my
own flesh and blood. We need to support them, to keep
the village school open so their children have a chance
to better themselves. Just think of all the wasted talent
if you'd never been taught to add a column of figures.
You'd never have discovered your own abilities, never
had the chance to get so far in life."

His eyes gleamed as he spoke, his face was animated;
he was clearly passionate about the subject.

"One of those children might end up being the next
Shakespeare or Sir Christopher Wren." He glanced out
of the carriage window and waved his hand at the narrow, crowded streets. "I've seen the results of a lack of
education, a lack of options, both here in London, and
during the war in France and Spain. It's awful. Children
forced to beg and steal, to work in foul conditions for a
pittance. Young girls selling themselves for a scrap of
bread. We owe it to our tenants to give them that chance.
A new landlord might not be so caring."

Georgie nodded, delighted that his thoughts on the
subject so closely correlated with her own beliefs. Wylde
was the polar opposite of her cousin; Josiah firmly believed that the lower classes should stay where they had
been put and be grateful.

Feeling the need to lighten the atmosphere, she sent him a sparkling glance. "You're so lucky to have had such adventures. And a brother. I confess I'm a little jealous. Juliet was never daring enough for me. I could never convince her to climb trees or come sailing on the lake. It's always better with friends. To have someone with whom to say, 'Remember that time we—' instead of, 'This one time, I—' don't you think?"

Wylde sent her a smile that, while clearly meant to be more friendly than flirtatious, nevertheless warmed her insides with a happy glow.

"You'll get your adventures someday, Mrs. Wylde," he said. "I'm sure of it."

Georgie rather hoped those adventures would include *him*.

Soon they were rattling past Wapping and the West India Docks until they finally reached Blackwall, where Georgie's ships unloaded directly into Caversteed Shipping's warehouses.

It was low tide. The earthy, fecund scent of the Thames was stronger here, and she caught a glimpse of several mudlarks—filthy young children—scouring the water's edge for pickings amongst the mud and rubble of the shoreline, looking for anything they could sell.

The streets surrounding the docks were, unsurprisingly, filled with a vast assortment of businesses that not only catered to the demands of the shipbuilding industry, but also sold the wares that were unloaded every day. It was all so vibrant and bustling, so different from the sedate, genteel pace of Mayfair. Georgie felt infused with energy every time she came here.

Tea and coffeehouses, taverns, silk merchants, and spice vendors vied for space with cordwainers, sailmakers, and clockmakers. As they rattled down Poplar Street, past the inventively named Eel Pie Lane and the

Mayflower pub, Georgie knocked on the carriage roof with her knuckles to signal Pieter to stop.

A swinging sign above the door of the bow-fronted shop outside read, T. HARRISON, PRECISION MARINE INSTRUMENTS.

"Here we are."

Pieter handed her down from the carriage, and Georgie entered the shop with Wylde close behind. She loved coming here. Mr. Harrison was, in her humble opinion, a technical genius, and the shop interior reflected the chaotic yet brilliant state of the man's mind. Every way one turned, there was a new wonder to behold. The counters and shelves were crammed to bursting with scientific instruments, some complete and for sale, others in various stages of construction or deconstruction. A three-draw brass-and-leather telescope teetered next to a brass sextant and a hygrometer for measuring atmospheric pressure, while a mechanical figure of a monkey and an organ-grinder lay in pieces on one side.

Wylde sucked in a breath as he ducked his head to avoid various barometers and other instruments that swung from the low ceiling. A smile stretched Georgie's lips. He looked like Gulliver from Mr. Defoe's tale, a giant in a land of midgets.

"Marvelous, isn't it?" She bustled over to the shop counter, which was almost invisible beneath a pile of springs, cogs, wood shavings, and assorted tools, and rang a small bell. "Mr. Harrison?" She peered toward the back room. "He has a small foundry out the back," she explained to Wylde. "Sometimes he can't hear very well over the noise of the bellows."

Wylde was examining a complicated mechanism near his elbow. "What is this? A clock?"

"A marine chronometer. See how it is gimbled so it always stays level, even in the worst seas? Knowing the precise time of day is of vital importance when it comes to navigation. Mr. Harrison makes the best chronometers in the country. I have just fitted my entire fleet with them."

He raised his brows. "That sounds expensive."

Georgie shrugged. "It was. But a correctly functioning instrument can mean the difference between life or death at sea. Didn't you read about the *Arniston* last year?"

"I don't believe I did."

"She was an East Indiaman that wrecked off the coast of South Africa with the loss of over three hundred and fifty lives. It was in all the newspapers. The captain couldn't afford the sixty guineas for a chronometer, and the ship's owners were unwilling to purchase one. They even threatened to replace him with another captain if he refused to set sail without one."

Georgie frowned in renewed anger at the memory. "The crew had to navigate heavy seas using older, less reliable means, since the inclement weather prevented them from using celestial navigation to get a fix on their position. They headed north, thinking they'd already passed Cape Point, but they'd miscalculated, and instead, they were wrecked on the coast, with the loss of all but six lives."

She pursed her lips, both saddened and incensed by such senseless waste. "Even if the owners had provided the worst chronometer ever made, they would not have lost their ship, nor sacrificed men, women, and children for the sake of some short-sighted economy."

She shifted uncomfortably under Wylde's penetrating gaze, suddenly self-conscious. She often became a little too passionate in her arguments. Mother was always telling her to stop prattling on like the fishwives at Billingsgate. But this was a subject close to her heart.

"Your own father died at sea, did he not?"

"He did, although not for the lack of a scientific instrument. Still, the employees of Caversteed Shipping are as well-equipped as I can make them. If I can prevent just one family from experiencing a similar loss, then it's money well spent."

"You are an extraordinary woman, Mrs. Wylde," he said softly.

Georgie felt herself flush with pleasure at the sincerity in his words. Only Pieter, a sailor himself, appreciated the things she did for her workers. Perhaps, having been a soldier, Wylde could appreciate that reliable equipment saved lives.

She turned away, flustered. "Yes, well, you might want to suggest to your friend Admiral Cockburn that the Royal Navy supply all *its* vessels with chronometers too. They do not currently do so as a matter of course."

She was saved from further awkwardness by the appearance of Mr. Harrison. The old man bustled in from the darkened back room, wearing his usual uniform of a battered leather apron tied over a shirt and a wilting jacket. A halo of frizzy white hair surrounded his speckled head, and a delighted grin split his face beneath his wire-rimmed spectacles.

"Miss Caversteed! It's a pleasure to see you again. How are you? How are those chronometers working out?"

Georgie returned his smile. "Good day, sir. I am very well. And the instruments are wonderfully accurate, as expected. I received a report from the captain of the *Juliana* a week ago saying he had arrived in Constantinople a full two days sooner than expected."

"Capital! So, what brings you here today?" He glanced curiously at Wylde.

"May I introduce an acquaintance of mine, Mr. Benedict Wylde?"

Harrison nodded. "Good morning, sir. A sailor, are you?"

"I'm afraid not. Ex-Rifles, actually. Currently working for Bow Street." He withdrew the plans from the tube and handed them to the older man. "I was hoping you might be able to shed some light on these."

Harrison swept a forearm across the counter to clear a space and unrolled the papers. His bushy white brows rose as he studied them. "Well, well, what do we have here?"

"They're plans for a submersible craft," Georgie offered. Wylde's shoulder touched hers as he angled himself next to her on the counter, and she shivered in awareness. "Mr. Harrison, do you recognize this ship? Or any part of it?"

The old man bent closer. "Extraordinary," he murmured.

Georgie smiled as she recognized the same awed reaction she herself had exhibited the previous day. She pointed at the mechanical workings of the submarine. "Do any of these particular parts look familiar to you? Has anyone ever asked you to make any of them?"

Harrison's wrinkled face clouded as he searched his memory. "Now I think on it, yes. Yes." He pointed at a larger, close-up section. "I made that particular series of taps and gauges for a gentleman a month or two ago."

Georgie glanced at Wylde, scarcely able to hide her elation, but Harrison was still talking.

"I thought at the time it was an unusual commission, but he told me it was for some top secret Admiralty project. Some kind of weather-measuring device. It was for a submarine though, eh?" He wheezed a delighted chuckle. "How interesting."

Wylde leaned forward. "Do you happen to recall the name of the person who commissioned that piece?"

Harrison glanced up reluctantly from the plans. "I can

look. It should be in my receipt book." He bustled away into the back room, and Georgie turned to Wylde with a little bounce of excitement. He shook his head, a silent warning not to raise her hopes.

"Ah, here we are." Harrison returned, holding a large, leather-bound ledger book. "It was ordered by a Mr. Johnstone. Paid for in cash."

Georgie tried to keep the triumph off her face. "We'd be very interested to speak with this Mr. Johnstone. I don't suppose he left an address?"

The old man drew his finger across the handwritten entry. "He did, as a matter of fact. I had a boy deliver an extra set of hinges to him at . . ." He squinted, trying to read his own handwriting. "White Lion Yard, off Ore Street in Limehouse."

Georgie beamed. "That is wonderfully helpful, Mr. Harrison. Thank you so much."

The inventor indicated the curling plans on the counter. "My pleasure. I don't suppose I might keep these for a day or two, for a closer look?"

"I'm afraid we can't allow you that courtesy, sir," Wylde said apologetically. "The Admiralty wants them back with all haste."

"Pity. I'd give my eyeteeth to meet the man who designed such a contraption."

"That would be an American by the name of Robert Fulton," Georgie said. "Unfortunately, he's back in his homeland now."

Harrison sighed. "Ah well. If I can be of any further assistance, do let me know. I always enjoyed working with your late father, God rest his soul, and I'm glad you're following in his footsteps so admirably."

Georgie blushed. "Thank you, Mr. Harrison, that means a great deal. I shall call on you again soon. Good day."

Wylde rolled the plans and replaced them in the tube, and together they stepped back out onto the street. Georgie took a deep satisfied breath. "Well, that was a stroke of luck. I never dreamed we would be quite so successful."

He shot her a condescending look. "Beginner's luck."

She punched him playfully on the arm. "Unkind, Mr. Wylde! Give credit where it's due."

He sighed theatrically. "Very well. You have been enormously helpful. Thank you."

She accepted that with a jaunty smile. "My pleasure. Now, since Caversteed Shipping's offices are just around that corner, how would you like to see my warehouse?"

Pieter, holding the head of the lead horse beside the carriage, rolled his eyes at her shameless attempt to prolong the outing, but Georgie ignored him.

Wylde offered her his bent arm. "I would be delighted."

She shot Pieter a winning smile. "I do believe we'll walk, Pieter, and I know you don't like to keep the horses standing. Perhaps you can take them for a slow drive until we're done? We shouldn't be above half an hour."

Pieter sent Wylde a frowning glare that clearly warned him to be on his best behavior or face dire consequences, and climbed reluctantly up onto the driver's seat. "As you wish, miss."

Georgie smiled up at Wylde. "This way."

Chapter 24.

As soon as Pieter had driven off, Georgie turned to Wylde. "So, next stop Limehouse?"

He let out a bark of laughter. "No chance. My Bow Street colleagues, Alex and Seb, and I will take things from here. We need to proceed with caution, not just go blundering in there, asking questions and frightening people off."

"I wouldn't do anything like that."

His skeptical look made her want to stamp on his foot.

"Believe me, I've dealt with situations like this before," he said. "We need to know how many people we're dealing with, for starters. You said it yourself; Johnstone could have a whole team of people working with him. They could be armed. I'm not putting you in that kind of danger, Georgie, so you can forget about trying to convince me otherwise."

Georgie closed her mouth against the urge to do precisely that. He had a fair point. He *was* far more experienced in this sort of thing. And his desire to keep her safe from harm was rather sweet. Misguided, of course, but sweet.

As they rounded the end of the street, the wide bowl of the harbor came into view. Georgie grinned at the familiar sight of bobbing, jostling ships and tugged him toward the wharf. There was always something happening here. Cranes and winches were busy unloading crates of produce, while the air swirled with the smell of the refuse floating in the grey-brown water. She shuddered at the bobbing corpse of a bloated rat. She'd once seen a group of boys playing a disgusting game whereby they actually threw the inflated rats at one other, like some sort of revolting exploding missile. It was so unsanitary, she couldn't even begin to comprehend it. No wonder people said the docks were no place for a lady.

And yet her father had always allowed her to come here with him to watch their ships come in. She'd found it endlessly fascinating, spinning tales in her imagination of all the exotic and wonderful places the goods had come from.

Wylde took her arm, his fingers gentle at her elbow, and they dodged a couple of sailors with tarred pigtails and an oyster seller with his wheelbarrow. Georgie pointed to a vessel farther down the wharf with a proud smile. "That's one of mine."

He shielded his eyes against the low, weak sun and read the painted nameplate on the bow. "The *Lady Alice*."

"Named after my mother." Her smile was bittersweet. "Father was always aware that he couldn't provide her with a real title, despite his wealth. He knew the *ton* looked down on her for being 'tarnished by trade.' This was the only way he could make her a lady."

"There's a measure of security in a title," he agreed easily. "Just as there is in wealth."

She nodded, glad he understood. "That's why Mother's so keen for my sister to marry a peer. She wants Juliet to have all the advantages she never had." She gave a half laugh, half sigh. "It drives me mad, but I can't fault her for it."

Wylde nodded at the vessel. "What kind of ship is she?"

"A brig. They're popular among pirates because of their speed and maneuverability, but we use them as standard cargo ships. She's just about to head off to Boston."

They stood side by side and watched as men loaded crate after crate of oranges onto the deck.

"What are the oranges for?"

"One thing the navy discovered while fighting Bonaparte was that citrus fruits, like oranges and limes, prevent scurvy. Our sailors stayed healthier than the French thanks to a regular supply of lemon juice and fruit. The Americans call our sailors 'Limeys' now because of it." She glanced up at him. "After reading Dr. Lind's *Treatise on Scurvy* I decided to adopt it as a health measure on my own ships. I haven't lost a man to scurvy in three years."

"That sounds like thrilling bedtime reading," he mocked gently. "I applaud the care you take for your crew members, but I truly believe I'd rather read a whole volume of Mr. Pettigrew's verses than a medical treatise on scurvy."

Benedict shook his head as he tried to reconcile the vibrant, multifaceted woman beside him with the first impressions he'd made of her. He'd imagined she would turn out to be a prim, haughty, ice princess with no care for anything except the cost of her gown and the elevated title of her next dance partner. He couldn't have been more wrong. She was astonishing. Her natural aptitude for the scientific and mathematical was as delightful as it was surprising. He admired her business-like brain, her sharp wit, and the fearsome intellect that challenged him on so many levels. She was in her element here, he realized, surrounded by the cutthroat hustle and bustle of trade.

She didn't need to work. She could have done nothing with her life and lived off the interest of her fortune, wallowing in luxury in the safety of Grosvenor Square. Instead, she'd chosen to take on the challenge of running a business, to prove her mettle in an overwhelmingly male-dominated environment. His respect for her went up another notch.

He shouldn't be surprised, though. War had shown him that people were rarely what one expected. He'd seen huge brawny fellows full of braggadocio before a battle cowering and whimpering like puppies by the side of their canon when the battle was in full flow. And he'd seen a skinny drummer boy, pale with fright, bend and pick up the fallen colors and face the enemy with a bellow of defiance. It was what a man—or woman—did when they were tested that showed their true worth.

He'd proved himself during the war. Despite the gut-wrenching, ball-tightening fear, the horror and misery of countless battles, he'd come out of it as a man secure in his ability to face adversity. Georgie wanted to prove that she was worthy of her fortune, of carrying on her father's legacy. She was doing an admirable job.

She was responsible for the welfare of not just her immediate family, but for the hundreds of other people who relied on Caversteed Shipping for their livelihoods, and yet she shouldered the weight of that responsibility with apparent ease.

The fact that he found her competency arousing was

barely worth mentioning. He seemed to find everything about her—from her expressive grey eyes to the sly curl of her lip when she thought something was funny—arousing. Just being near her was an exercise in restraint.

He glared across the river at the barren, boggy opposite shore known as the Isle of Dogs in an attempt to ignore the pull of her. The air was foggy, the weak sun filtering through the clouds. He'd forgotten the damp chill of England in March. It was such a contrast to the searing heat of Spain, the harsh glare. He missed the warmth, but not the bullets flying at him. It was infinitely preferable to be standing here with this woman on his arm, chilled or not.

His overstimulated brain dutifully provided a hundred different ways in which he could warm her up. Very few of them required clothes.

She tugged on his arm. "My offices are in that building there, above the warehouse. Come on."

He followed her toward the large red brick building, smiling at her enthusiasm.

"I come here every month to look over the books and discuss things with my business manager, Edmund Shaw."

"Can't he just bring the books to you?"

She smiled up at him guilelessly, and he felt the familiar tug in his groin. Blasted woman. Why couldn't she have been ugly? And dull. And unavailable.

"He could, I suppose, but I love coming here. It makes me feel closer to my father. And besides, I don't have to hide how good I am at figures here, as I do when I'm in the *ton*." She shook her head with a sigh. "Mother and Juliet don't understand. They have no interest in the business. They just want to go to parties and routs."

"And what do you want?"

She wrinkled her nose. "When I was younger, all I ever wanted to do was jump aboard one of our ships and sail away to see the world. I wanted to visit the Mediterranean, India, the Americas. Father and Pieter were always catching me trying to stow away in the hold." She laughed. "I vowed that as soon as I was a widow, I would go on a grand tour, just as the men do. Venice, Madrid, Vienna." Her face clouded. "I doubt Mother or Juliet could be persuaded to leave London, though. And adventures are no fun unless you have someone to share them with."

Benedict bit back his instinctive response—that such a trip should be a honeymoon, with him. *Impossible*. They were too different. He spent his time in seedy backstreets among thieves and drunkards, murderers and pimps. A world of sweat and ale, sawdust and spit, vomit, mud, and blood. She was Grosvenor Square—bright, sparkling silver, unchipped china, rugs that weren't threadbare and faded by the sun, warm wood polished with beeswax.

There would be no honeymoon. After the wedding, they would go their separate ways.

He forced a casual shrug. "You could still go once we're officially married. You could find a companion to go with you."

Another woman, he added silently. The thought of her sharing it with another man made his blood boil. He wanted to be the one she turned to with a breathless smile to point out some crumbling old ruin.

She nodded, blissfully unaware of his seething thoughts. "Yes, that's exactly what I need. A partner in crime. I suppose you've seen quite a lot of Europe during your time in the army?"

Benedict hid a grimace. He's seen battlefields, mainly. His tour of the Spanish peninsula had consisted of the sieges of Ciudad Rodrigo and Badajoz, the battles of

Salamanca, Pamplona, and Valencia. Then it had been a slog through France and Belgium culminating in the bloody fights at Quatre Bras and Waterloo last year.

Perhaps it would do him good to go back and see the same places not covered in dead men and horses, to see how the land was healing. Or maybe it would just bring back memories too painful to reexamine. He still had nightmares, odd moments when a particular sound or scent would plunge him right back into some hellish time he'd rather forget.

He shook his head. If he ever revisited those places, he'd make it his mission to replace the bad memories with good ones. Georgie would love Salamanca—the hilltop fortress and the great cathedral. And *he'd* love kissing her senseless up against the sun-warmed walls until she was soft and pliant in his arms. He'd make love to her by the window of some grand *pension*. She could admire the view before he made her lose her mind . . .

He bit back a groan as his body reacted predictably to his heated visions. From the corner of his eye, he could see the tempting curve of her neck, the smooth line of her jaw. The coils of shimmering hair that made his fingers itch to unpin it. A red lust clouded his vision and a slow heat rose in his limbs. His throat tightened. He imagined her hair spread around her in waves, her naked body lifting, arching up toward him, the sounds she would make—little breathless gasps—as he drove into her.

"Benedict?"

What had she asked him? Oh yes, his travels.

"Mmm," he managed hoarsely. "Yes, I've seen quite a bit of France and Spain, I suppose."

He was saved from elaborating when she nodded to the sentry guarding the entrance to the warehouse. The man doffed his hat at her in recognition.

"Hello, George. Is Mr. Shaw here?"

"Just popped over to the Royal Ensign to get some lunch." The sentry pointed to the public house a little farther down the wharf. "He'll be back in a bit."

She nodded and entered the enormous building, drawing Benedict in her wake.

Chapter 25.

Georgie watched Benedict inspect the vast warehouse with a swell of pride at his obvious admiration. The sight never failed to impress her either.

"My God, how rich *are* you?" he breathed, taking in the row upon row of neatly stacked shelves.

She couldn't hide her smile at his plain-spokenness. No one had ever asked her that outright, although she was sure everyone had wanted to. Trust Benedict to go straight to the point. She decided on equal candor. "Well, I suppose you could say I'm extremely rich. If one were being vulgar about it."

His smile was slow and melting. "There's a lot to be said for vulgarity." He stepped into the first aisle and bent to inspect a newly opened crate of tea leaves, and Georgie stole an appreciative glance at the way his breeches clung to his long thighs and outlined his taut rear. He was right; being vulgar definitely had its advantages.

She inhaled deeply, loving the combined scents that filled the air. The warehouse always smelled so wonderful, of spices and perfumes, lumber and tea. Aromas so seductive they conjured up all kinds of intoxicating, romantic images. She thrust her hand into the tea crate and let a handful of the wizened black leaves trickle through her fingers.

"You smell that? It's a special kind of black tea flavored with bergamot oil. We sell it exclusively to Jacksons of Piccadilly." She brought her palm up to her nose and sniffed appreciatively. "The oil comes from a fruit, the bergamot orange, which grows in Italy."

Her heart twisted painfully. Father had always smelled of tea leaves and sandalwood, like fragrant pencil shavings. Being subtle about it, she leaned closer to Benedict and took a surreptitious sniff. He smelled gorgeous. Of the sea, the sun, the earth. Like she imagined the breeze from a Mediterranean island might smell as it wafted over the sea, a clean, masculine version of rosemary and pine, with a delicious salty tang of skin beneath. She groaned silently as her knees turned to jelly.

"This place always reminds me of that children's rhyme," she said. "You know, the one that goes: 'Sugar and spice and all things nice. That's what little girls are made of.'"

He nodded. "I know it. Little boys are made of slugs and snails and puppy dogs' tails. Hardly flattering. There's a second verse too. 'Ribbons and laces and sweet pretty faces, that's what young women are made of.'"

His eyes roamed her face, and her heart skipped a beat. "I'd prefer to be associated with something a little more exotic," Georgie managed. She waved her hand at the surrounding shelves. "Like ambergris and sandalwood, jasmine and kohl." Scents that could seduce and stupefy the senses. She wanted to be the type of woman who had that effect, who made men dizzy, who could bring a man like Wylde to his knees.

She almost snorted aloud. *Some hope.*

She cleared her throat. "Tea imports are some of my most profitable shipments. We trade British woolens and Indian cottons for Chinese tea, porcelain, and silk."

"Do you import opium?"

"No. The East India Company does, though." She frowned. "I understand from Mr. Pettigrew that poets like Byron use it for inspiration, but I can't say I'm convinced. I suspect it's one of the reasons my cousin is in such debt. Have you ever tried it?"

"Never smoked it. But I was given laudanum when I was wounded in my shoulder. It helped with the pain, but not with my dreams. It made them even worse, even more vivid." He stopped abruptly, and a flush crept up his neck as if he were embarrassed to have revealed such a human failing.

"Do you recall unpleasant things from the war?" Georgie ventured cautiously.

"Sometimes. Yes." He cleared his throat. "I don't really think about it much, but sometimes, when I'm asleep, or very tired, memories come back to me, so real I think I'm back there." He shrugged. "I can understand why some men might want to drug themselves in an effort to gain oblivion, but I'm not sure it's the best way to deal with it. A life spent half asleep isn't much of a life at all. I'm glad you don't sell it."

"Yes, well, there are equally profitable cargoes that don't endanger people's health." Georgie waved a hand at the goods on either side. "Like silk. Velvet. Glass."

The existence of her fortune always provoked fierce and conflicting emotions in her breast. When she'd come out, aged sixteen, and found herself instantly popular with the gentlemen, she'd been flattered—until she realized they were only after her money. She'd found it hard to make female friends too. Her peers had resented her ability to afford expensive jewels and gowns and spread jealous gossip about her.

Georgie had spent years wondering how she would ever know if a man really loved her.

The only way to be sure would be to remove her fortune from the equation, which was almost impossible. In weaker moments, she'd imagined running away and starting a new life, incognito, where she'd have the potential to be sincerely loved. But the truth was, she appreciated being rich. She was glad she never had to worry about her next meal, or whether she might be able to afford a physician if her mother or sister fell ill. She gave generously to numerous charities—anonymously— to relieve other, less fortunate souls of the same burden.

The contract she'd made Wylde sign in Newgate had been the best solution she could find to weed out fortune hunters.

Wylde turned to her with a teasing smile. "I am seriously regretting signing your bloody bit of paper now."

Georgie blinked at the way he seemed to read her mind, then smiled at his unabashed honesty. "I *am* still paying you a thousand pounds," she reminded him. "In fact, if you'll step upstairs to my office, Mr. Wylde, you can have your first installment."

She headed up the spiral staircase, hotly aware of him close behind her, and entered the office reserved for her use. The leather-topped partners desk had a concealed drawer, released by pressing a lever underneath, which held her ledger books and a stash of banknotes. Georgie counted out three hundred pounds then rounded the desk and leaned against the edge as she held the money out toward him.

He shook his head. "I haven't earned this. A stroll around Vauxhall and one morning call to your house is hardly enough to convince the *ton* I'm courting you seriously. Nobody saw us together at the Westons'." He held his arms out to the side, as if offering himself as a servant to do her bidding. "Are you sure there's nothing else I can do for you, my lady? Here I am. At your service."

His voice had an ironic, slightly mocking tone, but whether it was aimed at her or himself, she didn't know. Georgie immediately imagined several, outrageously improper, things he could "do for her." The air between them became strangely charged. There was some emotion in his face that made her stomach knot. He called to every wild and reckless part of her.

His gaze dropped to her lips. "I may not have brought money to this marriage, but I can certainly bring experience." His eyes burned into hers as he allowed her to see the hunger there, the desire. "Are you sure you won't reconsider my offer?"

Her heart began to pound. She didn't need to ask which offer he was talking about. She'd thought of little else for days.

Taking him as her lover would be morally reprehensible. She was, technically, paying for his company. Which would make him—what? Some kind of male concubine? Her brain went a little fuzzy at the thought.

But she'd wanted a lover, had she not? And here she was, legally married to this ridiculously attractive man who sounded more than willing to accept the role. He wasn't pretending to love her. He was simply offering physical pleasure in response to a blistering mutual attraction.

What was the worst that could happen? There was a risk that she could conceive a child, but according to Tilly, there were ways to prevent such things. Georgie was rather vague on what they were, admittedly, Tilly not having been forthcoming with the details, but a worldly man like Wylde would know what measures to take, surely.

Her heart thudded against her ribs as he took a step closer.

"As a matter of fact, I've been giving serious thought to what you said the other day," she managed.

"Have you indeed? And what have you concluded?"

She gripped the edge of the desk. "That I should like to take you up on your offer."

He stilled, and she thought she saw a flare of triumph in his gaze. And then his focus flicked to the desk behind her, as if he were actually contemplating taking her right then and there. Her knees almost buckled. He took another step, deliberately crowding her between his hard body and the edge of the desk, and she swallowed, almost sick with anticipation. To be pursued with such purposeful intensity was terrifying. And wonderful.

She gave a half laugh, half gasp. "I didn't mean—"

Without a word, he lifted her by the waist and sat her on top of the desk. The money rustled against his shirt as she splayed her hands on his chest. Her knees parted automatically, and he stepped between them. His body was vibrating with desire, his heart pounding beneath her palm. Only a few layers separated them—his breeches, her skirts. She could feel the heat of him.

Their eyes met and held as he grasped the hem of her skirts and slid his hand over her knee. The rustle of wool and cambric was deafening. Suddenly impatient, Georgie reached up, caught his nape, and tugged his head down to hers. She parted her lips, desperate for a taste of him, just as Edmund Shaw's jovial shout echoed up the stairs.

"Are you up there, Miss Caversteed? I do apologize. I just went to get some lunch. I wasn't expecting you. Is there something I can help you with?"

They sprung apart guiltily, and Georgie was sure her own face held the same look of burning frustration as Wylde's. She cleared her throat and called down.

"No, no, it's quite all right, Edmund. This was an impromptu visit. I was just giving Mr. Wylde a tour. We must be getting on now." There was only a slight, betraying quaver in her voice, thank goodness.

Wylde's hot smile made her pulse skyrocket. He gestured for her to proceed him downstairs. "Quite so. Important things to do," he murmured as she brushed past him.

Georgie barely remembered taking her leave. Pieter was waiting with the carriage outside, and she got in, scarcely able to look at Wylde as he settled himself on the seat opposite her. Her stomach churned. Where had she found the nerve? She'd actually propositioned him!

The carriage lurched forward, and she kept her eyes on her hands. The silence became almost unbearable.

"When?" His low baritone sent shivers through her.

She couldn't look at him. Doubtless the other women he'd made such arrangements with knew exactly how this game was played. They'd be bold and flirtatious, breezily confident. She was finding it hard to breathe, caught in a tumult of conflicting emotions.

"Will you come to me at the Tricorn?"

The question was soft, almost lazy. With infinite implications. It made her pulse flutter and her heart pound. She sucked in a shocked gasp. "What, now? It's the middle of the day! Pieter—"

"Look at me, Georgie." His tone was teasing, gently amused.

She did what he ordered and was struck once again by just how ridiculously attractive he was. Like some wicked fallen angel. Good Lord, what was she getting herself into? How could she possibly handle a man like this?

"Breathe."

She let out a sharp exhale.

"Stop worrying. There's nothing to it, believe me." His smile made her insides quiver. "You're going to enjoy every minute, I promise."

Could a person expire from anticipation?

"Can you get away this evening?" he asked. "I can send Mickey with a carriage. You can slip out and meet him at the corner."

"I'm supposed to be attending the Evans' rout, but I could say I have a headache and leave early. Mother won't check on me until morning if I say I'm going straight to bed."

"Perfect." His appreciative gaze roved over her face and lingered on her lips as if he were already imagining the taste of them.

Georgie decided to press her luck. She leaned forward and rapped on the roof of the carriage.

"Yes, miss?" Pieter shouted down.

"We'd like to make a stop on the way home," she called out before Wylde could speak. "Ore Street in Limehouse."

Wylde sent her an exasperated look, and she arched her brows at him, suddenly confident.

"We're going to need something seriously distracting to get us through the next few hours, don't you think?" she whispered.

He gave a reluctant sigh. "Oh, very well. You shall have your adventure. But I warn you, if there's the least sign of trouble, we'll be leaving, understood?"

She sent him a delighted nod of agreement.

Chapter 26.

Pieter dropped them off at the corner of Ore Street, and they entered a bow-fronted coffeehouse directly across from the entrance to White Lion Yard. Georgie glanced around the dimly lit interior. She'd never set foot in a coffeehouse before, and this one appeared delightfully dingy. Clusters of patrons, from bootblacks to bewigged clergymen, lounged around rough wooden tables and argued nosily over the contents of the day's newspapers. The strong scents of tobacco, coffee, sweat, and warm beer assaulted her nose.

Wylde thrust her into a vacant booth in the bay window and ordered two coffees from the bored-looking barmaid. Georgie stared down at the steaming brew with mingled disgust and delight.

"'Black as hell, strong as death, sweet as love,' as the old Turkish proverb goes," Wylde murmured dryly. "Drink up." He clinked his tankard against hers.

She took an experimental sip and discovered her fears were unfounded. The coffee was exquisite. She groaned appreciatively, then blushed as she caught Wylde's intense gaze. Tension arced between them as she licked a drop from her lip, deliberately provoking, and enjoyed the way his jaw tightened. He desired her.

The knowledge of her newfound feminine power was like a drug. She wanted his hands on her, his mouth on hers, like a fever in her blood. Desire pooled low in her stomach. In a few short hours, this man was going to make her a woman. She would be a virgin no more. She couldn't wait.

"Stop it," he growled.

She shot him an innocent glance from beneath her lashes, her confidence bolstered by the fact that they were in a public place. It was safe to taunt him here. "So, now what?"

He tilted his head at the cluster of buildings opposite. "Now we watch and wait. This is the boring part of undercover work. I can't tell you how many hours Seb, Alex, and I have spent sitting around waiting for someone or other to show up."

And wait they did, for over half an hour. Georgie squinted through the grimy window, but there was no movement from the warehouse. There were no deliveries. Nobody went in or out. She puffed out her lower lip and blew the hair up from her forehead with a little gust of air. "This is dull."

Wylde, who had availed himself of one of the crumpled, coffee-stained news sheets and proceeded to ignore her, tilted down the corner and peered at her. "I told you." With a sigh, he flicked his long fingers and summoned one of the scruffy-looking potboys who were lounging near the fire.

"What's to do, guvn'r?"

He tilted his head across the road. "See that building there? Go and knock on the door. If someone answers, ask for Mr. Keating. There won't be any Keating there, so say you must have been given the wrong address. Then come back here."

"Woss in it fer me?" The boy sniffed.

"A shilling."

The lad touched his forelock. "Done." He scampered out into the street, and Georgie held her breath as he raced across the road and only narrowly avoided being trampled by a horse pulling a cart full of barrels. He rapped at the warehouse door and waited. When there was no response, he shrugged and jogged back across the road.

Wylde flipped a coin into his outstretched hand, and Georgie shot him a pleading look. "There's obviously nobody there. Can't we take a little look? Just a peek?"

He sighed. "Oh, all right." He turned to the boy again. "What's your name?"

"Mouse, guv."

"All right, Mouse. Another shilling if you'll stand watch and whistle if anyone comes."

"Done." The boy nodded eagerly. "I can whistle good."

Wylde bypassed the front door of the warehouse and instead tugged her into the narrow alleyway that separated it from its grimy neighbor. A short flight of steps led down to the river at the far end, and Georgie put her hand over her nose to mask the fetid stench coming from the piles of refuse heaped amid the rusty shipbuilding materials that had been abandoned on either side. Thank goodness she'd worn an ugly dress. She'd burn it after this.

Wylde dragged a wooden crate under one of the warehouse's dirty windows and climbed up. She was about to tell him he had little hope of seeing anything through such filthy glass when he produced a pocketknife and flicked open the casement with a practiced turn of the wrist. With a grin, he turned and offered her his hand.

"Ladies first."

She sent him a scornful, doubtful glance. "You want me to climb through the window?"

"This was your idea, remember? If you want to get back in the carriage—"

That did it. Georgie grasped his wrist and let him haul her up. She gasped when he caught her around the waist and lifted her effortlessly onto the sill, then gathered her skirts, swiveled around, and dropped into the empty building. Wylde followed close behind.

She brushed the cobwebs off her skirt as her eyes became accustomed to the gloom. Dim light filtered down from a series of grimy skylights in the roof, enough to see the iron rails that ran along the floor to help launch a ship through the double doors at the far end, and the workbenches laden with woodworking tools. In the center of the space stood the unmistakable shape of the vessel she'd seen on paper.

Georgie let out an awed breath. "That's it! Fulton's ship. Look."

She ran her hand along the rough planks of the ship's side. Externally, at least, it looked like any other boat, with a wooden mast and spar, rudder, and anchor dangling from a chain. The familiar smell of fresh-cut wood and tar—used to waterproof the planks—filled her lungs.

Desperate to see how much had been completed, she stepped up onto the ladder that was propped against the side and peered over the rail. Unlike on a conventional boat, the deck was completely enclosed. There was just one funnel-shaped opening in front of the main mast, with a hatch to allow entry inside.

"I'm taking a closer look," she whispered down to Wylde. He nodded, steadying the ladder for her, and she

clambered onto the deck and peered down into the workings of the beast.

The inner chamber was around six feet square and
curved on either side like a barrel, following the shape
of the ship. She could just make out the twisted shapes of
various pipes, handles, and levers in the gloom.

"It looks almost complete," she called, her head
still down the hatch. Wylde's body brushed hers as he
crouched beside her, and she bumped the back of her
head as she jolted in shock. His nearness made her quivery, as if snakes coiled in her belly.

"There's the handle and crank for the anchor," she
muttered, "and the bilge pump. Those other controls
must be for the letting in of water or air for ballast and
flotation."

Wylde's gravelly voice sounded directly behind her.
"Have you ever noticed the preponderance of double en-
tendres in maritime terminology? It seems to me there's
an alarming number of hand pumps, cocks, and screws."

Georgie stifled an unladylike snort. "I've never really
thought about it." She brought her head back up, and he
waggled his eyebrows at her.

"I mean, *bilge pump*? I don't even know what that is,
but it sounds filthy."

She rolled her eyes. "That is so—"

A shrill whistle interrupted whatever she'd been about
to say.

"Shit," Wylde said. "Someone's coming." He nodded
at the hatch. "Quick. Get in there."

Chapter 27.

Georgie didn't waste time arguing. Someone was already scrabbling at the front door, trying to put a key into the lock. Panic filled her as she lifted her arms above her head and dropped down into the darkened hull.

She fell back onto her bottom just as Wylde slipped in beside her. He banged her head with his elbow as he closed the hatch, and the scant light shut off abruptly. Without a word, he tugged her down so they were both lying prone, squashed together like two sardines packed in a jar.

She hardly dared breathe. Above her frantically beating heart, she could hear muffled male voices and the sound of heavy footsteps coming closer. Oh, God. They were bound to be discovered.

Her eyes gradually became accustomed to the semi-darkness. Thin bands of light filtered in between the unsealed horizontal planks and through the one tiny porthole at the front of the funnel. She could just make out Wylde's profile, tiger-striped and shockingly close, as he brought his index finger up to his lips in an unnecessary signal for quiet.

She lay on her back. He'd propped himself up on one elbow by her side, with one of his long legs draped partly over her to allow his larger body to fit into the restrictive space. Georgie closed her eyes as the scandalous nature of the position flooded her senses.

"Where do you fink 'e wants 'em?" a rough voice rasped.

"Just leave them over there," came the reply.

The sound of something heavy being dropped echoed around the room. The footsteps receded, only to return a few moments later with the same series of clatters, grunts, and thuds, presumably some sort of lumber de-livery. Georgie prayed that whoever it was would finish their task quickly and leave. It was warm inside the sub-marine, as if they'd been swallowed by a dragon. They were inside its belly, trapped within its curving ribs.

Wylde's long body pressed against hers, his warm breath mingling with hers. Her heart beat in her temples, and she took rapid, shallow breaths as the darkness be-gan to crowd in on her. Had Wylde shut the hatch com-pletely? Wouldn't they run out of air?

He seemed to become aware of her growing distress; his hand settled gently on her breastbone. "Breathe with me," he whispered, his lips just brushing her ear, a mere thread of sound. "Slowly. It's all right. Just breathe."

His hand was warm through her clothing, a reassuring weight. She felt her rib cage rise and fall and matched her breaths to his. In and out. Slower. Calmer. The panic receded, only to be replaced by a greater sense of aware-ness—of him. As if to compensate for her lack of vi-sion, all her other senses became more acute. She could feel the texture of his clothing, the buttons of his coat pressing into her side, every single place his strong body touched hers. A lingering trace of coffee and smoke still clung to him, but beneath that was his own familiar scent, which made her heart thunder against her ribs.

She glared at him in silent reproach, as if their ridiculous predicament were somehow his fault. He shot her a droll glance in return, as if to say, *I warned you*.

The delivery was still going on outside. Muffled sounds of scraping wood continued mere feet away, on just the other side of the planks, but Georgie could barely concentrate. All she could think about was Wylde's proximity.

He shifted restlessly, his body pressing against hers, and then he closed his eyes, as if the feel of her against him caused him physical pain. She watched the apple in his throat bob down as he swallowed.

His hand was still resting lightly on her chest. Georgie shifted her shoulders, trying to get more comfortable, and the unexpected movement cause his hand to slip sideways. His palm cupped her breast, and Georgie sucked in a shocked gasp. Their eyes met—and a jolt of pure erotic tension flashed between them. Her stomach flipped.

"Georgie—" Wylde groaned hoarsely. His fingers tightened on her breast for a split second, before he seemed to realize what he was doing, and tugged his hand away as if she burned.

Georgie almost moaned at the loss. She wanted him to keep touching her. His breathing was deeper than normal, as if he'd been running, and as he shifted again, she became aware of the rigid length of him pressing against her leg. Her eyes widened in sudden realization. He wanted her!

He dropped his head against her shoulder with an odd, muffled sound, then gave a slow despairing exhale near her ear. "That's what you do to me," he whispered. "Every minute of the day. You make me crazy with wanting."

He lifted his head and met her eyes. Only a few inches separated them. His lips were so close that their breath mingled, and Georgie quivered as longing liquefied her insides. Unable to help herself, she gave into impulse and lifted her hand to trace the outline of his lips with her fingers as if she could learn their contours by touch alone.

He stilled, then sucked in a shuddering breath and shot her a *what-do-you-think-you're-doing* look. "We can't," he whispered. He tilted his head to indicate the muffled sounds still coming from outside the hull.

But Georgie didn't care where they were, or who might hear. She slid her hand around the side of his neck, lifted her head from the wooden boards, and sought his mouth.

"Georgie—" he groaned again, almost in despair, and she waited for him to turn his head away, but instead, his lips found hers and her heart kicked against her ribs. His tongue flicked out to taste and tease, and then he was kissing her, openmouthed and full, and she nearly swooned with pleasure.

He tasted of coffee and sin. Georgie threaded her fingers through his hair and pulled him down to her, greedy, wanting more. Languor kindled into a hunger, a craving, in a heartbeat. His hand returned to the swell of her breast, deliberately this time, molding and kneading, and she arched up, inciting him, as her own hands stroked his neck, his shoulders, wherever she could touch.

She wriggled against him, and he gave an almost inaudible hiss, then caught her hand and drew it down his body, over his chest and abdomen, down to the bulge in his breeches. She almost pulled away when she realized where he was leading her, but curiosity got the better of her, and she let him mold her fingers around the rigid shape of him. *Oh, dear Lord.*

"Yes," he breathed against her mouth. "God, yes, Touch me."

Intrigued, she tightened her fingers and felt him flex against her palm. He closed his eyes in silent pleasure and lifted his hips, arching into her hand for a brief moment before he caught her wrist and lifted her hand away.

"Enough."

His nose nuzzled her jaw. He pressed kisses to the sensitive spot behind her ear, and Georgie closed her eyes against the impossible, forbidden pleasure of it. She was panting, her every nerve ending pulsing with a slow, drugging heat. Oh, this was a wicked game, but the danger of discovery only added to the thrill. She wanted his clever hands on her, that sinful mouth on hers. To hell with the noise, she wanted to go wherever he would take her.

In one swift move, he rolled up and over her, supporting himself on his forearms, settling into the groove between her legs. Georgie stilled, certain the rustle of his movement would be detected, but the noise from outside did not cease.

Their chests were barely touching, but from the belly down, they were a perfect fit. The potent weight of him pressed between her thighs, his heat burned her even through the layers of clothing that separated them.

Her pulse seemed to have relocated to between her legs, a sweet, brutal ache. Some soul-deep instinct told her that here, here was the answer to her craving. His body held the key. If only she knew what to do. She squirmed against him, unable to keep still.

He kissed her slowly, lingering and sweet. "Do you want me to show you what you've been missing?" His voice was so low, it was more vibration than sound, a deep rumble against her chest, a wicked secret in the dark.

Her pulse leapt in response, and she nodded her head emphatically. Yes! She *wanted*. She wanted with a feverish desperation. Wanted more of those kisses, those wonderful hands on her, making her burn.

For a long moment, he simply stared down at her in the shadows, and then, as if coming to a decision, he rocked his hips against her. The hard length of him nudged between her legs and a jolt of pleasure speared through her. She took a sharp, shocked intake of breath, and his lips curved into that wicked, conspiratorial smile she knew so well.

"Shhh!" he chided softly. "We don't want them to hear."

Dimly, Georgie realized that the muffled sounds of the workmen still resonated outside. She bit her lip to stifle a moan. Wylde rocked against her again, forward then back, a slow insidious rhythm that somehow managed to hit that maddening spot between her legs perfectly every time. It was exquisite torture. A sheen of sweat formed at her hairline as her body twisted and begged. Something was building inside her, and she ground against him, reaching for it, but the sensation was like an object bobbing on the water—always just out of reach.

She was so focused on where they touched that she barely registered the slam of the warehouse door, but Wylde stilled and she groaned in frustration.

"They're gone," he panted. "We should—"

"No! I don't care! *Benedict!*" She bucked again, urging him to finish what he'd started. "Show me!"

With a half laugh, half groan, he claimed her mouth and drove his tongue deep, deliciously demanding, drinking her in, and her limbs dissolved to water. And then his hand was under her skirts, over her stockings, sliding up the smooth skin of her thigh, and she parted her legs eagerly, desperate for his touch there, where it ached. His fingers found the slit in her drawers, and she groaned into his mouth as he found the center of her body and circled the little button of flesh, sending jolts of sensation spearing through her.

Good God. She'd had no idea she could feel like this.

Both of them were panting now, their breath mingling together. Georgie arched up as his finger mimicked the action of his tongue and slid *inside* her. She let out a shocked gasp, torn between amazement and bliss, even as her body clenched around him. He played, in and out, winding her tighter, higher, closer, and she began to tremble as the pressure built and built until it was almost unbearable.

He seemed to know exactly how to touch her. She threw her head back, held her breath—and everything inside her shattered. She was falling, pulsing, burning up. Her vision dimmed as pleasure washed over her in endless pounding waves.

A glorious lethargy suffused her limbs. When she could finally breathe again, she became aware of Wylde, propped up on his elbow, watching her in the darkness with a faint satisfied smile.

"Now you know," he said softly. He reached out and stroked her flushed cheek with the back of his fingers. "That really was a pleasure, Mrs. Wylde."

Chapter 28.

Benedict couldn't believe his voice came out as steadily as it did, considering that his hands were trembling and his heart was near to bursting out of his chest. That had been the most intense, most erotic encounter of his entire life—and he hadn't even climaxed himself. He was still rock-hard in his breeches, and yet he wanted to laugh in sheer primitive triumph. With joy.

He gazed down at the woman below him. Her pupils were huge in the half light, her hair delightfully mussed. He swallowed. The scent of her, of what he'd done to her, filled the small space and made the ache in his cock even worse. Desire still pounded in his blood. He wanted to be inside her, right now. No preliminaries, no more playing. Just hard and fast against the wooden boards, deep and full, until she cried out his name, and they both lost themselves in pleasure and oblivion.

He took a deep breath and strove for control, then rolled off her and tried to rearrange himself into a more comfortable position—as if that were possible. He was fiercely glad that he'd been the one to give her this first taste of passion. He wished he'd been able to see every nuance of her expression as she'd reached the peak, but even in the dim light, she'd been beautiful. So sweetly responsive. He'd loved her frown of concentration, the uninhibited trust of her climax.

He tilted his head, listening. No sound came from the warehouse beyond. He sat up awkwardly in the cramped space, taking care not to hit any of the pipes and gauges that protruded from the bulkheads, then hauled himself out of the hatch. He peered down at Georgie and offered his hand with an inner smile at his belated chivalry.

That had been no courtly wooing, no pretty poetic romance. It had been hot and sweaty and glorious. A frenzied blur of passion and limbs in the darkness. He swallowed and tried to slow his racing pulse. This was only the beginning. God, the things he had to teach her.

He wondered if she was embarrassed by what they'd just done, or merely incredulous. He was rather stunned himself.

She accepted his help back up, took a deep lungful of air, and made a big show of trying to right her rumpled clothing. "Well, that was, ah . . ." She seemed lost for words, which pleased him immensely.

"Exciting?" he provided wryly. "Amazing, Benedict? Positively the best experience I've ever had?"

"Something I'll never forget," she said finally.

He chuckled at her return to formality, even as he tried to ignore her becomingly flushed cheeks and the fact that her lips were still puffy from his kisses. "It was an honor and a privilege," he said solemnly.

"Not a duty?" She looked up at him then, and he sent her an easy smile, determined to banish any awkwardness. He wanted her to glory in what they'd done, not be ashamed.

"Never. You have wood shavings in your hair."

She put her hands up to remedy that, but he batted them away and plucked several stray curls of wood from her rumpled coiffure. He descended the ladder and then braced his arms on either side to steady it for her. When she reached the ground, he didn't step back, but instead trapped her between his body and hugged her into his chest.

"That was just the beginning, Georgie girl. Lesson one of many. I can't wait to show you the rest." He released her and forced himself to step back and return to business. "So. What do you think we should do with this?" He gestured at the submarine. "Disable it? Destroy it?"

"Not it," she muttered. "Her. All ships are feminine."

"What shall we do with *her*, then," Benedict amended dryly.

She shook her head. "Surely the Admiralty want her back? To destroy her would be a dreadful shame. She's an amazing feat of engineering." She patted the unfinished planks. "She isn't seaworthy yet—she still needs to be tarred to make her waterproof—so you have some time to set a watch and catch this Johnstone fellow in the act."

Benedict made a quick inspection of the rest of the warehouse and let out a low whistle as he pulled back an oiled sheet and found a neat stack of wooden barrels in one corner.

"What are those?"

He sniffed one to confirm his suspicions. "Gunpowder." The peppery scent was unmistakable, an old friend. He'd spent years with this smell during the war, could still recall the bitter taste on his tongue from when he'd ripped open the tiny paper twists of powder with his teeth to pour them down the muzzle of his Baker.

"It must be for the floating bombs that Fulton detailed in his plans," Georgie said.

Benedict searched around until he found a pail full of grey river water, then uncorked the bung on the top of each barrel and trickled a thin stream of liquid into them, soaking the contents. "That scuppers that plan," he said with satisfaction. "Nothing worse than wet powder." He replaced the oilskin and nodded toward the window. "Come on, I'll give you a boost."

Georgie spent the trip back to Grosvenor Square alternating between amazement, mortification, and shameless anticipation of what was still to come. What Benedict had done to her body inside that submarine had been a revelation. She'd never imagined a man's touch could affect her in such a way.

She was sensitive in places she'd never even taken note of before, and she felt strangely free and unencumbered. She glanced over at Benedict in the carriage.

He sent her one of those questioning, enigmatic looks, as if she held the answer to something he sought, some riddle he couldn't solve. Her insides tightened. He'd said there was more, but what more could there possibly be?

She'd never discussed intimate matters with her mother, but having lived in the countryside, she had a fair idea of the basic mechanics of procreation. The idea that the man's member must surely fit inside the woman, however—as a stallion fitted into a mare when he covered her—was so preposterous that she couldn't truly imagine it. Clearly, the place where Benedict had put his fingers was the same place he would fit into her body. But judging from the size of the appendage she'd felt through his breeches, such a thing was impossible. Georgie's cheeks flamed. The very thought made her hot and achy . . . and slightly apprehensive.

Did a man need to mount behind the woman, like a horse? It seemed unlikely, but she supposed she would find out this evening. Benedict had promised that she would enjoy it, and she trusted him.

When they pulled up at the Tricorn Club, he stepped down and rested his arm on the carriage door. His expression promised all manner of wickedness. He lifted her arm to his lips and kissed the inside of her wrist. "Until later, Mrs. Wylde."

Chapter 29.

Georgie attended the Evans' rout that evening with the sole aim of taking her leave as quickly as possible. She'd already mentioned to her mother that she thought she had a headache coming on. And then she caught sight of Benedict, heart stoppingly handsome in dark evening clothes, conversing with his friends on the opposite side of the room. Heat raced over her skin. What was he doing here?

He glanced up as her name was announced and caught her eye. His too-innocent smile made her stomach flutter. What game was he playing now?

She pretended to ignore him and seethed impatiently for a full twenty minutes before he made his leisurely way across the room and bowed low before her mother. His eyes crinkled at the corners. "Mrs. Caversteed."

Her mother smiled warmly. "Good evening, Mr. Wylde. How good to see you. I'm afraid Juliet is dancing with Lord Birkenhead at present, but—"

"I was hoping the elder Miss Caversteed might honor me with a dance."

Mother sent Georgie a look that was part congratulatory, part surprise. "Oh, of course. I'm sure she'd be delighted. Off you go, dear."

Wylde chuckled as he steered her toward the dance floor.

"What are you doing here?" Georgie whispered. "I wasn't expecting to see you until later."

"I'm upholding my side of our bargain. You're paying me to court you publicly. So here we are. Courting. In public." He sent her an admiring look that nobody watching could fail to interpret, and Georgie cursed the day she'd ever suggested the foolish idea. Yes, they needed to prepare the *ton* for an announcement, but she hadn't envisaged how difficult it would be to pretend to be strangers under society's ever-watchful gaze.

After this afternoon, they most certainly weren't strangers. They weren't precisely friends either, but she wasn't quite sure how to define their odd relationship. Coconspirators maybe?

Benedict took her hand, and she tried not to think of what those strong, elegant fingers had been doing to her only hours before.

The movement of the dance made conversation difficult, but as they dipped and swirled, Georgie came to the startling realization that her seduction had already begun. Every one of his slight, casual touches seemed choreographed to increase her state of tension. The innocuous graze of his fingers at her waist, the subtle brush of his thigh against hers—all achieved despite maintaining a perfectly decorous distance. The man was a menace.

"Lovely dress," he murmured politely.

"Thank you."

"I can't wait to take it off you."

She stumbled, but he caught her effortlessly and righted their steps.

The beast. He loved discomposing her. His piercing gaze seemed to assess her from the inside out, as if he saw into every secret corner of her soul, every womanly, shameful, hot, desirous dream she'd had of him. Georgie wished she'd brought a fan. A dizzying anticipation simmered in her blood. How could anyone miss the heat between them? She felt as if she were glowing with desire, obvious to all, like a beacon, a lighthouse.

As the dance brought them together again, he murmured, "I'll send a carriage for you at midnight." She could only nod, tongue-tied by embarrassment and desire.

When the dance ended, he returned her to her mother, bowed quite properly, and took his leave with the parting shot, "Thank you, Miss Caversteed. Until we dance again."

Mother watched him leave with pursed lips. "Mr. Wylde seems to be showing you marked attention, my love." She took a sip of ratafia. "There's no denying he's a handsome devil, but according to Caroline Cowper, the family's practically destitute. His father left a passel full of debt. He's a fortune hunter, you mark my words. Just like all the rest of them. Still, you're in no danger from him now, are you?" Her silent *because of your impetuous marriage* was left unsaid.

Georgie stifled a snort. If only she knew. Benedict Wylde was the most dangerous man she'd ever met. He was like a force of nature, a hurricane, a typhoon.

Mother looked at her oddly. "Are you quite well, Georgiana?"

She seized her chance. "Actually, no. I've an awful headache. Would you mind if I asked Pieter to drive me home? I'd like to go to bed."

Mother sent her a sympathetic look and patted her hand. "You poor lamb. I know just what it is to be the victim of a megrim. Go on, dear. After all, it's Juliet who needs to be seen, not you."

Georgie sighed at her mother's unintentional slight. "I'll send the carriage back for you."

"Thank you. Oh good! Juliet's dancing with Ponsonby. He's third in line to inherit from the Duke of Milford Haven, you know."

Georgie left her to it. When Pieter delivered her home, she went straight up to her room and paced nervously, pressing her hands over the fluttering in her belly. She caught sight of herself in the mirror and grimaced; she looked wild, her cheeks a hectic red, her eyes bright and glistening.

What was she doing? Sleeping with Wylde would undoubtedly change everything between them. It would certainly complicate matters. The thought of making love to him, of giving herself to him fully, was something she both anticipated and dreaded. His very presence made her breathless; he produced a sensation in the region of her stomach that felt like she was taking part in some precarious high-wire balancing act, like that of Madame Saqui at Vauxhall. Like terror, like exhilaration.

Georgie frowned. Affairs of the heart were far more complex than business deals. Would he lose interest in her once he'd had her? She'd heard that was true with many men. But all adventures involved an element of risk, did they not? What would have happened if Columbus had stayed in Spain, or Marco Polo had never ventured from Italy, too afraid of the unknown to risk setting sail? She was no coward. She wouldn't back out now. This would be an adventure she chose for herself.

Mother and Juliet returned just after eleven, but neither came in to check on her, and by the time she slipped down to the kitchen and out the back door, the house was quiet and still. She nearly jumped out of her skin when Pieter's large frame loomed out of the stables.

"And where do you think you're off to, missy?"

Georgie clapped her hand over her heart. "Pieter! You scared me half to death!"

"Thought you were feeling under the weather?"

Her cheeks heated as she realized there was no explanation she could give except the shameful truth. She set her chin. "If you must know, I'm going to meet Benedict Wylde."

She could see Pieter's scowl, even in the dim light.

"Well, I know you ain't eloping," he said sarcastically. "Because you've already married the cove. So what's to do?"

Georgie squirmed. Really, this was too humiliating. Pieter was like a father to her. In his eyes, she was still an innocent, headstrong little girl. To confess, quite baldly, *why* she was going to meet Benedict made her cringe. She squared her shoulders. "The man is my husband. And I have decided to visit him."

"At midnight," Pieter supplied. He suddenly dropped his head and rubbed the back of his neck, as if embarrassed himself. "Ah, Georgie. You're a grown woman now. I know it. And God knows I've never been able to talk you out of anything once you've set your mind to it. Yer just like yer father in that respect. I just hope you know what you're doing with him, that's all."

So do I.

He stepped aside, and she let out a relieved breath. "His carriage should be at the corner," she said quietly.

Pieter nodded. "Just make sure you're back before the household rises."

Georgie gave him an impetuous hug, and he pressed a quick kiss to her forehead.

"I hope that bastard realizes what he's got," he grumbled.

Mickey's huge bulk was instantly recognizable atop the plain black carriage that was waiting at the corner. Georgie climbed in, and in her agitated state, the ride to St. James's seemed to take only moments. She felt daring and adventurous. Glad to be alive. The carriage slowed to make the turn into the stable yard at the rear, but as it drew level with the front of the club, the door opened and a bouncer appeared with a struggling figure caught roughly by his collar. Amid furious shouts and obscenities, the man was forcibly ejected.

"And stay out," the manservant called out after him. "The Tricorn don't welcome those who can't pay their debts, *sir.*" The last word was issued with a curl of the lip and a dismissive sneer that made the title an insult.

The man stumbled down the front steps, reeling drunkenly, and to Georgie's dismay he staggered heavily against the side of the stationary carriage. She let out a little shriek of alarm as his body hit the side panel with a thud. The man wheeled around, using the carriage door as support, and Georgie gasped as she caught sight of his face.

Josiah's cheeks were mottled a furious red, his eyes bleary and unfocused. For one awful moment, he squinted into the carriage and she shrank back against the seat, terrified he'd recognize her. He issued a stream of invectives that shocked even Georgie, then slammed his palm against the wooden side and wheeled away into the night.

She released a shaky breath. Good God, Josiah had looked awful. Almost demonic. She'd had no idea he frequented the Tricorn Club. And what on earth had he done to get himself expelled so disgracefully? The doorman had said something about not paying his debts. A wave of fury assailed her. She'd just given him five hundred pounds! Had he squandered it all already?

The carriage entered the stable yard, and Wylde was there, opening the carriage door. Georgie practically fell into his arms. "I just saw my cousin! Your doorman threw him out."

Benedict frowned. "Seb must have reached the end of his patience. He didn't see you, did he?"

"No. I don't think so."

He took her hand and drew her inside. "Then stop worrying about it. Your unpleasant cousin is the very last person I want you to be thinking of tonight." His smile made her anxiety ebb and her blood heat. "The only person you need to be concentrating on is me."

He led her up the stairs and into his apartment; the key turned in the lock with a decisive click. Georgie glanced round, nervous again. This was it. The stage for her willing seduction. Only she had no idea how to begin.

"Why don't you take off your cloak?" Benedict suggested. She did so, draping the heavy fabric over the chair and adding her reticule. He was only wearing a shirt and breeches; he looked comfortable and relaxed. He crossed to a sideboard and picked up a cut glass decanter. "Brandy?"

She nodded. A fortifying shot of liquor sounded just the thing to bolster her confidence. His fingers touched hers as he handed her the tumbler, and she took a tentative sip to quell the quivering that had started in her belly. If they did this, she would be his wife in truth. Their marriage would be consummated. Legal. Binding.

She jerked when he reached up and stroked her cheek. Brandy sloshed onto her wrist.

His mouth curved in an endearingly crooked smile. "Stop thinking, Georgie girl." He raised her hand and licked the brandy from her skin, leaving a trail of heat in his wake. She shivered in anticipation, but to her surprise, he stepped away and slid open a drawer in his desk.

"First things first." He withdrew a sheaf of banknotes and counted out fifty pounds onto the leather. "Here. Take it. I'll pay back everything, including the five hundred from Newgate, as soon as I can. I won't sleep with you if I'm taking your money."

Georgie's spirits plummeted. "What? No! You need that money. I know you do."

He shook his head. There was a determined glint in his eye that said he wouldn't take no for an answer. He left the cash on the desk and stepped back to her. "Let's make one thing perfectly clear." His gaze held hers, and her knees went weak at the intensity that burned in his eyes. "I am going to sleep with you for no other reason than because I am *dying* to do so."

Georgie bit back a moan. An element of doubt had still persisted at the back of her mind, an ingrained mistrust of his motives that said this was all too good to be true. A man like him couldn't possibly desire a woman like her. And yet the hoarse yearning in his voice was unmistakable.

She felt like an ancient explorer, Marco Polo or Vasco da Gama, about to set sail. Unsure of the mysteries and dangers that lay ahead, but certain they were out there, just over the horizon. Tonight, Benedict was her uncharted territory. And she couldn't wait to uncover his secrets.

She put down her glass. "All right then, Mr. Wylde. Show me what I've been missing."

Chapter 30.

Georgie sucked in a breath as he advanced until only a few inches separated them.

"To start with, I should remind you that I am not like other men in the *ton*," he said.

She raised her eyebrows at that understatement. He was like no man she'd ever met.

He reached up to her hair, found one of the pins that was keeping it coiled up on top of her head, and tugged it out. "What happened this afternoon was ample demonstration. I'm not one of your courtly lovers, all talk and no action."

He tugged another pin, and the weight of her hair uncoiled lopsidedly then fell down her neck. He was so close, she could feel the heat rising from his body, smell the addictive scent of his skin. Two more pins, and the whole lot untwisted. He drew the shining mass over her shoulder, and she shivered as his fingers smoothed its length, tracing to the very end where it finished just above the peak of her breast.

"Allow me to demonstrate the difference between courtly love and real life."

"There's no need," she croaked.

"Oh, I insist." He ran his fingers down her arm, caught her hand, and raised it to his lips. "A courtly lover might kiss your hand, for example. Like this. Suitably reverent and correct." He trailed one finger over her collarbone and down the center of her chest. Her ribcage expanded as she took a deep breath, and he paused teasingly at the edge of her bodice, just above the shadowed valley of her breasts. "A courtly lover would say your skin is like petals, or silk, or cream."

He traced a maddening pattern back and forth, light as a feather. "A true and proper knight would probably faint if he imagined doing this." His finger dipped beneath the lace edge of her dress. "He'd liken your nipples to berries, or cherries, or some other such nonsense."

Her breasts felt full, aching for his touch. "You wouldn't say that?" she croaked.

"No." He withdrew his finger and stroked his hand down the side of her breast, over her ribs and back up. She gasped as he cupped her in one large, capable hand. The warmth of him spread through her dress and saturated her skin. Her nipple hardened under his palm. His eyes bored into hers.

"I'd just say that you have skin I want to lick. To bite. I'd just admit that I'm hungry for you. I want to eat you up."

Georgie could barely draw a breath. "You do?"

"Oh yes." He dropped his hand, and she let out a long exhale and tried to find her equilibrium. Every one of her senses was afire, anticipating his next touch.

"A courtly lover would offer a chaste peck on the cheek." He leaned forward and matched action to words. "But that's rather insipid, don't you think? Rather uninspiring." He took her face between his hands, and his thumbs stroked her chin. "I'd rather kiss you here." The pad of his thumb dragged over her lips. "I dream about your mouth," he whispered. "It's perfect."

He exerted the slightest pressure to tug her forward, and when his lips met hers, she couldn't prevent the little moan that escaped her. So sweet. So lush. So *right*. He angled his mouth and pushed deep, his tongue stroking hers, and she closed her eyes and let herself dissolve. Heat rose, and urgency, and she wrapped her arms around his broad shoulders, anchoring herself to him, a port in a storm.

She was hungry for him too. For taste, for sensation.

He caught her lower lip in his teeth—an erotic tug that sent a corresponding tug straight to her belly—then released it and kissed her again, full and commanding.

When he pulled back, his eyes were glittering, and Georgie sucked in a breath.

"Do you want a courtly lover, Mrs. Wylde? Or do you want me?"

"You," she gasped. "I want you."

"Turn around."

She did as he ordered, and he made quick work of the row of tiny buttons down her back. Her dress pooled at her feet, and he caught her shoulders and turned her back around. Georgie watched, mesmerized, as he untied the front lacing of her short stays and drew them off her. She was left in her stockings, shoes, and shift.

He took her hand and led her through into his bedroom, but she barely had time to register a huge fourposter bed and tones of deep burgundy before he took her mouth again. Her head spun, her blood pounded in her ears, and the next thing she knew, the back of her knees hit the edge of the bed and she was falling backward onto the mattress. Wylde followed her down. She gave a little squeak of surprise, and he pulled away, supporting himself on his hands, his hair tousled and his lips glistening.

The lower half of her legs were still off the bed. He pushed himself upright and stood looking down at her with a hungry expression.

"I want to see all of you, Georgie. Take off your shift."

Shaking with anticipation, Georgie gathered her courage and caught the hem in her hands. She lifted it, shifting her hips, and felt a cool rush of air as she exposed her stomach and breasts to the night air. He sucked in a breath as she tugged the cotton garment over her head. The movement snagged the chain around her neck, and with a sinking feeling, she remembered her wedding band. The metal dropped back against her chest as she tossed the chemise aside and faced him in just her shoes, stockings, and garters. A hint of uncertainty plagued her. Benedict had had numerous lovers, women far more beautiful than herself. Would he find her lacking? Would he be disappointed?

"Georgie," he breathed softly, and the reverence in his voice, the look of sheer yearning on his face, put paid to her fears.

He reached out and snagged the wedding band and raised his brows. "Nice to see you wearing this." He smiled. "Couldn't bear to take it off?"

She squirmed a little at how tellingly close to the truth that was. He lifted the chain over her head, careful not to let it tangle in her hair. She thought he'd put it aside, but instead, he rolled the ring between thumb and forefinger, then trailed the warm metal down the slope of her breast. She sucked in a gasp as he placed it over her nipple, encircling the tight peak within the golden hoop.

His lips quirked in amusement. "A courtly lover would *never* do *this*." He bent and placed his lips over the ring; cool metal, hot mouth, and her body went up in flames. His tongue pushed through the central hole, and desire speared through her like a scalding tide.

"Benedict!"

Her skin flashed hot, then cold. She threaded her fingers through his thick hair, pulling him closer as he let the band drop away and took even more of her into his mouth. He licked and sucked and bit. Her eyes widened. Oh, God.

"You taste so good."

The vibration of his low groan rippled through her body. She closed her eyes, drowning in sensation. He shifted, pressing his nose and forehead to the soft skin of her stomach, breathing her in, and she fell back against the covers. She twisted, trying to urge him lower, to put his hands between her legs where he'd been before. Now that she knew what he could give her, she wanted it with a shocking, blinding intensity. She wanted that glittering peak again.

But Benedict seemed in no hurry to oblige. In fact, he drew back again, and she bit back a moan of frustration. He lifted first one foot, then the other, and rid her of her shoes; they hit the rug in a succession of quiet thuds. Then he slid his hand up her shin until he reached the ribbon tie of her garter. With the slightest pressure, he urged her to bend her knee and open her body to him.

Georgie shivered, even as her skin flushed with embarrassment. A small lamp had been left burning in the room, and when she complied, she knew she was completely open to his gaze. He hadn't been able to see her in the submarine; she'd been shielded by her skirts and the darkness. Now, he could see everything, demand everything. No modesty. Complete surrender.

He was still completely clothed. Suddenly shy, she slid her hand down and tried to cover herself, but he kissed the sensitive skin on the inside of her knee.

"Don't hide from me, Georgie. Let me see you."

He slid his hands higher, up to her thighs, and pressed a kiss there too. Her stomach tensed in anticipation, but he simply looked at her, and the heat in his gaze somehow transferred itself to her skin. She burned. He licked his lips, his gaze between her legs. "Now this? This is worthy of a stanza or two." His fingers crept higher, and she fought the urge to beg. "I can see how a man might be inspired to write a sonnet about this." His expression turned wicked. "Of course, anticipation is sometimes the best part. Will you be hot? Wet?"

His fingers found her, a slow caress that circled with agonizing leisure.

Oh, yes.

"What will you taste like, I wonder?" he murmured dreamily, and she frowned as her slow brain struggled to made sense of the words. *Taste?*

His breath warmed her skin a moment before his mouth joined his fingers.

Oh, God.

Pleasure hit her like a lightning strike, and she almost bowed off the bed. It was agony. It was sublime. He licked her deeply, penetrating her, drinking her in. Georgie writhed and bucked, but he steadied her with a hand on her hip, urging her to accept his glorious ministrations. He lifted his head, and his cheeks were flushed. "Sugar and spice and all things nice," he murmured. "That's what Mrs. Wylde tastes of."

He bent again, and she tightened her knees around his shoulders as he used his tongue in a wicked counterpoint to his nimble fingers. Heat built, and tension, and she clutched his hair, trying to hold him closer.

Yes. So close. More.

Just when she thought she could take no more, a rush of cool air hit her. She almost screamed in protest. Benedict knelt between her legs, his chest heaving, his jaw taut with strain. "Not without me," he panted, stripping off his shirt in a blur of frantic movement. "Not this time."

He kicked off his breeches, and she had the briefest glimpse of his body, a vast expanse of smooth, muscled skin, and then he was over her, full length, and all she could feel was heat, the incredible sensation of skin on skin.

"I need to be inside you."

His chest pressed against her, abrading the points of her nipples. His thighs bracketed hers, all solid muscle and tickly hair. The hard length of him nudged her slick folds, and she bucked against him, desperate for the *more* he'd promised.

More and more and more.

"Show me," she panted, curling up for a kiss. She tasted herself on his tongue, a musky, earthy scent that enflamed her further, and he dropped to his forearms, bracketed her face with his hands, and kissed her as if it was the last time he'd ever have the chance. As if his whole soul belonged to her.

She writhed against him in unbearable anticipation. He rocked his hips and entered her just a fraction, a burning, stretching ache that made her tense at the un- familiar intrusion. He was larger than his fingers. He pressed again, inching deeper, and Georgie tilted her hips to ease the ache. He stilled, his chest heaving, and rested his forehead against hers. "Slow," he panted rag- gedly. "Don't want to hurt you. God."

Georgie caught his face and kissed his jaw, her heart swelling with the care he was taking with her. "It's all right," she whispered. "Do it."

He gave a deep groan and pushed his full length into her, one deep thrust, and Georgie cried out. The momentary discomfort quickly gave way to an astonishing feeling of fullness, of completion. With a harsh breath, he withdrew almost completely and seated himself again, and this time the slipperiness of her body eased the way, and he slid in with a delicious friction that made her entire body jerk in response. Her vision blurred.

"Touch me," he rasped, and she realized her arms had fallen to the bedcovers. Suddenly greedy, she ran her fingers over his shoulders, glorying in the muscles in his arms, the smooth contours of his back. He was tall and elegantly formed, all long, fluid lines, and she could feel the tremors in him, the taut control as he struggled to restrain himself.

She didn't want restraint. She wanted abandon. She arched her back, urging him on, and he groaned deep in his throat, an animal sound of pure pleasure. And then he began to move within her. He slid his hand under her bottom and lifted her hips, and the change of angle sparked a familiar curl of pleasure. She dug her heels into the mattress and reached for it, jerking in awkward counterpoint to his thrusts until she found the rhythm, and suddenly they were moving together in perfect synchronicity. He caught her thigh and urged her leg around his hip, and she was climbing higher, higher toward that glorious point of light.

"Come for me, Georgie," he breathed in her ear, and her body convulsed, fracturing in endless joyous beats. Flashes of light exploded behind her eyelids as she dissolved in mindless bliss.

He cursed as her body clenched around him. He gave one last thrust, withdrew from her body, and pressed himself hard against her stomach, holding her tightly in his arms with an incoherent groan. Jets of warm wetness coated her skin as every muscle in his body went rigid. He collapsed in shuddering exhaustion, his body heavy on hers, and Georgie closed her eyes as a wonderful, drugging lethargy claimed her limbs.

So *that* was the "more."

She smiled sleepily. It was certainly worth the wait.

Chapter 31.

Benedict returned to earth with his heart hammering against his ribs as if he'd faced a squadron of French dragoons. His entire being was suffused with an overwhelming feeling of contentment.

When awareness returned more fully, he realized he was squashing Georgie beneath him. With a murmured apology, he rolled to one side, relieving her of his weight but keeping one arm slung over her body, reluctant to sever contact with her entirely. The scents of their lovemaking filled his nose, and he experienced a surge of primitive triumph.

He let out a rueful laugh. "I meant to go slower than that, you know. In respect for your first time. But things got a little . . . out of control."

He'd meant to be gentler, to rein himself in. He hadn't wanted to frighten her with the full depths of his desire. But her untutored caresses had inflamed him so much that he'd forgotten every intention for a leisurely seduction. He'd been lost in mindless instinct. Lost in the wonder of her.

She gave a sated sigh. "Well, I thought it was perfect."

He almost purred with satisfaction but couldn't resist teasing her. "What do *you* know? That was your one and only experience. You don't qualify for an opinion until you've tried it at least ten times. It's like eating a strawberry bonbon and then declaring it's positively the best flavor in the world, when you haven't ever tried lemon or sherbet or cherry."

"I see your point," she murmured sleepily. "I wouldn't want to make any rash decisions. Not about something so momentous."

"Good. Because there's still a lot to discover. That was only lesson two."

He would teach her everything he knew, he thought dreamily. Show her the heights to which she could climb. God, it would be an honor. A delight.

His forearm was still draped over her ribs. She stroked it idly with her fingertips, and the contact sent a soundless shudder of pleasure through his body. After a few moments, he propped himself up on his elbow and used his discarded shirt to clean her belly. She tensed at his ministrations, and a charming blush spread down her throat and across her chest. He chuckled. "Don't tell me you're embarrassed *now*, Mrs. Wylde?"

He glanced at her face and saw her brow wrinkle. She gestured at her stomach. "Why did you . . . ?"

"Pull out?" he finished, shaking his head at her charming naivety. "Because we don't want any little Wyldes making an appearance in nine months' time, do we? And that's one of the best ways to ensure it doesn't happen." He studied her expression, searching for any hint of what she thought, but apart from a little frown, her face was inscrutable. He wasn't sure whether she was relieved or disappointed that he'd retained enough working brain cells to finish outside of her body.

Oddly enough, the idea of her round with his child didn't fill him with horror. On the contrary, it made his chest ache with a strange combination of wistfulness and yearning. She would make an excellent mother, fair and loving. The precise opposite of his own mother.

He shook his head, dismissing the ridiculous notion. The amazing coitus they'd just had must have disordered his mind. There was no future for them, not one that included children. They were simply going to enjoy themselves until the season ended and then part ways as friends.

He pulled the bedclothes over them both and rolled her so she was facing away from him then tugged her close, his body curving around hers so she was cocooned in his arms. She gave a soft sigh and wriggled her bottom against him. To his weary astonishment, he felt himself grow hard again. She had the most amazing effect on him.

Her uninhibited ardor had been immensely gratifying. She'd trusted him to guide her in her first foray into lovemaking and he was fiercely glad he hadn't betrayed that trust by hurting her or by being selfish.

She gave a sleepy yawn. "I can't stay much longer. I have to be back before the servants get up."

Benedict glanced at the clock on the mantel. There were still a few hours until dawn, and God knew, he would gladly spend the rest of them making love to her, but she was right. There was no sense in risking a scandal. Everything she'd done up to this point had been to avoid such a thing. Her coming here had been risky, but he wouldn't have changed it for the world.

With the greatest reluctance, he drew away from her and left the bed. He slipped on his breeches to spare her maidenly blushes, then scooped up her simple cotton shift. "Come on, sleepyhead," he said, tugging on her arm until she sat up, grumbling. "Let's get you dressed." He threw the garment over her head, then went out into the sitting room to retrieve her dress and give her some privacy.

It struck him that Georgie was the first woman he'd ever brought here, to his rooms. Despite the rumors about his profligacy, he'd only had two lovers since he'd returned from France, both discreet widows, and each affair had lasted only a few weeks. He'd visited both ladies at their own residences and had always left to spend the night in his own bed. He'd had no desire to linger.

He wished Georgie could stay. He wanted to drift off to sleep with her in his arms, to wake her slowly with a kiss and make love to her again, lazily, as dawn broke over the rooftops.

Impossible.

She was sitting cross-legged on the bed when he returned, a rumpled goddess amidst the messy sheets. His heart thudded to a stop. She looked so damned tempting there in his bed that he clenched his fists in her dress to stop himself pushing her back and kissing her breathless all over again. His cock throbbed in silent encouragement.

She was like one of those sirens that lured sailors to their doom with just a smile. He felt a sudden kinship with poor, mythical Odysseus, tied to the mast of his ship, valiantly trying to resist the promise in a glance, the temptation of a song. Her skin was flushed, her lips delightfully puffy, and he experienced a surge of deep satisfaction that *he'd* been the one to put the pink in her cheeks, that twinkle in her eye.

Georgie sucked in an admiring breath as Benedict reappeared shirtless in the doorway. The man was impossibly handsome. His skin glowed with health, and his breeches rested low on his narrow hips.

She'd barely seen him during the frenzied blur of their earlier lovemaking, but now she looked her fill. The soft glow of the oil lamp on the nightstand caressed his body in the same way her fingers itched to do, and her pulse galloped as she studied the intriguing ridges of his sculpted stomach and chest.

He was hard and lean, muscled but not bulky, as if every part of him had been honed to perfection by grueling necessity. His skin was tawny, darkened by the sun like a sailor's, not pale and paunchy like most gentlemen's of the *ton*.

Her heart squeezed at the sight of him. His dark hair was tousled in glorious disarray, and she felt a kind of wonder. He'd done things to her that were as astonishing as they had been pleasurable. It was like discovering a whole new continent where the map had shown nothing but empty sea. An entirely different landscape of sensation she'd never known existed.

She'd never imagined the all-consuming pleasure of making love with a man. She'd thought it would be pleasant in the same way it was nice to have Tilly rub her shoulders, or the way a bonbon dissolved on her tongue. Not so. It was pleasant in the way of the most fearsome of storms—exhilarating and overwhelming, terrifying in its power. But now she'd weathered it and come out safe the other side, she felt elated and reborn. Glad to be alive.

She sent him a tremulous smile, determined to be as cool and sophisticated as his other lovers. "So, will I see you tomorrow at the Cavendish garden fête? I'm fairly sure that after your performance at the Evans' this evening, the book at White's will be filling up with bets about us announcing our engagement."

He chuckled. "The last time I checked, it was fifty to

one against your acceptance. Your reputation proceeds you, my lady. You're a hard nut to crack."

"Well, I'm sure the odds will have shortened now," she said wryly. A sudden thought struck her. "You know, you could make yourself a whole stack of money if you just bet that I'll marry you."

He shot her a mock-wounded look. "Whatever you think of me, Mrs. Wylde, I do have *some* scruples. Entering into a bet with inside knowledge and a certainty of winning would be extremely ungentlemanly. I won't do it."

She nodded, perversely glad that he'd withstood the temptation to solve his financial woes by resorting to such underhand tactics. He had both integrity and personal honor. He was, in fact, the polar opposite of Josiah, who pretended to have impeccable morals, but bent the rules when he thought no one was looking.

Father would have approved of Benedict Wylde. He was exactly the type of man he'd always urged her to find, someone strong and constant, with a good heart. He wasn't always truthful, of course, and he could be annoyingly high-handed at times, but he was utterly loyal to those lucky few he chose to be his friends.

Georgie shook her head at her own foolishness. If she wasn't careful, she'd find herself besotted with her own husband. Or worse. "So, will I see you tomorrow?"

"I'll try to come. It depends on what happens with Johnstone."

She took her dress from his outstretched hand and put it on, not bothering with her stays. "You mean you'll be going after him?"

"Yes. Alex, Seb, and I will wait in the tavern we visited today. As soon as he enters the building, we'll pounce."

Georgie sighed. "I wish I could be there."

"You've done enough." He smiled to soften the sting of rejection, drawing her in for a kiss.

Georgie melted against him as her limbs went weak.

It was he who pulled away. He turned her and silently buttoned up her dress, as efficient as any lady's maid, and she shivered as he pressed a kiss to her exposed neck. "I'll ask Mickey to take you home," he murmured softly.

Pieter had left the back door unlocked, and Georgie sneaked into the house without incident. She entered her room and fell onto the bed in a state of exhausted bliss. Did she feel different now she was no longer a virgin? She made a quick mental catalogue of her body. She felt wonderful. A little sore and achy, slightly more sensitive to the touch of her clothing, but definitely *good*.

Her long-held goal of taking a lover had been achieved, and she already wanted to do it again. And again.

She remembered the incredible sense of peace and warmth she'd felt when they'd been lying together. Tucked against his body, enfolded in his arms, she'd felt cherished and protected and . . . loved. She pulled herself up short. He probably made every woman feel like that, as if she were the center of his universe.

Part of her hoped her obsession with him would burn itself up quickly. It would hurt when they inevitably parted ways. He would become bored by her lack of experience. She'd have to watch him transfer that blinding heat and teasing laughter to some other lucky recipient and pretend she didn't care.

She shoved that depressing thought away. She would take Benedict's advice and seize the moment, enjoy their time together, no matter how brief.

But first, she needed sleep.

Chapter 32.

Georgie woke to a scratching at her door and sat up as Juliet slipped into the room and bounded up onto the bed like an overeager puppy. She studied Georgie's face with a close, laughing scrutiny. "What were *you* up to last night, you naughty girl?"

Georgie frowned as a guilty flush warmed her cheeks. She pushed her hair out of her eyes. "What do you mean?"

"I mean, you weren't in bed when I came in to talk to you," Juliet accused. "I wanted to tell you about Simeon kissing me in the Evans' hothouse, but you weren't here."

Georgie stifled a groan.

"So where were you? And with *whom*?"

Juliet waggled her eyebrows, and Georgie couldn't prevent a smile at her gleeful prodding. There was nothing her sister liked better than an intrigue. And really, if Georgie hadn't been so fixated with Benedict, she would have remembered not to underestimate her sibling's ability to sniff out a scandal. Juliet was like a bloodhound, able to scent the merest whiff of impropriety at fifty paces. Most of the time it was all in her fertile imagination, of course, but this time she'd hit upon the truth.

"All right. I have a confession to make. I'm not actually married to a sailor, as I told you and Mother. I'm married to Benedict Wylde."

Juliet's eyes grew as round as saucers. She clapped her hand over her mouth and gave a little squeal of delight. "Ha! I knew there was something going on the moment I saw the two of you together! Those looks he sent you!" she crowed. "Tell me everything, Georgie, quick!"

Georgie did so, starting with her visit to Newgate but omitting any mention of Bow Street, Johnstone, or the submarine. She glossed over the events at the Tricorn Club, and settled for the rather inadequate phrase, "—and so we decided to, ah, consummate the marriage, and it was . . . very enjoyable."

Juliet clapped her hands in delight. "Oh, this is a famous! Worthy of one of Mrs. Radcliffe's novels. You're supposed to be the sensible one, you know!"

Georgie sighed. "I don't know what came over me. I only wanted to keep Josiah at a distance and gain some independence for myself. This whole situation has become far more involved than I ever intended."

Juliet sobered. "Do you care for him, Georgie?"

"Who, Josiah? Absolutely not."

"No, you goose! Wylde."

"I don't know. I mean, yes, of course, I like him, but—"

"Do you love him?"

Georgie stilled, reluctant to face that loaded question. She certainly loved what he did to her body. But physical attraction faded. Love, a marriage, needed more to survive. It needed shared interests. Compatibility. Respect. Trust.

"I think I *could* love him, if I allowed myself to," she

finally admitted. "But that would be a very foolish thing to do. We have an agreement. Once we're wed in the eyes of the *ton*, we're going to go our separate ways. He has no intention of making it a long-term arrangement."

Juliet looked crestfallen. This, apparently, was not how fairy tales were supposed to go. "What if he changes his mind?" she urged. "What if he realizes he doesn't want to let you go? Simeon would never—"

Georgie pleated the bedcovers. "That isn't going to happen, Jules. Benedict is nothing like Simeon. Simeon worships the ground you walk on. He loves you with his whole heart." She sighed again, more heavily. "It's not like that between Benedict and me. Men like him don't settle down with just one woman."

They were silent for a moment, then Georgie brightened. "So, what happened at the Evans'? You said Simeon kissed you."

Juliet closed her eyes in remembered rapture. "Oh, yes, he did, and it was wonderful! Just as I knew it would be. And guess what else? He *proposed*! He wants me to become Mrs. Simeon Pettigrew."

Her tone made it sound like that was a title equivalent to "Empress of India and Queen of the Known Universe." Georgie stifled a groan. "You know Mother still has her doubts about Simeon, Jules. She thinks you could do so much better than a penniless poet."

Her sister's lips formed a perfect pout. "I don't want a man with a title. None of them love me as Simeon does. He doesn't care a fig for how much I'm worth." She stood and straightened the bedcovers with a thoughtful expression. "Maybe I should take a leaf out of your book and present Mother with a *fait accompli*."

"Don't do anything rash," Georgie warned quickly. "She'll come around. She only wants the best for you, after all. Just give it some time."

"I know. I just hate pretending I'm considering other people when Simeon's the only one I will ever want." Juliet bent and gave Georgie an impulsive hug. "I know I don't always show it, Georgie, but I'm so glad you're my sister. I'm heading to Hatchard's this morning with Mother. Is there anything you'd like?"

Georgie shook her head at her sibling's mercurial changes of mood. "No, thank you, Ju. I'll see you at lunch."

It was only after Georgie dressed that she realized she was missing her wedding band and chain. She flushed; she must have left it in Benedict's bedroom. She felt oddly naked without it, as if it were some lucky talisman, her private link to him. Even more irritating, she discovered that Benedict had put the fifty pounds she'd refused in her reticule. Stubborn man. She would have to find a way to slip it into his pocket when he wasn't looking.

Juliet and Mother left for the shops in a flurry of skirts and perfume. Georgie had just entered the drawing room in search of breakfast when Tilly came in, holding a folded note.

"Letter for you, miss."

Her heart leapt as she took it. "Thank you, Tilly."

She glanced at the clock. Perhaps Benedict had changed his mind about letting her take part in Johnstone's capture? She unfolded the missive with shaking hands and squinted at the scrawled, almost illegible writing. It took her a moment to decipher it. *Meet me in the park. Copse near Tyburn tree. B.*

Georgie frowned. She'd never actually seen Benedict's handwriting, except for his signature on their marriage documents, but she'd have thought it was neater than this. He must have written it in haste.

She donned her pelisse, cloak, and bonnet and accepted Charlotte's offer to accompany her "for a breath of fresh air." As soon as they entered the park, however, she told the elderly maidservant to rest on one of the benches overlooking the ornamental lake and headed north, toward the strand of trees as she'd been instructed. She let out an amused huff as she searched the vista for Benedict. Mysterious assignations in parks were more Juliet's style.

There were very few people around at this unfashionably early hour. The *ton* wouldn't make an appearance until around four o'clock this afternoon when they would stroll down the walks and parade along Rotten Row in their curricles as slowly as possible in order to show off their latest fashionable acquisitions.

A cloaked figure loitered amongst the trees, and Georgie left the gravel path and headed that way. He disappeared behind a trunk, and she hastened forward, soaking her leather boots in the dew-damp grass. She entered the copse, peering around, and gasped when a hand shot out from behind a tree and captured her wrist.

"What's—?" She recoiled in horror. "Josiah! What are you doing here?"

Her cousin's smile turned her stomach. She'd been hoodwinked. Benedict hadn't written that note at all.

"Well met, Cousin. You look a little peaked. Did you have a late night?"

She tugged on her wrist. "I did, not that it's any of your business."

His lip curled. "Oh, that's where you're wrong. It is very much my business."

At this close distance, she could smell stale alcohol fumes on his breath and clothes.

His fingers tightened cruelly. "I saw you. At the Tricorn. I may have been drunk, but even four sheets to the wind I can still recognize my own cousin." His eyes glittered. "You little tart! You were going to Wylde, weren't you?"

She pressed her lips together.

Josiah shook his head. "At first I thought you'd taken a fancy to him after he defended you at Vauxhall. That you'd fallen into his arms out of gratitude," he sneered. "But there's more to it than that, isn't there?"

Her heart hammered against her ribs, and she tried again to free her wrist, but his hold was inescapable. "I don't know what you mean."

"Oh, I think you do, love. This morning I had a rather unexpected visitor. Tell me, does the name Knollys ring any bells?"

Her blood ran cold.

"You've gone pale," he mocked cruelly. "Cat got your tongue? I'll tell you, then. Mr. Knollys is the turnkey of Newgate prison. A rather revolting character, I'm afraid, but a man who possesses an excellent memory. As luck would have it, Mr. Knollys was present at a cock fight I attended in Blackheath recently. He heard someone shout my name across the pit and recalled another Caversteed he'd dealt with just recently. He decided to pay me a visit. Imagine my surprise when he told me he had some interesting information about *you*, dear heart." His sickly grin made Georgie want to retch. "What do you think he told me? Hmmm?"

"I can't hazard a guess."

"He made the outrageous claim that you and Wylde are man and wife." Josiah rounded his eyes in mock horror. "I didn't believe it, of course, but then he showed me the marriage register from Newgate, and there it was, clear as day: your signature and Wylde's. Married not five weeks ago." He shook his head, his expression changing to one of disbelief mingled with fury. "You vindictive little bitch. You did this to spite me, didn't you?"

His cheeks, already spidered with veins, grew even redder and more mottled. Georgie had never seen him in such a passion. Her heart began to thump in fear but she didn't bother to deny it. "Yes. I did. Because I'd rather be married to a Newgate felon than to you."

His laugh was ugly. "You think he doesn't want your money? Of course he does. I bet you paid him a pretty penny to go along with your plan, didn't you?" He snorted in disgust. "God, that bastard must have laughed himself silly. You spring him from jail then let him slip between your legs."

Georgie winced at his crude summation. "What do you want? More money? You won't get it. I won't give you another shilling. Benedict was right. You need to take responsibility for your own actions. You're a grown man, Josiah. Act like one. Now let me go."

"It's not about money anymore, you little whore."

She almost laughed in hysterical disbelief. Josiah not wanting money? The world had gone mad.

"It's you I want now."

"Well, you can't have me," she snapped.

He tilted his head, and the calculating look in his eye made her shiver. His voice was almost a caress. "Ah, Georgie. I could have understood if it was just business. But to see you whoring yourself out to him? I can't bear it."

Georgie had heard enough. She dug her heels into the soggy ground and bent her knees to get free of his grip, tugging with her whole weight behind her. Josiah cursed, and a flash of white fluttered in her peripheral vision as he pulled a handkerchief from his pocket. Before she could react, he pressed the fabric over her nose and mouth, cutting off her air. She cried out in panic and kicked at him, but he caught her in a crushing grip around her ribs. She tried to inhale, to bite him, but it was impossible. The edges of her vision grew fuzzy and narrowed like a tunnel closing in. She heard Josiah laugh.

"Shhh, sweeting."

She'd been so stupid.

Her knees grew weak, and her lungs burned. She scratched at his hand, desperate to remove the fabric so she could breathe. Then his fingers pressed into the side of her neck, hard against her pulse, and everything went black.

Chapter 33.

She awoke in a moving carriage. Her head felt heavy, her throat raw. Sounds came and went, as if she were beneath a pillow or under water; the blowing of the horses, endlessly pounding hooves. A painful jolt as the wheels bumped through a rut.

She didn't want to open her eyes. This didn't smell like her own carriage; it was musty and filled with a strange, smoky odor. Opium. She knew the scent from Blackwall—many sailors, especially those from the east, favored the stuff over regular tobacco.

She cracked her lids apart, praying she was alone, and suppressed a groan. Josiah was sprawled haphazardly on the opposite seat, watching her with a smug, satisfied expression. A small oil lamp burned on a wooden crate next to him, and as she watched, he held the bulbous end of a long pipe over the flame and took a deep inhale. His exhale sent a thin stream of blue smoke in her direction.

She opened her eyes and struggled to sit up and found to her fury that her wrists and ankles had been tied. She coughed and waved her bound hands in front of her face to dispel the cloud. Anger warmed her veins. She'd been abducted! In broad daylight, by her slug of a cousin. She'd never imagined him capable of such stupidity.

Josiah sent her a blissful, relaxed smile. "Ah! You're awake. I did worry I'd been a little rough with you. I'm glad that's not the case." He coughed, and it turned into a high-pitched giggle. He sounded unhinged. Had he lost his mind? She could escape him if he were slow and incapacitated. If only she could get free of her bonds. If he'd missed the knife in her boot she might have a chance.

She wriggled into a more upright position and scowled at him. "This is ridiculous, Josiah. Where are we going?"

He sent her a dreamy smile, took one last puff of the pipe, then set it aside and extinguished the little lamp. "Somewhere we can be completely private." The way his gaze roamed over her body made her stomach curdle. "Always thought you were pretty," he murmured. "Not as sweet as Juliet, of course, but I like your haughty manner. More of a challenge." His lip curled, as if he'd been reminded of something unpleasant. "Wylde accepted that challenge, didn't he, eh? You're a real woman now. Know what it's like to have a man between your legs." He licked his lips. "You'll find out again soon enough."

She quelled a whole-body shudder.

"You think he's shagging you because he wants you?" Josiah continued, his voice soft. "The whole *ton* knows he needs cash. His estates are mortgaged to the hilt. His brother's scarcely managed to keep things afloat since their father cocked up his toes and left them neck-deep in debt."

He smiled at her furious expression. "Ah yes, I've done some digging on your Mr. Wylde. He's tried everything to make a shilling, you know. Cards. Horse races.

Sharp-shooting contests. Those didn't last long—he was too good. Nobody's stupid enough to accept his challenge now." He shook his head and shot her a sorrowful look of mock-sympathy. "His other women have all been beautiful. Experienced. Sophisticated. Why'd he want a fumble with a virgin, eh?"

"You don't know anything about it," Georgie snapped, stung to respond. "He knows he can't touch my money. He signed the contract I had drawn up. He—"

Josiah scoffed. "He's playing you like a fiddle. Just biding his time, waiting for you to fall in love with him, so you'll change your mind and *insist* he has access to it all."

Her voice shook with tightly controlled rage. "That's not true!"

But Josiah's words were like poison; he voiced every negative thought she'd ever had about her interactions with Benedict, all her insecurities. *Was* he only taking advantage of what she offered so willingly? Was he laughing at her eagerness? Her inexperience? Did he *pity* her? That would be unbearable.

She leaned her aching forehead against the cool glass pane of the window, even though it rattled horribly, and stared at the drab landscape flying past. It looked as though they were on the outskirts of London, but she had no idea where.

Josiah was wrong. Benedict wasn't conning her. There was more between them than lust. They were friends. They enjoyed each other's company, made each other laugh. And it went deeper than a shared sense of humor; they both believed in protecting family, no matter what. She would do anything for her mother, sister, Pieter. He would do anything for his brother, and for his family-in-war, his comrades at the Tricorn Club.

The difference between Benedict and Josiah was that

Benedict wouldn't sacrifice his own sense of honor to achieve his ends. He was a decent man beneath his cynical, playboy veneer. He'd earned her respect. Georgie blinked as everything came into sudden focus. Benedict didn't just have her respect.

He had her heart. Her love.

Her chest pounded, and she almost laughed, despite the dire situation. How simple it was. She was in love with Benedict Wylde. Her own husband.

Josiah was still talking. "I'll bet a rake like him's taught you all sorts of whore's tricks, hasn't he? I used to think you were so cold." He laughed, a thoroughly unpleasant sound. "It's true what that say, though. Blood will out. You're no highborn bitch with ice water in her veins, are you, Georgie? You're your father's daughter, a merchant's brat. No better than a tavern wench."

She was saved from answering when the carriage took a sharp turn between a pair of low stone markers. They hadn't passed another dwelling for some time—only ploughed fields flanked the narrow track—and her sense of panic increased.

"Nearly there," Josiah said cheerfully. "This is about the only place I haven't had to sell. Used to be Great-Uncle Rupert's hunting lodge. No one will disturb us here."

That's what she was afraid of.

The vehicle rocked to a stop, and Josiah climbed down and spoke briefly to the driver. Then the door on her side opened, and he reached in and grabbed her waist. Not wanting to risk being dropped, Georgie suffered his touch until he'd placed her on the patch of overgrown gravel, then she used the few inches of slack rope between her tied ankles to hobble away from him. She looked up at the tumbledown building in front of her with a sinking feeling.

"Hunting lodge" was too grandiose a description. The place was barely more than a cottage, with a roof that looked like it was about to collapse and several broken panes of glass in the front windows.

She tottered wildly around to face the driver. "Sir, please. Whatever he's paying you, I'll triple it."

The man, a skinny, rat-faced fellow with sunken cheeks and dead eyes glanced at Josiah, then pretended he hadn't heard her. He flicked the reins over the horses' backs, and Georgie bit back a howl of fury as the carriage lumbered away.

"A hundred pounds!" she called after him desperately.

He didn't even pause.

So much for helping a damsel in distress, the swine.

Josiah chuckled and unlocked the front door. It had dropped on its hinges, and he had to push hard to get it to open, but with a shriek of protest the wood scraped across the flagstones and he stepped inside.

"This way, my dear."

With no other option, Georgie hobbled after him and into the first room on the right, a tiny front parlor with a fireplace filled with ashes and dead leaves, a shabby chaise longue, and an overstuffed armchair that seemed to have been recently inhabited by mice. The straw stuffing spewed out of it onto the floor as if it had been disemboweled.

Josiah indicated the chaise longue—only slightly less moth-eaten than the chair. "Have a seat. I'll see if I can make a fire."

As soon as he'd left the room, Georgie felt for her knife in her boot. Hell and damnation—it wasn't there. He must have searched her whilst she was unconscious. The thought of his hands sliding over her body made her nauseous.

She made a quick search of the room, looking for

anything she could use to free herself or use as a weapon, but there was nothing except a small mirror-backed wall sconce. If she could break it, she could use a shard of glass to cut her bonds. A few heavy-looking books sat on a bookshelf, their leather bindings dusted with white mold, but she doubted she'd be able to lift them with her hands tied.

Her stomach churned as she tried to imagine what Josiah planned. Did he mean to rape her? She clenched her jaw. If so, she wasn't going down without a fight.

Josiah returned with an armful of logs and set about building a fire in the grate.

"Now what?" Georgie asked stonily.

"Now we wait."

"For what?"

"Your husband." He almost spat out the word. "He's going to bring us the funds we need to get to the Scottish border. And I'm going to kill him." He smiled at her horrified expression. "You'll be a widow before the day is out, my dear. When we reach Gretna Green, you'll marry me, without some ridiculous contract restricting my access to your fortune."

Georgie tried to keep her voice calm. "How will Benedict know where to come?"

"I've sent instructions to the Tricorn."

Her stomach dropped. "He won't be there." He'd already be in that tavern on Ore Street waiting for Johnstone.

"Then it will take him a while to get here. I'm sure we'll be able to think of something pleasant to pass the time."

Chapter 34.

Benedict, Seb, and Alex converged in the Tricorn's checkered hallway at precisely ten o'clock. A familiar sense of nervous energy swirled between them. How many countless times during the war had they met like this, about to set out on a mission?

Alex shot Ben an eager grin as he tugged on a pair of leather gloves. "Remember the ambush we set up in that gorge above Talavera? Six hours, sweltering on a rocky mountainside, before we got our man. At least this time we can wait for our target in a nice comfortable tavern."

Seb nodded. "So, what's the plan? Wait until Johnstone arrives, barge in, and arrest him?"

"That's about it," Ben said. "Let's just hope he shows. Admiral Cockburn wants us to commandeer the submarine rather than destroy it—he wants it sailing down to the Royal Navy dockyards at Woolwich, but I'll be damned if I know how to get it there. Either of you know how to sail?"

Alex grimaced. "Don't look at me. I spent the entire

crossing from Belgium casting up my accounts, if you recall. I get nauseous if I look at a puddle."

Seb shook his head. "I've only ever manned row boats."

"Well, Bow Street only wants Johnstone," Benedict said. "If Cockburn wants the vessel, he can bloody well send someone to get it. When we've nabbed Johnstone, one of us can guard the warehouse until the Admiralty arrives."

Georgie could have sailed it, he thought. She'd studied the plans, knew how the infernal contraption worked. She'd be miles better than anyone the Admiralty could send. Perhaps he'd suggest it to Cockburn. She'd be in no danger once Johnstone was in custody.

He wondered where she was now. Probably still in bed, catching up on much-needed sleep. The thought brought a smile to his lips, and he realized how impatient he was to see her again. That in itself was unusual. With every other woman, he'd found that sleeping with her invariably got her out of his system. His curiosity was assuaged, the itch satisfied. Not so with Georgie. Making love to her, knowing her more intimately, had only tightened the strings that bound them, increased his curiosity. He wanted her again. Maybe tonight, she—

Seb's hand, waving in front of his nose, reclaimed his attention, and Benedict felt an uncharacteristic heat flush his neck. Christ. He was acting like a besotted schoolboy.

"Distracted by your lady love?" Seb teased mercilessly, uncannily accurate as ever.

Benedict scowled. "Let's go."

He reached for the brass doorknob at the same moment an urgent hammering sounded on the other side. A scruffy lad was panting on the steps. "Benedict Wylde?"

"Yes."

The boy thrust a folded letter at him. "I was told to give this to you."

Ben broke the seal, scanned the letter, then swore fluently and long. "That *bastard*. I should have put a sword through him when I had the chance."

"What is it?"

He thrust the paper at Alex.

"'I have your wife,'" Alex read aloud. "'Tell her sister to retrieve her jewels, along with any cash in the house, and deliver them to me at Rupert's place in Hounslow. Juliet can give you the direction. If you do not do as I say, I will enjoy my cousin as you enjoyed her last night. Come alone and unarmed, or I will hurt her. Josiah Caversteed.'"

Benedict turned and headed back into the Tricorn. He already had his trusty Baker rifle—the strap of its leather case was strung across his body in anticipation of dealing with Johnstone—but he took the stairs two at a time and went back into his apartment. He retrieved a pair of dueling pistols from his desk drawer, loaded them with the ease and efficiency of long practice, thrust them into his belt, and hastened back downstairs.

Alex and Seb were still in exactly the same place on the doorstep. Ben leapt down the steps toward the stable, shouting for one of the grooms to saddle his horse. His friends were close behind him.

Seb frowned in sudden recognition. "Caversteed? Not that cheating whoreson I had thrown out of here last night?"

"The very same."

Seb whistled. "Her cousin, eh? He's a nasty piece of work."

Ben mounted his chestnut stallion and motioned to his friends to get out of the way.

"You're off to rescue the damsel in distress, then?" Alex said.

"Of course I bloody am. She's my wife." Benedict

scowled. "I swear, if he's harmed one hair on her head, I'm going to make him wish he'd never been born." He kicked his heels to the stallion's sides and clattered out of the yard.

It took him less than ten minutes to ride to Grosvenor Square, and he cursed every slow-moving cart, stray dog, and suicidal pedestrian that got in his way. He turned into the square to find a traveling post chaise pulled up in front of the house and Juliet standing on the steps, a traveling trunk and several band boxes piled at her feet.

He clattered to a stop behind the chaise. "What's all this?" he demanded sharply. "Where's your mother? Where's Pieter?"

Juliet's face paled, and she clasped her hands to her bosom.

"Don't even consider fainting," Benedict growled.

She swallowed visibly. "Pieter's visiting his sister, and M-mother's having lunch with Lady Cowper."

Benedict narrowed his eyes at the luggage. "And what are you doing?"

Juliet managed to look both flustered and extremely guilty. "Oh, you mustn't say anything! Simeon and I are eloping. Don't try to stop us, Mr. Wylde, I beg you." She achieved a wonderful imitation of a tragic Greek heroine, all wrinkled forehead and glistening eyes.

Ben kicked his boot from the stirrup and dismounted. "I don't give a tinker's damn what you do. Your cousin's taken Georgie."

Juliet's eyes grew wide. "What do you mean, taken her?"

"I mean, he's kidnapped her for ransom. Now go inside and get me her jewels and any cash you have in the house. Quickly now." When Juliet just stood there gawping, he snapped. "Go!"

Juliet went.

"Don't talk to my fiancée like that!"

Simeon's shaggy head appeared from inside the chaise. Benedict took a deep breath and reminded himself not to smash his fist into the boy's face. It was bad form to hit a man with glasses. "Button it, Pettigrew. I don't have time to deal with you now."

Juliet returned, panting from her exertions. Her hands held a bulging reticule with a drawstring top. Part of a necklace peeked out, and Benedict recognized it with a pang as the one Georgie had worn at O'Meara's, the one she'd tried to pass off as fake—a fortune in diamonds and emeralds. His stomach clenched. He had to get to her.

"Where are you supposed to take them?" Juliet asked.

"Rupert's place in Hounslow. Your cousin said you'd know the direction."

Juliet's perfect forehead creased. "Uncle Rupert had a hunting box there. Father took us a few times when we were little." She screwed up her face. "But that was years ago. I can barely remember how to get there. I never took much notice. All I remember is that it's a few miles out-side of the town, past a tavern called the Dog and Duck." She glanced mournfully at the bag as she handed it over. "You're not really going to give those to him, are you?"

"No. I'm going to beat him to a bloody pulp," Benedict said. "And then I might just shoot him for good measure."

Juliet raised her chin, a very unladylike spark of violence flashing in her blue eyes. "Well, good. If he's done something horrid to Georgie, then he deserves everything you give him."

Benedict remounted, and she placed her hand on his booted foot. "Please bring her back safe, Mr. Wylde."

"I will." He wheeled his horse and found Alex and Seb, both mounted, blocking the end of the street. He frowned at them. "Why aren't you on your way to the docks?"

Alex shrugged. "We sent a message to Bow Street. Willis is going to watch the warehouse. We're with you. If this woman's important to you, she's important to us."

Ben swallowed a lump in his throat. Thank God for such friends. The bond he shared with Alex and Seb was so much stronger than blood. It had been forged in sweat and tears, in shared misery and elation. And countless instances of finding humor in the blackest of situations. "This isn't your fight."

Seb grinned. "Don't be ridiculous, of course it is. Remember that time near Badajoz when you saved me from that sniper? I owe you. Your fight is our fight, remember?"

Alex chuckled. "Not to mention I've been praying for a decent scrap for months. London's deadly dull when it comes to proper fighting."

"All right," Ben said gruffly. "Let's go."

They headed west, and when they were obliged to stop and pay fourpence apiece at the Kensington toll gate, Alex said, "I must say, this is the first time any of us have chosen a girl over a mission."

Ben glared at him. "Either one of you would do the same."

Alex and Seb shared a skeptical look. "For a woman?" Seb said. "I doubt it. For her *fortune*, maybe . . ."

"It's not about her money. Why does nobody believe that? I care for her. I don't want her hurt."

Ben scowled as he set his mount to a gallop again and curbed the impulse to push the animal even harder. He'd get nowhere on an exhausted horse. Worry churned in his gut, mingling with a deep and furious rage.

He could count on one hand the people he cared about, those he feared losing. His brother John. Alex and Seb. And now Georgie. Somewhere in the past few weeks, she'd wormed her way into that select little group. Wormed her way into his heart. She'd become more than an acquaintance, more than just a friend, or a challenge, or a body to be discovered. He needed her. Wanted to be with her, to tease her, to share some story or anecdote to see how she'd react. He wanted to hold her and keep her safe from the Josiahs of this world. There was more than a casual connection between them now. There was something new and binding, and he was horribly afraid he knew what it was. Love.

His mount tossed its head as he inadvertently jerked at the reins. *Oh, shit. He was in love.*

And like a French sniper's bullet, he hadn't even seen it coming.

Benedict slackened his hold on the reins and patted his horse's lathered neck in silent apology. His stomach pitched. This was a disaster. A surefire recipe for misery. They couldn't possibly have a future together. What did *he* have to offer her—the girl who could afford everything? A mountain of debt. A drawer full of medals he didn't deserve.

Benedict narrowed his eyes. If her idiotic cousin laid so much as a finger on her, he would pay dearly. Any man who used his physical superiority to bully a woman or intimidate someone weaker than himself didn't deserve to draw breath.

Blood thundered in his ears, the same way it did before battle, bringing with it the bright anticipation of mayhem.

Seb trotted up beside him. Alex drew level on his other side and pounded him on the shoulder. "We'll get her back."

Ben grunted. At Hammersmith they slowed the horses to a walk, and he fought a rising sense of frustration. Time seemed to slow to a crawl, every mile a chore. He fought off a superstitious feeling of dread as a single magpie landed on the road in front of him and he recalled the old children's rhyme: *One for sorrow, two for joy*. He prayed it wasn't an omen—and felt immeasurably reassured when a second bird joined its mate, cawing loudly before they both flew off in a flutter of black-and-white wings.

Two for joy. He would not fail Georgie.

Finally they came to the village of Hounslow, just before the infamous heath, the setting for many an audacious robbery. It was no great work to locate the Dog and Duck public house.

Ben glanced at his companions as they headed out of town. "Stay out of sight. I'll go in alone."

They nodded in unison, not needing further instruction, and he appreciated the certain knowledge that they had his back.

Hold on, Georgie girl. I'm coming.

Chapter 35.

The sound of hooves on the gravel drive made Georgie glance toward the grimy window in sudden panic. Relief and terror swirled in her chest. Only one rider—Benedict had come alone. And he was walking into a trap. She tried to warn him, but the only sound she could make was a muffled grunt; Josiah had stuffed a rag in her mouth and tied it with the same handkerchief he'd used to overpower her.

He sat in a spindle-backed chair he'd brought in from the kitchen, facing the door, a loaded pistol resting on his knee. His fingers twitched on the wooden stock, and he bounced the heel of one foot compulsively against the chair leg. She'd never seen him with any sort of weapon before. Did he even know how to use the thing? She prayed not. Benedict had been in the army—the Rifles, for goodness sake. Surely his greater experience with firearms would give him the advantage here?

Boots crunched, and she heard Benedict's achingly familiar voice shout, "Caversteed? Show yourself."

"In here, Wylde," Josiah called.

Her eyes teared with fright. She thumped her bound feet down on the wooden floor as loudly as she could, trying to alert him, and Josiah sent her a mocking glance for the futile gesture. Benedict appeared in the doorway, and her heart stopped at the sight of him, tall and strong and windblown. His gaze swept the room, taking in Josiah and his gun in one glance, then fixing on her. He seemed to breathe a sigh of relief, and she nodded emphatically, trying to explain that she was unharmed; Josiah hadn't yet made good on his threats to molest her.

He turned his attention back to Josiah, apparently unfazed by the muzzle pointing directly at him.

"Did you bring the jewels?" Josiah demanded, his voice high-pitched with strain.

Benedict glanced down at the small, lumpy bag he carried, and Georgie recognized it as her favorite beadwork reticule.

"Here." He tossed the bag carelessly onto the floor. A puff of dust flew up and a pile of jewelry slithered out across the dirty boards. Diamonds caught the light, sparkling even in the gloom.

"Well done." Josiah smiled and lifted the pistol.

A deafening report echoed through the room. Georgie screamed behind the gag and swung to Benedict, expecting to see a terrible red stain spreading over his chest, but he merely sent her a cocky smile that made her heart trip over. It took her a stunned moment to comprehend that he was holding a smoking pistol and that it was her cousin who was bent over in his chair, clutching his arm and wailing in agony. Blood dripped onto the dusty floor beneath him.

"You shot me!" Josiah screeched.

Benedict stepped forward and used his boot to kick

away Josiah's pistol, which had fallen to the side of the chair. "Stop sniveling," he said harshly. "I was in the Rifles. I once shot a man on horseback from eight hundred yards away. You're lucky I didn't blow a hole in your forehead, you bastard. How dare you take her?"

Josiah cringed. Benedict caught him by the collar, jerked him to his feet—and punched him clean across the jaw. Josiah's head snapped back, and he slid to the floor in a boneless, unconscious heap.

Benedict stepped back, a look of utter contempt on his face, then glanced over at Georgie. In two strides, he was in front of her, ripping the gag from her mouth and pulling her into his arms. Georgie let out a whimper of relief and buried her nose against his shirtfront. His hold on her was so crushingly tight, she could scarcely breathe.

"God, I thought he'd hurt you," he groaned, kissing the top of her head.

She tried to shake her head against his chest, but he'd left her no room to move. She wriggled, and his hold slackened. "It's all right. I'm fine," she gasped.

He clamped her cheeks between his palms, searching her features with a fierce expression, and then he pressed his mouth to hers in a desperate, hungry kiss.

A thousand conflicting emotions flowed into her: relief and desperation, fury and desire. Georgie yielded to them joyously, loving the rough tenderness of his hands in her hair, the frantic kisses he pressed to her nose, her cheeks, the corners of her eyes. Her hands were still tied, trapped between them, so she couldn't wrap her arms around his neck as she wanted to, but she leaned into him.

Then his lips were back on hers, and she matched the fierce tenderness of his kiss. Her chest ached with a sharp consciousness of how close she'd been to losing him, how fragile and precious life was. Tears threatened, but she choked them back, losing herself in the wildness of his kiss.

It seemed forever before he pulled back, and for a few moments they just stood there, swaying together. She pressed her forehead against his sternum and closed her eyes, sinking into his sheltering strength and absorbing his solidity, his integrity. He was as big as Pieter, but the Dutchman had never held her this way, as if he could shelter her from the whole world.

This man, her heart said.

She lifted her head. "I thought you were supposed to be at the docks catching Johnstone?"

"I was. Your cousin's note arrived just as we were leaving."

Her heart gave a little skip; he'd chosen to come for her over catching his foe, for which she would be eternally grateful.

A footfall outside made her jump, but Benedict merely smiled and released her. "Don't worry. That's Seb and Alex."

"They came too?"

He nodded, and her amazement increased. The fact that two complete strangers had also abandoned their mission to come for her was humbling—although not entirely surprising. Benedict seemed to inspire 'til-death-do-us-part loyalty in almost everyone he encountered.

He produced a knife and made quick work of the ties at her wrists, then knelt on the dusty floor to cut the rope at her ankles. Georgie quelled a brief wistful pang as she took in the sight of him kneeling before her as if he were proposing marriage. She shook her head. Foolish yearnings. He'd come to her rescue because he was a good and honorable man. He would have come for Juliet or Mama too.

She glanced over at Josiah, who was still insensible on the floor. A trickle of blood marred the corner of his mouth and a livid purple bruise was already forming on his jaw. Served him right, the idiot.

"What are we going to do with him?"

Benedict sighed. "I don't want to leave him here. What's to stop him from trying something equally foolish again?"

A sharp whistle of warning sounded outside, quickly followed by the clatter of horses and the unmistakable creak of a carriage. Georgie looked through the cracked windowpane as a black-and-yellow traveling chaise rocked to a stop outside. By the time she reached the cottage door, the steps had been let down. She gasped as Juliet leapt down and barreled into her arms, hugging her tightly around the neck like some fragrant-smelling octopus.

"Oh, thank goodness you're all right!" Juliet sobbed. "When we heard Josiah had taken you, we were so worried."

Georgie disentangled herself from the embrace and eyed her sister suspiciously. "We? You mean Mother's here too?"

Juliet's cheeks pinked. "Oh, no, I mean, well—"

"Afternoon, Miss Caversteed," Simeon said.

Georgie suppressed a groan as the full implications of his presence sank in. "Please tell me you have Charlotte or Tilly in there with you?"

Juliet bit her lip. "No, actually. If you must know, Simeon and I were about to leave for Gretna when Mr. Wylde arrived with your note."

"You were eloping? Oh, *Juliet*."

"Yes, well, we didn't in the end, did we?' Juliet said crossly. "Because I demanded to come after you instead. You're welcome."

Georgie glanced back at Simeon and dropped her

voice. "You might as well have eloped, Ju. Word of this is bound to get out. You'll be ruined."

"I don't care," Juliet said mulishly. "I want to marry Simeon, and he wants to marry me. That's all there is to it." She glanced around. "Where *is* Cousin Josiah, anyway?"

"Inside. Benedict put a bullet in his arm then knocked him a facer. He's out cold."

"Good."

Simeon jumped down from the carriage—and stumbled over his own feet. He righted himself. "I'll just go and see if I can help, shall I?"

Juliet beamed at him. "Oh, yes, Simeon, that would be perfect."

Georgie sighed. "Well, at least you've solved one problem. Josiah sent his carriage away, and I assume Benedict rode here." She gestured at the carriage. "We can put Josiah in there to get him back to London."

"You should dump him in the Thames," Juliet said.

"I have a better idea."

Chapter 36.

The trip back to London was rather jolly. Georgie, Juliet, Simeon, and Josiah all squashed into the chaise.

Josiah had been efficiently bound and gagged in the same way he'd bound Georgie, which gave her a great deal of satisfaction, and when he finally roused from his stupor, his furious attempts to free himself entertained everyone in the vehicle.

Benedict and his two companions—Alexander Harland, whom she recognized from Lady Langton's, and another equally handsome specimen he'd introduced as Sebastian Wolff—rode alongside. A flash of memory caught her; this must be the Mr. Wolff Benedict had told her to send his five hundred pounds to in Newgate. She studied the man's olive skin and saturnine features. Juliet had whispered that he was the youngest son of the Duke of Winwick.

Simeon produced a notebook and pencil from his jacket. "I do believe I should write a poem commemorating this great victory," he said. "Iambic pentameter, do you think?"

Georgie glanced out of the open window and caught Benedict's eye as he rode parallel to the chaise. His comic expression of horror made her chuckle.

She couldn't help but wonder what Simeon would have done if Juliet had been kidnapped. He was far less physically intimidating than Benedict, but he clearly held strong feelings for her sister and love made people do extraordinary things. Perhaps he would have surprised them all.

She stifled a little pang of jealousy at the adoring looks Simeon sent Juliet across the carriage, as if she were the air he breathed and the gravity that kept him anchored to the earth. She could imagine them as an old married couple, still exchanging such glances, even when their hands were gnarled and their eyes rheumy with age. If only Benedict looked at her with the same adoration.

She glanced at him again, admiring his large hands guiding the horse and the strength of his muscled thighs, and a sudden intense recollection of what they'd done in the night came to her, of his body pressed over her, his mouth at her neck, her breasts. Heat scalded her cheek at her inappropriate thoughts.

Benedict caught her eye with a knowing look, and she just *knew* he knew what she was thinking. His wicked glance promised a repeat of such pleasures the next time they were alone. Would there be a next time? She fervently hoped so.

When they reached Hyde Park, Benedict's companions bade their farewells. Georgie told a grumbling Simeon to get out and walk home, amid assurances to Juliet that she would put their case before Mother and lend her support to a proper, non-clandestine marriage.

Instead of returning directly to Grosvenor Square, however, Georgie told the driver to convey them to Blackwall.

The *Lady Alice* was still anchored by the quay—all three hundred majestic tons of her—and Georgie smiled as she stepped down onto the wharf, tottered up the gangplank, and hailed the captain. He snapped to attention and greeted her with polite surprise.

"Miss Caversteed! We are honored. Is anything amiss?"

"Afternoon, Captain Moore, and no, no, nothing is wrong. Are you still off to Boston at high tide, as scheduled?"

"Aye. Everything's stowed and ready."

"Excellent. In that case, I was wondering if you have room for one extra passenger?" She indicated Josiah, who had been unloaded from the carriage and stood on the dockside, wriggling furiously in Benedict's grip. "You see there my cousin Josiah, who has found himself in somewhat, shall we say, *uncomfortable circumstances* here in London."

The captain noted Josiah's gag, black eye, and bound hands, and shot her an amused, knowing look from under his bushy brows. "As you say, ma'am."

Georgie smiled. "Confronted with rather dismal prospects on this side of the Atlantic, I'm pleased to say that he's taking my advice to start over in America."

"Righto," the captain said. "I'm sure we can find room for one more. He won't cause me no trouble, will he?"

"Oh, no, but I would advise you not to undo his bindings until you're a good way out from port. He may be rather reluctant at first, but I'm sure he'll come around if you put him to work. He really ought to be made to pay for his passage, don't you think?"

The captain chuckled and gestured to the ship's longboat, which carried a noisy assortment of livestock for the crossing—pens for sheep and pigs in the bottom, ducks and geese on a deck laid across the gunwales, and on top of all, crates of hens and chickens. "Very good, ma'am. He can make himself useful tending to the animals."

Georgie chuckled. "Perfect, Captain Moore. How long do you think it will take you to reach Boston harbor?"

"As long as the weather holds, we should make excellent time. Nineteen to twenty days, I should think, now we have our new chronometer to chart the course. You can tell Mr. Harrison it works beautifully, ma'am."

"Oh, good. He'll be so glad you think so."

She went to the rail and indicated for Benedict to escort her cousin aboard. Josiah glared at her over his gag and clearly tried to remonstrate, or perhaps beg forgiveness, but she was in no mood to listen.

"Josiah, stop." She fixed him with a baleful glare. "I have had quite enough of your foolish spite and jealousy. The only reason I am not having Mr. Wylde take you straight to Bow Street and charging you with unlawful kidnapping and the attempted murder of a peer"—she paused, to let the severity of that sink in—"is because it would reflect badly on the rest of the family."

Josiah's eyes widened as he realized she was serious.

"I have no desire to see you incarcerated in Newgate and hanged from Tyburn tree, but if I see your face on these shores again, I will not hesitate to press charges. Nod if you understand me."

Josiah's head bobbed up and down.

"Good. I am hoping that once you have been forced to make your own way in the world, you will appreciate the value of hard work and find a measure of the happiness that has eluded you here."

She nodded to Juliet, who passed her the reticule Benedict had filled. "Because I am not entirely heartless, I will not send you away with nothing but the clothes on your back." She opened the drawstring and pulled out the diamond and emerald necklace. "This I will keep"—she glanced at Wylde—"because it has fond memories attached to it, but I give you the rest as a gesture of goodwill. There's also fifty pounds in there." She shot Benedict an accusing glance.

Juliet gasped in outrage at her generosity, but Georgie ignored her. She handed the bag to the captain. "Captain Moore can keep these safe until you reach your destination. Goodbye, Josiah, and Godspeed. Captain Moore, I wish you fair winds and a calm sea."

The captain saluted and gestured for one of his crew to escort Josiah below. Georgie turned her back on her cousin and accepted Benedict's arm down the wooden gangplank.

"That was well done," he murmured, as he helped her back into the carriage. Her heart glowed a little with pride.

Juliet climbed in after her and collapsed on the opposite seat. "Well, that was far more than he deserved, I must say," she huffed. "Now we must go home and face the wrath of Mother." She sighed gloomily. "Do you suppose there's even the slightest chance she won't have found out about Simeon and myself?"

"Not a chance," Georgie said. "We'll just have to make the best of it." She turned to Benedict and suddenly found herself unable to speak. There was so much she wanted to say to him, but she couldn't form the words at all. "I don't know how to thank you," she said finally.

He sent her an easy smile. "Don't mention it, milady. Rescuing damsels in distress is our specialty. All in a day's work for a Bow Street runner, I assure you." His hand covered hers where it rested on the door of the carriage, and he gave a brief, reassuring squeeze. "I have to catch up with Alex and Seb, but I'll be in touch soon, I promise."

Georgie nodded as the carriage pulled away.

Chapter 37.

Juliet puffed out her cheeks as they clattered toward Grosvenor Square. "Well, I'm glad that's over. Whatever was Josiah thinking, the nodcock?" She rearranged her skirts and sent Georgie an arch look. "And Mr. Wylde coming to your rescue was the most romantic thing possible, don't you think?"

Georgie grunted, and Juliet sent her a laughing, chiding frown.

"Oh, don't deny it! He put himself in harm's way for you, Georgie, like a real chivalric knight!"

"I am very grateful to Mr. Wylde for—"

"Grateful? Pish! Why are you so afraid of admitting you're in love with the man?"

Georgie bit her lip. Was she afraid? Juliet wasn't ashamed to declare her love for Simeon to all and sundry. She threw herself headfirst into it and trusted that all would be well. Such complete abandon could be admired *in theory*, but the thought of risking it all on one person still terrified her. It was the shipping equivalent of putting one's most valuable cargo on a single ship and sending it straight out into a storm without a compass.

It wasn't unreasonable to want to protect herself from hurt, was it? Just look at how her own mother had been affected when their father had been taken from her. It had taken her years to be merry again. And yet Mother had often said that she'd rather have had those years with their father—even knowing the heartache that would follow—as opposed to a life spent without him.

Georgie blinked as the blur of London rolled past the windows. Love, it seemed, was like Mr. Johnstone's submarine—there were no half measures. You had to fully commit. To close the hatch, put your life in another's hands, and trust you wouldn't drown. It was easier said than done.

Should she tell Benedict how she felt? What good could it do, when their arrangement was only temporary? He hadn't asked for her to fall in love with him; he'd probably just feel guilty and awkward because he didn't return the sentiment. What he felt for her was lust, not love.

Their return to Grosvenor Square elicited the expected flurry of concerned scolding from their mother. Tilly the maid had been cajoled into telling all, and no sooner had Georgie and Juliet been ushered into the drawing room than Mother demanded to know what on earth had possessed them both. Georgie was reprimanded for abandoning Charlotte in the park and "disappearing heaven knows where." She was given no chance to explain, however, before Juliet was subjected to Mother's patented *what-did-I-do-to-deserve-such-a-trial-for-a-daughter* glare.

"Eloping?" she wailed. "*Why*, Juliet? And with that penniless poet Pettigrew!"

Georgie tried not to snort at the unintentionally amusing alliteration.

Juliet firmed her jaw. "I love him, Mother. We make each other happy. I don't want to marry anyone else."

Mother dabbed the corner of her eyes with her handkerchief. "But to be seen leaving with him in a carriage. Unaccompanied. In broad daylight! And then to return home *un*wed? Oh, the shame!"

Georgie coughed to interrupt what promised to be a fit of dramatic sobbing and general palpitations. "If you'll just listen for a moment, Mother, I can explain. Yes, Juliet and Simeon were planning to elope, but they abandoned their plans to come and help me. I was kidnapped from the park by Josiah."

Juliet threw her a grateful look. Mother clutched her handkerchief to her quivering bosom and gasped. "Kidnapped? Why on earth would Josiah do that?"

"Because he's gambled himself into a hole and thought the best way to get himself out of it was to demand all my jewelry in exchange for my safe release."

Mother gaped at her. "Why, that little weasel! I always knew he was a bad one. You didn't oblige him, did you?"

"I did not. Luckily, Benedict Wylde intervened. He succeeded in subduing Josiah and returning my jewels to me."

Mother frowned. "*Wylde* rescued you?"

Georgie pasted a bright smile on her face. "Yes. It was the most amazing coincidence. He just happened to be passing by."

Mother seemed to digest that. "Are you quite sure he wasn't in on Josiah's plan? It sounds awfully convenient. Perhaps they cooked the scheme up together so he could play the gallant rescuer and impress you."

"I can assure you it was nothing like that. Mr. Wylde

has no love for Josiah. In fact, he helped me send him off to Boston with his tail between his legs."

"Boston? In Lincolnshire?" Mother echoed, bewildered. "What's there to do in Boston?"

"No, Boston in *America*," Georgie clarified, with a satisfied grin. "Josiah threatened me and tried to shoot Mr. Wylde. So we took him to Blackwall and put him aboard the *Lady Alice*. He'll make no more trouble for anyone."

Mother sat back in her chair. "America? You've dispatched your own cousin to America? Good heavens, Georgiana!"

"He deserved it," Juliet chimed in supportively. "And Mr. Wylde really was quite heroic."

Mother shot her a glare, apparently reminded of her indiscretion. "Well, even if Josiah can't make any more trouble, it hardly matters, since you've brought scandal upon us all anyway." She sighed dramatically. "Oh, Juliet. I had such high hopes for you. But if it's truly this Pettigrew you want, then I suppose you'll *have* to marry him now."

Juliet blinked at this sudden about-face. "I can marry Simeon?"

Mother nodded. "I suppose so. I can't say I'm not a little disappointed at his lack of title, but if you really love him, then that's not such a bad thing. I married your father, after all, despite him not having a title, and I never regretted it for a moment. Just promise me you'll appoint someone like Edmund Shaw to look after your assets. Mr. Pettigrew doesn't seem particularly skilled when it comes to financial matters."

Georgie chuckled at the irony of Mother presuming to lecture anyone on budgeting. Her idea of "economizing" was wearing a dress more than twice in one season, but since she made sure to disguise the fact by purchasing new shawls, hats, gloves, and earrings to match—which inevitably cost more than a new dress—there was no saving whatsoever.

Juliet gave a watery squeal. "Oh, yes, I promise! Thank you, Mama!" She leapt from the sofa and went to embrace her, but Mother waved her off, already in full planning mode.

"If we announce your engagement immediately, it should put a stop to any gossip, especially if we hint that the two of you have had a private agreement since before you even came to town."

Juliet danced toward the door. "Oh, I must write to him at once and tell him the good news!"

Georgie watched her sister's rapturous departure with a sense of utter fatigue. The day's events had left her exhausted. "If you don't mind, I'm going to have a lie down before dinner."

"Of course." Mother nodded absently, already deep in thought about how to handle Juliet's forthcoming betrothal and, presumably, the wedding of the decade.

"We missed all the fun," Seb said gloomily, as soon as Benedict strode into the Tricorn's dining room. "Willis and his men nabbed Johnstone while we were larking about in Hampstead with your woman."

Benedict stopped in the doorway. "What? Truly? Bloody hell." Biting back a howl of frustration, he crossed to the sideboard, poured himself a generous splash of brandy, and took a healthy swallow. The alcohol warmed his belly but did nothing to ease the bitter taste of disappointment. "There goes five hundred pounds of reward money, then. Bollocks."

He sank into a comfy leather wing chair beside Alex, who nodded in confirmation.

"We stopped in at Bow Street after we left you. They've got Johnstone and another of his men in the cells. Admiral Cockburn was there questioning them, but neither one was talking."

Benedict groaned. That five hundred pounds could have started the repairs on Morcott's stable roof or paid off a chunk of mortgaged land. Damn it all. Why in God's name had he tried to impress Georgie by refusing to take her money? He couldn't afford such stupid, quixotic gestures.

"I told Cockburn you knew someone who could sail the submarine down to Woolwich," Seb said. "Didn't tell him it was a girl, of course. He thinks all women are useless gossips, like his wife. He would have refused on principle. So I told him you'd found a lad who was a powder monkey at Trafalgar. He said to go ahead."

Benedict closed his eyes and rested his head back against the chair. He tried to feel some sense of satisfaction that Johnstone had been contained and the scheme to rescue Bonaparte foiled, but he failed miserably. Patriotic sentiment was all well and good, but it didn't solve any of his financial problems. Or the conundrum of his wife.

"I'll tell Georgie," he murmured. "She can meet us at the Ore Street warehouse one night this week."

She'd be delighted, he thought with an inward smile. The challenge of sailing an unmanageable boat down the Thames in the dead of night was exactly the kind of caper she'd relish. At least with Johnstone in custody, the risk to her would be minimal. As long as the damn thing floated, she'd be fine.

His blood still boiled when he thought about the danger she'd been in that afternoon. Thank God her cousin hadn't had time to molest her. He doubted he'd have been able to restrain himself from killing the bastard if he had. Georgie was his wife, even if only a few people knew it. It was his duty to protect her. He should have been with her. She could have been killed.

Ben took another deep draught of his drink. The thought of the rest of his life without Georgie in it was unimaginable. As provoking and disruptive as she was, he couldn't contemplate a world without her vitality, her determination, her sly sarcastic wit. He needed her. Not just as a temporary diversion, but as a permanent requirement for his future happiness.

He'd never thought he'd find a female he could trust and admire as much as Alex and Seb. He'd had no female friends, only acquaintances, lovers. Sex and friendship had been neatly compartmentalized in his mind—women in one camp, men who'd earned his respect in the other. But Georgie had broken down those barriers; she was both friend and lover, temptation and muse.

He gazed moodily into the fire. Did she feel the same way about him? Or was she just using him—an experienced male she found relatively attractive—to rid herself of her unwanted virginity and gain worldly experience? He ground his teeth. No. She might not love him, but she certainly desired him. She wouldn't have responded so ardently to his touch if she didn't want him. Wouldn't have given herself to him without trust.

Was she still thinking their time together was limited? That she'd be moving on to another lover in a couple of months' time?

Never. Not while he drew breath.

She was his wife. And heaven help him, he wouldn't give her up to anyone else.

Benedict stilled as the irony of the situation struck him. He'd been thrown into a marriage of convenience with a stranger, exactly as his parents had been, but that was where the similarities ended. His parents had had nothing in common. No shared interests, no underlying bond of compatibility. They must have felt some momentary attraction, at least in the beginning—they'd managed to sire two sons, after all—but they'd barely tolerated being in the same county by the end of their marriage.

It wasn't like that between Georgie and himself. Yes, there was lust, a sizzling animal attraction that continued to stun him. But more than that, they shared a love of adventure, found the same things funny. She was full of wild ideas and schemes. He could see himself being interested in her, fascinated by her, for the rest of his days. He didn't want to stand up in church in a few weeks' time and have her think he was *pretending* to love her. He wanted her to know that he meant every word, that he was sincere in his desire to be joined with her forever.

Was it fate? All he knew was that he'd dodged more bullets than one man should reasonably have survived, so somewhere the cosmological odds must have been in his favor. Maybe this was the same. He'd found the one woman he could be happy with. With whom he could break the pattern set by his own parents.

The fire crackled and reality made an unwelcome, crashing return. *Impossible.* His lack of money would always be an insurmountable obstacle. He couldn't even give her the title her mother so desperately wanted. He could give her nothing but himself, and how could that ever be enough?

"You're frowning," Seb murmured unhelpfully.

"Shut up." Benedict glared at him, but it was without heat.

Unease and despair bloomed in his chest. Time was running out—only a few short weeks of the season remained. He and Georgie would announce their engagement, marry, and then she'd leave him. She'd go back to the wilds of Lincolnshire or set off on some years-long grand tour of Europe without him. And he'd have to let her go, loving her, wanting her. Unable to burden her with the admission of his love.

He might as well cut out his own heart.

Alex refilled his glass and gave his shoulder a sympathetic pat. "Women, eh?"

Benedict grunted. *Carpe diem*, that was his motto. He still had a few weeks left with her. He would enjoy each moment as it came. His knee started to bounce, his foot tapping in a jiggle of impatience as he calculated when he could see her next. Make love to her next.

He wanted a full night with her, not a few furtive, stolen hours. He wanted the luxury of time to savor her, to learn the feel of every part of her, from the smooth, fragrant valley between her breasts to the texture of her nipples under his tongue. He wanted the creamy skin of her inner thigh, the sleek, supple muscles of her belly, and the warm, heaven-scented slickness at her core. He wanted to hear the sounds she made, that sharp intake of surprise followed by a moan of pleasure.

Alex murmured something to Seb, and Benedict blinked as he surfaced from his drowsy reverie. Christ. He was hard as a rock. He had to stop.

He shook his head. "I'm going to bed."

Chapter 38.

Simeon surprised everyone that afternoon by casually announcing he was the sole beneficiary of a distant great-aunt's will.

"A gold mine? In Wales?" Mother echoed, almost dropping her teacup in astonishment.

Simeon, unaware of the magnitude of the grenade he'd so casually exploded in the drawing room, gave an absent-minded smile and gazed soulfully at Juliet. "Hmm? Oh, yes. Great-Aunt Wilhemina. I was always a favorite of hers. I used to send her a poem every year on her birthday. Hard name to rhyme, Wilhemina. Anyway, it turns out she's left the whole thing to me. Lock, stock, and barrel, as they say. She said I was the only one in the family who would appreciate the romance of the place."

"What's it like?" Juliet breathed, at the same time as Mother said, "Does it produce any income?"

Simeon answered Mother first. "Oh, yes. Around five thousand a year, by all accounts. There's a house and some land and whatnot too." His wispy mustache twitched as he took Juliet's hand. "Actually, when I say 'house,' it's really more of a castle. It has turrets. And a moat."

Juliet looked as though she could scarcely breathe for excitement. "A castle?" she sighed. "You own an honest-to-goodness castle?"

"Near Carmarthen. Built in the 1200s, parts of it. Legend has it there's even a cave nearby with a dragon."

"There aren't any dragons in England," Juliet whispered.

"This is Wales," Simeon said. "They have a dragon on their flag. Who knows what we'll find?"

"That is excellent news, Mr. Pettigrew." Mother helped herself to another biscuit in delight. "I can't tell you how relieved I am that you will have the means to support Juliet in the manner she deserves. I only wish you might have told me of your improved financial status earlier."

Simeon gave her a perplexed look. "Oh, but Juliet loves me for who I am, not what I own."

Mother snapped her mouth closed, and Georgie stifled a smile at how neatly she'd been put in her place. By Simeon, of all people. A bittersweet ache coiled in her chest. Simeon had articulated her own desire—and problem—perfectly.

What should she do about Wylde? Was it just too foolish to hope that he might grow to love her? For all her money, she couldn't buy the thing she desired most: his love.

As predicted, the announcement of Juliet's engagement to Simeon caused a minor sensation and successfully overshadowed the potentially scandalous gossip that she and her beau had been seen alone together in a traveling chaise. Always desperate for entertainment, the *ton* had whispered, but had turned an indulgent eye to this lapse in behavior since it had resulted in a betrothal. It was generally supposed that the couple had anticipated their vows; a baby, eight months after the wedding, was the gossips' consensus.

A few high sticklers tutted at the lax morals of the modern youth, and several disappointed suitors had declared themselves heartbroken that the divine Juliet was off the marriage mart, but all in all, everyone was looking forward to the wedding. Society had been thrilled to learn that Juliet had insisted upon the fashionable St. George's, Hanover Square, and banns were to be called for the next three successive weeks before a mid-May wedding.

Georgie had smiled until her cheeks ached as she accepted well-meaning felicitations on her sister's happiness and endured some less-than-subtle digs at her own still-unmarried state. She'd been sorely tempted to tell all those snide busybodies that she was, in fact, also engaged to be married, but since she and Benedict hadn't discussed when, precisely, they would make their own announcement, she held her tongue. Doubtless their betrothal would create even more of a stir than Juliet's, and she didn't want to overshadow her sister's moment of glory.

She hadn't seen Benedict all week. He hadn't made an appearance at any of the events she'd attended, and she'd found herself desperate for even a glimpse of him. His note, telling her to meet him at the coffeehouse on Ore Street that very evening, had been delivered six days ago, and Georgie could barely contain her excitement. This was the adventure she'd always craved, the chance to test her skills and help with something truly important.

"Pieter, I need to disguise myself as a boy."

It was a testament to the old Dutchman's years of service that not a whisper of surprise showed on his weather-beaten face. "Of course you do. May I ask why?

I can only assume it's because you're about to involve yourself in some scheme that is—"

"—a terrible idea?" Georgie finished fondly. "Yes, quite probably." She reached up and kissed his whiskered cheek. "But you'll help me, won't you? I promise I'll be careful."

The old Dutchman sighed. "Ah, you're yer father's daughter, Georgiana Caversteed. Ever one for a lark, he was. An adventurous spirit who could never be contained." He gave a suspiciously watery sniff and blinked hard. "Of course I'll help you. But tell that Wylde, I'll wring his neck if anything happens to you. What do you need?"

"Breeches will be fine. And a jacket. Something rough and inconspicuous. Oh, and a cap, to disguise my hair. I need to look like a powder monkey or a chimney sweep."

"And what exactly will you be doing, dressed up like that?"

"Helping deliver an important cargo to the navy shipyards in Woolwich."

Pieter grunted, but went to do her bidding and returned a few minutes later with a bundle of clothes. "Here you go. What time do you need to be at Ore Street?"

Georgie turned her mind to the task at hand. "Since Woolwich is downstream from Limehouse, we'll need an outgoing tide to draw the vessel along. Tonight's high tide is just after midnight, so we'll have to wait until then. I've arranged to meet Benedict at eleven."

"I'll have the carriage ready at ten thirty, then. What have you told your mother?"

"She and Juliet are attending the opera. I've said I hate *Don Giovanni* and I'll see them in the morning."

Pieter nodded. "So, you'll be sailing a boat, eh? Remember what I taught you. The Thames is a completely different kettle of fish to that pond you have back home.

Stay away from the mud banks and watch out for the currents. At low tide, the water's only around three to four feet deep, but high tide is twenty-two feet or so."

"I'll be careful, I promise."

Along with his note, Benedict had sent her the tube of rolled plans, and she'd studied them again just in case she needed to know how to operate the strange vessel. She eventually decided there would be no need to submerge it fully; they only needed to sail down the river, after all, which could be achieved by steering with the rudder and using the conventional sail and the power of the outgoing tide to propel them.

As darkness fell, excitement coiled in her belly. The breeches fitted snugly over her hips—clearly meant for someone without feminine curves. She donned the clean shirt and shapeless jacket Pieter had provided, then tied her hair in a pigtail like a sailor and stuffed it under the squashy cap. She tied a red spotted handkerchief around her neck as a jaunty final flourish. A glance in the mirror confirmed she looked a perfect urchin, and she practiced hunching her shoulders forward to hide the telltale lumps of her breasts.

Pieter smiled when she met him in the stables and cuffed her playfully on the shoulder. She'd seen him do the same thing to the cabin boys and younger crew members onboard ship; it was the highest form of masculine affection.

"All right, Georgie Porgie," he said, referencing the nursery rhyme he'd often hummed to her as a child. "Let's go. And no kissing the boys to make them cry, you hear me?"

Georgie shot him a wide-eyed look of devilry. "Who, me? I wouldn't dream of it."

Chapter 39.

It took Benedict less than three seconds to recognize his wife as she slipped through the coffeehouse door. He scowled. She probably thought she was being unobtrusive, keeping her head down so the cap shaded her features, but he was so intensely aware of her that he couldn't believe no one else saw through her disguise.

She slid onto the wooden bench next to him. He glanced at the front of her shirt, buttons straining over her small, pert breasts, and prayed for strength. Her slim legs were encased in tight brown breeches, which outlined her rounded derrière in the most tempting way possible. They weren't touching, but he caught a whiff of her perfume, the intoxicating scent of her skin as she moved. That unmistakably feminine smell would be a surefire giveaway to anyone who got close to her. Not that he'd allow anyone to get close to her.

He pressed his palms flat on the table to stop himself grabbing her by the lapels, hauling her outside into the alley, and ravishing her up against the wall.

Bloody hell.

"Evening, George," Alex murmured across the table.

She nodded at him, then at Seb, who was slouched in the corner, cradling his second cup of coffee. Ben glanced over at the large tavern clock positioned next to the bar. Not long to go. He ordered a chocolate for Georgie, and she sipped it dutifully.

Despite the fact that it was nearly midnight, the place was still lively, but the crowd thinned a little as they waited for the tide. He, Alex, and Seb had gone over the plan in detail. After they slipped into the warehouse, they would slide open the rear doors and launch the vessel into the water. He and Georgie would navigate it to the Royal Navy dockyards, while Alex and Seb would remain to dismantle the rest of the smugglers' paraphernalia and look for further evidence that might incriminate Johnstone and O'Meara.

Benedict kept an eye on the masts of the boats moored in the small dock behind the warehouse. The pool was separated from the main flow of the river by a set of thick wooden gates that could be swung open to allow access. As he watched, the boats turned on their anchor chains, swinging around to face the opposite direction with the turning of the tide. "All right, it's time."

He was about to stand when a scruffy figure sidled up to the table, and he raised his brows as he recognized the newcomer. Jem Barnes wiped his nose on his sleeve and gave an eloquent sniff.

"Evenin', all." He nodded at Ben, Seb, and Alex, cast the briefest look at Georgie, and added, "Miss."

Ben snorted. So much for her disguise. Nothing got past a sharp one like Jem. "What are you doing here?"

The scruffy lad hiked up his trousers, which seemed to be held up with gardener's twine. "I been following Johnstone, just like you said, guv."

"Then you'll know he's in Bow Street. I hope you don't think you're getting paid for telling me that."

Jem shook his shaggy head. "No! That's what I come to tell you. You ain't got 'im."

"I saw him myself in the cells," Alex said.

"No, you ain't. Your boys scooped up the wrong man. They arrested *Fergus* Johnstone, 'is cousin. He's the coxswain. They look almost identical."

Ben and Alex shared a glance. "Are you sure?"

"Yeah. I went to Bow Street meself, pretendin' to take 'im a meal. It's Fergus, all right."

"So where's Tom Johnstone, then?"

"A brothel in Covent Garden. With three of 'Ammond's old crew." He glanced at Benedict. "You know 'em. Shadwell, Finnegan, and Daws. They all dodged the Gravesend raid."

Benedict cursed under his breath. Those three had been the most vicious cutthroats in the smuggling gang.

"Johnstone thinks he's safe, seeing as you think you've got 'im locked up," Jem continued. "'E's coming to move that boat."

"Johnstone's on his way to launch the sub tonight?" Alex repeated.

"That's what I said, ain't it? You got about 'arf an hour, maybe less. They wants to catch the tide."

Benedict blew out a breath. "Good job, Jem."

He reached into his pocket and pressed a gold sovereign into the boy's grubby palm. The cheeky blighter had the audacity to test it between his teeth before he slipped it into his pocket. He caught Seb's look of astonishment and sent him a gap-toothed smile. "Can't be too careful, can yer? Not wiv all these crooks and coiners around, eh?"

Benedict glanced at his colleagues. "Ambush?"

Two sets of eyes twinkled in anticipation. "Oh yes."

He glanced at Georgie and his stomach pitched. Bloody hell. He'd never intended to involve her in anything so risky. He needed to get her out of here. "Perhaps we should come back another night."

Three sets of eyes glared at him in astonishment.

"And let Johnstone get away with the submarine?" Georgie growled. She sent him a scornful look that clearly maligned his manhood. "Never. Stop worrying about me, Wylde, and let's get in there while we still have time."

Her cheeks were pink, her eyes flashed sparks, and he wanted to grab the back of her neck and kiss some sense into her, the stubborn, headstrong wretch. She raised her brows at him in silent challenge, and her obstinate expression was indicative of an iron will behind that velvet facade.

"I do hope you're not going to forbid me from coming," she said, her voice flinty. "Might I remind you that I am the only one here who knows how to sail?" She crossed her arms over her chest as if that settled the matter. Which, in truth, it did.

Alex snorted in amusement and tried to disguise it as a cough.

"Have I mentioned how much I approve of your wife, Benedict?" Seb drawled.

Georgie sent him a sunny smile.

Benedict sighed in defeat. If they worked quickly, they could be out of there before Johnstone arrived. "All right. Jem, can you act as a lookout?"

"Aye-aye."

As the five of them crossed the road and headed for the shadowed warehouse, Ben caught Alex's eye. "Take one more look at her arse in those breeches and I'll flatten you," he muttered.

Alex shot him a wicked grin. "Can't blame a man for

looking. Not when the merchandise is so appealing. I'm just appreciating your excellent taste."

A muscle ticked in his jaw. Alex clapped him on the shoulder. "Easy!" He laughed. "Jealousy does not become you, my friend."

"Maybe one day you'll get yourself a wife, and then we'll see what you think of another man eyeing her up."

Alex shuddered theatrically. "Me, a wife? Never."

Leaving Jem at the front to keep watch, they slipped into the side alley. Seb and Alex climbed through the same window he and Georgie had used. Benedict caught her around the waist and hiked her up onto the barrel below the window. He meant to let her go, but the feel of her tiny waist beneath his hands turned his brain to mush. Driven purely by instinct, he tugged her forward, and when she planted her hands on his shoulders, he took advantage of her momentary imbalance to capture her mouth.

There was nothing sweet or chivalrous about his kiss. It was hard, brazen, lusty. An unmistakable statement of intent. After an instant of shock, she wrapped her slim arms around his neck and kissed him back greedily, as if she couldn't get enough of him. His legs almost buckled. He craved her, when he'd never craved anyone or anything before. "Georgie," he groaned. "You're killing me."

Her mouth pressed eagerly to his, warm and delicious.

A laughing cough came from inside the warehouse. "Are you two coming, or shall Alex and I do this on our own?"

He pulled away reluctantly, his legs unsteady and his heart pounding in his chest. "In you go." She turned on the barrel—which just positioned her delectable arse tantalizingly close to his face. Pure torture. *Later*, he promised himself. When all this was done, he'd take her back to the Tricorn and make love to her for hours. Days. Weeks.

The warehouse smelled of sawdust and tar, turpentine—and the unmistakable tang of fresh gunpowder. Benedict frowned. He shouldn't be able to smell that. There was no way the barrels he'd dampened could have dried out in just a few days. He strode across to the stack and flicked back the oilcloth. "Bollocks."

Alex materialized out of the shadows, silent as a cat. "What is it?"

"Johnstone's taken a new delivery of gunpowder. I ruined the last lot."

"Good thing none of us smokes, then, isn't it?" Seb added dryly.

They unlatched the double doors at the far end of the warehouse and slid them aside to reveal a slanted wooden slipway that disappeared into the dark water. The tide was fully up, lapping hungrily only a few feet from the top of the ramp. Intermittent moonlight glimmered on the murky water as the boats moored along the sides of the small harbor creaked and rocked on their ropes.

Georgie came to stand beside him. "We have a problem. The hull still hasn't been sealed with tar. It'll float, but the gaps between the planks will let in water."

"How much water?"

"I don't know."

"Well, Johnstone was obviously going to risk it. Let's get it in there and see if it sinks."

Benedict took hold of one of the mooring ropes attached to the boat's hull while Alex and Seb kicked away the wooden chocks that had prevented it from running along the metal launch rails. With a wooden groan of protest, the small vessel started to move, sliding down the angled slipway exactly as it had been designed to do, gathering speed until it entered the opaque brown water with a splash.

All four of them stood and looked at it.

"It floats," Alex said.

"I feel like we should give it a name," Seb added. "All ships need a name, don't they?"

Benedict smiled. "The *Georgiana*." He tugged on the rope so the vessel floated parallel to the ramp and clasped Georgie's hand. "Care to hop aboard, Mrs. Wylde?" When she nodded, he picked her up as if she were weightless and deposited her on the rocking deck. She crawled over to the hatch and peered down into the dark interior. "I can't see anything. Can you pass me a lantern?"

Alex produced a tinder box from his pocket and lit one of the paraffin lamps on the workbench.

"There's a slow leak," she confirmed, "but we should make it to Woolwich without sinking." She handed the lantern back to Ben, who extinguished it.

A sudden flurry of movement had them all glancing toward the side window. Jem dropped through the casement and landed in a scruffy heap on the floor. "Time's up, gents," he wheezed. "Johnstone's 'ere. Look sharp!"

Benedict beckoned him over. "Quick! Get into the sub."

The boy shied away. "No chance. I'm like a cat, me. I 'ates the water."

Judging from the layers of grime on his face, that statement was probably true. The boy looked like he even avoided washing with the stuff.

"Can't you swim?"

"No."

Ben sighed. "Well, hide yourself somewhere, then, quickly." He secured the rope to a metal cleat on the ramp and glanced up at Georgie. "You, get inside and stay down until we've dealt with Johnstone."

Chapter 40.

Georgie's heart was hammering in alarm, but she did as she was told. She dropped through the narrow opening and landed in the shallow puddle of water that had already seeped into the boat. Unable to bear not knowing what was happening, she peered out through the tiny circular porthole at the front of the funnel.

Alex took up position by the front window. Benedict and Jem hid behind a workbench, and Seb ducked behind a pile of lumber near the stack of barrels. Footsteps crunched outside and Seb tilted his head in silent warning. To Georgie's shock, all three of the men withdrew pistols from their clothing and exchanged nods of anticipation. Her heart lodged in her throat.

After an agonizing wait, a key scraped in the lock and the door to the warehouse swung open. Four men stepped through the narrow doorway, one holding a lantern aloft to light the way. There was a moment of ominous silence as they registered that the submarine had been launched, then murmurs of outraged disbelief.

The foremost man, a hulking figure with bushy ginger sideburns—presumably the elusive Tom Johnstone—bellowed. "O'Meara? You in 'ere?"

All four of the men peered around suspiciously. As one, they reached into their clothing and produced weapons: two pistols, two knives.

"I'm afraid not," Alex drawled. He stood, his pistol aimed at the nearest man. "You'll just have to make do with us."

All four swiveled toward him, and Georgie let out an involuntary cry as a cacophony of shots rang out, seemingly from every direction. Shouts and howls echoed around the walls as the flash of muzzle fire and puffs of smoke added to the general confusion.

She could barely see anything in the shadowy darkness, but caught a glimpse of Benedict throwing down his spent pistol and launching himself at Johnstone, just as Alex pounced on another man. The four of them started punching and wrestling viciously, like the sailors she'd seen once outside a tavern in Blackwall, brawling over a tart.

She gasped as a knife blade glinted in the moonlight. The awful scuffle of grunts and thuds, the sickening sound of fists hitting flesh, made her stomach churn.

One of the men had fallen to the floor and lay ominously still, sprawled in a pile of sawdust and wood shavings. Another had dived for cover behind a stacked pile of wood, but he'd hardly crawled there when Seb loomed out of the darkness and dealt him a vicious kick to the ribs then hauled him up by the collar and punched him across the jaw. The man slumped down just as Benedict threw Johnstone against one of the workbenches with an almighty crash of metal and wood. Johnstone shouted in pain and renewed his attack, and it was then that Georgie noticed the flames.

The lamp had shattered as the first man hit the ground,

and now the acrid scent of burning filled her nose. A wicked streak of flame snaked along the trickle of paraffin on the floor and set alight a bucket and paint brushes covered in tar. The whole thing caught with a wicked *whoosh*!

Seb rushed forward, scooped up the pail, and tossed it into the water next to the sub, but the burning paraffin had splashed liberally in several other places. Flames leapt, eagerly finding fuel in the wood shavings, oil cloth, and hemp ropes scattered around. Soon smoke, thick and black, began to fill the space, and Georgie poked her head out from the submarine in panic. "Get out of there!" she shrieked. "The gunpowder!"

Jem broke cover from behind one of the benches and darted toward the gangway, his fear of the flames apparently overcoming his dislike of the water. Georgie hauled herself out onto the deck and tried to maneuver the vessel closer to the side so the boy could climb aboard. She reached out her hand to help him just as the boat shifted away on the skittish tide.

Jem teetered on the edge of the sloping boards. He took a desperate leap toward the front of the boat but missed her outstretched hand. His fingers clawed the front of the deck, but there was nothing for him to hold on to, and with a strangled shriek, he fell into the water. Georgie threw herself flat on her stomach and reached out over the water as far as she could, trying to grab him as he splashed about. For a moment she thought she could get him, but then his head disappeared beneath the muddy water.

"Jem!" she screamed.

He surfaced a few feet from the side of the boat, and she caught sight of his face, white with terror. His arms clawed upward as if he were climbing an invisible ladder, and his mouth opened in a silent scream. Georgie stood, about to leap into the water, when Seb appeared from the smoky warehouse.

"Help him! He can't swim!"

Seb saw Jem flailing and leapt into the water, but as soon as he got near Jem, the boy threw his arms around his neck and they both went under. Seb pushed the grasping hands away and dealt him a sharp blow across the face, and before Jem could react, he grabbed him by the collar and started towing him toward the dockside.

"Kick your legs," he ordered harshly.

Georgie let out a sob of relief as Seb managed to drag the flailing boy to the set of wooden steps and haul him out of the water, coughing and spluttering.

Jem's mishap had distracted her from the commotion in the warehouse. She turned, searching frantically for Benedict through the choking smoke that was now billowing out of the double doors.

"Get going!" Seb shouted. He raced down the side of the wharf to the wooden gates that opened out onto the main body of the river and started turning the handle. The iron cogs groaned against the press of the incoming tide, but the gates gradually opened and a swirl of brown water swept in, making the little vessel pitch and toss.

Georgie grabbed the knife in her boot and hacked through the rope that restrained the sub. She saw Alex drop through the side window of the warehouse and stagger down the alley, and then Benedict lumbered onto the gangway.

The sub had already floated to the middle of the dock, out of reach, drawn by the irresistible pull of the tide. Benedict shook his head and sent her a teasing smile across the eddying water that separated them. He cupped his hands around his mouth. "Where do you think you're going?"

Before she could tell him that she had no way of

steering the vessel any closer, he stripped off his jacket, tossed it aside, and waded down the jetty into the water. "Bloody hell, that's cold!"

"What are you doing, you imbecile?" she screeched.

He ignored her, and when the water was up to his thighs, he launched himself forward and began to swim toward her with strong, athletic strokes. When he reached the side of the vessel, he caught the dangling end of rope and hauled himself up. Georgie grabbed the back of his breeches and tugged until he landed, panting and sodden, on the deck. His formidable build seemed to take up most of the available space.

He rolled over onto his back and let out a breathless groan that was half laugh, half pain. "No adventures without me, Mrs. Wylde. Is that understood?"

She sent him a chiding frown for doing something so risky.

"Now, how do we sail this thing?"

Georgie sprang into action. She raised the sail and swung the boom around so the cloth caught the breeze, then took the tiller and turned the bow so they faced the open water gate. She glanced up at Benedict, who had risen to his feet and was looking back at the burning warehouse with a satisfied expression.

"Where's Johnstone?" she asked uneasily. "Is he still in there?"

Benedict's jaw hardened. "I don't know. Shadwell and Daws are both dead, but Johnstone managed to slip away. I don't know what happened to Finnegan."

As if in answer to that, a hulking figure emerged from the rear doors of the smoking warehouse. In the blink of an eye, Georgie saw him raise a rifle to his shoulder and aim it directly at her chest. She choked out a cry of alarm at the same moment Benedict threw himself in front of her. The gun discharged with a crack. Benedict's staggering weight almost pitched them both over the side, and he gave a grunted curse as they fell to their knees on the deck. When he pulled back, a red bloom was seeping through the white of his shirt, near his shoulder.

"Benedict, you've been shot!"

He clapped his hand to his arm and glanced furiously back at the warehouse. "It's nothing. I'm fine." He pushed down hard on the back of her head. "Keep down."

The gunman, Finnegan, had managed to reload. Georgie saw Seb sprinting back along the dock to intercept him, but Finnegan lowered his head and aimed again. The crack of another shot echoed over the water and she ducked instinctively, but it pinged against the side of the ship with a spray of wooden splinters. Seb leapt toward Finnegan and took him to the ground just as series of mighty explosions tore through the warehouse.

Windows shattered, and an enormous fireball billowed into the sky as the gunpowder barrels exploded in a chain reaction of sound. Georgie felt a flash of heat against her face and then debris rained down, splashing into the water all around them. For some bizarre reason, all she could think of was the story of Guy Fawkes and his plot to blow up the Houses of Parliament.

"Seb!" Benedict bellowed, shielding his eyes with his hands. He scanned the ground around the burning building, and his shoulders dropped in relief when his friend crawled out from beneath a fallen advertising placard and sent them a shaky wave.

Seb stood, tried to brush the dust and debris from his coat, then gave up with an expression of acute irritation. "That's another coat ruined!" he yelled across to them. "It was a Weston too. You can damn well buy me a new one, Wylde!"

Benedict gave an amused chuckle. "Fair enough," he shouted back.

Georgie scanned the rest of the dock and saw Alex and Jem huddled together a safe distance away, on the street near the coffee tavern. With a breathy prayer of thanks, she turned away from the confusion and grabbed the tiller. They still had work to do.

She steered them through the water gate—the wooden boards were slimy and green with algae as they slid past—and the river caught them in its flow.

Chapter 41.

Georgie bit her lip in concentration and maneuvered them into the center of the river, grateful there were so few other vessels around at this hour of the night. The muddy, earthy smell of the Thames surrounded them and she shuddered as rank, rotting things probably best left unidentified swirled past in the eddying current.

It was choppier out here. The hull rocked with the slap of waves on the side, and strange clanking, slurping noises echoed from belowdecks. The wind raised goose bumps on her arms, and she found she was shivering both from the chill and delayed reaction.

Benedict thrust his head down into the hull and came up frowning. "Looks like we're taking on a lot of water. How far to Woolwich?"

"About six miles."

"It's going to be a close-run thing."

They gained speed with the current. The warehouse fire was soon just a distant glow as they followed the curve of the river past the huge hulking shapes of warehouses and wharves. The moon provided just enough light to see.

As they slid around the sharpest bend, where the Thames doubled back on itself, the banks became more sparsely populated. Soon, they reached the near-uninhabited, marshy, windswept spit of land known as Blackwall Point, on the Isle of Dogs. Georgie shuddered as she caught sight of the gibbet—and the iron cage swinging eerily from its wooden gallows-like frame. The dark shape of a body slumped within the bars.

She'd seen this sight before, one summer when Father had taken her down the Thames all the way to Dartford and the sea. Any sailor entering London would pass this point, which made it the ideal spot to display a deterrent to any would-be pirates. For over four centuries, convicts had been hanged at Execution Dock in Wapping, their bodies coated in tar and then displayed on these gallows for the length of three tides before being cut down. Her eight-year-old self had shivered in delight at the grue-some story. Father had said it was a warning to always be honest in her business dealings.

Georgie gazed over the brackish pools, and her chest contracted painfully. The gibbet was a stark reminder of how close she'd come to losing the man she loved. He'd been shot, hadn't he? He'd said it wasn't serious, but what if the wound became infected? Men had died from less. Oh, God.

She should tell him how she felt.

She clapped her hand over her mouth to prevent a shaky sob, but it slipped out anyway.

Benedict glanced over, then stepped behind her and wrapped his arms around her, tugging her tight against his chest in an embrace that left her right arm free to steer. His soaking clothes wet her own immediately, but she didn't care. The sensation was grounding. She melted back against him, took strength from the warmth of him seeping through the fabric, as if he were transferring some of his bravery, his vitality to her.

He pressed a kiss to the top of her head. "It's all right. It's over now. Breathe."

Georgie let out a slow *whoosh* of breath, then sucked air in, loving the feel of his strong arms around her. Her shivers calmed. She wished they could stay like this forever, just keep on sailing, down the river, across the sea. But the little ship was sinking lower and lower with every passing minute. They'd be lucky to make it to Woolwich, let alone anywhere farther afield.

She glanced down at the water; she did *not* want to go in there. It looked dark and terrifying, the current too strong to withstand. Pieter had taught her how to swim, but the still, flat waters of the lake at home bore no resemblance to this choppy, angrily swirling tide.

After a few more minutes the buildings returned, and they reached Blackwall dockyards. This part of the river was more familiar. Georgie made out the dark rectangle of the Caversteed warehouse among the bobbing forest of masts. A rogue wave splashed over the deck.

"Is there a bucket to bail?" she asked.

"No." Benedict glanced mournfully down at his wet footwear. "I could use my boots, I suppose." He sighed, as if in pain. "Hoby made these, you know. They cost two pounds and sixpence. They were just getting comfortable."

"I'll buy you another pair."

They navigated one final twist of the river, and she angled them closer to the southern bank. "We should be nearly there." She squinted into the darkness and pointed. "There! That must be it. The naval dockyards."

A lone sentry was guarding a series of wooden barriers, behind which a cluster of large ships bobbed at anchor. He was slumped half-asleep on a stool by the small hut, but he jolted awake and snapped to attention when Benedict hailed him.

"Ahoy there! Open the gate. Admiral Cockburn's expecting us!"

The guard sent their vessel—of which only a few feet was now visible above the waves—a curious look but did as he was told. They slid into the calmer waters of the dock pool and pulled up to the side in the shadowy space between two huge navy frigates. Benedict leapt ashore and secured the mooring rope, then grabbed Georgie's raised arms and hauled her up to stand beside him on the dock.

"Dry land. Thank God!" He laughed, and to Georgie's complete astonishment, he dropped his head back and let out a shout of pure elation, like a lunatic, a wild "Wahooo!" of victory. An answering smile curved her mouth as a ball of joy and relief filled her chest.

He turned to her, breathing hard. "We did it, Georgie girl!"

Water streamed down his face in rivulets, and his shirt clung to him, almost transparent in the moonlight. With a grin of triumph, he lifted her up on tiptoe against him, hard against his chest. His kiss was savage, joyous, and Georgie responded in kind. Her legs went weak, and she clung to him like a barnacle as their tongues tangled and danced. A wild, exultant fever warmed her blood, and her head started to spin.

Benedict drew back, panting, his eyes glittering in the darkness, and Georgie opened her mouth to tell him exactly how she felt about him. "Benedict, I—"

The sound of approaching footsteps interrupted her admission of love.

"Wylde! You've brought me my submarine. Good man!"

Admiral Sir George Cockburn strode along the shadowed wharf. Benedict saluted the older man, and when he lowered his arm, the admiral caught his hand and shook it enthusiastically. He turned to Georgie and did the same to her. "And with the help of this young fellow. Well done lad, you've done a fine job here tonight. You have the Admiralty's deepest thanks."

Georgie had lost her cap somewhere along the way, but her hair was still tied back in a low sailor's pigtail. She kept her head down, praying that the admiral wouldn't recognize her.

Benedict indicated the sinking vessel. "You may need to drain it out."

The admiral shrugged. "A bilge pump will sort that. What matters is that we've stopped that blackguard Johnstone from carrying out his dastardly plan. Exceptional work, fellows. Invaluable service. Rest assured, I shall be recommending both of you to His Royal Highness for a reward." He turned to Georgie. "What's your name, lad?"

Georgie groaned inwardly and tried to pitch her voice an octave lower than normal. "Um, George?"

Her wobbly baritone didn't fool the admiral for a moment. He gasped at Benedict in shock. "Is that a *girl*?"

Since further subterfuge was impossible, Benedict stepped forward and made the introductions. "It is indeed. Admiral Cockburn, may I present Miss Georgiana Caversteed, owner of Caversteed Shipping."

Curtseying would have been ridiculous, given her attire, so Georgie straightened, met the admiral's eye, and inclined her head in greeting.

"Good Lord. Well, I never," the admiral blustered. "What is the meaning of this?"

Benedict was unfazed. "I asked Miss Caversteed to accompany me. She has an exceptional grasp of all things maritime, as I believe tonight's success has demonstrated. I had complete faith she could accomplish the mission."

Her heart swelled with pride at his praise.

"Most irregular, sir," the admiral muttered. He sent Georgie a paternal glare, his white whiskers twitching. "Does your mother know you're gallivantin' all over town dressed as a powder monkey, my girl?"

She opened her mouth to answer, but Benedict spoke first. "If I might have a word?" He sent her a wicked, conspiratorial look, and she just *knew* he was about to do something scandalous.

"I should tell you, sir, that Miss Caversteed has done me the very great honor of agreeing to become my wife. I trust I can rely on your discretion?"

Georgie's gasp was drowned out by the admiral's jovial chuckle. "Married, eh? Well, congratulations, Wylde. Capital." He pumped Benedict's hand again.

Georgie stifled a snort. Discretion? She didn't believe for one moment that the admiral could keep such momentous news to himself. He wouldn't be able to resist telling his wife, and Clara Cockburn was the worst gossip in London. The news would be all over the *ton* by breakfast. Benedict might as well have taken out a full-page announcement in *The Times*.

The admiral nodded. "You look as if you could do with a change of clothes, Wylde. There are some spare uniforms in the mess if you'd care to use them." He indicated a series of dark buildings behind them. "And no doubt you're keen to get the lady home. I'll arrange for a carriage for you." He turned and strode down the dock.

Georgie lost no time in rounding on Benedict. "Why did you go and tell him that? Now there's bound to be a dreadful scandal."

He gave an infuriating shrug. "There'll be a scandal

whatever happens. It's your fault. You were the one who insisted on an adventure."

She was about to berate him some more when he shifted into the light and she caught sight of his shirt-sleeve. It was stained pink with blood. "Oh! I forgot. You're hurt!" She reached for him, but he stepped away from her questing hands. He tugged the neck of his shirt off his shoulder and inspected the damage.

"It's nothing, look. Just a graze. Not even a through-and-through."

It was as he said. The bullet had gouged a deep furrow on the outside edge of his bicep. The torn flesh was ugly, still seeping blood, but it was better than Georgie had feared. "Well, you still need to clean it out and bandage it," she said. "That river water is revolting. It could easily become infected."

He untied the neckerchief from around his throat and handed it to her. "You do it. I can't with one hand."

Her fingers shook as she secured the square of linen tightly around his upper arm. The touch of his skin made her shiver. On impulse, she slid her hand over his collarbone and then flattened her palm over his heart. His pulse beat, strong and steady beneath her fingers, and she bit back a sudden sob of relief. "You took a bullet meant for me!"

He frowned down at her and gave a dismissive shrug, as if embarrassed. "I would have done the same for Alex. Or Seb."

"You could have died," she persisted, her voice a little quivery.

"Jesus. Come here." He enfolded her in his arms, and it felt like the most natural thing in the world. Her throat closed and tears stung her eyes. She buried her face in the curve of his neck, trying to hide the damnable weakness, but he wouldn't allow it. He caught her face in his palms and turned it up. He kissed her eyelids, her cheeks, her temple. His hold on her was so tight, it was almost painful, as if he was trying to absorb her pain into himself, her tears.

After a moment he leaned back, and his expression was as serious as she'd ever seen it. "I would die for you," he said simply. "Don't you know that by now?"

It took her slow brain a moment to assimilate his words. "Wh-what?" She blinked. "What did you say?"

"I would die for you," he repeated. "There's only a few people I can say that about in this world, but you're one of them, Georgiana Wylde. I love you." He pressed a reverent kiss to her lips. "I don't expect you to do anything about it," he added quickly. "We can still keep to our agreement. You can leave me whenever you want. I just thought you should know, that's all."

Joy exploded in her heart, and elation made her breathless. "I love *you*," she breathed, and felt him jerk against her. He stared at her, stupefied, as if he couldn't believe his ears. Then, he closed his eyes as if in torment.

"You can't," he said brokenly. "That would be stupid. And you're not a stupid woman. You're a woman who can run a shipping empire, calculate interest payments, haggle for silk. You're far too clever to love someone like me."

"I love you," she said stoutly. "And there's nothing you can do about it."

He raked a hand through his dripping hair and groaned. "We cannot possibly be together. Don't you see? God, I hate your damned money!"

He let her go abruptly, turned on his heel and paced away, then pivoted and strode back to her, his expression thunderous. "How can I possibly prove that it's you that I want? I can't ask you to give it all away, just so I can stay with you without it. The only way we could reasonably be together would be if I had the same fortune as you. There would be equality. But that will never happen. I'll never have a fortune like yours."

Georgie wrapped her arms around her body, missing his touch. "You're thinking about this all wrong." Her eyes were brimming with tears, but she gave him a watery smile. "Just for a moment, imagine what it would be like if our places were reversed. If *you* were the one with an embarrassing amount of money. What if you knew, in your heart, that you loved me? Wouldn't you want to share everything you had with me? Wouldn't you want to share your body, your life—everything it entailed—with me?"

She gained confidence as she spoke. The words tumbled straight from her heart; she was certain of their rightness. He faced her, chest heaving, fists clenched at his side. But at least he was listening.

"Think of our marriage vows," she said. "Neither of us really meant them when we said them—I barely paid attention—but the answer was right there." Her voice was reedy, choked with emotion, but she soldiered on, desperate to make him understand, terrified of losing him.

"For richer or poorer. In sickness and in health. You'd stay with me if I were poor and sick, Benedict, I know you would. So, why won't you stay with me when I'm healthy and rich?" She shook her head. "It's illogical. And besides which, it's too late." She crossed her arms over her chest. "We're married, for better or for worse, so it's just something you're going to have to get used to. I refuse to let you leave me now, after all this."

Chapter 42.

Benedict studied the woman in front of him and felt as though his chest would crack open, his heart was beating so hard. Her cap had come off somewhere during their adventures and her furious diatribe had left her with flushed cheeks and flashing eyes.

"I love you. You love me," she said crossly. "I fail to see the problem."

A droplet of water slid down the side of her nose and down to the corner of her mouth, and he wanted to lick it away but he made one last-ditch effort to dissuade her. She could do so much better than him—a penniless rogue. "Men are supposed to provide for their women. That's the way society works. You should marry a man with a fortune equal to your own."

She made an inelegant snort through her nose. "Oh, stuff and nonsense. This is the modern age, Benedict. The world is changing." She saw he was about to argue and raised her hand. "I agree that marrying *only* for money, with no other sort of compatibility, is a huge mistake."

She had that right. His own parents were a case in point. His father might have supported his mother financially, but he hadn't provided for her emotionally. He hadn't loved and cherished her. He'd never been there for her through life's ups and downs.

Georgie's expression was an adorable mixture of frustration and pleading. "I don't need you to provide for me financially. I need you to *love* me. I need you to love me so much that you can overlook the ridiculous amount of money I have and accept that it's just part and parcel of who I am. Can you do that? Please."

It was the "please" that broke him; Benedict almost fell to his knees. She didn't have to beg him for anything. He was hers, body and soul. Happiness, acceptance, trickled through him, melting his resistance like a spring thaw.

"I suppose I must," he said, trying to joke, but his voice broke halfway through, giving him away. "Because I really can't imagine living without you."

Her smile was the sweetest thing he'd ever seen. She slanted him a teasing, haughty glance from beneath her lashes. "You do realize that you've never actually proposed to me, don't you?"

He frowned. "You're right."

He sank to his knees, there on the grass, and watched her brows lift in surprise. It struck him that he was no better than poor, besotted Simeon Pettigrew, standing outside in the rain. Here he was, wet and wounded, offering himself, lacking even fancy clothes or clever words.

He took her hand in his. "It will come as no surprise that I have no expectation of a sudden inheritance of a gold mine," he said gruffly. "Or even any army pension. I still have a bundle of debts. My profits from the Tricorn Club are being used to recover the family estate. That said, please take this as a formal request: Georgiana

Caversteed Wylde, would you please do me the immense honor of becoming my wife? Again. Forever."

Her eyes sparkled. "Yes."

He stood and pulled her in for a kiss so sweet, so full of promise and longing, that it took his breath away. Every one of his senses reached out to her and became entangled. Her skin, her hair, her lips. When they pulled apart, he shook his head, incredulous, almost afraid to trust the happiness blooming inside him. "I can't wait to be able to call you my wife in public, not just in my head," he growled. "I'm sick of having to sneak around. I want everyone to know you're mine."

Her breath came out in a rush. "Yes."

"Come back to the Tricorn with me. Let me love you."

Her satisfied sigh was all he'd ever wanted to hear. "Yes. Oh, yes. Please."

Chapter 43.

It was almost three in the morning, and as physically exhausted as she was, Georgie was too excited to sleep. Benedict held her close in the carriage as they crossed a near-deserted London. She rested her head on his shoulder as they rattled along, her heart singing with happiness. He'd availed himself of the dry clothes the admiral had offered, found some linen to bandage his wound, and now they huddled together under a thick woolen cloak.

When they arrived at the Tricorn, it was to find Mickey the doorman still awake, despite the ungodly hour.

"Alex and Seb made it back all right?" Benedict asked him quietly.

"Aye, sir. And that scamp Jem Barnes is dossing down in the front room. Seb said you might've been winged in the arm?" He shot Benedict a concerned glance.

"It's nothing serious, Mickey. No need to summon the sawbones just yet."

The manservant gave a relieved grunt. "Right. I've

kept the fire going in the kitchen. I'll bring you up a pitcher of warm water in a minute."

Benedict murmured his thanks and ushered Georgie up the stairs. As soon as they entered the apartment, she swung around and adopted a brisk, no-nonsense tone. "Let's clean off that wound, shall we? I don't want you to catch a fever and die, Wylde. Not now you've just started to be sensible. Take off your shirt."

His smile was thoroughly depraved. "I don't think I will ever tire of hearing those words come out of your mouth, Mrs. Wylde."

Without even giving her time to brace herself, he stripped off his shirt and stood there in just a pair of buff breeches and his top boots. Her mouth went dry and her insides knotted. The man really did have the most splendid physique. Mickey's arrival with a jug of hot water, clean linen bandages, and a bottle of brandy, prevented her from leaping upon her husband and ravishing him on the spot.

"Thought you might need these," the servant rumbled.

"'Night." He closed the door quietly behind him.

Benedict took a swig from the bottle and handed it to her. "Do your worst, then, woman."

She moistened a handkerchief liberally with the brandy.

"Easy!" he protested. "That's France's best Armagnac you have there."

She slanted him a prim look. "Imported foreign spirits are illegal in this country, Mr. Wylde."

He winked. "I may have stumbled across a few barrels of unclaimed contraband while infiltrating that smuggling gang." He washed the wound, turning the water in the bowl pink, then hissed in through his teeth as she pressed the liquor-soaked pad to his flesh. Georgie winced in sympathy. It must sting like the devil.

He looked down as she tied a clean bandage around the wound. "Kiss me. I need distraction from the pain."

She was more than happy to oblige. The nearness of him, the scent of all that smooth, bronzed skin was just too tempting.

He tasted of brandy and heat. His tongue slid against hers in a steady, sinuous rhythm she felt in her breasts and her stomach, between her legs. She smoothed her hands over the muscled expanse of his shoulders, loving the feel of him, the power, but pulled back when her fingers ran over the puckered patch of scar tissue just above his clavicle.

"I took a bullet at Salamanca," he said softly. "French sniper. I was lucky; it came right out the back." He guided her hand behind him, and she felt a corresponding ridge where the bullet had exited his body. "Didn't even touch the bone."

Georgie shuddered, and her stomach pitched weightlessly. The scar was so close to the throbbing pulse of his neck. It could so easily have been fatal. She bent and kissed the damaged skin, and his long body shivered in reaction. His hands went to the tie at the front of her boyish shirt and he pulled on the strings. It opened in a deep *V*, and she raised her arms to help him as he lifted it over her head and threw it aside.

She understood this time, knew exactly where it would lead. And she welcomed it. She wanted it all—the darkness, the passion, the heat. Him.

Her linen shift was tucked into her breeches and her heart thudded against her ribs as he tugged her forward by the waistband. The back of his hand slipped against her stomach as he undid the buttons at the fall.

"These damn things have been driving me mad all night," he growled.

She toed off her boots and stockings, removed the

breeches and her shift, and heard him draw in a deep breath when she stood naked in front of him. The look in his eyes made heat curl low in her belly.

He caught her and kissed her, holding nothing back, and she felt as if she'd been burned, scalded by his kiss, his strong body, and his big hands. He opened his mouth against her, tasting the corner of her lips with his tongue and then plunging deep inside. She threaded her hands through his hair and felt his fingers encircle her wrists. He didn't push her away; instead, he tightened his grip and held her in place, a thrilling, willing bondage.

Georgie quivered all the way to her bones. Lust dragged her down like a whirlpool, an undertow impossible to resist. She didn't even want to come up for air. She lost herself in him, inhaled his scent, drew him into her lungs, into her heart.

With staggering steps, they made it to the bedroom. She knelt before him as he sat on the edge of the bed and helped him remove his wet boots. He made quick work of his breeches and lay back, gloriously naked, and Georgie couldn't contain a breathless laugh of triumph. *Hers.*

She put her knee on the bed and prowled up his body, and for a while he was content to let her explore. She trailed her hand down, over the marvelous bumps and ridges of his chest and abdomen, down to the intriguing line of hair that started at his belly button and speared, like a wicked arrow, straight to his thoroughly aroused shaft.

Georgie swallowed, suddenly overcome by nerves. She hadn't seen this part of him the last time.

His eyes glowed. "Touch me."

She'd wanted to do this ever since she'd felt him through his breeches in the submarine. Gently, she wrapped her hand around him and gasped as he pulsed under her palm. He was shockingly warm, his skin soft with a layer of rigid muscle beneath. She stroked experimentally, and he groaned and arched up into her hand. "Do you like this?" she teased.

"Yes!"

"I love this sleepy, sulky look you get," she said. "It must be whenever you're thinking of *this*. It makes me all hot and muddled."

She bent and put her mouth on him. He hissed a breath between his teeth, as he'd done when she'd touched his wound with the brandy, but feminine instinct told her this was in pleasure, not pain. She flicked her tongue. Her senses reeled at the incredible feel of him, his taste. He filled her senses. There was only him, only delight.

"That's enough," Benedict groaned. "No doubt a courtly swain would let you have your wicked way with him all night, but a scoundrel like myself can only take so much." In a lightning move, he reversed their positions so she lay beneath him on the bed. He sent her an insolent pirate's leer, once again her beloved prisoner from Newgate. "Now, I have you in my clutches, Mrs. Wylde." He curled her hair around his fist and dragged it to his nose. "I know you, wife. I know your scent. The way you move. You're mine."

Georgie shivered.

"Let's see how much torture you can stand." He stroked her, from her throat, down the center of her body between her breasts, and back up. "I love your body's reaction to me. Your skin flushes, your nipples tighten to little peaks." He brushed his fingers over them to underscore his point, and Georgie gasped at the sensation. Jolts of lightning shot through her. He chuckled. "Your breath is coming in pants, Mrs. Wylde. Should I infer that you like this?"

Georgie arched up into his touch, and he took pity

on her and cupped her breasts. She moaned. His hands molded to the contours of her skin like water, a perfect fit. He leaned over and paused with his mouth suspended over her, one taut peak inches from his mouth. At the last moment he made a detour and traced the soft underside curve of her breast with his tongue instead.

"I surrender!" Georgie panted. "You win. Stop teasing."

His chuckle vibrated against her skin. She caught his hair and pulled him up to her breast, and he captured one nipple in his mouth. She let out a ragged sigh.

"I suspect you like this too," he whispered, and his hand slid down her stomach and over the springy hair below. He stroked between her legs, found the telltale slippery wetness, and groaned. "I want to be inside you."

"Yes!" Georgie gasped. "Now."

"Now," he echoed hoarsely.

He lowered himself over her, and she felt his hand at her inner thigh, guiding himself to her. He took her mouth at the same moment he slid into her, one sure, deep thrust, and he caught her soft moan of pleasure on his tongue. It was a shock, a revelation, a miraculous filling and stretching. He stilled, fully inside her, and looked deep into her eyes. Georgie felt the connection right down to her soul.

He was buried deep, hard and hot. And then he started to move, and she arched her back and caught the rhythm. Soon, she was trembling, lost in that dark, wicked place where there were no words, only sensations. He increased the pace, deeper, harder, until she was straining for more, gasping his name. She hovered on the peak of agony for what seemed like forever, and then she hurtled over the edge, and it was like Guy Fawkes and his gunpowder again—only this was her own personal detonation. Blistering. Earth-shattering. All-consuming.

He let out a soul-deep groan, and his entire body went

rigid over hers. Instead of pulling out of her, she felt him pulsing deep within her in his own blissful release. He collapsed onto her chest, then rolled them both to the side and lay breathing hard, great gusts of his chest, as her own heart hammered and pleasure liquefied her limbs.

"Say it again," she panted. "What you said at Woolwich."

He stroked her hair away from her temple. "What? That I love you? Yes." He pressed a kiss to the end of her nose. "My love. My life. Stay with me. Always."

"Always," she breathed.

Chapter 44.

She awoke in his arms, with the light of morning hardening on the wall, and sat up in a flurry of sheets. The clock on the mantel showed almost eight o'clock.

"Oh, goodness, I have to go home and tell Mother we're engaged before she hears it from somebody else. Admiral Cockburn's wife will make it the talk of the town by lunchtime."

Benedict's sleepy chuckle warmed her heart. "Would you like me to come with you? We could speak to her together."

Georgie shook her head. "No, it's all right. I'll talk to her on my own first. You can come over for tea this afternoon. She should be over the shock by then."

He tugged her back into his arms and kissed her thoroughly. "All right." He left the bed and strode, unashamedly naked, over to a mahogany dressing chest, giving Georgie a wonderful view of his long back and firm buttocks. He opened the doors to reveal three sliding drawers below a space for hanging garments and selected a clean shirt for her to wear. It was too big, but it smelled of him.

Georgie grimaced as she pulled on the grimy breeches from the previous day. She couldn't wait to have a bath. She padded over to join him and a forest-green garment caught her attention. "Is that your uniform?"

He stroked the jacket's sleeve affectionately. "Yes. The Rifles."

"Why isn't it red, like the rest of the army?"

"The Rifles are sharpshooters. Snipers and skirmishers. We're supposed to blend in. You have to admit that red is a ridiculous color for a soldier. It makes the perfect target." He leaned over and reached inside a cut glass bowl, apparently searching for something. A muddle of assorted items swirled around haphazardly, and Georgie gasped as she caught sight of his campaign medals lying carelessly amongst the cufflinks and penknives.

"Why don't you ever wear your medals?"

He let out a tired sigh. "Because I don't deserve them."

"What? Of course you do! You were at those battles, were you not?"

"Yes."

"Then why—?"

He stared at the bowl as if struggling to find the words. "I suppose I still feel guilty, for making it through the war almost unscathed when so many of my friends didn't. I didn't earn those medals for anything other than staying alive. I couldn't control whether a bullet hit me or the man next to me. I couldn't change the trajectory of a shell. It was more dumb luck than skill."

Georgie's chest contracted at the pain in his voice.

He glanced over at her and met her eyes. "That's why I work for Bow Street now. If I can foil plots like that one yesterday, maybe *then* I'll have done something actually worthy of a mention in dispatches."

She wound her arms around him and hugged him tight. "Well, you're *my* hero, Benedict Wylde, whatever medals you've earned. And we should both be extremely proud of what we achieved yesterday. Think of the trouble Napoleon could stir up if he ever escaped St. Helena."

He grunted in grudging agreement. "Ah, here we go." He hooked a familiar chain from amid the clutter, and Georgie saw it was her wedding band—which had been joined by his plain gold ring. The last time she'd seen that, she realized, was at Newgate; she'd assumed he'd pawned it or sold it.

He uncoupled the clasp of the chain and slid both rings free, then took her left hand and solemnly slid hers onto her fourth finger. Her heart glowed with pride and love.

She winced when his fingers touched her palm, however, and he frowned as he turned her hand over and noticed the skin was red and torn from handling the submarine. "You idiot," he chided softly. "Why didn't you tell me you were hurt?"

Georgie shrugged. "I truly didn't notice at the time."

He pressed his lips to the tender skin on the center of each palm, then straightened and kissed her mouth. "God, the next month is going to be torture. We'll have to wait three whole weeks for the banns to be read, and we'll be under the eagle eye of the *ton* the entire time. I'll actually have to behave myself."

She chuckled, and he looked into her face with a wry smile and a shake of his tousled head. "I still can't believe you want to be married to me. Are you sure you know what you're doing? What if I turn out to be a terrible husband? I don't have the first clue how to be happily married. My own parents barely spoke to one another. They ended up living apart for almost twenty years."

"We are nothing like your parents, Benedict. I'm sure we'll figure it out."

He tilted his head as another thought struck him. "I still need to introduce you to my brother, John. He'd have been a far better choice for you, you know. He's the earl. He's solid. Dependable. Steadfast. He can run an estate. Organize tenants. He doesn't run around getting himself thrown into prison."

Georgie shook her head. "You're a good man, Benedict Wylde. Despite what you might believe. It's you that I love." She sent him a teasing glance, determined to lighten the mood. "Do you think it's actually legal to marry the same man twice?"

"Of course. One wedding doesn't cancel out the other. That's not how it works. We'll just be doubly married." He bent and kissed her again. "Besides, I don't care. I'll marry you every week if that's what it takes to keep you happy." His expression clouded, and he glanced down at her warily. "You don't want to get married at St. George's, Hanover Square, do you?"

"No. The Caversteed family will provide the *ton* with quite enough entertainment with Juliet's wedding there. How do you feel about a small, select wedding at my home in Little Gidding?"

He let out a sigh of obvious relief, gave her another quick kiss, then swatted her playfully on the behind. "Perfect. Now, go and tell your mother."

"Mother, I have a confession to make."

Georgie, freshly bathed and dressed in a flattering morning gown of sprigged muslin, strode into the drawing room. Juliet and Simeon had gone for a drive in the park. Mother looked up from pouring the tea with a questioning look, her brows drawn together.

"Not another one. Really, Georgiana, I do think you should consider my poor nerves. I've come to live in *dread* of you saying things like that. What is it this time? Should I brace myself for the revelation that you're leaving us to join the circus? Becoming a clairvoyant?"

Georgie stifled a laugh at her mother's peeved sarcasm. "Cousin Josiah was blackmailing me."

"Blackmailing you? About what?"

"My husband. Josiah discovered the truth about him."

Mother sniffed. "Oh. Well that's hardly a surprise. I told you marrying a convict was a recipe for disaster, didn't I?"

"Yes. You did. But I didn't actually marry a convict. I married Benedict Wylde."

Mother appeared temporarily struck dumb—a miracle in itself. She opened and closed her mouth a few times then managed to croak, "Wylde? Morcott's brother? *That* Wylde?" She closed her eyes as if praying for strength, then sent Georgie the patented *what-did-I-do-to-deserve-this* glare. "Georgiana Caversteed. Well, I never."

"Since our first marriage was a secret, I'm going to marry him again," Georgie said. "I'd like to announce our engagement and have banns called as soon as possible."

Mother's teacup clattered in her saucer. "Good heavens above. Do you love him?"

"I do."

"And does he love you?"

"He does. And before you ask, yes, he's already signed the contract. I know for certain that he doesn't want my money."

Mother sank back on the chaise longue like a deflated balloon. "Well, then. Good gracious." She took a fortifying swig of tea, and her eyes grew suspiciously moist. "Would your father have approved of him, do you think?"

Georgie crossed the room and sank down next to her mother. She gave her a fond hug. "I'm sure of it. Mr. Wylde is everything he ever wanted for me. He is loyal and brave and decent."

"And penniless," Mother added forlornly. "And untitled."

"That too. But it's not as if we really need any more money, is it?"

Mother reached for one of the little iced cakes on the tea tray and sniffed. "I suppose not. And if this is what makes you happy, Georgiana, truly happy, then of course I don't object. It's all I ever wanted for you, you know. For you to be happy."

Georgie gave her another loving squeeze. "I know."

The next moment, Mother seemed to perk up as renewed energy flowed through her. Georgie recognized it with an inward smile as her *I-have-a-project* look.

"Who would have thought it?" She chuckled gleefully. "Both of my daughters to be married within the space of two months! I must get to work! Heavens above, what shall I *wear*?"

Chapter 45.

Predictably, the "confidential" news of their engagement had spread from Admiral Cockburn to his wife, Clara, and thence like wildfire through the *ton*. To Georgie's amusement, the announcement only served to increase her popularity. At every event she attended, she was besieged by gentlemen wanting to dance or perform menial tasks for her.

She finally sorted these men into two distinct camps. The first paid her attention because they were determined to find out what it was about her that had captured the attention of a man like Benedict Wylde, or to discern whether she was being hoodwinked by a fortune hunter.

The second group were those who still fancied themselves as potential suitors. They were praying for her to come to her senses and call off the engagement. Their attentions held a certain comical edge of desperation. Georgie could barely contain her laughter as Elton and Coster cracked heads when they both bent to retrieve her ostrich feather fan. Freddy Cadogan brought her continuous glasses of champagne. Five different men offered to show her various aspects of the gardens, fountains, shrubbery, and hanging lanterns. Even Sir Stanley Kenilworth renewed his efforts.

Benedict found it vastly amusing. "It's sadly predictable." He'd chuckled as he whirled Georgie around Lady Ashton's ballroom. "The fortune hunters sense that time is running out. They're trying to besiege you. A last-ditch effort, as we say in the army." He let out a sigh of mock-regret. "If only they knew you were already married. Just think of the broken hearts."

"Ha! There wouldn't be a broken heart among them. All they see when they look at me is the matched set of horses they'll buy at Tattersall's, or the brand-new racing curricle they'll order before the ink is even dry on the marriage register. None of them see *me*."

He sent her one of those looks that made her stomach flip. "*I* see you," he said softly. "I see a woman who is brave and headstrong and secretly rebellious. I see a woman who is witty and clever, and who doesn't go fainting all over the place or falling into hysterics at the drop of a hat."

Georgie felt heat climb into her cheeks at his sincere flattery. How far they'd come from the two strangers who had married in Newgate.

"You know, there are already bets in the Tricorn's betting book about the arrival of my son and heir in nine months' time," Benedict whispered. He laughed as her cheeks flamed even hotter.

"That is not the case!" she whispered back. Her monthly courses had arrived on schedule last week; Benedict's lapse in control had not resulted in a baby. Georgie had been surprised to find herself rather disappointed by that. "They'll lose their money."

He sent her his pirate's smile. "Ah, but that's assuming

I can keep my hands off you between now and the wedding. I'm not sure I can, Mrs. Wylde. And besides, would it really be so bad? I'd love to give you children. If that's what you want."

Georgie's heart stuttered, and she gave him a radiant, breathless smile. "I'd like that very much indeed, Mr. Wylde."

"God, don't look at me like that in public," he groaned. "I want to ravish you on the spot. Please tell me Lady Ashton has a pagoda or a library we can sneak off to."

"Behave. I'll come to the Tricorn later, and you can show me all manner of depraved acts."

He sent her a hard glare. "Fine. In that case, distract me."

She laughed. Teasing him was so much fun. "All right. Did I tell you that I received a letter from Captain Moore? The *Lady Alice* arrived safely at Boston harbor. Cousin Josiah has apparently resigned himself to his fate during the voyage and indicated his decision to find himself a rich American heiress."

"That sounds about right," Benedict said scornfully. "It's just like him to look for the easy way out. Heaven forbid he should actually work for a living. Let's hope the ladies of Boston are as discerning as their English counterparts."

"Since we're exchanging news," he continued, "instead of doing debauched things to one another, I should report that Seb and Alex tracked down Tom Johnstone. He's currently in debtor's prison, awaiting trial. Seb says he's writing a book about his adventures."

"And what about O'Meara?"

"He hasn't been charged with anything yet. Lord Castlereagh's looking into reports that members of the Bonaparte family transferred substantial funds to London over the past few weeks, but I'm not sure they can link it to O'Meara. Still, with Johnstone's ship and Fulton's plans now back with the Admiralty, I think it's safe to say that this particular threat has been eliminated."

"I think we make an excellent team," she said smugly.

"I couldn't agree more."

Chapter 46.

The wedding of Juliet Caversteed and Simeon Petti-grew was, according to all who attended, the most lavish event of the season. The groom took the unusual step of reading aloud a sonnet he'd composed in honor of the celebration, but apart from that mystifying anomaly—during which one slightly deaf old dowager was heard to remark querulously, "I thought poems were supposed to *rhyme*?"—it all went off without a hitch.

The rings had been specially commissioned from rose-colored gold mined from the groom's very own Welsh gold mine, and the bride was acknowledged to be as beautiful as a fairy-tale princess in a silver lamé gown that had been modelled on the one worn by Princess Charlotte at her own wedding some weeks before. The bride's mother was resplendent in a ridiculously impractical hat by Madame Cerise, which boasted no fewer than three different artificial fruits and obscured the view of everyone unfortunate enough to be seated in the three rows directly behind her.

Georgie and Benedict's own wedding, a few weeks

later, was a far less fussy, more intimate affair. It took place on a glorious summer day. White cow parsley and pale-green grasses bobbed like froth in the hedgerows, butterflies chased one another in lazy helixes, and fat pigeons cooed contentedly in the trees. Only a handful of selected guests weaved through the avenue of ancient yews to the crooked porch and crowded into the tiny Norman church at Little Gidding, but the atmosphere was one of quiet celebration.

Georgie wore a simple cream dress with a small amount of lace at the bodice and sleeves, and carried a posy of peonies and sweet peas. Juliet was beautiful as matron of honor in pale-blue sarcenet, and their mother had come prepared, clutching her handkerchief and smelling salts in the expectation of happy tears and possible faintness.

Benedict, in a dark coat of navy superfine and buff breeches, was accompanied by his two groomsmen, Alex and Seb, both of whom looked exceedingly handsome in pale grey. Alex had, apparently, ruined no fewer than six cravats before he achieved the perfect knot.

When Georgie walked down the aisle on Pieter's arm and got her first glance of Benedict waiting for her at the altar, her breath caught in her throat. The proud expression on his face made her heart swell with love.

The service proceeded with all due solemnity. Georgie, comparing this wedding to her first one, in the dark and gloomy bowels of Newgate, shook her head in wonder. Who would have thought that such an inauspicious beginning would end so happily? This time, there was no hint of uncertainty or trepidation in her breast. She meant every word of her vows, and she was equally confident that Benedict meant his.

She couldn't wait to start their life together. Benedict was a far cry from some idealized courtly lover, but life with him would never be dull. It would be fun, irreverent, playful, breathless, and passionate. It would be the best adventure ever.

There was a moment of levity when the vicar came to the part in the ceremony where Benedict promised to endow Georgie with "all his worldly goods." Benedict rolled his eyes and sent her a droll glance, and she had to bite her lip to prevent herself from laughing out loud. And when the vicar pronounced them "man and wife," Benedict swept her into his arms and kissed her so soundly that she dropped her wildflower bouquet. Mother resorted to her smelling salts.

Now, three blissful weeks later, Georgie sat in her new office in the town house she and Benedict had rented a stone's throw from Grosvenor Square, and gazed at her handsome husband across the large leather-topped desk.

"What is it?" Benedict asked. "You said you wanted to see me. Is anything the matter?"

She smiled at his concern. "No, nothing's wrong. It's just that I had Edmund Shaw drop these off a short while ago." She tapped her fingers on the two folded vellum pages in front of her. "It's just a small business matter we need to attend to." She unfolded the first document and handed it to him. He took it reluctantly, and she watched in amusement as his brows lifted.

"This is the contract I signed in Newgate."

"It is, indeed. Would you mind throwing it on the fire, please?"

He frowned at her, uncomprehending. "What? Why?"

She broke the red wax seal on the second document. "I have a different agreement for you to sign."

He let out a good-natured groan. "Not another one. You're obsessed, woman. What is it this time? Names for our future children?"

"No." She rounded the desk, took the paper from his hands, and carefully ripped it in half. Then in half again.

And then she threw it on the fire. The dry vellum burned cheerfully in the grate.

Benedict looked at her as if she'd lost her mind. She waved at the paper on the desk. "That new document gives us both equal access to my fortune. With sensible stipulations, of course. Any withdrawal of over five thousand pounds will require joint signatures, for example."

He seemed to be a little dazed. "That's—very sensible."

"All of our children, no matter what gender, will inherit an equal portion of the estate when we die."

He seemed to be getting over his shock. "How very modern of you, Mrs. Wylde. That sounds alarmingly progressive." He frowned. "You don't have to do this, you know. I'm not interested in your money."

"I know. But it makes me happy. And I trust you. With my heart. With my happiness. It's stupid if I don't trust you with my money as well."

He caught her in his arms. "In that case, I promise I will never give you cause to regret your decision," he said gravely. He gave the desk behind her a speculative glance and backed her up so she was trapped between the hard wood and his strong body.

Georgie's pulse quickened. He reached around her and pushed the silver inkwell and paper to one side with distinct deliberation. Her limbs turned to water.

"I don't think I've ever shown you my husbandly appreciation on a desk before," he mused. "A bed, yes. And several chairs, certainly. The sofa in the sitting room."

"Don't forget the bath," she reminded him judiciously, as a slow curl of excitement twisted in her veins. "That was particularly memorable."

"How could I forget the bath? But a desk? No. Never."

"I don't believe so," she said breathlessly.

"In that case, allow me to—"

"Letter for you, sir!"

Benedict swore roundly as the cheerful voice of Jem Barnes carried down the hallway. They'd retained the little terror as a general stable boy, errand-runner, and cook's assistant, as a means of providing him with a regular source of income and food. He slept in the rooms above the stable, and his boundless energy paired with his youthful cynicism was usually a source of much amusement. Now, however, his presence was most unwelcome. Georgie pushed her skirts back down just as he bounded into the room without knocking.

"Letter just come," he repeated, his face glowing with excitement. "Look, 'ere. It's from the king!"

Benedict took the proffered envelope and frowned down at the embossed royal crest. "So it is."

Georgie peered over his shoulder as he broke the seal. "What does it say?"

"It's a summons, from Carlton House," he said, reading slowly. "The Prince Regent has been instructed by his father the king to bestow an honorific title to—good God—to *Benedict Wylde*, in recognition of 'invaluable services to the crown.'" He looked up with an astonished, bewildered expression. "He's making me an earl. We have to go to Carlton House for the investiture at the end of the month. Bloody hell."

Georgie threw her arms around him and hugged him tight.

Three weeks later, in a private ceremony, Benedict knelt in front of the rotund Prince of Wales and became the newly minted Earl of Ware. Alex and Seb were also present and were made the new Earl of Melton and the new Earl of Mowbray, respectively. All three of them were wearing their medals.

"We know you're well used to dealing with crooks, gentlemen," the prince said jovially. "And sad to say, they're not limited to the slums and docklands of this metropolis. Oh no. Plenty of 'em right here in Belgravia. And at Westminster too." He sent each of the three men a steely look. "As earls, you can keep an eye on the House of Lords for me." He chuckled, his belly shaking in mirth, then his gaze focused on Benedict.

"We are aware of the debts amassed by your father, Wylde, and your efforts to repay them. I wish you and your brother luck." He shot Benedict a commiserating look. "Believe me, I know *all about* difficult fathers." For a moment he looked aggrieved, and then he shook his head, dismissing the thought. "Admiral Cockburn tells me you took a bullet in the process of stopping this fellow Johnstone?"

"Yes, sir."

"Brave man." He glanced over Benedict's shoulder and beckoned Georgie forward. She swept a deep curtsey before His Royal Highness and the prince smiled at her approvingly. "And you, Mrs. Wylde, who I hear had no small part in the adventure, are now Countess of Ware." His blue eyes twinkled. "What do you think of that, eh?"

Georgie glanced sideways at her husband and smiled. "I like it very much, Your Majesty. And if I may say so, I think my husband will make a very good earl indeed."

Coming soon. . .

Don't miss the next novel in
The Bow Street Bachelors series

To Catch
an Earl

Available in May 2020 from
St. Martin's Paperbacks